# UNGIVEN LAND

*Silverlands Book Three*

## DONNA MAREE HANSON

# AUTHOR'S NOTE

*Please note:*
*British/Australian spelling conventions are used in this book.*
*For example, words like color are spelled colour, recognize are recognise,*
*traveling are traveling and so on.*

Copyright Information

First published by Aust Spec Fiction (Donna Maree Hanson) in 2017.

Copyright © Donna Maree Hanson 2017.

The moral right of the author has been asserted.



CIP National Library of Australia

Title: Ungiven land / Donna Maree Hanson.

ISBN: 9780648041504 (paperback)

Series: Hanson, Donna Maree. Silverlands; bk. 3.

Subjects: Fantasy fiction, Australian.

Best friends--Fiction.

Imaginary places--Fiction.

Creator: Hanson, Donna Maree, author.

Ebook format ISBN: 978-0-9757217-9-7

Edited by Kaaren Sutcliffe.

Cover design by Frauke, Croco Designs

Proofread by Jasan Nahrung

Map by Russell Kirkpatrick

To report a typographical error, please email donnamareehanson@gmail.com

❀ Created with Vellum

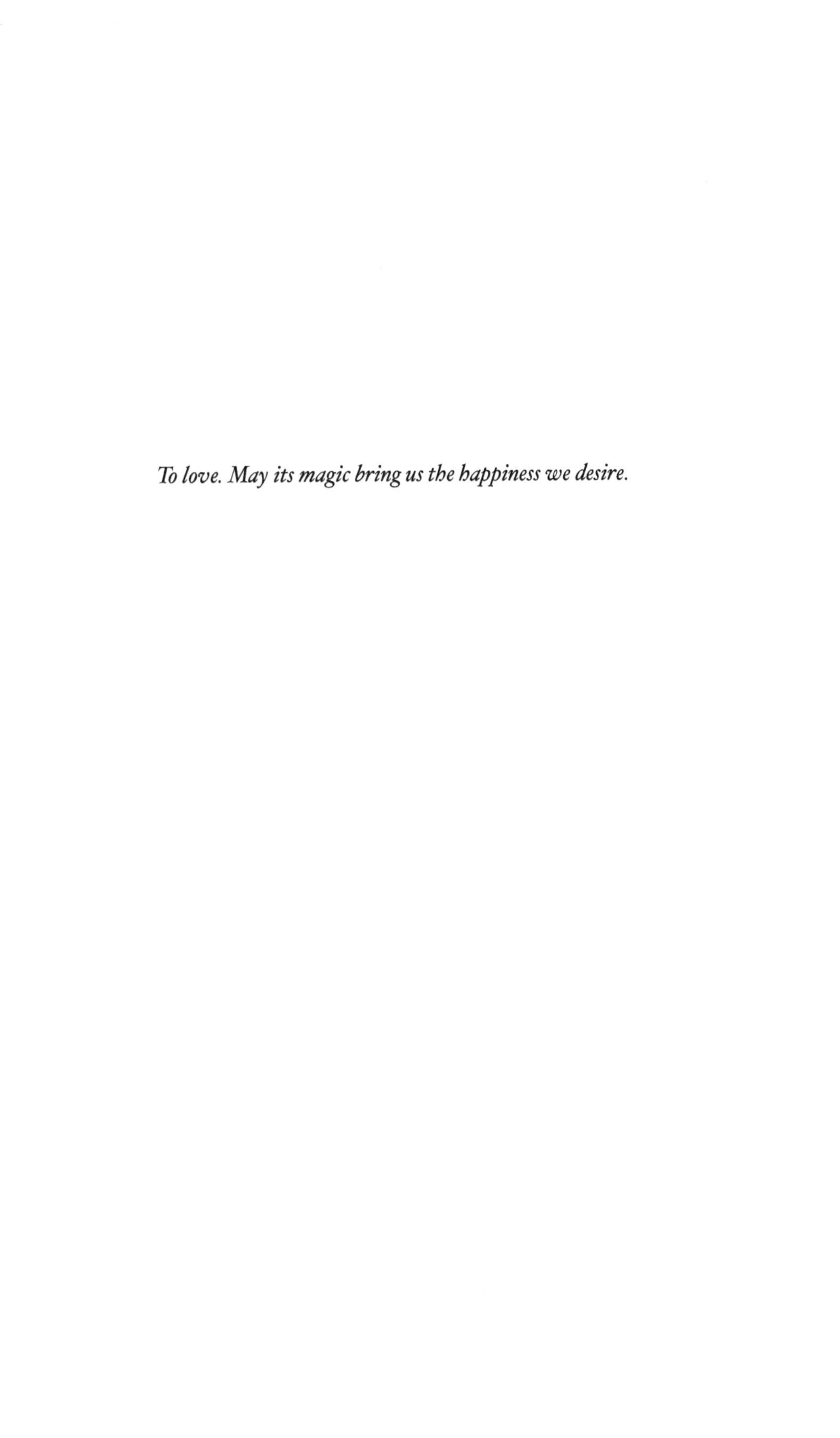

*To love. May its magic bring us the happiness we desire.*

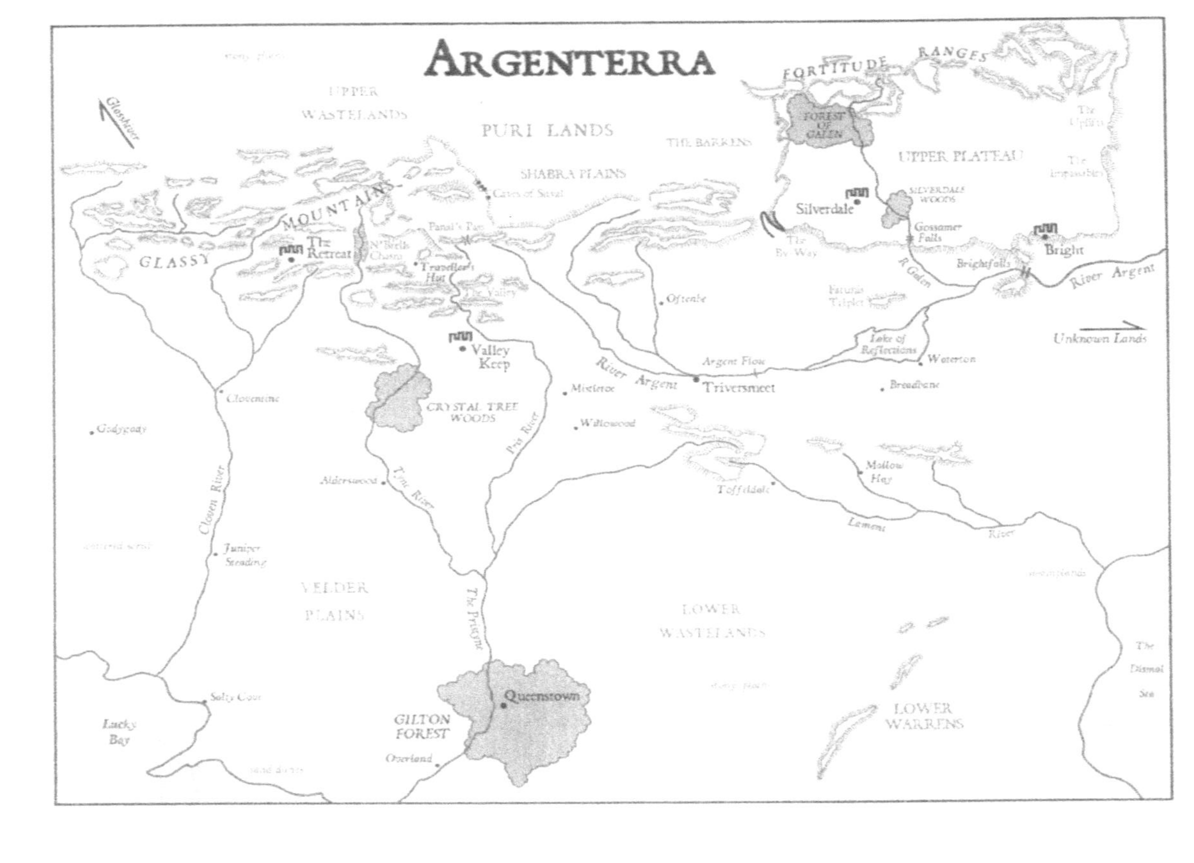

ARGENTERRA
Glenhour
UPPER WASTELANDS
PURI LANDS
THE BARRENS
FORTITUDE RANGES
FOREST OF GALEN
UPPER PLATEAU
The Uplers
The Impassables
SHABRA PLAINS
SILVERDALE WOODS
Silverdale
Caves of Saval
MOUNTAINS
Panal's Pass
Gossamer Falls
GLASSY
The Retreat
N'Beth Chasm
Traveller's Hut
The Valley
The Ev Way
R Galen
Brightfalls
Bright
River Argent
Oftenle
Favouro Triplet
Valley Keep
Lake of Reflections
Waterton
Unknown Lands
CRYSTAL TREE WOODS
Mistletoe
River Argent
Argent Flow
Triversmeet
Breadbens
Cloventine
Pin River
Godygony
Willowood
Mallow Hey
Cloven River
Aldersivood
Tyne River
Toffdidale
Lemont River
Juniper Steading
VELDER PLAINS
The Pristyne
LOWER WASTELANDS
LOWER WARRENS
The Dismal Sea
Salty Cove
Queenstown
Lucky Bay
GILTON FOREST
Overland

## ❧ I ❧

# THE DEADLANDS

W ind rippled a strip of her torn and scorched clothing as she lay inert on the ground. Another gust dumped grit onto her head and spilt dirt onto her face. With a splutter, she woke, wiping at her nose and mouth and licking her dry lips. Sitting up, she coughed and then groaned as a sledgehammer of a headache slammed behind her eyes. She knew only pain—toes, fingers, knees, elbows, and even the tips of her ears radiated agony.

Wincing, she cracked open her eyelids. Blinking was like rubbing broken glass against her eyeballs. She was in a strange, barren place. Empty and dead. Nothing moved, only the dust. She hadn't stumbled far from where she'd found herself at first...but what about before that? Her memory was a blank wall of nothing, impenetrable. She just knew there was something before, before this.

As she scanned her surroundings seeking a place to hide, she fought against a rising panic. Who or what did she hide from? All around was a dirty, grey landscape, streaked with sulphurous yellow smears. Barren, dry and lifeless. Probably toxic, too. The same muted colours smothered the sky, the worn, pallid rocks, and distant haze obscured the hills. An inhalation of stale, tainted air added weight to the feeling that death and isolation. This was a nothing place, a forgotten place. She could breathe the atmosphere, but there was no indication that anyone else lived here; no sign of life.

How long would air alone keep her alive? She exhaled, the taint of old smoke lingering on her tongue. She continued to scan the landscape, coughing a few times as her lungs drew in more of the left-over air. The pull of tender ribs, cuts and scrapes all over her body made her wish her cough would ease. What had happened to her? A quick inspection revealed scraps of clothing, looking burnt and torn. But when she tried to remember her head only ached more. It looked like she had fallen. From where? She angled her head up to the sky. Nothing except the stringy strands of dirty-looking cloud. She was just here.

Alone.

Afraid.

Confused.

When her eyes adjusted to the light and the texture of the place, she discerned more geographic features. Behind, the land rose up to form a scarred ridge, marked with clefts and tiny holes. Hidden behind the yellow-grey clouds was a sun that did little to lift the miasma of old smoke. Not far away, she saw a pale, blurred patch. It looked like a wood, except there was no suggestion of life or abundance. No green leaves. White, spindly growths speared out of the ground, stretching up to the sky like the limbs of drought-stricken trees.

The wind picked up, nailing small pebbles into her arms and legs. She scrambled up, shielding her eyes, and yelped as each little missile pricked her skin. With three dust devils at her heels, she aimed for the shelter of the ghostly wood. Sharp rocks cut into the soft soles of her boots, hampering her progress. At times, she crawled with eyes scrunched shut against the wind-blown debris, picking her way carefully through the rocky obstacles and occasionally falling, only to leave drips of blood on the stones along her path.

Whimpering, she reached the edge of the wood and panted, relief coursing through her as the wind was less in the shelter of the trees. The air cooled around her and, shivering, she took in her new surroundings. The distorted trunks made her think of tortured, naked bodies. Edging further in, she picked her way carefully around roots and holes, like puncture wounds in the ground. Clawed roots clung to the ground as if someone had tried to rip them out and they hung on for dear life. Dry twigs crunched under her feet and dead leaves rolled out of her way as she trod carefully. Dry brown vines and long fingers of dead leaves reached down from the sparse canopy, like a testament of a once vibrant past.

Large folds of roots created waist-high valleys, dark hollows that appeared to lead to burrows beneath the trees. These dark gaps unnerved her, made her think she was being watched. She avoided looking into them. A faint memory of lightless, closed-in spaces made her shiver anew.

Choosing a large, thick root to park herself on, she decided to check the damage to her toes and the soles of her feet. Slipping off her tattered boot, she began to clean her big toe with a bit of spit on her finger. It hurt but that particular spot did not appear too bad.

The longer she sat, the more her injuries advertised themselves and the wearier she became. The light grew dim, a slow leaching of day. With dusk, the tree trunks glowed brightly, illuminating everything. With a yelp, she jumped up. Staring around her in amazement, she saw the leaf mulch was black against glowing roots grasping soil. She stepped further into the wood, pressing through black drapes of leaves and vines. Scanning alternately overhead and along the ground, she searched for life. Nothing moved. Ahead was a large tree with thick, raised roots that embraced a bed of leaves like loving arms. She headed to it and, kneeling, checked there was nothing living in it and then lay down to sleep.

When she next woke, stiff and sore, it was morning. The tree trunks no longer glowed and the pallid sky indicated the sun was up. What had woken her? She drew in a breath. Sounds assaulted her ears: *click, click, clicking.* Her heart skipped a beat. What was that?

Swinging her head around, she tried to detect where it was coming from. Behind her, beside her, in front of her, beneath her: it kept changing, moving.

Surging to her feet, she pushed her hair out of her face and scampered over the roots, heading deeper into the wood. Soon she was surrounded by pale, dead trees. The sound of her panting was overly loud. Turning in a full circle, using her hand on a high, fat root to balance herself, she looked to the tops of the trees, seeing nothing except the empty, grasping limbs. The click, click, clicking returned, more deafening than a forest full of chorusing cicadas in mid-summer. Trying to calm her panic, she put her fingers in her ears. The sound would not be shut out.

What was it? Where was this place? Who was she? The memory of who she was hovered there, just out of reach, if only she could grab it and hold it for long enough. The sounds overwhelmed her, stopped her thinking, and filled up her mind with fear. The noise grew even louder and she screamed for it to stop. Her voice was drowned out and she despaired, but abruptly the crescendo of clicks stopped. Her breathing relaxed and her ears ached.

Into the empty space she heard a voice calling a name. It was coming from a long way off. Surprised, she began to make her way out of the wood. Her progress was slow, hindered by the roots that had to be navigated or climbed over. The voice was deep and drawing closer. "Sophy. Soooophhyy?"

A familiar voice—she didn't understand her reaction to it. Her stomach clenched and fluttered as if hundreds of butterflies were taking flight. *Sophy? That's me! That's my name.*

The voice was now in the wood. The trees deflected the sound, making it hard to pinpoint. The clicking sounds were rising again, over the sound of crunching twigs. Whatever was approaching was large enough to smash its way through the trees. She heard a ripping sound, then a crash followed by a mindless screech. A sound that made her shake uncontrollably. She no longer headed towards the voice. It was moving in her direction. She turned and ran.

The *click, click clicking* drowned out the encroaching voice. Her eyes darted around. She could hear movement around her, like cockroaches swarming. Then a tree collapsed near her, bringing down another one with it. Panicked, she kept running, then stumbled. Looking down, she expected a tree root was the cause, but there was a multitude of tiny brown hands around her ankles.

"Argh!" she cried as horror swept through her. Yelling, she tried to stamp her feet but as soon as she lifted one, the hands tugged and she dropped to her knees. A scream escaped her when she saw the gaping black hole she was being tugged into. She did not want to be pulled down into the ground, down into the dark places.

Between her panicked screams, she heard the approaching voice again, the one that ignited a strange fear. The ground-hands tugged urgently. Now thigh deep, her legs were dangling into the empty space beneath the trees. The hands pulled at the strips of her clothing, pinching her thighs, her buttocks. She dropped into the hole, just managing to snag the root above her head with a desperate grasp to halt her fall. She gritted her teeth, fighting the pull of the many hands.

A crash sounded as another tree fell. In the aftermath floated that voice, caressingly soft, yet loud enough to hear. "Sooophyyy! Come to me. Come to your angel."

As if they too were listening to the voice, the clicking noise the creatures made subsided but the grip of the hands strengthened.

"Sooophy," said the sweet angelic voice. "Come to me, my sweet. I know you are there waiting for me."

Sophy let go of the root in preparation to cup her hand around her mouth to call out a reply. But before she could draw breath, the hands jointly yanked her down into the dark and hands covered her mouth, stifling her voice. Eyes wide in the dark, she sensed hundreds of creatures were there with her, moving around her and on top of her, crowded in. As one they hushed as the creature with the seductive voice drew closer. Through the gap made by her passage, she could see the world, as if on a television screen. As he came into view, she saw a tall, grey-skinned, hairless being, with bat wings and red glowing eyes. Saw him sniff the air with a rat like nose. "Know you are here, little one, little jewel. Come to me now."

When she gave no answer, he sniffed again. *Did that mean he could smell her?*

"You may hide for now, little jewel. But you will come to me eventually. There is no life here, no food, no shelter. I am your only hope. *She* wants to talk to you. Only talk. No harm will come to you if you come now and freely."

Even if she had wanted to go with him, the hands held her firm and quiet. The image of him was familiar. The memories came back, painfully and slowly; she had to fight to get them to the front of her brain. Rufus. His name was Rufus and he meant danger. There was more there, she could tell, but she couldn't remember other than the sensation of danger and of past history where he had abused her, hurt her and those she loved.

Loved? There were people she cared about. A vision of wide green eyes loomed large. She could not remember the details and could only recognise the gap in her life where these others she cared for had existed. Perhaps other memories would return, like the one of Rufus. Now at least she knew her name: Sophy.

A loud thump drew her from her reverie and then another. More trees crashing to the ground marked the passage of Rufus as he ploughed through the wood. After a while the wood grew quiet. The air smelt stale in the dark place and she could feel the little creatures moving against her, like a wave of rats. Revulsion at the thought of rodents made her thrash and one by one the hands dropped away from her mouth. The creatures began to click again, soft, gentle clicking.

They had saved her, prevented her from giving herself up to Rufus. That meant they had intelligence—and a prior knowledge of this Rufus. Perhaps this was where Rufus came from. More memories were hovering, but they splintered and drifted out of reach. No point in forcing it or being angry with herself. If the memories were there then they would return. They had to.

Now that she had recovered from her fright, the sound of the little creatures relaxed her. Her panting eased, her heart ceased thumping painfully and echoing against her rib cage. Without sunlight, she could not see the creatures but she could sense them, hundreds of them. Yet they did not move to harm her, or bite her, or make any other threatening gestures. So, what next? She couldn't stay down in this little hole forever.

Before she could assess her surroundings, the hands snatched at her again, dragging and pushing her flat on the ground. Then lifting her, they tugged her along what appeared to be a tunnel, her body running over hands like a conveyor belt. Her nose brushed the ceiling, and occasionally an elbow or knee caught the earthen sides. Fear took hold of her, particularly when fine grains of dirt rained down on her face, so she closed her eyes and let the little creatures take her. It wasn't as if she had a choice. A scream perched in her throat, waiting to pounce.

Time passed slowly. She scrunched her eyelids shut as she was trundled along like a parcel in some automated post office, the smooth transfer from little hands to more little hands appearing seamless. Then came a change: the air felt cooler, fresher, and the feel of the soil being so close subsided.

Opening her eyes, she found that she was in a small cavity dug into the ground, suffused with dim light. The hands lowered her to the ground and the creatures moved away. She sat up, her head gently brushing the ceiling, in time to see the tail ends of the creatures disappear into a multitude of holes. She shook her head, not sure what she had seen. Curling into a ball, she huddled, waiting for what came next. An hour passed, maybe more. There was nothing except the occasional soft hissing click. She could, if she tried, stretch out here and lie flat. There was only enough room to stand doubled over. Better to crawl, she realised, if she wanted to move around. As her eyes adjusted to the low light, she saw about twenty dark holes in the sides, roof and ground, which appeared to be tunnels leading away—a dark, tiny labyrinth. At the base of the opposite wall was a small pool of water.

On all fours she shuffled forwards. The creatures stared out at her from the tunnel openings, a series of small glowing lights that she reasoned must be their eyes. She could hear the soft clicking noises they made. Were they afraid of her? Why? They had grabbed her and dragged her down here, so why would they be afraid of her?

"Hello?" she said quietly. "Is anybody there?"

A rising choruses of *click, click, clicking* responded. None of the creatures dared to put in an appearance. "Bugger," Sophy said to herself. "I guess I'll have to sit here while you guys work up the nerve to let me go or at least talk to me."

Her stomach grumbled loudly. "I'm hungry. Is there food?" No answer, not even one click. Using a hand-to-mouth gesture she mimicked eating, exaggerating the movements and making noises. Then she paused, looked around the tunnels and saw lots of glowing eyes staring at her. Had they got the message? "A bit of food would be nice. Steak, medium rare, roasted potatoes and don't forget the gravy." Scooping out a seat for herself in the soft soil, she sat down. Another suggestion came to mind while she was fantasising about food. "A pizza maybe—with the works."

Once seated, she eyed the pool. Dipping her fingers in, she licked the tips. It tasted a bit musty. Her mouth was dry. She rubbed some of the water on her dry lips. Her tongue darted out. She may as well drink. Cupping her hands she scooped more water into her mouth, and then drank deeply. It eased her hunger, lifted her mood slightly. She wasn't going to die today, which was a nice thought to have.

More clicks and then the sound of scampering feet echoed around her. She wondered what they were doing. Could they have understood her? Sophy was tired and her fear had lessened somewhat. Yet if she thought it through, there was not much hope. She was in a strange land, with barely any idea who she was or why she was there. These creatures had provided some shelter, or was it an early tomb? Without food she wouldn't last long. At least her headache had eased somewhat.

"Think, think, damn it. How long can you last on water alone?" She stared at the pool, wondering. Yet what point was there staying alive anyway? What was going to happen? What was she to do? A black wall of nothing in her mind was her only answer. Rufus was looking for her. He knew who she was and why she was there. Instinctively, she was afraid of him. Yet he seemed to be the only way ahead, unless she regained her memory. Casting a look around the little hollow, she reminded herself of the world above. She wasn't going to last long in this place.

Curling herself up into a ball again, she tried to sleep, or at least nap. The sound of Rufus's voice tormented her as soon as she closed her eyes. The recollection of the trees shattering and crashing to the ground made her jump and twitch in her sleep. She groaned once or twice, trying to clear her head. Well rested, she might be able to deal with her new circumstances. Danger, she understood, but the loss of memory made things more difficult. There was something she should be doing, but for the life of her couldn't remember what. Someone needed her but she didn't remember who or why.

✣ 2 ✣

## A QUEEN RETURNED

**M**aralain followed the adepts who carried Jeff's body to the retreat. He was Prince Daken of Valley Keep, but had been Jeff to her so long that that was the name she held in her heart. Jeff stood for the life they'd lived in another world far from Argenterra—and from oaths that couldn't be broken. After Sophy had vanished through the Crystal Gate, and the gate itself had dissipated in a swirl of colours, they had found Jeff lying dead just below where the gate had been.

The adepts, only knowing him as Prince Daken who had vanished long ago, carried him to a room in the lower floors of the retreat. An adept turned to her, causing her to pause. An older man, with a grey beard and soft blue eyes, the adept bowed to her. "Please wait while we see to him."

The adept's words barely registered as she watched Jeff's body being lifted onto a table inside the room and the door closing her out. She stood in the hallway in a daze, conscious that her face was wet from tears. Her body and mind were numb.

"Mum?" Aria's voice sounded from behind her. Aria's hand reached out and squeezed hers. "I can't believe this. I'm going to miss him so much." Her daughter's voice was clogged with tears. Jeff had been a father to her; the only one she had known. Aria stepped closer, put her arms around Maralain's neck and wept.

Maralain held herself distant, fortified with barriers. Too much pain. Too much hurt. But Aria's sobbing broke down her defences. A sudden wail leapt out of her mouth and she bent her head to weep on her daughter's shoulder. Life-crushing sobs, such that she had never experienced. He was gone. There was no way to comprehend that. It was sudden and violent and unexpected. All she could understand was that life was different now.

The door opened and the adept stood poised, waiting until she lifted her head. He beckoned her in, his cream-coloured robe rippling with his gesture. Aria waved for her to go first. The adepts had tried to tidy his body up, to cover his wounds. She touched his foot, ran a hand up to his knee, and then touched his shoulder with her other hand. The burn marks where his eyes had been were hidden by a cloth and her gaze rested on his lifeless face, composed now in deathly slumber. How she wished that he was asleep, that he would wake, but she knew he never would. He was gone. Gone forever. She snatched at his hand. "Jeff!" And then the tears flowed. "Oh Jeff!" she wailed.

Aria cried quietly beside her. Maralain lost track of time. Her sobbing eventually eased to silent anguish. She was alone: Aria must have gone. Mutely, she stared down at her dead lover and her mind lost itself to memory.

"Will you retire now, my lady queen?" the adept asked as he returned to the room. "We shall prepare him."

"No. I will stand vigil tonight. Bring me fresh water and towels, and a robe. I wish to bathe and dress him."

The adept bowed and left the room. "Now, my love," she whispered. "We say goodbye." She stripped off his clothes and thanked the adept who unobtrusively brought her a bowl of water and towels. As the widow, this was her duty. His skin was cold to the touch, but she wiped him with warm snow-melt, scented with rose oil. When she was done, she dressed him in white adept's robes for burial. While she worked, she talked to him, to the spirit of him that remained, and told him all the things she had kept hidden: the secret pain of leaving her son; the unspoken dreams and the longings for family and her home in

Argenterra. She spoke also of the love and life they had shared and how dear those memories would always be. Sprinkled amongst those truths were tears of grief.

WHEN THEY CAME TO TAKE HIM FOR BURIAL, MARALAIN WAS standing still, looking down on his face, not a thought left in her head. She was empty.

Then he came: Dellbright. Maralain could not look at him. He did not speak to her, nor approach his father's body. He watched. Dark, brooding Dellbright. When the procession moved, she tried to make eye contact, but he refused to even meet her eye. Aria would have come to say goodbye if not for Dellbright. Maralain did not blame her daughter for not coming, not after such strange violence. There was more to their situation than met the eye, but she couldn't engage with it, not then. Not until she said goodbye. Not until the pain lessened.

Cocooned in a burial cloth, Jeff was carried to the burial place, which was outside with the mountains towering above them and a breeze cutting through their clothes, shredding warmth and words. Steel-grey clouds roiled above them. A dull roar of distant thunder presaged a storm.

An adept said the words of parting. Maralain crinkled her brow. Were they meant to console her? Well, they didn't. The adept told her that Jeff was to be interred in a cave, for the ground was too rocky and cold to bury the dead. So Jeff would join the adepts at their rest.

Then when it was done. All trace of Jeff was gone from the surface of the world, she turned to the retreat. She had a lot to do.

"My children and my home need me."

OAKHEART HAD WEPT ON AND OFF DURING THE NIGHT, overwhelmed by all that had occurred and his inability to act as he chose. Duty and honour warred with his heart. Now, in the morning light, he lay back on the sheets and stared at the ceiling, a mind-numbing emptiness opening up inside. *Sophy!* The comforting tether of their bond was gone—as if it had been savagely cut from him.

Too tired and sore to get up, he lay listless on his bed. His body ached as if he had been tumbled down into one of the Glassy Mountains' many gorges and then dragged up the other side. He acknowledged this mood as a depression. Expected, he supposed. It was a frame of mind he did not have time for. Had he been light of spirit, perhaps his physical aches would not loom so large.

Sophy was gone through the Crystal Gate. That was a cold, hard fact. That might not have been so bad if he had been able to follow directly, but the gate had snapped firmly shut behind her. None at the retreat could open it again, despite his urgings and pleadings. What use was all their learning if they could not do that one simple thing? Previously in his heart, he had cherished admiration for the adepts. Of late, that had crumbled to dust. Too much had happened. Now, he could only look upon them with a jaundiced eye, perhaps seeing them for what they really were: flawed.

Then began the debates about what had really happened, about where Sophy actually had gone. Had she been taken or had she left of her own accord? He ground his teeth. He knew what had happened, despite his mother opining that Sophy had gone home to her own world. There was no argument as far as he was concerned: Unesta's minion, Rufus, had snatched her. He longed to believe that she was safe at home, despite in accepting that story it would be a mark of her rejection of him. He dared not believe it to be true. His fist clenched. *Rufus!*

But now there was war and duty to add to this ineffectual situation. Word had come from Silverdale that the Puri had made war on Argenterra and, duty-bound, he must go with speed to their aid. He could not help Sophy. By the *given* it was more than he could bear. Three times he had failed her. First, when he failed to stop her falling into Rufus's trap in the Lower Warrens, second through weakness after her retrieval so that just when he needed to be strong, he allowed her to be snatched away by Nasheen. And now a third time through inaction. He could not follow: thus he could not save her. To fail her again. How could she ever forgive him? How could he forgive himself?

A knock at the door sent him diving for his clothes. He was doing up his breeches when his mother came in. Now that she was here, he found he resented the intrusion and the expectation she appeared to have that he would accept and respect her without any recriminations about her past actions. "Lianal sends word that Veld calls on the talkstone. Will you come?"

"Straight away." Drawing on a shirt, he noticed his mother inspecting him. He lifted an eyebrow. "Mother?"

She shook her head. "Nothing." However, she lifted her shoulders and tilted her head. "It's just you're so like your father, but I see me in your eyes. You're a man now. It's hard to take in."

Oakheart closed his eyes. Her manner of speaking was so like Sophy's it made his heart clench. "You chose to leave. There is little use in repining to me."

Her eyes widened and her mouth opened in a wounded look. "You're heartless," she replied, voice low. "I didn't expect that from you."

"What did you expect? Love, honour, obedience?" Oakheart barked out a laugh.

Her expression hid her thoughts and she turned away. "Hurry. Veld is waiting to speak to you."

Oakheart studied her face. Red blotches indicated she'd been crying. Then he knew he'd inadvertently missed Daken's funeral. He had not shown his mother the courtesy of witnessing her grief. "I am sorry for your loss, mother. I...I did not absent myself from Daken's burial on purpose. I was...indisposed."

She lifted her gaze to his, her expression distant. "He's gone now. There's much to do."

"I am sorry for speaking to you roughly. You are new to your grief, as I am to mine. Forgive me."

Her gaze passed over him. "There is nothing to forgive. I realise he was nothing to you but the source of your pain." She turned away.

Oakheart repressed a sigh as he followed after, wading through a rising tide of mixed emotions and remnants of past trauma.

OAKHEART ENTERED THE ROOM WHERE A LARGE CRYSTAL HUNG suspended in chains, hovering over a stone pedestal. An adept viewing a smaller stone acknowledged him with a nod and rose to pull up a chair. The high king was called and soon his face loomed in the stone.

High King Veld had aged since Oakheart had last seen him. Although the old man tried to hide it, Oakheart saw the tear drops smattering his ruddy cheek when he spoke of Mara's return. He knew his father still loved his wife, knew that he would forgive her for all she had done. Brokenly, Veld had passed on words of welcome to convey to her and charged Oakheart to ask Mara, if she would so have it, to garner fighters around her, then to make haste to Silverdale to assist in their defence.

"Father. There is more."

A white eyebrow lifted. "More?"

"Aria, the Gift of Crystal Tree Woods. She is my sister."

Veld recoiled. "Sister? But...but that means Mara..."

"Yes, Mara carried your child out of Argenterra. She said as much. Seeing her and knowing her, I know this to be true. Aria is your child."

"And married to Dellbright?" Veld's voice was strained.

"Yes, and there's more." Oakheart looked down at his feet, hating to tell his father the next part. "All is not well with their marriage, father. Dellbright abused Aria, raped and beat her. He took their child away and withheld food and freedom. Such a wrong has been done to her that it could not be disguised. You know she ran away from him and is here at the retreat?"

Veld let out a sob. "My dear child! My dear daughter? Such a mess. By the *given* I will see her soon. And her child? My grandson?"

Oakheart squeezed his hand into a fist. "Yes, Gillcress is your grandchild. I have not seen the child since I returned him to Valley Keep. Aria says she was not allowed to be with her son."

"He has no right to do this, to take the child from her. What ails the man that he should do this to one he loves?"

"I do not understand it, either. Something dark has influenced him, lives within him. The loss of his mother in such a violent way has wounded his spirit."

They regarded each other in silence. Veld brought a cup to his lips and drank deeply.

Oakheart waited and then ventured to speak again. "My king, I will come to your aid as soon as I can but Sophy, my wife, is lost beyond the Crystal Gate..."

Veld sat back, his face drooping with shock. Too much bad news all at once, on top of the situation in Silverdale. Oakheart was frustrated not to be there to support his king, but torn because his duty was to Sophy, too. Never had his role in life been such a burden. "My son, I know not what to advise you. I can see Sophy is dear to your heart. You want to go to her. But I need you here. Soon. I am trapped within a nest of spiders and doing my best to hold them back so our people will be safe."

"Is it really Hanal and his Puri horde?"

Veld nodded and wiped a hand across his forehead. "Perhaps I should have harkened to your earlier advice and allowed you to marry Lyant, thereby giving Hanal of Puri what he wanted—an alliance. What I did, I did for the best and based on my own understanding."

Oakheart lifted an eyebrow, which Veld caught.

His father looked sharply at him. "Yes, yes, you are right, I will admit it. My own prejudices blurred my thinking. There, I can see the error of my ways, late though it is. Yet, I find it hard to regret that one denial. You have Sophy, who is more important than a mere Puri ally. Perhaps I could have offered Lyant another: Fern, for instance. Too late to repine now."

Oakheart's heart pounded at the mere mention of Sophy. "You know that Sophy held a portion of the land's *given* within her? Thus, with her taken from here, Argenterra is weakened, perhaps for good?"

Veld nodded. "I do not know how we will live with a decrease of the *given*. Already there is panic here as the lessening spreads to the Upper Plateau. The Puri may want what we have, but the fact is what they want may no longer exist."

"It is more than just the *given* being harder to work. Oaths are weakening. The Puri raiders have not killed in the past. They have hurt, they have stolen property and abducted women, but never slaughtered. They have always held true to the binding oath, father. If that oath weakens much more then there could be killing."

Veld shook his head, shoulders slumped in misery. "I know."

"How did they manage it?" Oakheart asked.

Veld lifted a fist. "They came from the north and Glasshiver warriors ride with them. No oath binds those from Glasshiver—before or now."

Oakheart started. "The north?" he blurted. "How is that possible?" All their plans for the defence of Silverdale centred on Brightfalls and possible attacks from the Unknown Lands. They had thought Silverdale unapproachable. The Upper Plateau should have been sufficient to deter any invader. Glasshiver too. They had always been a remote but friendly trading partner.

"Our scouts report that Glasshiver warriors had been working on excavating a pass, in a box canyon in the Fortitude Ranges." He checked a document that was shown to him. "Glass Cutting Canyon, we think. The canyon wall was known to be thinner there, but no one thought that it could be breached. The north has always been secure."

Oakheart pulled on his lower lip. "Then there was no warning. No declaration of intent either?"

"No. Hanal did not make a declaration. The Puri just appeared and started running the farmers off their lands, coercing them by taking their women, burning homes." Veld rubbed his hand over his face. Oakheart had never seen him look so worn, so defeated.

"How many?"

"So far there is only a handful of Glasshiver warriors. My scouts estimate one thousand Puri."

Oakheart considered the threat. It was severe, but not insurmountable. "That is not a lot of warriors."

"In a surprise attack and through the north, it is plenty. We could not deploy a force to fight them when they swarmed over us. We could only bring people inside the walls and prepare for a siege before they reached the gates."

Oakheart rubbed his cheek as he thought of possibilities. "Still, they are few in number. We could—"

"I see what you are thinking," Veld said, shaking his head. "There will be no easy victory. All I can hope for is that you can raise an army to come to our aid."

"Of course, I will do all I can. Have you any word from the By-way? Is it clear?"

"I have no news. But be prepared, Oakheart. Hanal is no fool. He will secure the By-way and cut you off. They are tightening the noose."

Oakheart bit his lip. The defence of Silverdale was always built around the impregnability of the Upper Plateau and control of the By-way that allowed access to it. A narrow switchback pathway up the face of the plateau, it was of strategic value. From the top of the By-way, any attack could be repelled by only a handful of warriors. Argenterra's one strategic advantage had been turned against them. Once the Puri controlled the By-way, there was little that could be done to provide relief. Some serious thinking would be required to make any headway. Hopefully, there were some military-minded men to be found outside Silverdale.

"Time is of the essence," Veld said, leaning forwards so that his face dominated the talkstone.

"Then we will leave as soon as we can. Tomorrow, I think. But I have not many men with me. The adepts may lend us a few fighting men and women. We must gather warriors as we ride." Oakheart was going to insist that those fighting adepts who had fought against him when he searched for Sophy be included in his forces. Maybe they would teach him the technique with the *given*. It was still hard to understand how the *given* could be used as a weapon. Maybe it would give them an advantage.

"We both know who has the most fighting men outside of Silverdale."

Oakheart's head jerked up and he ground his teeth. *Dellbright!* He narrowed his gaze at his father. Should he warn him how the change in his cousin may affect the discussions?

"Leave that negotiation to me." His father looked to the side, distracted by someone entering the room. "I must go. Something urgent has come up."

"Before you go, may I ask a boon of you, father?" Oakheart asked, gazing steadily at his father's image in the talkstone.

"Ask," Veld said, head held in his hand as if it ached beyond measure.

"When we have gathered fighters and delivered them to you, allow me to return here to find Sophy. The retreat is looking for a way to operate the gate. I do not know when it will be, only that I must come when the way is found. One less man fighting will not change the outcome."

Veld looked up, mouth agape. "You do not wish to fight for Silverdale?"

"I do, father, but I cannot leave Sophy to her fate. If, as Mara says, she is free and happy in her own world, then I will leave her there, if that be her wish, and return straight away. But I believe Rufus has her and, if so, she will be in danger, suffering needlessly at his hands. I must do all I can to save her, however late I may be."

Veld nodded. "I agree, though it grieves me. You have a way to galvanise the men and you are a great leader and warrior in your own right. It will be a disadvantage for us but I will not hold you back. When the time is right, you may go. Will your mother come to Silverdale, do you think?"

"Yes, I am sure she is already rallying those adepts who will fight by our side and is busy organising supplies for our journey. We should be able to leave tomorrow morning."

"I will speak to you again after I deal with this problem that has arisen here. I will speak to Aria too."

After saying farewell, Oakheart left the room where the talkstone stood. Outside the door Mara waited for him, an impatient look marring her features, twisting her mouth. "What word do you have?"

"I told him we would leave tomorrow." He started to walk away, and she trailed after him. "We need to gather troops and supplies. I must speak with Lianal to see what adepts he can spare."

"Wait!" She grabbed at his shoulder, then withdrew her hand. "I want to talk to you."

Oakheart turned. Maralain stood very still, chin high, her bearing regal. He let out an impatient sigh. "We leave tomorrow on a journey of many weeks. We will have plenty of time to talk then."

He stalked away but she followed him back to his room.

"Oakheart! Wait." Short of shutting the door in her face there was little he could do to exclude her. With a slight bow, he let her pass inside. Once in his room, Mara strolled about, looking at his things, touching them with the tips of her fingers and surreptitiously casting her gaze at him, sizing him up. "I thought perhaps you would join Aria and me for breakfast."

Oakheart rolled up a shirt and placed it in his pack. Wasn't time supposed to be of the essence? "You invite me to eat with you and my sister?" He let out a sigh, realising that he was being boorish. "That I would gladly do."

Mara nodded, her face solemn. "You don't forgive easily, do you, son?"

A breath huffed out of him. He thought he was doing a good job of being civil and hiding his feelings. "I do forgive you, mother. 'Tis just not easy to adjust. So much has happened and there are so many calls on my duty that I can barely think straight. Of course, I would like to get to know you again. But I worry about the possible impact you might have."

Her gaze leapt to his. "What do you mean?"

"I worry that you will hurt father. He never stopped loving you, you know."

"Pfah! What did he ever know of love? What did he care then? I was a thing, a necessary thing. He was oblivious to me."

Oakheart finished organising his gear so he could join them for breakfast. "You will find that you are mistaken, and perhaps your recollection is obscured by emotion and time. He suffered greatly when you left. Still does."

"You're only saying that to make me feel guilty. I won't be forced to take the blame; it's as much his fault as mine." Bristling with anger, Mara preceded him out of the door.

Oakheart repressed a groan. She had to understand that she was still a beautiful woman and still capable of breaking his father's heart all over again. Yes, she grieved for Daken. Yes, she said she did not love her husband. Perhaps she did hold many grievances against the high king. He was not privy to what had gone on between them, only what he had witnessed as a child. But she was here now. Her oath was still there, weaker perhaps, but still in force. She could take no other, and Veld would never force her to do anything she did not want. There was ample opportunity to break Veld's heart all over again. He feared such a happening: it would be the end of Veld.

⌘

ARIA PLAYED WITH HER HAIR WHILE SHE WAITED FOR THE REST OF her family to join her for breakfast. Her grief at the loss of Jeff was still with her. She hadn't been able to bring herself to see him buried, not when he was there too. Her jaw ached from the blow he'd dealt her, even after receiving healing from adept Aran. It had to be enough, supporting her mother and sharing her grief. And Sophy was gone. Just like that. Leaving her here to deal with everything, leaving a hole in her life. *Oh Sophy, I hope you're okay. Please be okay.*

Aria had other problems. Dellbright was still at the retreat—a fellow guest, as she was. She could feel his evil presence nearby, like a throbbing ache smack in the middle of her head. It was probably her oathbond that gave her that feeling. Her sensitivity to the *given* was increasing and as the oathbond was something made of the *given*, it was natural to assume that this was so.

More than anything she wanted to be gone, far away from Dellbright. His presence this close weighed her down, brought back memories, gutted her confidence. Clenching her fist, she pressed it against the table. It was necessary to fight these feelings or she would never be free of Dellbright and the effects of his abuse.

In her own right she was a princess, with intelligence and a talent with the *given*. None of that she owed to Dellbright. Damn him for being there. His brooding presence complicated everything.

Her and Fern's original plan for leaving Argenterra had been that they would return to her world, then go to her mother and live with her until they sorted their lives out. But Maralain's sudden appearance through the Crystal Gate and the consequent revelations of her true identity and past events changed everything. Yes, she still loved and wanted Fern, but it was all so complicated now. Fern had not taken the change in their situation well, and Aria hadn't had much time to talk to him about it. They had both been caught up in a swirl of activity ever since the surprise arrival of her mother and the loss of Sophy through the gate. How she wished Sophy was there to advise her with her good sense. When she did try to talk to Fern, he was sullen and uncommunicative. That made her angry and hurt. Why couldn't he be more understanding?

It was enough to convince her that men were not worth it and that she had abominable taste in the opposite sex. It made her question her assessment of her intelligence. But smarts didn't relate to emotions, did they? A long, slow sigh escaped her.

A knock at the door broke her out of her reverie. The door opened and an adept came in, followed quickly by another. Together, they laid covered platters of food on the table. "Thank you," she said to the one who entered first.

She thought she saw him tremble when he nodded to her. "I am sorry, but are you all right?" she asked him. His companion inclined his head and left the room.

"Yes, princess. I am called Rany. I will be joining you to fight for Silverdale." Her gaze rested on his hands. When he noticed, he held them up closer to his eyes. "Oh!" He threw her a grin. "I am shaking because I am excited, that is all."

Aria nodded again and smiled. "How very brave of you. I thank you."

The young adept blushed and quickly shut the door behind him. Aria lifted a lid on one of the covered platters just as her mother and Oakheart came in.

"Morning," Aria said with more brightness than she felt. Her mother's expression was strained and Oakheart had dark shadows under his eyes. Yet he moved with grace and more strength than he had in the weeks since Rufus nearly snuffed out his life. That lifted her heart. He was finally returning to his normal physical strength.

"Looks like hot toffelporridge and syrup," she added after finishing her inspection.

Her mother's eyes brightened. "Toffelporridge? I never thought to taste that ever again. Jeff—I mean Daken—loved a good bowl of it and often yearned for it in the mornings..."

Aria blushed and glanced under her lashes at Oakheart. He had sat down and started heaping some porridge into his bowl. He didn't appear to react to the reference to Daken. Maralain dabbed at her eyes. Her grief was still close, as was to be expected. Aria leant across the table and squeezed her hand. "I'm so sorry. Jeff was a good father to me."

Oakheart's head shot up and his eyes flashed. "But he was not your father, was he? You were effectively stolen away from your true father, your family, your home. If only we had known who you really were, events would have taken a different course. You would not be in the situation you are in now, or made to suffer at the hands…"

When Aria's mouth fell open, Oakheart lowered his head and dropped his spoon to clench his hand. She had rarely seen him so tense. That he thought of her touched her. For a fleeting moment, she wondered what her life would have been like growing up with him as her brother.

Closing her gaping mouth, Aria slid her gaze to her mother, whose face was clouded with anger. "You cannot change what has happened!" her mother began hotly. "I told you before, I did not know I carried Aria when I left here."

"And would that have changed things? Would you have stayed if you had known?"

Maralain paused in lifting her spoon, an angry expression twisting her mouth. "I repeat, the past cannot be changed. I did what I thought was best at the time."

"Best? For you and your womanising lover? Face it, mother, you acted selfishly without regard for any of us. Did you ever spare me or father or Aurore a second thought when you took Daken to your bed in your new world where oaths are nothing?"

Aria gasped as she saw the colour leak from her mother's face. "Oakheart, you shouldn't talk like that…" Aria whispered urgently. "Maybe…calm down…a little bit."

"It's okay, Aria," her mother said. "I understand Oakheart's difficulty."

"Really? How can you? If only you had told Aria who she was, or at least what Argenterra was, so that she knew something of her history when she came here."

Maralain bit her lip and Aria thought there were tears in her eyes. "I..."

"Better still," Oakheart went on. "You have been through the Crystal Gate. Perhaps you know of its workings. Perhaps you can help me fetch my wife."

Her mother shook her head. "Jeff was the one who studied it." Maralain screwed up her napkin, fingers working with nervous tension. "He was able to predict when it would arrive." Her glistening eyes met Oakheart's angry gaze. "I know nothing about—" She shrugged, and let go of the napkin, which slowly expanded from its tight ball shape.

Oakheart stood up, scraping his chair on the floor as he pushed it back. "Forgive me. I fear that I am upset by events." He tossed down his own napkin.

Before Oakheart could do or say anything further, an adept rushed in. "Please, Oakheart. High King Veld is back on the talkstone."

He acknowledged the adept with a nod. Turning to Aria, he bowed quickly. "Please excuse me, I must speak with Veld." He did not look in his mother's direction.

Aria was so stunned she couldn't say anything as Oakheart stormed out of the room, with the adept hurrying after him. Maralain started to cry as soon as he was gone. Forgetting about her breakfast, Aria went to comfort her mother. Oakheart's words blazed across her heart. Selfish, he said. Did he mean her too? She had been going to leave Gilly behind and run off with Fern. *Oh lord, I'm so confused.*

She respected Oakheart and wanted to always be held high in his esteem. Never had she witnessed him so angry before, so out of control. Did the loss of Sophy affect him that much? With a sinking heart she realised it did. Just when he'd thought he had got her back for good, she was snatched away. Talk about a difficult love life. To top it off, Sophy had indicated that she hated the idea of being a princess and was livid that he, her husband, was the high king's son and heir. Sophy had been very angry at Oakheart—and Aria—for keeping that fact from her and asking others to do so. Of course, being Sophy she would have gotten over it and forgiven them, such was her nature.

As Aria soothed her mother, she reminisced about when Sophy had been caught in Rufus's trap. Oakheart had fulfilled his oath and placed Aria's abducted son, Gilly, back in Aria's hands, and then he went straight back to the Lower Warrens and risked his life yet again to save Sophy. Indeed, his life had been attached to his body by the merest ethereal tether as he lay helpless, mortally weakened by Rufus. So, Sophy had been taken and Oakheart had dragged himself across Argenterra to find her. Of course he must be conflicted now.

She had to consider his words just now about what might have been if she had known who she was. Would she have married Dellbright if she'd known she was a princess of Argenterra? Not straight away, as she had. She looked down at her mother, feeling a twist of the knife of regret. Then Sophy would have been the bride. No, that was never going to work. Sophy and Dellbright never liked each other. Aria and Sophy would have both gone to Silverdale with Oakheart and things would have been different. But it was best not to walk down that path. She couldn't change it now. What was done was done. *Damn that cliché. It is so fitting!*

Poor Oakheart. He must be devastated that he could no longer feel his oathbond. *Lord, I wish I didn't feel mine.* That otherworldly bond still existed between her and Dellbright, forever a reminder of their connection. She managed to dampen it down, to exclude his malice. Her oath tether was enough to let her know he lived, and if she lowered her defences she'd taste the dark wall of emotion and anger. Just the thought of what lay beneath the surface of him made her shudder with revulsion and, she had to admit, fear. Would she ever be free of her terror of him?

Too much was happening to let herself be drawn into the complexities of "what if". She had to accept Adept Aran's offer to teach her basic healing and anatomy while she was at the retreat. That was the best use of her skill. Then even without access to Sophy's power, she could treat casualties with the *given*.

ONCE BACK IN HER ROOM, MARALAIN LAY DOWN ON HER BED AND

stared at the plain walls and lost herself in reminiscences. The breakfast meeting with Oakheart had not gone well, she thought sarcastically. In fact, it was over before it began. Aria understood her better. She supposed that was right: she was her daughter, a daughter who faced similar decisions in life. And Maralain had been there for her for all of her life until she had been snatched way by the wanderer and brought here to Argenterra. However, if she were honest, there had not been a day since she had first left Argenterra that she hadn't thought about Oakheart, hadn't grieved for her bonny son, so strong and clever—and so very left behind.

Jeff was dead. Tears came again. They'd had nearly twenty years together, happy years, enjoying each other, escaping from the trouble of their lives in Argenterra. Other than missing her son, Maralain had not reflected much on her previous Argenterran life. Jeff had the philosophy of living in the now and pursuing dreams, and she had followed along. It was only her insistence that they seek out Aria that had led him to summon the Crystal Gate. She had no one to blame for his death but herself.

In her not-so-secret heart, she had hoped that Vorn had died, leaving her free. Was that such a bad thing? However, as soon as she stepped through the gate, the oath had snapped shut around her. Funny that it was Daken who had felt no bindings or echo of his oath. Aurore was dead, leaving him free. It had been a brief instant of happy realisation for him before his life was prematurely taken. And she barely had time to register his passing before other things intervened: Sophy stepping through the gate, leaving her son broken-hearted; Aria holding hands with that upstart Fern; Dellbright hurling accusations and sneering at them all, and news of Puri raiding Silverdale.

Puri in Silverdale? Unthinkable. That was her home, the home of her ancestors. Funny after being away so long how quickly the old loyalties were rekindled. Daken would not see it again. Not that they had made such plans. Her yearning to know her daughter was safe had driven them to return and led to his death. It had been her fault, all of it.

❧ 3 ❧

# SILVERY, SOFT TARGET

Hanal stood at the entrance to the canyon, taking in the unnatural sight of severed stone and plundered earth, and wondered what he was doing there. Licking his lips, he wiped at the sweat on his forehead and tried to quell the turbulence in his gut. What had led him here? His thoughts took him back to that day. The day he touched Sophy's power and everything changed.

That day in the summer tents...

Hanal had blinked but had been unable to move his arms and legs. He was not quite sure he could breathe as every muscle was locked tight. Shouts! Cries. Footsteps outside. A groan escaped his lips as he focussed his vision. Umri lay across from him unconscious; blood stained her clothes. He tried to move but it hurt. He radiated hurt. Was that blood in between Umri's legs?

Sophy's power. He'd touched it. Pure *given* magic he was sure. It was on his tongue. His mind was white with the power. Slowly as he breathed painful breath after painful breath, the power bled away, leaving him empty.

The blood. He blinked. Why was Umri bleeding? Legs crossed his line of sight. "Hanal?" said a panicked voice. More people came in.

Some went to Umri. Another, his brother, Tarkel, came to him, helped him to sit up. "What ails you, brother?"

Hanal groaned. It hurt to move, even though he made no effort to engage his own muscles. Being moved hurt. He focussed. Sophy was long gone. She'd slipped through his fingers. Rae had helped her. Rae had betrayed him. *Rae!* He would never forgive her.

Awareness of his surroundings came slowly. Hanal looked into his brother's dark eyes. "Your child. I'm sorry."

Tarkel nodded, sparing Umri a brief glance. "There will be others. My wife is hale."

Hanal looked up as Umri was carried out. "Rae?"

Tarkel shook his head. "Gone. We await your orders to pursue."

"Why are you waiting?"

Tarkel steadied Hanal as he drew him to his feet. "An envoy from Glasshiver. There is news."

Hanal shook his head slightly. "Glasshiver?" His mind wasn't working right. There was something he couldn't quite remember.

"Yes. An ambassador."

Hanal swallowed. "Then I will see him. Bring him food and wine. I need some time, delay him."

"It will be done. Rae? The outlander girl? Do you have orders?"

Hanal took a faltering step and leant heavily on his brother's arm. "Leave them for now. We can track them later. They will not go far."

With the aid of his brother, he was able to wash and dress. His wounds were small but painful: a cut at the back of his head, burns along his torso, a sprain in his thigh muscle. All survivable. It could have been worse.

He sat in his audience tent, his plaited hair hidden beneath his head cloth, a pot of tea steaming by his knee. Umri parted the curtain, bowed and then entered. Her complexion was pale, her movements stiff. He had not requested her presence and couldn't be bothered dismissing her. She obviously had her reasons for being there.

"Bring in Rexford of Glasshiver," he said to his brother.

Tarkel bowed and left the tent. It was but a few moments, even then Hanal did not look to Umri. He didn't know what to say to her.

His feelings were mixed. He was responsible for her actions. She had urged a certain method but it didn't work. They were lucky to be alive. He was still waiting for the euphoria to kick in, the innate sense that he had survived the unsurvivable. But it didn't come.

The man from Glasshiver strode in, feathers arranged on his head, along his back and like a skirt around his middle. Leather belts crossed his chest, embellished with silver. Jewels ringed his fingers. He bowed from the waist. "Honourable Hanal of Puri. I bring news."

"Will you not sit?"

The man, Rexford, looked around him, a grin on his face. "I would rather stand."

Hanal let out a breath. *Let the man stand*, he thought. He was not about to bring him a chair.

"What news have you?"

"It is done. The breach in the Fortitude Ranges is complete. The Argenterrans call it Glass Cutting Canyon." The man grinned. "Appropriate name, I say."

Hanal stilled, then his gut twisted. "You cut into the earth?"

"Yes, the wall of rock was thin in that canyon. It did not take much. Your way into Argenterra is secure. You can approach Silverdale with stealth."

Hanal lifted an eyebrow. "And what is in this for Glasshiver?"

"As discussed, some items of treasure, free trade in Argenterran goods. And an alliance."

Hanal frowned. While he had been in negotiation with Glasshiver to the north, it was for arms and warriors. Their previous ambassador had brought word of their plan to hack through a canyon but Hanal had thought it impossible. He could not do it, or order it done, as it went against his beliefs. Yet they had gone ahead anyway.

He smiled at Rexford. "An alliance? I asked for warriors."

Rexford inclined his head in acknowledgment. "Yes, you did. We can spare ten."

"Ten? What use are ten?"

"You have your own men."

"I do indeed."

"So will you invade? Will you sweep into Silverdale?"

Hanal poured a cup of tea and sipped. "I have not decided yet. I believe a tent is ready for you. I will send word of my decision in the morning."

Rexford's gaze slid to Umri, who knelt in the corner, quiet but watchful. "Very well."

When the Glasshiver man withdrew, Umri edged forwards. "You must take this opportunity."

Hanal turned to her. "Opportunity? To risk my people?"

"No, to be king in Silverdale. I have seen it in a vision. You will rule there."

A sudden chill raced up his spine. "You had a vision?"

"Yes!" Umri edged closer. So close he could feel her body heat. "I had a vision. Your blood will be in the line of kings to rule all of Argenterra. Our people will be equal with the Argenterrans. We will have plenty. We will have more of the *given*."

His eyes narrowed. Umri knew him too well, knew what his heart desired. "I don't believe you. You seek to manipulate me."

Umri threw herself to the matting, abasing herself before him. "No. I speak true."

Hanal breathed through his mouth, waiting, watching.

She lifted her head, tears trailing down her cheeks. "The vision came to me as I recovered from Sophy's power. It was the *given* magic that gave me this vision. Your name will live forever. You will replace the Vorn spawn who inhabit the throne. It will be yours. Your children, your sons will follow after."

Hanal quivered with excitement. Her words stroked his secret hopes. Part of him didn't want to believe, but the other part did. She had proven she had a gift. Now her gift was telling her what path to take. "What do you suggest?"

"Take what Glasshiver is offering. Invade Silverdale before they find out about this breach in the mountain range. Too long have they sat there afraid of no one because of their physical isolation."

"Without declaring war?"

"Yes, it must be so. It is the only way you can win. Take them by stealth, before they have a chance to defend."

Hanal growled his frustration and thumped the matting. "Why doesn't Glasshiver move against them? They hope to let us spend our efforts and they can sit back and take the rest."

Umri shifted around to meet his gaze for he had turned his head away. "No. It is because they do not want us as enemies. Glasshiver only wants bounty. The wealth of Argenterra is the *given*, something they don't understand and can't carry off with them."

Hanal shifted in his seat, feeling the strength of Umri's argument. Still he demurred.

"You only have one chance at this, Hanal. One opportunity to gain all that you desire."

He pierced her with his gaze. "If I don't take it?"

"Then Glasshiver will move against Silverdale. They will plunder it all and leave nothing for us. Then they will be our mighty foe. They will turn on us."

Hanal's eyebrows drew together. "You saw this?"

"No. I can reason this myself. If you do not take this opportunity, they will. It's the only thing that makes sense. If you conquer Silverdale, you will be merciful. Your rule will be just. Forget the Argenterrans. You will make the Puri great."

Hanal raised a hand to his forehead. The after-effects of the power explosion were still with him. "Very well. Umri, I want you to use your gift. Make sure these plans are what you truly see. You have been injured and there may be some mistake. In the morning, when you have a clear head, we will talk and then I will decide."

Umri lifted her head, a fleeting smile crossing her features. "As you command, Hanal of Puri. And what of Rae and Sophy? Will you do nothing to bring them back, nothing to punish them?"

Hanal growled, then ground his teeth. Umri was good at poking his sore spots. "If what you say is true, they no longer matter."

Alone in his bed, Hanal could not sleep, could not rest. Umri's words swirled around in his head. Excited by them, entranced by them, he could not close his eyes. Plans cascaded and reordered themselves. When the morning came, Umri told him of her further visions. Of their trek along the wastes and their victorious capture of Silverdale, of

Veld bowing before him, vanquished. Hanal grinned. He liked the thought of that.

Later he called for his brother. "Tarkel. Give the orders to the clans. Warriors will ride. We take the northern route across the Shabra Plains and The Barrens and will we slip into Argenterra through the Fortitude Ranges, through this pass that Glasshiver had made for us."

Without even a flicker of an eyelid Tarkel heard the news then bowed. "We will be ready." Had Umri told him of her visions? Was Tarkel in accord?

As Hanal made ready, he was interrupted. Nasheen burst into his tent. "Hanal!"

Hanal turned. The insolent clan leader did not even bow. "You cannot do this!" The older man's girth jiggled as he spoke. He really was past his prime. Yet there was pride in his stance and the thrust of his oiled beard. Hanal didn't need an explanation of the man's complaint.

"I can and I will," Hanal replied, and turned back to his preparations.

"It is not honourable," Nasheen said. "You must not."

Hanal lifted his head and turned. "You speak to me of honour? I think you do not know the meaning of the word. I think you are afraid, a coward."

"Me?" Nasheen replied, falling back a step. "Me, a coward? It is you who are a coward. This is a cowardly act. To invade without warning, without a declaration..."

Hanal's mouth drew into a hard line and his eyelids narrowed as he surveyed the clan chief. "Did you not steal Sophy from Oakheart? Did you not betray him, take his wife out of his arms? Were you honourable then?"

"This is different. That was a woman. This is a town."

"No, Nasheen. This is a crown." Hanal was full of righteous anger. How dare this man question his honour? He would remember this. Nasheen and his clan would pay for this outrage.

"What do you need with a crown or a town? In the wastes you are the master, the leader of us all."

Hanal walked away from him, to stop himself from lashing out. *How dare he speak so!*

"It is not for myself I do this. It is for our people. They should be equal. They should have access to the *given*."

"Are you certain about that? Our life is hard but we are free, happy here with our own culture, our own ways. What you seek to do will change us all. Perhaps not for the good."

"Get out, you fool!" Hanal snapped, his ire burning in his gaze.

Nasheen glared at him a few moments more, then lowered his head. "Forgive me. I cannot join you."

Hanal jerked up and then tried to mask his surprise. Nasheen defecting was a big thing. Ordinarily he should imprison the man and his clan to stop the rot. "So be it. Speak to no one of your decision and you will be free to leave."

"Very well, I will do as you ask."

Nasheen left the tent and very soon after Hanal heard the sounds of his clan's departure. Nasheen would regret this betrayal but now he had better things to do.

And so it was that Hanal came here to the border of Silverdale lands and faced the monstrosity of Glasshiver's creation.

THE CUTTING OFFENDED HANAL'S SENSE OF RIGHT. IT WAS A weeping, savage wound. The Puri did not shape the earth as others did. He did not know why it was so, only that it was. His people lived in harmony with the land. They nestled in caves, sheltered within the ground, or abided in tents atop it, leaving no lasting harm.

Glasshiver had wounded the fabric of the mountain here. Piles of broken rocks were pushed up against the sides of the canyon wall like a scab on a sore. Rexford spoke of what they had done to bring it down. He spoke with pride, but Hanal burned with shame.

Would they have committed this act if not for his desire for war with Veld? Glasshiver sought bounty. The cost of the war, the risk, was all Hanal's and his Puri warriors'. Yet as he looked through the opening to the Forest of Galen, he knew it was an opportunity not to be missed. If he did not take it, Glasshiver would. In that Umri was right. Then Hanal would have to choose: fight for Argenterra against Glasshiver, or fight with Glasshiver and get the leavings. He shook his head. No, the decision was made. The conditions set. He could only move forwards now.

The surprise attack could only happen once. For when discovered, the breach in the canyon wall would be guarded by warriors and easily held against attack. Any future skirmish through this route would cost lives, time and would fail. Stealth was his ally now.

"What do you think?" Rexford asked him. "Is it not a feat beyond your imagining?"

"Yes," Hanal responded truthfully. He faced the feather-adorned man and considered his bright gaze as he surveyed the destruction of the canyon. "These explosives you used. Did you invent them?"

"No," Rexford replied, shaking his head. "We traded with people further to the north west. You do not know them, I think. They have not ventured this far south."

Hanal nodded slowly, pretending knowledge where there was none. True, they had some legends from the First Comers, but direct knowledge of these "explosives"? No. He did not want to know these people who could blow up mountains. He repressed a shiver and nodded to Rexford. He put the knowledge of these people in the back of his mind for future reference. The Glasshiver man left his side to join with the warriors that accompanied them.

"Tarkel!" Hanal called to his brother, who served as his second.

Tarkel rode up. Umri sat astride her mare, and followed him. Tarkel spared her a look, but that was all. The rest of his men were arrayed behind them.

"We march. Give the word," Hanal said to his brother.

Tarkel acknowledged his command and propelled his horse ahead, yelling orders as he rode along the line of men and horses.

Hanal glanced over to Umri, who remained by his side. Her eyes glittered and she grinned, then hid her face with the tail of her headdress like a coy maid. He wondered what was going on inside her head. Was she excited to see her visions play out or was she full of doubt as Hanal was? He thought it was the former.

A heel to his mount's side sent his horse lunging forwards into the gaping breach in the rock. Umri fell in behind as Hanal led his people into the Forest of Galen and the lands surrounding Silverdale beyond.

❧

THE OUTER FARMS FELL EASILY AS HIS TROOPS SWOOPED DOWN ON the unsuspecting farmers and their families. Surprise was his ally. That these were peaceful dirt grubbers concerned with growing things and protecting their families was his weapon. A knife to the throat of a wife or child had the men walking off their land, dropping their tools without a backwards glance. He cared not where they went as long as it was not to warn Veld in Silverdale. Many slipped into the forest or lingered aimlessly along the road behind his troops.

Umri rode up close to him. "Have your men take the women hostage. The men will not fight if their families are in danger."

Hanal turned to her and grinned a savage grin. "We have used that tactic already to great advantage."

Umri lifted her chin, her dark eyes glittering. "Then give the unbonded women to your men as a reward. The Argenterrans will run away at your approach when they hear of it."

Hanal's eyebrows lifted. "Take them as wives?"

"Only if you think the women worthy. They are weak, prudish Argenterran maids, hardly worthy of our hardy Puri men."

Hanal considered this. Argenterran women were prized by his people. By report they were soft and pliant. If willing they'd make nice sport for his men, something not smiled upon within their own culture. Sure, he'd had Rae without a vow and she had borne the brunt of that with ostracism. Only his position of leader gave him some leeway with the rules. This was war. This was different.

"Very well. I will tell my men of this reward. Only the ones willing to lie with my men should be gratified with Puri seed and only those worthy should be offered a vow."

Umri nodded her head. "I will spread the word."

Hanal watched her ride off. It worried him that she was eager for

37

his men to sate their desires in soft Argenterran women. Yet, she was his seer. She saw things he did not.

It took two days to empty the farms, to round up the men and keep them quiet while they approached Silverdale proper. Overcoming the resistance was like carving cream.

The walled town loomed ahead.

❧ 4 ❧

## A NEW CHILD OF PURI

Rae fumbled as she untied her pack from the saddle with numb fingers. Her horse was useless to her now. The poor thing had served her well. She staggered away from the mound of dead flesh, dragging her damaged foot behind her. The exhausted horse had fallen, snagging her leg as it tumbled to the ground. It had taken her all morning to free herself from under its bulk. Her knife had been useful to take some of the horseflesh, although there was no salt to dry the meat and no time to dry it. Now she was all alone in the cold, windswept wastelands between the Puri's summer camp and the path Hanal had taken.

For a moment she wished she had sought out her father instead of choosing to pursue Hanal. Too late now: she was on this path and it was Hanal or nothing. Either he would welcome her back with love or spurn her for her betrayal. There was no middle ground that she could see. Yet, despite the risk, she had to follow him. He was her love and her life. As she limped, her womb contracted sharply.

Stopping and bending over, she breathed through the pain and sucked in a breath. That pain was stronger than the last. Bad timing; there was no one here, no tribe's people to give her aid. Ahead was some shelter amongst the rocks and a water hole. An oasis of sorts.

Hanal's people had passed this way. How had Hanal recovered enough from Sophy's discharge of magic to go marching to war? Had that been his plan all along? She guessed so. The clans had already gathered even before Sophy had come amongst them, distracting him with her power. She recalled that he had been angry when a leader was late, or when all the leader's followers had not accompanied him to swell their numbers. Nasheen had been a good example. He had left men dotted around Argenterra. Surrendering Sophy had been the only thing that had saved him from absolute disgrace.

It hurt her back to carry the backpack, so she dragged it by the straps to trail along behind her. What point was there in carrying it? She had no water left and only enough horse meat for one more meal. This trek, coming hard after the one with Sophy, taxed her. Foolhardy as that gesture had been for her actions had made no difference. Hanal was gone. He had left the encampment before she had made it back. Not one finger did he lift searching for Sophy or Rae. Her actions had changed nothing.

At the summer camp, the old women would say only that Hanal and his men had headed for Silverdale. Then they spat on her and turned their backs, offering her no shelter or food or warmth. She was nothing to them without Hanal's protection. Her being heavily pregnant, they could not ignore the fact that she had been in Hanal's bed. Any chance she had of him giving her an oath before the birth had evaporated. She was alone.

So, taking what she could steal from unsupervised tents, she snuck back out of the Puri camp. Left her life behind and walked into the unknown. Hanal was taking a strange path to Silverdale—one that skirted the Upper Plateau. He must have found a way through the Fortitude Ranges to approach Silverdale from this direction. That added to her concern that this invasion had been long in the planning. Chewing her bottom lip, she fretted. Silverdale would not be expecting an incursion from that quarter. The route she followed was barren and difficult. Hanal was taking his men by a hard trail, for an evil purpose. He went to conquer and Rae's soul ached with the knowledge. Ignoring the usual track to Panal's Pass, Hanal and his army were crossing the plains to approach from the north. She puzzled at it. Was there even a route to Silverdale by this road? In all the tales her father had told, none spoke of a trail to Argenterra this way.

For five days she had followed Hanal's trail. Now, her horse was dead and she was not any closer to catching up. Hanal and his men did not travel by night and day so surely she should have caught up. But then, they did have a head start. She tried to estimate when Hanal had departed. The old women on the camp would not give her details. She knew not whether Umri was alive or dead. She guessed alive, but perhaps no longer with child. She remembered the blood between the woman's legs after Hanal had touched Sophy's power, nearly destroying himself in the progress.

Another pain, stronger even than the last one; the promised shelter of the rocks ahead was still too far away. She supposed she could give birth here, out in the open. But at the oasis there would be water and a boulder to lean against, a place to shelter the new baby from the wind while she regained her strength. This time she counted out the steps between the contractions. Her dragging gait rolled her along thirty steps before the pain began low in her belly and spread out. By the *given*! She grunted with effort. The pain was long and sharp. She barely managed to stay on her feet. The baby was coming soon.

Then when the contraction eased she lurched on again, counting slowly—one, two, three, intent on the shelter of the rocks. She must reach them. She made twenty steps before the pain snaked down into her legs, making her fall to her hands and knees. Rae thought of Hanal, thought of her love for him, thought about herself. She would live. She would birth this child and present him to Hanal. If he shunned her then maybe she would die, maybe she would not. How would she feel about this child inside her?

What if it was not the son Umri said she was carrying? Umri, the deceiver, the manipulator. Rae now understood that Umri had never been a friend, just a schemer for her own ends. Her influence had corrupted Hanal, made him do things no honourable man would do. Even Hanal of Puri meant nothing to the seer. His physical beauty did not touch her, only what he could give her: status, control, wealth.

Her heartbeat thundered. She was afraid. Alone. Scared.

How ever was she going to do this? Rae knuckled a tear from her eye and pulled herself to her feet to continue walking—*one...two... three...keep going to the rocks*. If Hanal would not have her, then she would die of an empty heart. Not quite: if he took her child and turned his back on her, she would die. But had she not betrayed him? Would he forgive her? Perhaps, if he understood her motives, the reasons that drove her to take Sophy away from him. Jealously, first and foremost, and concern for him, concern for the danger the girl represented. Moreover, concern for what he was doing to himself, sullying his honour and setting out along a path from which it would be hard to return.

The pains grew worse, and closer in interval. The rocks ahead had dark clefts, nooks where she could brace herself for the birth, water close by to quench her thirst. She *must* reach that spot before the baby came. What if she could not move afterwards? What if she gave birth only to die of thirst? *No!* She would not let that happen.

The next set of pains she walked through, breathing loudly through her mouth, pushing forwards with effort. Finally, she made the edge of the rocky outcrop and crawled the last stretch to the rock, with warm liquid leaking down her legs. The pains came sharp and hard. She panted and gritted her teeth while she fumbled with her trousers. Behind her was a dark crevice, a place where she could lean and push down in privacy. Although there was no one about, she did not wish to be stumbled upon by some Puri travelling to the oasis for water. And if something untoward happened to her, the child had a chance to be found. Scanning the landscape, she could see no sign of other travellers. She was thirsty yet she did not have time to struggle over to the water's edge and drink. A scream left her parched throat, hoarse and raw. Something moved. Something gave as she pushed. The child was coming—now.

LATER, SHE CRADLED THE LITTLE GIRL IN HER ARMS, WRAPPED IN material from her headdress. It was the only item of clothing that was clean, being kept in her carry bags for many days. Her fingers stroked the little arm. The baby girl was perfect in every way. The potential for dark skin was evident already, a pale cream-brown.

Rae ran her index finger down the sleeping child's face. Would the child have Hanal's eyes? Now that the child was born she was happy it was a girl. Not only to overturn Umri's predictions but also to lessen the threat that Hanal would take the child and cast her out. A son would have been a prize to him, even one born in shame. He would let her keep the girl if he threw her out. She prayed that he would not discard them both, but she now knew that she would not die as she had thought. As a mother, she had a duty. Having no memories of her own mother, she knew the lack of that all-important relationship. Rae had to live for her daughter. She would tell the child the stories of the First Comers, of Goslien of the Valley and of Hanal of Puri.

For a day and a night, Rae rested by the oasis. She ate the last of the horse meat and drank from the water. Her feet were sorely used from her trek—red, swollen, blistered and bleeding. One was more swollen than the other from where it had got caught under the horse. Scooping pungent mud from the water hole, she covered her feet and let it dry.

As she washed the caked dirt off the next morning, the redness was gone and the swelling had lessened. Not entirely cured, but better able to move ahead. After offering the child her breast, she refilled her water containers and prepared to leave. She had little to stem the blood flow resulting from the birth. Her clothes would be ruined if she did not take steps.

She looked to the clump of weeds where she had buried the afterbirth and considered whether she could use them. Perhaps another day of rest and preparation would help. Placing the child in view, Rae broke off fronds and laid them in the sun to dry, then before sunset she bundled them together to make a wad to capture the blood as she walked. The rest of the fronds she put in her pack. Nearby was a marker, advising that it was three days to the next oasis. Perhaps at the next one she would find more traces of Hanal.

That night, she tucked the child beside her, listening to the buzzing of insects. Already the child suckled well. Her milk would come soon. Her breasts were tender and throbbing. It was a long walk to Silverdale and this route was hard. No lush pastures and food growing by the roadside. Why did Hanal come this way instead of through the Argenterra, where food lay for the taking?

A grey dawn greeted her and the sound of the child crying rang loud in her ears. Her nipples tingled and her milk let down. Using the dried fronds and some cloth torn from her tunic, she made fresh coverings for the babe and fed her.

The wind lifted with the sunrise and she tugged her clothes around her. Her food situation was not good. Tying the child to her, she scouted around the rocks for something edible. Nothing was left on the vines. The men who had passed before her had taken everything. She kept searching. Then around the bend, in amongst the stones, was a bruised melon. She swept down on it, broke it open and ate the flesh, even the bruised portion. She supposed she should have kept some back, but she was so ravenous. After further searching she found a dropped portion of flat bread. This she dusted off and put in her pack for later. The child whimpered and she stroked her lightly furred head. It was time to leave and with luck there might be more dropped bounty on the way.

## ❧ 5 ❧

## DARK DEALS

Dellbright leant back on his chair as he waited for one of Veld's lackeys to summon the old king to the talkstone. With his booted feet resting on the retreat's talkstone stand, he rocked back and forth, whistling quietly to himself.

During the night, an idea had come to him. That old slut had stayed with his father's body so he had been denied a private viewing. He had tolerated her presence at the burial and then turned his back on them all. Only she came to the funeral, though. Not the others, Oakheart nor Aria. His wife was too much of a coward to face him.

Dellbright grieved for his father but beneath that emotion there was seething resentment, betrayal, feelings of abandonment. He wished things could have been different and that he had had some control over his life back then. Now that his mother was gone, there was only Gilly. And his son was not enough to fill the void. As he thought about his plan, his smile widened.

The news of Silverdale's predicament had filtered through to him. How he hated the Puri scum; hated that some of their blood flowed through his veins. If not for that blood, he would be king in Silverdale. Of that he was sure. He had had time in the night to think things through while the adepts treated his wounds. Healing bark and some treatment was enough to get him on his feet again. *Given*-brewed wine helped soothe the hurt.

Veld's predicament gave him leverage he could use. He had the best fighting force outside Silverdale—if Veld wanted it, he had to accede to his wishes—and Dellbright wanted a lot. He would enjoy Veld's pain, enjoy seeing him squirm.

A face appeared in the talkstone. "Your highness? His majesty is on his way." The face looked away, peering to a part of the room that was not visible to Dellbright. "One moment, your highness, the high king is here to talk to you now."

The king's aide gave no sign he recollected their previous exchange. Dellbright had demanded to speak to Veld and he had threatened to do some interesting things to the adviser when he saw him in person if he did not act swiftly enough to suit him. Dellbright supposed the adviser had never been spoken to like that. Well, it was a new world and everyone had to adjust, even Veld.

Veld's face hovered in the talkstone. Dellbright had forgotten how big the old man was and how red his face got when he was in his cups or upset.

"Prince Dellbright of Valley Keep," Veld's voice boomed through the stone, the over-politeness dripping off his words. "You wished to speak with me, old friend, kin of my blood?"

"Yes, I do, high king. I have heard of your plight there in Silverdale."

"Terrible upstart, that Hanal. He has already taken the choice farmland, cut off our food supply and taken hostages."

"So you are helpless?" Dellbright liked the old man's discomfort.

"We are holding our own, but if our friends do not aid us, yes, the situation could worsen."

Dellbright placed his elbows on his knees and stared into the talkstone. "Where were you, high king, when the Puri attacked my land, my people?"

Veld coughed once and someone next to him passed him a goblet. He took a sip and then spoke. "If you needed my aid you only had to ask. I acknowledge that I did not send aid when I did belatedly hear of your troubles. By then things were a little out of hand."

"So you expect me to aid you when you did nothing for me?" Dellbright scratched his chin and stared at the corner of the room, hoping to give the impression that he was barely interested in Veld's excuses.

Veld sat back and his expression hardened. "I expect nothing. I ask for your aid. If you had sought mine, I would have provided it. Our situation is dire and we need your help."

Dellbright smiled. "I understand. My fighters could swing the battle in your favour, release you from a siege, but..."

"But what? Look, Dellbright, let us be frank. I don't know what ails you but something obviously does."

Dellbright laughed. "Ails me? Why, nothing ails *me*, Veld." The high king blanched at the use of his name without title or respect.

"You are so changed since the last time we spoke on the occasion of your marriage," Veld continued. "I heard about Daken's death and I am sorry for it. 'Tis not the time to open old wounds. Many were affected by that affair. Me, in particular, if you recall."

"I am not changed, Veld. Do not discuss those events without my permission. My father is dead. You will not speak ill of him."

Veld leant his head to one side, assessing him. "As you wish."

Dellbright sat back in his chair and looked Veld in the eye. "I would gladly aid you. There are conditions, though."

"Conditions?" Veld squinted at him and shifted his shoulders uneasily. "What conditions?"

"You may have heard that my beauteous wife has left me to go rutting with that nephew of yours."

"What are you talking about? You mean Fern? Not possible!"

"Very possible."

"So you say, but I have heard nothing about it. Your oathbond would prevent them, I am sure."

"Like mother, like daughter, they say. Your family are not good with fidelity, are they? Experts on betrayal, too."

Veld leant forwards, white eyebrows meshed over the bridge of his nose. "Look, I am very busy. Please be clear in your meaning. I have no notion what you are talking about."

Dellbright's smile vanished. "Do you mean Oakheart did not advise you of the events here?"

Veld blinked a few times. "I have been informed of the high queen's return, the sad passing of your father and that Aria, Gift of Crystal Tree Woods, is my daughter." He sat back in his seat, resulting in the image of his face becoming smaller. His voice when it filtered through the talkstone was frail and shaky. "I do not know what has happened to cause a rift between you and my daughter. As you may guess, I knew nothing of our kinship before she wed you. The day Mara left Argenterra was the worst day of my life."

Dellbright saw someone exchange the high king's goblet for another. The old man took it with a shaky hand and took a few swallows. After handing the goblet back, he wiped perspiration from his forehead. "I am sorry that you have lost your father. I—"

"Pah, what do you care about what I have lost?"

Dellbright's anger boiled. He did not want to hear platitudes from the old fool. He wanted him to suffer, wanted all of them to suffer—as he had.

"Oakheart is on his way to talk to me. After I have spoken with him I will have more time to consider what is happening there. I fear for her, for Aria. You are a changed man."

"It may be that I am a changed man." Dellbright leant back in his chair and grinned. "Changed for the better, in my mind. You can talk to Oakheart all you want, but here are my conditions." He sat up straight and stabbed the air in front of him. "Aria must return with me as my wife."

Veld's eyes widened. "But..."

"There will be no marriage in name only. She will open her legs and let me at her whenever I say so. I want a large family, brothers for Gilly. I want peace and tranquillity in my home. You will make me the heir of Silverdale after Oakheart. As Aria is my wife, it is my right to claim that place in your line. You will banish Fern from Argenterra after Silverdale is delivered from a siege. If he survives, that is.

"You will keep your nose out of the affairs at Valley Keep. Oakheart is to resign as your ambassador and never step foot in Valley Keep again." It was out! It felt so good. His rage simmered. Would it ever be enough?

Veld was silent, his gaze assessing. Dellbright shifted to the side and saw that the scribe was writing his words down. *Good, they should take it down because I will not budge.*

Veld coughed and when he spoke his voice was croaky, hoarse with emotion. "I thank you for your offer of assistance. I will respond to your conditions after I have consulted with my advisers and Oakheart. I would also consult with my daughter before I make commitments on her behalf."

Dellbright stood up and leant over the stone. He knew that his face would take up the whole image, that his features would be distorted and intimidating. That was just what he wanted. "I will await your response. Except I am not happy with you talking to Aria. She has no say in this: she made a binding oath to me, one none can break. Your role is to force her to do her duty, nothing more."

Veld stood up and leant into the talkstone, his face filling up the image, confronting Dellbright in the same way. "That may be your desire, Dellbright, but I have yet to lay eyes on my daughter. I will talk to her before I agree to anything. This discussion is over for now."

The high king turned abruptly and swept from the room. One of his advisers covered the talkstone with a cloth.

Dellbright stared at the dulled gem and then laughed. "Talk all you want to who you want, it will make no difference. I will make sure you never see her, Veld. Your family are sluts, betrayers and destroyers of lives. I will make sure my son takes your place on the throne and I will make sure Gilly is never tainted by his mother's presence. If you had not been so weak, such an idle fool, your wife would never have seduced my father and taken him away, taken him from me."

Dellbright slammed from the room, raged at the adept standing outside the door to seek him out when Veld summoned him to talk again. Dellbright knew that Veld would. Silverdale was in trouble and needed Valley Keep's help. The people of Gilton Forest might send some aid but not enough and not in time to be of use. There were other settlements spread out over Argenterra. That could yield them some fighters, if they took the young ones, too, the young men and girls, who could shoot an arrow or wield a hoe. Again, such a call-up would take time, weeks lost riding from one village to the next. Dellbright found his mirth overwhelmed him. He let go a full belly laugh and winced. The burns on his chest ached, and when he returned to his quarters he demanded more healing bark from the adept who serviced his quarters. Before shutting the door he summoned his second in command. He had some planning to do.

❦

WHEN OAKHEART ENTERED THE TALKSTONE ROOM HE PAUSED AS HIS father's image loomed in the stone. Protocol meant that it was he who had to wait and not his father. *There must be new developments.* He tried to shake off his bad mood and clear his mind. The angry words he had spoken to his mother at the breakfast table were not planned, they just spilled out of him. He regretted them, even though there was truth in what he said. Yet the time was not right to address these things. His mother still mourned her lover. They were all adjusting to the change in circumstances, in relationships. He should have shown more control over his emotions and his mouth. He mentally noted to apologise the first chance he got.

Before he sat down, Veld near yelled at him: "That Dellbright is deranged!"

Oakheart blinked a few times, rearranging his thoughts. Dellbright had been well enough to discuss the situation with Veld? That was a surprise. All his enquiries about his cousin had met with a negative response. Dellbright would not see anyone. He was too unwell. Then it sunk in. Dellbright was deliberately avoiding contact. That thought sent a shiver through Oakheart's gut.

Oakheart cleared his throat. "I am sorry I...er...what happened?"

When his father continued to glower, Oakheart took a seat and said carefully, "Dellbright sought an audience with you?"

"By the *given* he did, and how I wish he had not. Vorn's Blood! And Aria is married to him!"

Oakheart's heart sank. "Yes, she is, but...father, Dellbright has changed these past months, since his mother's death. Has he refused you aid?"

Veld swore again. "He will aid us...but with conditions."

"He wants Aria back," Oakheart guessed. Why had he not anticipated this and sent Aria away beyond Dellbright's reach? His stomach churned. Still, there could be conditions placed on Dellbright if Aria did choose to return. His chest tightened in mere anticipation of her fear. She could not do it. "But..."

"No, do not even go down that road. He was explicit. She's to be a *full* wife, give him more children."

"No!" He tried to think of ways to spirit her away while delaying Dellbright.

"There's more. You are banned from entering Valley Keep and must provide a *given*-witnessed vow to that effect."

Oakheart could hardly keep his seat. "You cannot agree to this! There must be another way." With dismay he watched his father's face churn through emotions: anger, distaste, desperation.

"He has five hundred men, already mounted and trained. Our situation is desperate. Wait, there is more..."

Oakheart's heart skipped a beat. *More? Was not surrendering his poor sister to Dellbright already too great a price?*

As Veld read out the conditions, Oakheart's anger boiled over. What madness drove his cousin? His hands clenched and unclenched. That Dellbright dared to utter such conditions was criminal. How had someone so dear and close to him become so tainted, so different? It was like he was possessed. *Possessed?*

His mind came to an abrupt stop. *Rufus? Could that being's power extend so far?* Indeed, he had possessed a dead body, why not someone living, someone with weaknesses that could be exploited? He thought back to the blood from Aurore's murder that had sunk into and spread through the fabric of the keep. Dellbright had lived with that for months. Could the taint have damaged him in some way?

When Veld finished reading out the conditions, he waited for Oakheart to speak.

"But that would mean we would be effectively giving Aria to him to do with as he wished and none of us would be permitted to see her again. You cannot allow it, father. He beat and raped her. He is not normal, not the man that he was."

Veld took a sip of wine, the redness in his cheeks fading back to normal now that his anger had lessened.

"He was always unstable," Veld whispered, almost to himself. "Ever since that business..."

"Yes, but not like this. Rufus did something to him. The murder of his mother changed him."

His father could not meet his gaze. Hope leaked out of his heart. "You cannot do this. You cannot give her to him. She will die in the end but not before he has beaten her, destroyed her spirit. Say that you need time to get to know her first."

Veld shrugged. "I could do that but what about this slur on her character, this business with Fern? He called her a slut. This is serious, Oakheart."

Oakheart lifted his gaze to meet his father's glare. "I do not underestimate the seriousness of the situation."

"Do not play coy with me, Oakheart. Tell me what is really going on."

Oakheart lifted a shoulder and placed a loose strand of hair behind his ear. "Ah well, there is some truth to the Fern allegations. Fern fell in love with her when she escaped from Dellbright. She had been beaten, raped. The wrong done to her body emanated from her. No one that saw her could help but be affected by her plight, to feel an up-swell of pity. It was extremely difficult to ignore. Fern could not help himself, despite my urging. I could see nothing but heartbreak for both of them. Normally, Fern would be able to keep his passion to himself as his heart is not easily touched, but the situation was different, extreme.

"And her oath was weakened by the depletion of the *given*. She cannot consummate her love for Fern but I think they came pretty close. I have not asked her directly about it. Dellbright caught them together when they were trying to leave Argenterra through the Crystal Gate. She was going to leave her son and her husband like..."

Veld nodded slowly. "Like her mother did..."

Veld buried his head in his hands. His shoulders heaved. After a few minutes, he lifted his head. "I will speak with her. It is my right as well as hers. I would behold my daughter with my own eyes before I decide her fate."

"Very well. One hundred men are with me, including some fighting adepts and other volunteers. Without help from the Valley we could garner another fifty fighting men and women on our way to Silverdale, perhaps a few more. If the forest folk join us, that would swell our number to two hundred, maybe three hundred."

Veld shook his head. "It's not enough. Dellbright has five hundred men, more if we can urge others, the young men and women who would defend our land."

"What about talking terms with Hanal?" Oakheart ventured.

"Give him Silverdale and exile ourselves to the wastelands? I will not."

"Is that what Hanal seeks?"

"I have not asked him. Nor has he demanded anything from me. He just came and took..."

Oakheart burned to ask more, to persuade further, but he could see that Veld was not in a listening mood.

"I will request another talkstone to take with me on the road. Do you wish to speak with...with my mother?"

Veld's grey eyebrows rose. "Ask me that later...I have not...the heart to do so now. I need to prepare myself for that..."

Oakheart left the talkstone room and made his way to the lead adept's office. The hallways once full of adepts were now bare of company. Much had happened here to lessen his fondness of the retreat and its inhabitants. He was not sure he would ever feel at home here ever again. Near Lianal's door, he recalled how two adepts had used the *given* against him as a weapon. At the place where truth was to abound, he found it elusive. There were only shadows of truth, hiding amongst the lies. Adage was gone forever and even that event had been marred by the strange adepts' motives. Only Adage had understood the deeper meanings within the land. Oakheart suppressed a groan before requesting admittance to the lead adept's office.

Once admitted into Lianal's presence, he saw straight away that the adept wanted to apologise for all that had transpired. "Excellency..."

He made a chopping motion with his hand. "We do not have time to discuss that. There is much to do and little time to do it in. I would like to request a talkstone to aid us on our journey and in the defence of Silverdale. I hasten to add that we need it urgently, within the day if it pleases you."

Lianal walked around his desk, smiling at Oakheart in an avuncular fashion. "I have already anticipated you, Oakheart. One is being prepared. It should be ready before you leave. One thing before you go: I hate to mention it, but you appear to be depleting the retreat of its recruits."

"Many seek to join us in the defence of Silverdale. It is home to many, I imagine."

"Yes, I am sure it is. I am hoping you will send them back when they are done." He lifted an eyebrow, a smile reaching the corners of his mouth.

Oakheart nodded, relaxing slightly. Perhaps the retreat was not such an enemy after all, but it was still hard to trust. He had yet to talk to Veld about all that had transpired. He was not sure how his father would take the story of the treatment of Sophy and the rest of his party. Particularly the use of the *given* as a weapon against the heir to the throne.

"I will do my best, Lianal. However, there is much that I need to discuss with my father."

Lianal looked down, avoiding his gaze. "I hope that you will understand our motives in our dealings with you and your oathbound. We had the best intentions."

So that was it. They were looking to make up for what they had done. Oakheart stood rigid.

"Intentions? Well, your intentions were not good enough. If you want to make reparations for all that you have wrought, put your best scholar onto researching the Crystal Gate. I want to know how to summon it and how to control it. You will call me when it is done. I will return, and when I do, I want to go after Sophy and bring her back."

Lianal bristled at Oakheart's tone and when he heard Oakheart's intention his eyes widened. "You intend to bring her back? Through the Crystal Gate? Then we have another chance to drain the power and return it to Argenterra?"

Oakheart bit down on his frustration. "Let the *given* bear witness: if Sophie wishes it, I will bring her home to Argenterra. This I do vow. Whether she consents to let you drain her of power, I cannot say. But I will tell you this: she wanted nothing of power and I am hoping she will want to be rid of it. Then perhaps we can have a life together, one without the Ancient Evil threatening us."

Lianal stepped around the desk, hands outstretched. "Then we will make sure we do as you ask. You have set alive in me a hope that something can be salvaged from this mess." He tugged on his robe. "We will send word via the talkstone when we have made some inroads in discovering what you ask. We found some more writings in Adage's room. Perhaps he has left some clues."

"Adept Aran mentioned that Daken had made notes, and that these were in an archive somewhere."

Lianal nodded. "I will make sure they are found, Oakheart. His work on predicting the Crystal Gate's appearance will assist us. Every effort will be made, I assure you."

"Very well, I thank you. When you know enough to operate the gate, send word and I will return. And that mess you speak of? 'Tis my wife. Your future queen. I would be careful if I were you in how you talk about her. When she returns you will also be very careful how you treat her. Is that understood?"

"I understand, Oakheart. I will remember."

Oakheart turned to go and Lianal followed him, saying, "Oh, and do not forget about the young adepts. Take care of them. The retreat depends on them to survive."

He paused and turned back. "Ah...you remind me. You will ensure that those who can fight with the *given* are sent with us. It will increase the chance of all of your charges returning. Also, I want them to teach me. You will instruct them to do so."

Lianal bowed and Oakheart left the office. In the corridor he checked himself and reprioritised what he had to do. It was important to talk to Aria before her audience with their father. He had to prepare her for what Veld would say to her. How would she bear such news?

Thinking of the situation in Silverdale made him chew his bottom lip. He would have to do better if he was to outsmart Hanal. So far he had not handled his father well, had upset his mother and had underestimated his cousin. Hopefully, his sister would be easier to manage, but he doubted that would be so. How was it possible for her to even contemplate agreeing to Dellbright's demands? He did not want her to but neither did he want to leave his father powerless against the Puri.

❧   *6*   ☙

## THE UGREALS

Sophy woke from her huddled doze, wondering for a moment where she was. Her stomach roiled, and if she'd had food in her belly she would have vomited. When the queasiness passed, she opened her eyes to the grim light of the below-ground cavity and her recollections shuffled themselves. She stretched out her legs and wished that she was better dressed. What had happened to her clothes? She was sure she didn't normally dress like this, dressed in scraps of rags. Images of pretty dresses came to mind, and comfortable trousers.

The cool dryness of the burrow made her skin rise in tiny bumps. Then she detected some stickiness on her thigh, where she had a burn and some scrapes. Sitting up and squinting, she gasped at a film of white sticky substance on parts of her skin. Checking her other injuries, minor though they were, she discovered that these too were covered in the slime. Blinking, she decided the layer of film was not a normal body fluid. It was too white and opaque for that.

Her head jerked up at a grinding sound. Without moving her limbs, she angled her head around and saw a small, furry creature chewing on what looked like a twig. With spine-stiffening surprise, she watched it

57

edge closer to her thigh and spit on her. Its furry tongue rasped and tickled somewhat as the creature spread some of the white stuff on a long scratch on her thigh. Suddenly, another creature was by her foot; it too spat and began to spread the gauzy film over a graze.

With a shrill squeal she jerked her foot away, recoiling as if they had bitten her. The creatures promptly dropped their twigs and flitted back into the tunnels, like mice disturbed in their nocturnal wanderings.

Sophy panted, and as her panic subsided she examined the substance clinging to her wounds. She probed the edges gently with a forefinger, testing the substance and her level of pain. On what looked to be older bandages, the film had dried to a white powder. When she prodded, it brushed off and she saw that underneath the wound was healing. Hastily reviewing her other injuries, she could see no redness or signs of corruption. With a sigh, she realised that whatever the wood bark and spit were, they were helping her.

She peered into the dimness and stared at one of the tunnels one of the little creatures had escaped into.

"Sorry, little one," she said in a soft, coaxing voice. "You frightened me, that's all." She could see the light reflecting off its little eyes. The clicking sound started, and many low clicks combined and grew to sound like humming. Her gaze travelled over the openings to the other tunnels. Lots of eyes stared right back at her. The little creature she had seen was about the size of a large rat, with a little cotton ball tail, dexterous forearms and cute little hands. Its coat appeared grey in the dull light.

Sophy's stomach grumbled loud and long. "Oh dear, sorry about that. I am awfully hungry. You wouldn't have some food, would you?" She mimicked putting food in her mouth and chewing. When that didn't elicit any movement, she knelt and moved along the walls, patting the dry surface and ceiling, hoping to find an exit. The tunnels were too small for her to crawl through. How on earth had they got her in here, even in that conveyor belt way they'd used? "What's the point?" she said and then crouched.

The creatures clicked again and she heard them moving around in the tunnels. The glowing eyes vanished, leaving the cavity darker. She didn't want to destroy their warren so she figured she would have to be patient. Sitting down, she dozed again, thinking that she would climb out later and search for food. Just the thought made her stomach go all queasy. The air was so dry. Her eyes snapped open and she crawled to the little pool of water and took sips. Then she dozed again and dreamt of dying there and being found years later, a dehydrated corpse, a mummy for some explorers to wonder over.

She jerked awake. Next to her on the ground was a piece of white wood. It hadn't been there before. She prodded it with her finger, then picked it up and examined it. Not wood, exactly, a kind of root.

One of the creatures slowly climbed down out of its hole in the wall. She watched it carefully as it moved slowly. In its hand it had a small piece of root, which it began to gnaw on. Its little teeth scissored, removing the outer crust. Then tiny shavings were sucked up into its mouth. It paused, looked up at her and waited.

"You want me to eat this?" she asked gesturing with the root in her hand. *It could kill me. So would not eating.* The creature eyed her speculatively as it swallowed. Then she sniffed the root, dabbed her tongue on it. It smelt musty although the root was clean. She copied the little creature and gnawed on the root to expose the white inner flesh. Then she bit into it and a clean taste burst onto her tongue. It tasted like sherbet but that wasn't quite it—more citrus tasting and pasty at the same time, with just a hint of sweetness. As she chewed on it, moisture flooded her tongue, released from the fibres. She wasn't sure how long it took to eat the root, but her jaw ached when she was done. Her hunger had dissipated and her mouth was less furry and dry. She crawled over to the little pool of water. It was nearly empty. She scooped what she could but she was still thirsty. "More water?"

The creature stiffened, then bolted into the closest hole. The *click, clicking* started up again, like a deafening forest of cicadas.

Wiping her mouth, she inspected the holes. Obviously the creatures were intelligent. They had brought her food so maybe they could take her outside. She wished they'd stop with the racket, because the cavern amplified their clicks and made her ears hurt. "Water," she said, pointing to her mouth. "Must have more water."

The clicking died away. She sensed movement in the tunnels. She listened, waiting patiently. The clicking was there again, distant and broken up, like a conversation.

A sudden approach of little feet and she lowered herself to a squat. About ten of them fell out of a hole in the wall onto the floor. She almost laughed aloud at the comedy of it. But then she saw it was a rather smooth movement, which allowed them to arrive and stand in a line. They clicked at her and their little arms waved. After regarding them for a minute or so, she asked, "You want me to go with you?"

The chirping increased. Sophy peered into the larger of the holes. "You want me to go in there? I don't think I can fit."

The thought of trying to tummy-crawl through the hole gave her goosebumps. Fear punched into her gut. She couldn't go in there—a dark, enclosed space. However, if she thought about it, she couldn't stay where she was, either.

More creatures poured out of the openings. Soon there were about a hundred of them covering the available floor space so she had to stand up and bend over. "Well now, can't keep calling you creatures. Have to give you a name, I reckon. What about ugreals? I mean, you're sort of weird and ugly and I'm not quite sure you're real either. I could be dreaming this whole thing. Ugly unreal things..."

The chirping increased. Soon they were tugging on the strips of cloth dangling from her buttocks. She got the idea that they wanted her to lie down. Carefully, without squashing them, she lay down. Straight away their little brown hands were on her. They were soft and waxy, lifting her gently, like Lilliputians lugging Gulliver, except they weren't that small and she wasn't that big. Her body began to glide along. She closed her eyes, blocking out the sight of the walls moving, of her head going last into a dark hole.

The ugreals whisked her through tunnels. Sophy let her body completely relax and trusted them to look after her as they bent her, curved her, pulled and pushed her as they conveyor-belted her through the tunnels. At last they stopped and put her down gently. The smell of water was tantalising, and she could feel moisture on her skin. To her disappointment this space was still underground, but perhaps not by much. Sitting up on the edge of the pond, she cast her gaze around while the ugreals huddled behind her and in the shadows. It was lighter in this space, and through one of the larger holes in the ceiling she could see a grey smear of the sky beyond the white, twisted bulk of a tree trunk. Its roots dove into the earth, supporting the opening. Underground but the surface was close and accessible. She crawled over to the water's edge and cupped a handful of water, drawing her face close to it. It looked clear, smelt clean, but tasted funny.

On her tongue was an overlay of the tree root she had eaten before. Either that was still on her palate or the water took on the taste of the roots. She supposed the trees reached into the water to survive. Nevertheless, there appeared to be no bad after-effects from eating the root so far, so she drank, content to have her immediate needs met. If she continued without ill effects she would eat more of the roots. So much for Rufus saying she would starve.

"Take that, Rufus, you bastard."

At the sound of her voice, the ugreals began clicking again, this time deeper in tone.

She studied them, trying to work out their reaction. "Rufus? You know Rufus, I take it."

Again the clicks, rumbling with fear. That appeared to be a 'yes'. "Do you know where he lives? Can you show me?"

The clicks turned to tiny screeches and all the ugreals disappeared like water being sucked down a plug hole, except in reverse as they flowed up into the various holes dotting the walls and floor.

To the empty space she said, "I guess that's a 'no'."

There were no responding clicks. Sophy took her time checking out the larger water cavern. She found a foothold that allowed her to poke her head out of the hole.

The larger cavern was better that the other small cavity. Sophy found a place to stretch out and nap without feeling the presence of the walls and roof surrounding her. Then as she closed her eyes she remembered her injuries and the regurgitated slime covering them. Jerking up, she checked on them. On more of them, the film had gone whitish but was not quite dry. The others looked nearly the same, turning opaque with some gunk still visible. Tentatively, she probed the edges. The skin surrounding it felt numb. Some kind of anaesthetic, she realised. No sign that any of the wounds were infected. Smart little ugreals.

62

## 7

# FOR THE SAKE OF OTHERS

ria sat across the table from Oakheart, the skirt of her robe twisting in her hands. Not only had she spent most of the day soothing her mother and helping her adjust to her new life, now she had to listen to what Oakheart said about Dellbright's machinations.

"I won't do it. You can't make me go back to him."

Oakheart took her hand in his, stroking it. "I would not dream of making you...I do not want you to return to him. Perhaps we can think of another way to get his fighters to assist us."

With compressed lips, Aria shook her head, letting her hair fall down over her face. A shaky breath and then she wiped at a tear. She would not cry. It was time to be strong and not fall into a heap. Oakheart had advised that her real father wished to speak with her within the hour. Hand over her mouth, she stifled a groan. What a topic of discussion for her first conversation. The fact that she had run away from her husband, forsaken her oath and, as it turned out, planned to repeat the deeds of her mother by leaving Argenterra with her lover, leaving a son behind. The irony was not lost on her.

How could her father even look at her when so much about her would remind him of Maralain's painful betrayal? She could not even begin to think of how that scenario, the reuniting of her mother and Veld, would play out. She had no doubt it would take place. From her discussions with her mother and the knowledge of her intentions to rally forces to lift the siege of Silverdale, she had no doubt that her mother wanted to again be high queen and maybe the wife of the king in name only? Perhaps it was how her mother was dealing with the loss of Jeff, or should she say Daken? By throwing herself into actions and plans, she didn't have to think about her grief or what the future would bring. Aria could understand that; she would probably do the same. No, she couldn't think of going back to Dellbright, of living with him, of being in the same room. Just the thought of all that sweetness turned to bitterness and hate made breathing more difficult. Never mind the beatings...the rapes...

Hands all a-tremble, she raced to the bathroom. Oakheart stood up when she left the room, and then stood again when she returned. The only bright spot in Dellbright's proposal was that it would allow her to be with Gilly. Longing infused her, spreading like an ache. But would Dellbright allow her to be with her son? A thread of doubt niggled in her mind.

Previously, he had called her a curse. Did he still think so? Was he sufficiently over his aversion to her that he would allow Gilly contact? And what about Fern? He had hardly spoken to her since their aborted attempt to flee Argenterra. How angry would he be when he heard of this proposal to return her to Dellbright? She so very badly needed Fern's sage counsel right at this moment, but he wouldn't talk to her.

Aria studied Oakheart's haggard face. His eyes lifted to hers and she sensed the sadness in them. Sophy was gone. Her hands clenched and then she reached out to squeeze his hand. "Brother," she whispered. "How good it feels to say that."

He placed his free hand over hers. "Aria. Sweet sister."

"Sophy would not have abandoned you willingly. I'm sure of it. She is loyal to the bone."

Oakheart nodded. "This I believe."

"Yet, our mother has a point. The gate was open to our, I mean, Sophy's, home world."

Oakheart lifted an eyebrow. "No one appears to be an expert on the workings of the gate. I know what my mother believes and I know what I feel. Sophy could be in danger and I..." He broke off, lifted hands to rub tired eyes. "I can do nothing."

These were the saddest words. She sniffed, finally succumbing to emotion. "But...I know she is strong and brave."

"I know that too."

They sat for a few minutes, then Oakheart lifted his head. "About Dellbright..."

Aria stood up and walked to the corner of the room. "Can't we make a counter proposal?"

Oakheart's eyes widened. "Like what?"

"I could pledge not to leave Argenterra. I could even—" She bit her lips, then released them. "I could live at Valley Keep, look after Gilly and supervise his household. I could be civil, if that would work. What do you think?"

Oakheart let out an explosive breath and shifted in his seat. His gaze brushed hers and then he looked at a spot on the wall behind her head. "His conditions state he would not suffer a marriage in name only. He would require unfettered access to you, to your...er...bed."

Aria's cheeks grew hot. "What? He would dare to demand such a thing? After what he did to me? He has lost his mind!"

Oakheart shrugged, unable to answer her question. Not for one minute would she consider letting Dellbright touch her. Soberly, she took the seat opposite Oakheart again, folding her arms as she thought furiously. Go back to Dellbright as his wife. She couldn't do that. Shifting position, she wrung her hands together, sticking her nails into her palms. In a heartbeat, Oakheart was next to her, drawing her into his embrace and stilling her hands, lifting them to his lips to kiss them.

"Do not fret so—it breaks my heart to see you so distressed. I would not ask it of you. But I am not Veld and I am not in Silverdale surrounded by Puri raiders. I do not know how to aid you unless I stand against our father in his hour of need. I have told him my thoughts on the matter. He says he intends to discuss it with you. Would that it was a happy family reunion and that Dellbright and war were not the topics of conversation."

Aria pulled away from him and looked him hard in the eyes. "I could not ask you to go against your...our...father. I will wait and see what he...our father has to say. Perhaps one of his advisers has come up with an alternative plan since you last spoke with him; perhaps he will take pity on me and not ask me to do something so against my heart."

Oakheart's sympathetic expression undid the last of her self-control. Aria buried her face in his shoulder and sobbed noisily.

"The trouble with politics, dear sister. How I like the sound of that —sister. It warms my heart to know we are such close kin."

Oakheart nuzzled his nose in her hair. She felt the air expel from his mouth. "Ahhh...what about...not an easy subject...Fern? He will not take it well if you return to the Valley."

"Oh, brother, Fern will barely talk to me as it is. I can do nothing and say nothing to anyone until I talk to Veld. Then I will know what I must do and Fern will just have to bear the decision, either way. I realise now our romance was hopeless from the outset. I should have had more strength."

"You were vulnerable and Fern was persuasive."

She eased away so she could look Oakheart in the face.

He smiled tenderly. "You have courage, Aria, and intelligence to match. You will make the right decision."

Aria groaned. "Don't do that, don't confuse me. Let me rest my head on your shoulder and stay quiet. I need to think and time is running out." With those words, he sat there holding her, stroking her back until it was time to speak to Veld.

Aria closed her eyes, just letting herself be in the moment and revel in Oakheart's warmth and strength. A tap on the door and a muffled voice announced Veld's call.

"Coming," Oakheart called out on her behalf. Lifting her chin to look into her face, he asked, "Do you wish me to come with you?"

"Maybe to the room...and...close by, in case I need you."

Her knees shook. This was the first and most important conversation of her life as part of her true family. It would forever shape the relationship she would have with her real father. In her childhood, she had known that Jeff was not her real father. There had always been something hovering between them to distance their relationship. Perhaps it was that her blood line, her kinship and resemblance to her true father were always there. Although Jeff had never been cruel to her, this factor would explain many things; his looks, words and treatment all shifted and reassembled to make a new perfect sense.

Aria stepped through the large door, which a female adept held open for her. The chamber was large and dominated by a pedestal, above which hung a large faceted crystal with a smoothed front, held in place by chains. Light refracted around the crystal and sparkled on the walls. She moved closer, heading for the chair the adept guided her to. When she sat down the image of a large old man with a red face and white hair filled the talkstone. He was so like Oakheart that she gasped.

The attendant left and quietly shut the door. Aria's pulse quickened and, with effort, she willed herself to relax although she felt like throwing up at any moment. The face gazed at her, still and quiet, as if he was staring at a sunset slowly disappearing with the encroaching night. Then she heard a sob. "'Tis true," he said. "You are my daughter —so like her, so beautiful, so dainty, so regal." He wiped a tear from his eye, and another and another fell unchecked. Someone passed him a white cloth and he blew his nose loudly.

Aria's nervousness evaporated. She was moved, and teary too. Letting herself gaze at the high king in turn, she contemplated his resemblance to Oakheart, and the shape of the brow and the slight dimple in the chin that matched the characteristics of her own face. She couldn't find the words. Her heart was so full. It would have been best to meet in person, but Dellbright's demands had precipitated this first meeting via the talkstone. They could not touch and hold and embrace. It was not to be.

"You cannot know how much joy it gives me to see you," Veld said. "I always wanted more children, a girl to take after her mother. And there you are, all grown up and your life chosen before I could give you one word of advice, one word of caution or guidance."

Overcome by tears, she listened to him talk. She hadn't waited for or listened to any advice as far as her decision to marry Dellbright was concerned. Had she listened to her true heart, heeded Sophy's warning, then her life would be less complicated now.

But how could she blame herself; her mother set things in motion years before.

Not that she blamed Maralain, but she couldn't help wishing things had been different. Regret was hard to swallow along with the tears. Now she knew who she was, it made sense that Argenterra had seemed so welcoming, so overwhelming, and why she could use the *given* when Sophy could not. That meant that it was Sophy who was the Gift of Crystal Tree Woods, and not her at all.

"I see your mind runs wild with possibilities and what-ifs," her father said. "I have also been engaged in such thinking. Waste of time. We have to deal with the facts of now. We cannot undo what is done. Silly to even try to. You are here and married to Dellbright. Not the man I would have chosen for you."

Aria lifted her head. "Really? Who would you have chosen?"

"Not Fern, if that is what you are thinking. As a princess of Silverdale your marriage would have been made to further our interests, seal an alliance perhaps."

Aria was suddenly angry. Fern was who she had been thinking about. Her father's comments brought her out of a dream. "I suppose you would have married me off to Hanal of Puri, without any thought of love or my happiness?"

"Come to think of it, that's quite a good suggestion. Hanal is an excellent specimen. Pity about his heritage."

Her chin lifted. "How dare you even suggest such a thing. To marry me off for convenience. I wouldn't stand for it."

Veld chuckled. "I like your spirit. You are going to need it."

Aria's breath froze in her chest.

Veld met her gaze. "I suppose Oakheart told you about your husband's conditions?"

"Demands," she hissed through her teeth.

"Yes, a much better description."

"What will you have me do, father?" she asked, not liking how her voice shook and how her pulse throbbed painfully in her neck.

Veld frowned and she could see clearly the muscle jumping in his jaw. He let out a breath. "You know what the situation is here so I have no need to detail it to you. You know what kind of man Dellbright is." He paused as if waiting for her to speak.

She nodded. "Yes, I know those things. What would you have me do? What are your orders?"

"Orders? In this I can give no orders or make directions. I do not know you well enough and I cannot call upon our relationship in the way I can with Oakheart. I have watched him grow up and know his strengths and his weaknesses. In this case there is only duty. It is you who must decide what your duty is. Is it to yourself? Is it to Dellbright? Is it to Silverdale, or something else entirely? I beg leave not to make the decision for you. I trust that you will make the right one."

Aria stood up with fists clenched. "What do you mean? You can't do this. You have to make the decision. Tell me what I should do!"

Veld chuckled. "Very good. If I tell you to run off with Fern, you will blame me when Silverdale falls. If I tell you to sacrifice yourself to your upstart and unstable husband, you will blame me for the outcome. There is no middle road here. No clear path. No one, not me, not Oakheart, will ask of you something you cannot do. You must decide your own path."

Aria wanted to run from the room. This was not what she had expected.

Her father continued, looking her straight in the eye. "You are a princess of Silverdale. Oakheart told me many months ago about his impressions of you, how you were born to be a princess. Make that true, Daughter. I wish that I was there so I could hold you. I wish that your friend, Sophy, was restored to us. I wish that Rufus had never stepped foot in Argenterra and that the very substance of our lives, the *given*, was not under threat. However, whatever I wish for is useless idleness and fancy. There is only the now—and the decisions we must make for good or ill—and then the consequences we must live with.

"Do not decide now. Think on it."

"I don't need to think about it," Aria said through clenched teeth. She wanted to punch something. *Why, why, she thought to herself, did it have to be like this? Why did he have to be so kind and yet not tell her what she must do? Why did he have to be so right?*

"Yes, you do. You want to cloak yourself in anger and feelings of uselessness. You want to rage at me, at your mother and everyone. In the end you will make up your mind and we will all accept it."

Aria groaned and ground her teeth. On one hand she thought he was opting out, avoiding the issue; on the other hand, the truth sang out to her. "Please, has no one thought of an alternative?"

"Not yet. I have people thinking of various strategies. For example, we could do nothing. We could let the Puri overrun us. Or we could try to parley with Hanal but what have I got to offer? A daughter already wed, and a son too. It is too late for that. I made a mistake. Oakheart was right. I should have let him make that marriage to Lyant. But I heard about that girl, that friend of yours, Sophy, and I had this feeling that she was important and that she would be right for him. I had heard of the beauteous Aria, but it was this strange girl, pale like snow and ethereal like she wasn't really there, that held me bound. There is where I thought the real power lay, why I hoped that Oakheart would take her for his own. When I met her, I saw there was honesty in her and no real sense of trickery, even though you could not see her in the *given*. If you took the time to look, there was Sophy revealed for all to see.

"You, my child, are different. Like your mother you may be in looks and ways and also inside of you there is part of me. It saddens me, what you have suffered. Yet we all suffer in some way in this life, always there is some hurt that has to be borne. To know happiness, you must taste sorrow. So for now you must choose and I must plan and act based on what you decide. You know what responsibilities I have and I know you will take them into consideration."

"But...but father, that's not very helpful. I cannot tell if you want me to sacrifice myself or not."

"Ah, but I do not want you to suffer, my child. No father wants that. Now I must go. I pray by the *given* we shall meet in person and that the circumstances are better than the ones we suffer now."

And then he was gone, and the talkstone was covered up by a cloth while she sat there staring at nothing. She wept into her hands. She didn't hear the door open and the attendant enter. Then her sense of the world around her intervened so she dried her eyes, stood up and walked out. Oakheart looked up as she exited the room. "I'm all right. I need to be alone."

He stepped aside and she made her way back to her quarters, pushed the door open and paused on the threshold. Fern and her mother were waiting for her, sitting at a table. Evidently they had been arguing and her opening the door had cut off their shouts.

Aria guessed it was time to discuss things with them, but she was no closer to a decision than she had been when talking to Veld. In fact, all she had been prepared for was to fight the decision demanding her to be sent back to her husband. But that had not been laid before her. It was not so clear-cut.

Her mother stood up, scraping the chair across the floor. "Oakheart said you went to speak with Veld. What did he say? Did he..."

Fern stood up slowly and walked over to her, his gaze searching her face. Torn, she wanted Fern to hold her, but that would only confuse her. She put her hand on his shoulder and squeezed, then stepped past him and sat down at the table. She caught his expression—anger, betrayal and then confusion—before he hid it away. She saw him hesitate too, as if he were considering leaving.

"Please sit down, both of you. We have a few things to discuss."

Maralain glanced at Fern and at the same time they drew their chairs out and sat down. Both turned curious gazes in her direction.

"Veld has not ordered me to do anything at all. The decision is mine to make."

Fern's hand darted across the table, grabbing for her hand. "You cannot go back. The man is an animal."

Maralain's head snapped around. "He is no such thing. He's the son of a wonderful man...just misunderstood."

Fern shouted at her: "You are blind. You cannot know what he is."

Maralain sucked in a breath and her face reddened. She sat back. "What business is it of yours? That is my daughter's husband you are talking about." She cast a fleeting glance at Aria before diverting her gaze to Fern again.

"What business? I love her for who she is, not what she is. I would never harm her like...he did."

Her mother looked ready to fly into a rage. Aria stood up and thumped her fists on the table. "Enough! For heaven's sake, enough. What Dellbright has or has not done is not important right now. Neither of you know truly what I suffered at his hands. Mother, how can you defend someone you don't know? The man raped me on my wedding night and left me thinking I was inadequate, that there was something wrong with me, and I believed it, believed if I had been a better wife he would have no cause for complaint.

"Later something happened, something that ripped those cracks in his personality open and filled them with hate. If he was ever a good person that is completely gone now. I can sense him at the other end of our oathbond. I can't bear to even look there. It's too dreadful. Yet this man has my son, your grandchild. He stopped me from seeing my own baby. Left alone, he will fill Gilly with poison and create a mirror image of himself. I cannot allow that to happen. I don't know how I can stop it. I have to save my son. While I am doing that perhaps, just perhaps, I can help Silverdale."

*There!* She had made up her mind without even trying.

Fern's chair fell back with a crash when he surged out of his seat. "No!" he cried out, chest heaving with repressed rage. "You cannot!"

Maralain's expression stilled, yet Aria detected a hint of pride. She nodded as Aria locked gazes with Fern. "There's no point in arguing with me. Put your mind to something better. Find a way to free me from Dellbright, bring me home and Gilly. Find a way to bring us both home."

Oakheart entered quietly. Aria hadn't even heard him knock. He had caught the end of her speech. He stood there, showing no emotion. "So you will go to him? Are you certain?"

Aria nodded slowly but definitely. "Lord help me."

Oakheart frowned, pale eyebrows furrowed over eyes darkened with concern. "I will take over the negotiations and see what concessions I can gain from him." He turned to leave the room, opened the door a fraction and hesitated. In a low voice, he added, "I would that you were not..."

Aria stifled the sob so that it lodged in her throat. Turning away, she sniffed loudly. She hated what she had to do, yet at the same time knew it was right. She had this one chance to get her son back.

"My wonderful girl," her mother said. "You will not regret this."

Aria gaped at her mother. Could she admit that she already did? "I'm not being that noble. It is my last chance to be with my son. It will help Silverdale, of course. But I will see my Gilly once again. My motives are not so pure."

Was she prepared to forgive Dellbright? Not entirely, but she was prepared to give him one last chance. But she wanted an out, wanted a way to win clear of him if it fell into a mess.

"You will come for me, won't you Oakheart?"

"I will do what needs to be done." And then he was gone from the room.

Fern glared at her, then headed for the door, his eyes a dark storm grey. "You could do this?" His tanned skin was red with suffused anger; the hand gripping the door handle was almost white. "Deny us?"

"Fern..." Aria could not think about his pain. She had thought she loved him. Now she wasn't so sure. The future had changed and chances for their joint happiness were non-existent. "Try to understand."

"That I will never do." His words were forced out, clipped and hard. The door slammed shut, leaving her alone with her mother.

Maralain held her arms open. Aria nodded and allowed her mother to embrace her. Her cheek rested on her mother's soft breast, a place of comfort in her childhood days.

"I wish I had been there for you." Her mother's voice was soft, and her forefinger stroked her ear lobe. "It is I who am to blame for this," she continued. "I should not have let you go on that ghost tour and let you be taken away. I knew in my heart when Jeff said that it had been the wanderer that fate would bring you here. There was too much coincidence for it not to be the case."

Aria pulled back. "You took me away from this place, away from my real father, abandoned Oakheart and everyone. Things could have been so different if you hadn't. I wish you had brought me up here in Argenterra, where I belong."

She saw the look of horror in her mother's face at her words and rushed to ameliorate them. "I'm sorry. I don't wish things undone. Father said it is silly to do that. We must deal with the now. No point in bemoaning what we should have done; we did what we did."

Tears smeared Maralain's cheeks. She gulped, as if swallowing what she wanted to say, and nodded. "Who would have though Veld would be so wise?"

Aria suddenly realised that his words to her were also for her mother. There appeared to be a way forwards for them all.

ARIA UNPACKED HER CLOTHES AND LAID THEM OUT, THEN SHE folded them and placed them back in her bag. By mutual agreement they put off their departure for one more night. Aria had been all packed to go with her mother to join in the recruitment of volunteers to fight for Silverdale. Now her destination was in doubt. Most likely Aria would leave with Dellbright and head straight to Valley Keep. Maralain had departed for her bed; her mother had to be up early and promised to see her before leaving.

Fern had not returned. He had sent word by an adept saying he was preparing his men and supplies for the journey to Argenterra. Heavy-hearted, Aria knew it was over between them. She was returning to her husband, turning her back on Fern and their love. Was it love? She no longer knew. Inside of Argenterra, they could not live as man and wife, not while her oath still bound her to Dellbright. Had there ever been a chance for them? Not after her mother walked through the Crystal Gate and changed everything. It surprised her how easily she understood Fern. She was a prize. Now a prize denied, he no longer wanted her. It was all about him. Maybe she was being unfair.

It was well after midnight when Oakheart came knocking softly at her door. Her smile at Oakheart was weary, a bit sad.

Sitting next to her, Oakheart spoke. "I have spoken with Dellbright."

Her gaze was riveted to a spot on the opposite wall. Best not look at Oakheart and the sympathy he could not hide. "And what concession did he make?"

"He will let you see Gilly, let you bring him up. On that he did swear a binding oath."

"That's it? What was the wording of the oath exactly?"

Oakheart leant back his head. "I swear on the *given* that Aria will have daily access to Gillcress and have a say in his upbringing."

Aria savoured those words. It was hard to believe and she suspected there was something underhand but couldn't see where. Dellbright did not say his son, her son or our son? But he had vowed to let her see Gilly. Argenterran oaths were still a bit of a mystery.

"Anything else?" she asked softly.

"In other things he was less willing to agree. When he heard that you had chosen to return to him, he acceded to your wish to be with Gilly."

"I had hoped that you could have managed more, though I am grateful. I want to be with my son."

"You also have a new maid, Leyla. She will accompany you everywhere."

"A maid?" She looked sideways at Oakheart, not quite certain she had heard correctly. "How does that help things?'

"Leyla is an adept, one of Adage's special students, and he only taught the naturally gifted ones. She will aid you, protect you if the need arises."

"I see. Did Dellbright make a binding oath about that?"

"No, but he has agreed to allow her to accompany you. I would not let you go otherwise."

"I don't understand, brother. How does a maid help me, even one gifted with the *given*?"

"She uses the *given* to make herself stronger. She can fight with it. If you don't want her, I could use her myself. You could get her to teach you to use the *given* too."

Aria laughed despite herself. "I see. So when do I meet with this wonder maid? What if we hate each other—who will protect me from her?"

To her surprise, Oakheart stood up and opened the door. In walked a tall girl with long, dark red-brown hair, her adept's robes hanging off her thin frame. Her features were plain, her face long. Aria eyed her, wondering about this strength with the *given*. She did not doubt her brother's word, but it amazed her how much she relied on seeing to believe and on appearances. Then she closed her eyes and felt a slight tremor—so that must be what a special gift felt like. Reaching out with her senses, she detected a larger tremor emanating from Oakheart.

"Hello, Leyla. Thank you for agreeing to look after me as I travel with my husband."

When Leyla spoke, her voice surprised Aria because it was croaky and deep, almost a man's voice. "I am happy to serve others of Vorn's line."

Aria glanced at Oakheart, questioning eyebrow on the rise. Oakheart put his hand on Leyla's shoulder. "Leyla is actually descended from Adage's line, before he took his oath that extended his life. She is distantly related to us."

Leyla turned to him. "We are closer in blood than you think, but I will leave that discussion alone for now. Genealogy is not for the faint-hearted. It is nice, though, that you think me kin. Adage paid it no mind at all. His main interest was my ability with the *given*. I can teach you, Aria, I mean, my lady, if you wish it."

"I do wish it. Very much so." Aria went forwards and embraced the girl. The girl was stiff and unyielding. Aria stood back and thought about her future: a husband to stay clear of and a maid to get to know and like. She was dismayed that she did not like the girl at first sight; there was something strange about her. Aria tried to pinpoint it. Leyla was not feminine, nor was she entirely masculine. Gender neutral? Maybe that was it.

Aria did not like the thought of re-entering Dellbright's hostile household without an ally. Yet Leyla was not going to be much comfort unless they could become friends.

Leyla bowed curtly. "I will say good night now. I will meet you when your party assembles. I am to present myself to your husband in the morning. I fear he may not approve of me."

Aria frowned. "Approve of you? Does he need to? Oakheart?"

"A formality only. He has agreed in principle. But he does not know about Leyla's gift with the *given*. He believes her to be a child of adepts who has no use here and must find her place in the outer world."

Aria's eyebrows rose. "I'll keep her abilities to myself then." Aria smiled at the young woman. How was she going to face Dellbright? Thinking and doing were two different things.

Oakheart let Leyla out of the room then shut the door again. He sat on the bed next to her and took her hand. "Send word to me often. Leyla will see that any messages get through. She has a small talkstone. Contrive to have her with you always. If she is sent out of the room, make sure she stays by your door. She will intervene if Dellbright becomes violent. Do not worry, she can handle him."

"I grant you that's comforting, but as soon as she stands up to him, he will have her dismissed. Then he will be free to...to...do what he pleases."

"Leyla will send word if anything like that happens. We will come for you as soon as we can."

"Oakheart, I don't doubt you, but I wonder, what promise did he wrest from you? I am sure there is one if you managed to get one from him."

"I vowed never to step foot in Valley Keep again."

"Then you can't come for me?"

"Not personally, not within the boundaries of the keep. But that does not include my men, or Fern."

"It is enough though, enough to take hope out of my heart. I remember those first days, eating in the great hall and how exciting it all was to be in Argenterra, meeting Dellbright and you. Now it's all so different."

"There is more. He has made some conditions for Veld as well."

Aria bit her lip, her eyes brimming with tears. What more could he want? "What are they?"

Oakheart put an arm around her shoulders and squeezed. "Well, he has also demanded to be next in line to the throne after me. He claims it as his right due to his marriage to you. Veld has agreed in principle but has placed strict conditions in turn on Dellbright."

"Conditions?"

"You are to be brought to Silverdale once a year and be permitted to stay for six weeks, commencing once the siege has lifted. You are to be free to be seen by all in Valley Keep and when in Silverdale and must be healthy and happy or father will revoke his entitlement. If I am killed before I inherit the throne and without issue of my own, Dellbright is to step down from inheriting the throne of Silverdale and pass the crown to Gilly."

"I see. How did father manage that? Surely he made no binding oath."

"Oath no, Veld had no need of oaths. There are some technicalities he could revert to regarding the inheritance of the governance of Silverdale. He thought that Dellbright should never rule, but he did not mind if Gilly inherits the throne one day. In the end, it was your agreement to return to Dellbright that made him a tad more amenable than we had any hope to expect. After you are presented to Silverdale, Veld will have documents prepared that will outline the succession."

"So we say goodbye tomorrow? And what of Sophy?"

"Lianal is making sure research is undertaken. Hopefully when that is completed I will be able to operate the gate. I will go for her as soon as I can. In the meantime, I must fulfil my duty and go to the aid of my father. I will miss you, Aria. Study hard with Leyla. You have great potential. Do not let Dellbright make you think otherwise."

Aria nodded. "I'll do my best. I can't deny that I am very afraid. Afraid for all of us."

Oakheart sighed, his face revealing all that he had suffered. At the threshold of her room, she embraced Oakheart again. He whispered to her. "I have faith that we will win through this. I have made an oath to find Sophy and bring her home if she wishes it."

"Of course she does. She wouldn't leave you willingly. I know that in my heart."

He smiled fleetingly. "I wish our mother thought so. I do not need her assertions cutting up my peace." Then he was gone, walking slowly down the corridor to his room.

# 8

# NOT SO ALONE IN THE DEADLANDS

Sophy camped in the water cavern for many, many days. She didn't know how to measure time while she passed almost all of it underground. The hole above was shadowed by the tree trunk, except the sky glowed during the night, bathing the little cavern in bluish light. During the day, the cavern was suffused with dim light from the weak sun.

The ugreals had made her a latrine, though it was a bit of a squeeze for her to climb into. They had made it beneath a tree so that it could get the benefit of the nutrients. That was her interpretation of their actions. She remembered how the little things had got excited by her first deposit. They chirped like crazy so she guessed it had been a while since they had seen one so big. The little creatures did not understand privacy at all.

More time passed, she thought maybe weeks instead of days. She learnt how to scavenge for roots, which she now could eat quite quickly. Also, she could understand the ugreals quite well. Not to have a conversation but for her to communicate simply. They were never far away.

Rufus had searched for her twice since that first time. The ugreals had provided plenty of warning when she was above ground so she had been able to hide. She could tell the ugreals were outraged when Rufus pushed over the trees. To a casual eye the wood looked dead and yet there was life. While she'd witnessed the strange magic of the trees on her first night, it never ceased to amaze her. The sparse tree trunks and naked limbs glowed, twisted surreal shapes reaching for a dark sky, bathing the night in light. It was an ethereal beauty, a sad beauty. In the cavern below the surface, the roots glowed with light like the tree trunks, which made her life down there bearable.

The dark patches in her memory remained, but Rufus was the stuff of her nightmares. Faces and voices all crawling over one another, comprehension stalking her, yet staying out of reach. Close to remembering it all, she ached inside. Something important was missing from her life. She knew enough to know that she had come here from someplace else and that Rufus was the cause of her displacement. She had to know—she had to face Rufus.

Every day she asked the ugreals about Rufus and every day they reacted in the same way: shooting into their tunnels and clicking like mad.

One morning, while she was reclining on the bank of the water pool, gnawing on a large root, a few ugreals spilled out of the tunnels, sniffing and clicking their curiosity. She could never tell them apart. They appeared to be uniform, but if she looked closely there were slight differences in colouring, size and attitude.

She broke off some root she was eating and gave a piece to the ugreals who stood in the shadows watching her. One cocked its head, took the root, sniffed and then nibbled on it before passing it to the next one. She watched them and their black eyes stared at her as she finished her meal. Then she crawled over to them. The creatures stood their ground, brave now that they knew her better.

"So, little ones, I think it is time for me to find Rufus's place. Want to come along?"

This time they surprised her. They didn't flee to the tunnels and click; they stared at her. She frowned. Did this mean they would go with her, show her the way? She had become fairly good at navigating the tunnels, the ones that were big enough for her to crawl through. Many times when they went foraging, she lay down, went floppy and relaxed, and they took her, speeding her along the tunnels like a conveyor belt. "Okay, which way?"

They didn't move. More ugreals crept out of the tunnels, quiet and diffident. She raised an eyebrow at them, considering this new behaviour. "Well, well...em..."

As she watched, more ugreals crowded around her. She lay down on the coarse soil, calling on her body to relax. Next thing she knew they were lifting her up and she went feet first into one of the side tunnels. She closed her eyes even though she couldn't see anyway. Occasionally, smatterings of dirt landed on her face and she spat the grit out. The dirt tasted rotten. The tunnel they traversed levelled out and it went on and on for a long time. Occasionally, a lighter shade of dark meant that the roof of the tunnels breached the surface above. How far away were they taking her? Then a quick movement: she was almost folded over before she was spat out into a shallow bowl of earth. The ugreals clicked quietly, soothingly. It was still light, but it was fading fast. Sophy eased the stiffness from her neck and wiped her mouth with the back of her hand. That had been the longest, most difficult trip she'd taken in the Deadlands.

Outside, for the first time in ages, she saw how grimy her body was. What was left of her clothes stuck to her skin. All traces of her wounds were gone, either healed or covered in grime. The ugreals gathered on one edge of the hole. She belly-crawled over to them, keeping her head down. As the light bled way, she lifted her head over the rim of the hollow and gasped when she caught sight of the ruins. As the sun went down the darkness appeared to leap out from the skeletons of the buildings and crawl along the streets that were littered with debris. The signs of previous habitation must have been obscured by the ridge when she had first arrived and had taken shelter in the wood.

Once a town, maybe a city...she couldn't see the extent of the old roads and slumped and caved in buildings. They looked old, but somehow modern, too. Looking at them stirred memories, blurred the boundaries of her confusion. "That's where Rufus lives? Rufus?" she said and pointed at the same time.

A few of the ugreals closest to her clicked slowly. She took that for an affirmative.

Turning her head, she tried to orient this place to the wood, of which there was no sign. She frowned. How far had they brought her? Behind them were the remains of a ridge, with pockmarked passageways. She wondered if she was near the place she had first arrived, but wasn't certain. That had been so long ago and she'd been dazed, barely aware.

Nothing moved along the debris-strewn roads or within the broken spines of buildings. The quiet, except for her own breathing and the rustle of the ugreals, was eerie. Below was a pathway leading into and along the ridge. This far away from the ruins, she had some cover.

A few of the ugreals accompanied her. Darting into the first passage way she found, it inclined towards the top of the ridge. She ran up it, panting with effort. Halfway up she turned around and saw the ruins more clearly. Darkness was leaking into the abandoned town from the surrounding terrain. Back a few streets she saw a mostly intact building—low and squat with not many windows. She wondered if it extended underground. A faint light emanated from one of its few windows. A tremor passed through her; her breath stopped in her throat. Rufus!

Turning quickly, she bolted up the trail to make the most of the light and use the growing shadows for cover. Many other passageways snaked away from this main one. She stayed on the main one because it went straight to the tip of the ridge. At last, she made the top and saw down the other side. In the distance she could make out the wood. She tried to see where she had found herself that day, the day she came through...through the...gate. Yes, she had come through a gate.

What had come before the gate? Then ugreals started clicking, warning and urging. She turned on her heel and ran down the incline. Halfway down, the clicking broke off suddenly. Darkness tightened around her like a shroud. Everything appeared shrouded in a yellow-smeared grey haze but still she discerned details such as individual rocks in the distance. Some new sight? A side effect of her diet perhaps. The ruins of the city were a dark blob on the land. Her new visual acuity could not penetrate that.

She slowed her step and listened: something large was moving around at the end of the path. She stepped into a side passage, a pathway with high walls. It was a short dead end. The sound of movement drew closer. There was nothing to do but climb up the rock face in front of her to find a way out. In the gloom, she patted around for a foothold and something higher up to grab on to and then saw a hole in the wall to the side of her. Could she fit inside it?

The hole was made of something resembling hardened clay, not as giving as the substance of the ugreal-formed tunnels. Yet she had little choice. She pushed at it, wiggling to get her shoulders and then hips through. It too was a dead end but at least it served to hide her. There was no room to move her body. She was effectively blind and deaf. She hoped whatever was out there did not have a good sense of smell. She was ripe from weeks of being dirty and unwashed. In the small hole in the wall she had nothing to do but inhale her scent and fear that something was going to pluck her out of her hiding place. Immobile, she waited and waited. Until finally, she detected a soft nibble on her ankles. Then the clicking sound reached her. She pushed herself backwards with her hands, wriggling her hips to gradually work her body backwards out of the hole to slide down the wall.

A couple of ugreals cleared out of the way as she tumbled to the ground, missing her foot-hold entirely. Landing hard, she was winded but unhurt. As she lay there in a heap, drawing in cleaner air, they clicked at her in a syncopating rhythm. She thought they meant "hurry up".

A loud rumble: the ground shook, and a section of ridge behind her trembled. Dirt showered down the wall beside her and she ran out of the dead end to avoid being caught in its collapse. A crack formed in the section of ridge ahead of her and it collapsed in on itself and a wave of dust and debris came billowing towards her. Crouching, she let it roll over her, holding her hands over her mouth and nose. For a few moments she was seized by coughing, and then it eased, allowing her to see through watery eyes what the quake had revealed. There in the ridge face were larger caves and in front a deep depression where the earth had fallen away. Drawing her brows together, she worked her way around the larger boulders and upthrusts of stone and went to investigate. Her feet sank where the sand was loose so she trod carefully, hoping no ugreals were caught in the debris.

The closer she drew to the damage the more concerned she became about the darker patches in the loose rubble. On closer inspection she saw that these were indeed bodies of ugreals. There were other items in amongst the rocks and piles of dust: a mug, a twisted plate, a belt, bits of broken crockery. These littered the ground or were half submerged in the freshly disturbed earth. A steady but weak click, click, click reached her ears. Turning her head, she tried to hear where the noise came from. She saw dirt moving. Falling to her knees, she scooped and swept the dirt away to uncover the buried ugreal. The ugreal struggled to get free, its foot captured by a rock.

"There, there, just wait. You'll be free in a minute," she whispered to it soothingly, stroking it carefully on the head as she freed it. There was a small graze on its head but this did not seem serious. Other ugreals emerged, clicking like crazy, digging in the dirt. At first she thought there was another ugreal buried there, but it wasn't. Curious, she helped them dig. Something met her fingertips. It was a stone or something. As the dirt was cleared away, a long object with a knob at one end was taking shape.

Using a small stone, she raked the dirt off the length of it, realising that it was a long blade. The knob at the end appeared to be a hilt. It was a sword! Excited, she realised there had once been people here, in this very spot. Finally she cleaned the dirt off and grasped the hilt— and everything went blank. A scream tore from her throat as she was thrown back against the wall of the ridge. Her chest hurt and there was a glow of light coming from under her skin. Shaking her head to clear her mind, she stared dazed at the artefact for a while. Her hands throbbed as if she had been electrocuted, but there were no burns or other injuries.

The sword glowed faintly. *Power.* Gazing at her hands, she wondered what had happened. Had it tapped her life force? Was she just a crazy chick in a dead world experiencing hallucinations? Or did the sword have electricity inside it? But how could there be electricity here where there was nothing? No industry. No power plants. Not possible, there was nowhere to generate it. Surely if there was solar power it would not carry such a punch. She tilted her head. Gingerly, she crawled back to the sword. The ugreal she had rescued began to click rapidly. More ugreals appeared, sticking their heads out of small holes in the damaged wall. The ugreals clicked rapidly in conversation.

Then the ugreal she had rescued limped over to the sword and put its little brown hand on it. Nothing happened. Sophy chewed her lip. There was something about this that sparked a chord in her. Power. She put out a finger and brushed it against the hilt again. This time there was a tingling sensation, as if the hilt was drawing a mild electric current from her. The blade of the sword glowed again with a blue-tinged light. "Shit!" she said to no one in particular. "I'm the source of the electricity. How weird is that?"

She let some power drain into the blade, not at all perturbed by the sensation running through her finger. The ugreal she had rescued came up and sniffed her hand, touched her with one tiny hand and gazed up at her. Its dark eyes glittered and she nearly laughed because she thought she saw awe in its expression. She was taking her association with these creatures to a new level, where understanding and imagination whirled around with fantasy. With a shrug she removed her finger. She hadn't lost the plot. If she was going to, it would have happened already. Unless, of course, she needed her memory to totally lose her mind.

The ugreal clicked some more, nudged her hand. She rubbed between its ears. The sword was important. The power she put inside it was important.

The ugreals jittered again and scurried away. The earth shook beneath her feet and she dropped the sword. With a cry of dismay she saw it sink into the ground, as if it were swallowed by quicksand. She tried to grab for it but the quake grew violent and rocks tumbled down on the spot where the sword had disappeared. Desperation overcame her as she darted to the spot and tried to heave the stones away. The ugreals came out of their holes, chittering to her. She wasn't going to uncover the sword anytime soon. If she was going to try for the city, she needed to move. Taking a good look around her, she was certain she could find this place again.

Next stop was Rufus—and answers.

# 9

# CHOICES MADE

Aria clenched the reins and gritted her teeth. She hadn't been able to relax since they set out from the retreat. They were in the Valley surrounds, full with green fields and sparse homesteads, some now black, charred ruins. This made her think of Kushlan. Had he survived the razing of his home? No doubt Dellbright was behind this action for he had never liked Kushlan. With his additional malice, cruelty came easy to him. She hoped Rae's father was alive and well.

After her trek across Argenterra, Aria was now a competent horsewoman. She thought back to her first day in Argenterra and how insipid and stupid she'd been, riding with Dellbright and feeling all soft and stupid and mushy. Just thinking about it made her cringe.

She peered across at Leyla while they rode. Ahead, Dellbright rode stiff-backed, leading the way. To her relief he had hardly spoken to her. Still, his dark looks were like punches and did nothing to ease her anxiety. She was offended—she was the wronged one and not him. Thankfully, he had made no objection to Leyla and the adept made herself useful and unobtrusive by setting up their tents, preparing food and otherwise pretending she wasn't there.

The Valley men who had accompanied Dellbright to the retreat had mostly been handed over to Oakheart, with Dellbright retaining only a small honour guard for their return trip. More men were committed and would be sent on to Silverdale once they had arrived back at Valley Keep. In addition, homesteads and small villages were informed of Silverdale's need and about twenty or so young men and women followed behind their train—some straggling on foot, others in carts, and one or two on horses.

Dellbright had been true to his word, instructing his man-at-arms to train these recruits so they could contribute something when at last they reached Silverdale. Although this training was a bit haphazard, with half the recruits struggling to keep up on foot and not being there when the training started and then being too exhausted to participate once they had arrived. As more people joined them, the transport became a bit more organised. People were rotated between the carts and more carts were employed in transportation.

Some of those that joined them spoke of wanting revenge against the raiders who had burned farms and stolen livestock and grain. Some had lost sisters and maiden aunts to the raiders. Aria was uneasy when she heard this. *Why would the Puri take the single women? Ransom?*

Leyla brooded when she asked her and then finally commented, "You do not want to know what the Puri do to those women."

"Actually, I do. I don't understand."

Leyla looked away, her keen gaze assessing the landscape. Perhaps she was making sure there were no raiders nearby to snatch her away. Although, having the ability to protect herself should have built up her confidence.

Dellbright slowed his horse until he was close by. "They take the unmarried women to bed." His eyes glinted and he had a hint of a smile. Aria's stomach lurched. "It is the most harm they can do. The oaths of married women protect them."

Aria gasped. "You mean rape them?"

He shrugged. "Not all of them are unwilling if the Puri man is fair and asks nicely."

"But..." She looked down, fingering her reins.

"'Tis the worst thing to do to an Argenterran, polluting the bloodline with Puri taint. Their families will disown them if they are returned."

Aria raised an eyebrow. "I remember Rae telling me about Goslien of the Valley. Panal gave her an oath. She was happy to stay."

"Tales. Lies. Who cares? Those women are lost to the Valley now."

"But it's not their fault. Why should they be punished?"

Dellbright's mouth tightened. "Do not argue with me." His voice was tight and hard. He looked tense, as if ready to strike.

"I'm not. I'm asking questions."

Leyla glared at Dellbright, who noticed at once. The adept dropped her gaze, once more the quiet retainer, and he kicked his mount to move forwards. What Dellbright said made Aria uneasy. The Puri were taking the innocent as prisoners and their families would forever consider them outcast. He did not complain about them killing people, just the theft of goods and the destruction of property. Obviously they held to the binding oath or the binding oath held them. But would it continue to do so? How did it even work? There was no point in asking Dellbright.

Leyla and she urged their mounts on. "Leyla, how does one kill someone in Argenterra?"

"My lady?" Her handmaiden frowned at her.

"With the binding oath that prevents killing. How does it work? If someone aimed an arrow at someone's heart and let it fly, wouldn't that person get injured and die?"

Leyla looked away momentarily, licking her lips before speaking. "It is complicated. The oath works in a number of ways. It can take away the will to kill. Most people wouldn't think of killing someone. If someone, say in the heat of battle, set out to deliberately kill, then either they could not let the arrow fly or they would be compelled to not kill. Another way the oath might work is if they did shoot an arrow or throw a knife and their aim would inexplicably be off. They might injure their opponent, but not kill them. I have not seen this in action myself, you understand. Adage explained it to me. He said that the binding oath is part of the fabric of our world, and of us."

"The Puri are bound by the oath though."

"Yes, Shabra and his kin swore the binding oath when the First

Comers arrived through the Crystal Gate. Always they have been bound by it, even though the *given* is weaker in the wastelands."

"So this battle for Silverdale does not involve killing?"

Leyla pushed her hair over her shoulders and her gaze swept over Aria. "We do not know. It could, because oaths are weaker than they once were. The fabric of the *given* is unweaving. No one truly understands what the outcome may be. I have heard reports that there have been injuries, wounds have been taken that once would not have been. An arm lost, a leg, an eye…all grievous wounds. The binding oath does not protect all life, you understand. Some die accidentally in battles, or just preparing for battles." She shrugged.

"So there's no killing. Just the raping of women?" Aria's heart raced with fear and outrage. Surely Vorn did not envisage this when he worded the binding oath? How she wished she knew more, understood more.

Leyla's eyes lowered and she bit her lip. She took her time in answering. "I like it not, but that appears to be so. This is my first experience of war. At the retreat, I was neither male nor female. I was a student adept. Such transactions of the flesh are not known to me."

"You are a…you've not had a lover, is that what you mean?" Aria asked, feeling her face heat.

Leyla hesitated for a moment and then replied, "Yes, that's what I mean."

Aria realised that Leyla was afraid: she had no oath to protect her. Married women were not generally taken, not for sex anyway, because their oaths protected them. They could be slave labour, but the unmarried women were prey. Aria was protected from being ravaged by the Puri, but Leyla wasn't. Her gaze flicked to Dellbright. *He* could rape her, though, because she was oathbound to him. Her stomach lurched.

"Are you feeling ill, my lady?" Leyla asked.

"No, not really. Just heart-worn by what you have told me. Why must the women pay?"

Leyla bit her lip. "Single men are vulnerable too. It depends on the tastes of the captors. Rumour has it that the Glasshiver warriors have also joined the fight. It is said that some of them have a taste for young, pretty men."

Aria growled, making Leyla jump and her horse jerked up its head and pranced uneasily. "It is awful, regardless. I thought the binding oath a good thing, but it is flawed."

Leyla's eyes widened. "My lady! That is not a popular opinion. You best keep it to yourself."

They made camp, the last before they would reach Valley Keep. Their numbers had swollen with volunteers. Aria was assisting in setting up her tent when Dellbright walked up behind her. "You will share my tent this evening, Aria."

Aria spun around. She couldn't hide the surprise in her eyes or her sharp intake of breath. "Oh…that is kind of you to offer, but I prefer to share a tent with Leyla. We are almost set up."

"You have pledged your word that you will be my wife in more than name." His dark eyes assessed her coolly, a flame of anger in his irises.

She returned his regard calmly. "I am your wife. I'm indisposed right now and I would be an inconvenience to you."

He stared at her long and hard, his breath fast but controlled. "Very well." He marched away, his back rigid with affront.

Hands clenched, with sweat gathering on her neck and lower back, she stood there immobilised, seized by swirl of terrible memories.

"My lady?" Leyla placed a hand on her shoulder. She jumped and spun around. "Are you all right?"

Aria gaped at the other woman as she tried to calm her breathing. With a quick glance in Dellbright's direction, she replied, "For now. Once we reach Valley Keep that will be debatable." Looking at her shaking outstretched hands, she shook her head. However was she going to cope?

Leyla clasped her shaking hands between hers. "We will think of something, my lady. I know what was done to you. It will not happen again." Leyla drew her towards the tent.

"You don't know what it was like. How he can isolate me. Yet there are three hundred men at Valley Keep that need to be sent to Silverdale and I can't jeopardise that. My father is depending on me."

Once inside, they settled in the tent. Leyla undid Aria's hair and stroked the brush through it and, gradually, Aria let the tension go. She had to be brave. Like Sophy. Wind fluttered the tent walls and snapped at the open flap. Aria sighed as Leyla massaged the tension from her scalp.

The camp cook bellowed that the meal was ready. Aria garnered her courage and went to join her husband for the evening meal. Thoughts of running away loomed large in her mind. The thought of seeing Gilly gave her the strength to put a smile on her face. Leyla walked beside her, a firm presence at her side. Maybe things would be different this time. However, when she reached out with the *given* to the other end of their oathbond, she knew differently. With her heightened senses, she could read that Dellbright was even more dark and menacing than previously. He was putting up a front. She didn't want to be there when he dropped it and showed his real self, his real intentions.

Leyla leant in her direction. "Tonight I will start to train you to use the *given* as a defence. That way if we are ever separated you will be able to ward against harm."

Aria's head jerked around. "Really?" she whispered. Her attention was caught by Dellbright, whose dark eyes glittered as he watched her approach. She suppressed a shiver. As she stepped to sit where Dellbright gestured, she replied, "I would be most grateful."

Unfortunately Dellbright heard. "What would you be grateful for?"

Aria ran through some options in her head, discarding each quickly. Leyla spoke. "My mistress asks me to sort through her clothing once we reach the keep. She wishes to donate unwanted items to those refugees fleeing from their homes."

Dellbright glared at Leyla. Aria smiled. "It's a small gesture. You don't mind, do you?"

His mouth turned down. "You assume too much. I had your belongings burned. You have only what you have brought with you. You will need to make your own clothes. Valley Keep is no longer the fashion centre of Argenterra."

"Oh?" Aria was genuinely nonplussed. Dellbright's vindictiveness knew no bounds. Shaking off her disquiet, she added, "Never mind,

I'm sure I will cope with what I have. Thank you for explaining it to me. I am sorry I have nothing useful to offer the refugees, after all."

As it was, Aria could barely put a morsel in her mouth. What had she got herself into? With Aurore dead, the heart had gone out of the keep's industry. Aria had learnt a lot, but the looms, the spinning, dyeing, cultivating—that took a lot of people, and with the war with the Puri, perhaps there was no one to do any of the work. Knowledge would be lost. It saddened her to know that Aurore's legacy was gone. Aria didn't think she had the heart to revive it.

Dellbright made little effort at conversation, but eyed her gloomily as if he couldn't believe she was present. His eyes darted to Leyla often, a wary, calculating gaze. Aria did not feel safe.

After what seemed like hours, but was less than half an hour, she returned to her tent, her meal sitting like lead in her stomach. She let out a large sigh and turned to face Leyla, who said smugly, "You managed to avoid sharing Dellbright's tent, my lady."

Aria sat on her camp bed and ran her hands through her hair. "I have my monthlies. A mixed blessing."

"Why mixed?" Leyla asked.

"Because he knows and will work out when they are due to end."

Leyla frowned. "I think I understand. Should we start? With the lessons?"

Aria shrugged off her worry and let herself be cheered. "Yes, what do you want me to do?"

"We will meditate first. You must be able to detect, summon and command the *given*. The *given* within you, and also the threads of it nearby."

Aria closed her eyes and tried to coax her mind to relax. It was a battle. Her aches from the day's travel intruded as did images of Gilly and Dellbright, the tender moments with him and the more savage remembrances. Finally, her mind grew clearer.

"Yes, you are there. Now, send your awareness into your body because there is a reservoir inside of you. A large one."

Aria could not detect anything at first. She looked for bright light, a glow, a fire, a crystal—and found nothing like that. Then as she quieted her breathing, she sensed something in her core that was elusive and alive, a flicker of flame. She reached inwards to touch it, and it warmed at her touch. The throb of the *given* welled up inside her, a rich, fluid thing that threatened to overflow. So this was it. The more she meshed with the warm sense of being, the more it grew in light and colour until it grew to a deep green, with soft shafts of light emanating from within the centre. Tingles chased across her body. Her tongue detected every groove in the back of her front teeth. She smelled bread baking and heard a voice singing. For a moment she was the voice floating on the breeze.

Leyla's voice, as if from a distance, reached her. "Now come back out of it."

She blinked and was back in the moment, her limbs heavy and lethargic. "I feel so tired."

"You were absent for an hour."

Aria gaped and then shut her mouth. "It seemed but a few seconds."

Leyla stretched and took off her clothes, readying for bed. "No, 'twas much longer. We will try more tomorrow. You need to sleep now. The first excursions can drain your energy."

Aria thought of how close they were to Valley Keep. "In the morning?"

"Very well. I will wake you before dawn." Leyla smiled before extinguishing her firestick. "You are strong and have good control, but it will still take time to learn all I have to impart."

"The sooner the better." Aria extinguished her own firestick. "Good night, Leyla," she said to the gloom.

"Good night, my lady."

## ❧ 10 ❧

# RAE MEETS THE TRIBES

The wind was howling from the north, bringing cold and grit and all kinds of unpleasantness as Rae struggled through the wastelands. She was long past the Shabra Plains and deep into the Barrens now. No wonder the Puri did not dwell there.

The child cried no matter how well Rae wrapped her and sheltered her and offered her a breast. Normally, Rae loved the beauty of the wastes, the desolate land, burnished by sun and wind but seldom with rain. When the wind was calm you could enjoy the quiet beauty of the place, the shades of grey and brown and yellow. Yet like all things, there was a price to be paid for travelling there without preparation, without shelter. With the wind blowing it was most unpleasant. The blustery weather dried out the skin, took away moisture from the lips, mouth and throat. It made survival precarious; took away her strength. Constantly fighting to put one foot in front of the other, seeing into the distance was hard because the grit was constantly being hurled into her eyes.

She fed her daughter often so the baby would grow strong. She was so thirsty she worried that her body would be unable to produce the milk she needed. Perhaps she was defective—her soft Argenterran upbringing had not conditioned her for this.

After trudging along for a day or so she saw many hoof marks, dents in the drying earth. A welcome change from the hard ground that gave up little signs of the traffic that had passed over it. There must be another oasis nearby, for that was the only reason she could see prints. She followed the trail leading to wetter ground, hoping to find the Puri before they departed. Surely there were stragglers, please, there had to be someone to help her. She would die if she tried to go on alone. The oasis would offer some shelter for a short time, but not food. Not enough food. Going beyond this place to the next oasis could end her life and it would definitely end her child's. There *had* to be someone.

Her vision blurred and she tasted bile in the back of her throat. Stumbling on, she stopped abruptly to dry retch. Hunched over, she clutched the baby tight to her chest, then struggled on. The soles of her feet cooled with the touch of mud, a balm to her red and blistered feet. Glancing up, she saw something, thought she heard something. Ahead were smeared shapes. People rather than rocks! "Help me, please. Hanal. Take me to Hanal."

The shapes loomed closer. Her blurred vision picked out many coloured layers of robes. Blackness loomed at the edges of her vision and her head felt like it was floating away from her body. Hands caught her as she fell, arms protectively around her child. Her body was lifted, voices enveloped her, excited, concerned, the words familiar. At the sound of the Puri accent, she gave up the struggle for consciousness. Knowing that she was safe at last, she surrendered to fatigue.

THE PAINFUL ENGORGEMENT OF HER BREASTS WOKE RAE. SHE DID not know how long she had slept. She was in a small, triangular tent big enough for two people, although she was the sole adult occupant. These small tents were often used for single men when on herding expeditions. Glad that she was alone and not with a family, she thought of her baby. Pushing herself up on her hands, she scanned the small tent for the child. There, next to her propped on a clean tufted skin was her little sleeping babe. Lifting the child to her breast woke the child. Rae did not know if it was right to wake her, but the milk was there, leaking now that the child was close.

The baby cried, unused to the gouts of milk that near drowned her. The tent flap opened, letting in a waft of wood smoke and the smell of food cooking. The thought of hot food brought on a rumble in her empty stomach. She flushed hot and cold, like she had been sick with fever. A woman's head poked through the opening, nodded once when she saw Rae was awake and then left again. Soon after, she was back with a bowl of steaming water.

"I thought you might like to wash after you have fed the child. You were fevered for three days. We did not know if you would make it. The babe could not feed from you so we had to make do."

The woman came closer and, taking a look at Rae's efforts to breastfeed, grunted. "Here, try this." She held the baby at the back of the neck and aimed its mouth onto the breast. Rae squeaked as the baby latched on. "That's better. You just needed the right angle." The other woman looked on. "She's got the hang of it now. I don't think you'll have further problems."

Rae glanced up at the woman, dragging her gaze from her suckling child. The older woman had a kindly face. "Thank you," she said and then winced. Breastfeeding was painful.

"You best swap her over to the other breast. It will take a while to get used to it. You don't want to wear your teats out."

Rae gaped at the woman and then thanked her when she helped her change the baby to the other breast. Rae realised she was very tired and weak and was grateful for the assistance and the advice. At least the painful swelling of her breasts had eased. "Thank you for your help."

The older woman nodded her head, indicating the end of the bunk. "Your feet have been salved and bandaged. We were wondering what you were doing wandering the wastes without your kin. Your clothes are Puri but your accent is not."

"I am Tu Raenal, daughter of Kushlan. Recently I was in the household of Hanal."

The woman nodded, as if Rae's words confirmed her suspicions. "My name is Anwi, by the way. They said you called his name. Often you have talked when the fever took you. You asked him for forgiveness. Why do you seek it?"

"That is between him and me. Do you follow him on his quest to conquer Argenterra?"

The woman placed a cloth in the water and squeezed it. She leant over and wiped it firmly across Rae's brow. The scent of citrus teased Rae's nostrils, and she relaxed at the woman's touch. "We follow the rest of our clan. Orders came weeks ago for all Puri to leave the wastes and journey to Silverdale. Hanal has proclaimed it our new homeland."

Rae's eyes widened. "No!" Looking down at the baby, she fought tears. With the baby lying across her belly, she stroked its back. "That is unexpected." She glanced at the woman hopefully. "Are you sure?"

The woman rinsed the cloth and commenced washing the remainder of Rae's face. "It is true. Hanal has ousted the Argenterrans."

The woman wrapped the baby and rocked her, but seeing the babe was already asleep she placed it in the makeshift cradle. Taking Rae's arm to wash it, and then the other one, she said nothing for a while, her lips wrinkling as they pursed in thought. Anwi rinsed the cloth again and Rae took it to wash herself.

"I do not believe what you are telling me. Did not the Argenterrans fight back? Was there killing?" Her heart pounded as she waited for the answer. Had Hanal broken the binding oath? Was all hope lost?

"I have not been there myself, but I have heard tales. Not many killings as far as I know. Accidents mainly, where a horse was dropped and a rider injured. I have heard…"

A man's voice called Anwi's name from outside the tent. The woman paused. "I will be back."

The child made a sound and then screwed up her face, still asleep. Rae propped herself up and ran a finger along her daughter's cheek. Then when the child remained asleep, she continued to bathe herself with the water the woman had brought, appreciating the great kindness of warm scented water. She looked around for her clothes and found them to be clean and mended. It moved her to think that these people were kind to her. Perhaps they would not be so kind if they suspected she was Hanal's whore. She thought Anwi had guessed, but still she had been kind—unlike the women who lived in Hanal's settlement, the summer tents.

Men shouted orders and then the sounds of packing up reached her. She guessed they were on the move. Being left behind was not an option. If they were going where Hanal was then so was she, even if she had to trail behind them.

The tent flap pushed in and Anwi was there. "We leave soon. I have said you are well enough for travel. You will ride my horse and I will walk beside you."

"That is a great kindness. I am very grateful for all that you have done." Rae was concerned about receiving kindness on false pretences. While she thought Anwi had guessed who the father of Rae's child was, she had to be sure the situation was clear. She had to give the woman a chance to turn away from her. "I am not sure that you should help me. I am—" She lowered her head, not wanting to see the disdain in the other woman's eyes.

"We know all about you. We know who you are and who fathered your child. It makes no difference to us. You are welcome amongst us."

Rae's head shot up, her eyes bright with tears of gratitude. "Thank you, Anwi. I appreciate your help but I do not wish you to suffer for it. Hanal may have anger at me and I do not wish to repay your kindness by having him take it out on you."

The woman pursed her lips and absently reached up to adjust her headdress. "We understand the risks. It is not our way to leave people in need behind. Besides, Kushlan spent time with us in the upper wastes. We saw him before we came away. He is kin in blood and soul to us. We will aid his daughter, for his sake as well as your own. So, no more protests."

Rae nodded. "Thank you. May your waters flow with the *given* always."

Anwi scoffed, but there was a smile on her face. "Good, I will bring you food and then we will pack up. Do not worry if you see the others leave before we do. We will travel at the end of the train so we do not hold up the others. We do not fear attack here so we will be safe. And I have sufficient supplies on my animal to feed us if we are too slow."

TWO DAYS LATER, RAE SAT ON ANWI'S HORSE, NURSING HER BABY girl. Now proficient at feeding the child, she could breastfeed while riding. While it still hurt a little, she was more confident. The baby had filled out, her soft brown cheeks puffy, hands and legs chubby. Her milk was good, thanks to the water and food Anwi supplied. It gave her satisfaction that all was well with the child, even if she was not a boy as Umri had predicted. Rae clenched her teeth at the memories of Umri's treachery and manipulation. Deciding to let Hanal decide their fate first, Rae had not named her girl child. If he chose to ignore the child then Rae would bestow the name herself.

Despite fears of being left behind, because at first she was slow on the horse, they had managed to improve their pace so that they were within sight of the rest of their group when the sun set on the first day. Today, they were merging with a larger train. As she sat there waiting for one of the tribesmen to adjust his saddle bags, she saw the sun burst through clouds to bathe the plain in white light. The baby opened her eyes and Rae gasped as she saw the pale crystal blue, so like those of Hanal. The eyes of Goslien had passed successfully through the line. It brought her great joy and spoke of wonderful things for her daughter despite her rather difficult beginnings. Her child was going to be special, like Goslien had been, and like Hanal.

Rae's strength returned quickly once she was in Anwi's care. The fever she had had after the birth had dissipated. Her various cuts and bruises from her long trek healed steadily, if somewhat slowly. Ample food kept her, and hence her baby, well fed. Every day she could do more to assist with setting up camp. However, when she approached Anwi, the older woman snorted. "Be off with you. Feeding and tending that child is all you should be worried about. An old woman like me has nothing better to do than wash clothes and cook for others. Leave me at it and you will make me happy."

Anwi shoo-shooed Rae to a blanket. Rae complied and sat there gazing at the sleeping babe and then looking up occasionally as someone spoke or undertook some chore. Looking after herself and the child did weary her. The nights were broken with feeding and tending her daughter. She smiled as she realised that Anwi knew how she must be feeling and was grateful for the older woman's consideration. Added onto that physical fatigue was anxiety about Hanal, about this war on Argenterra and about her own role in what was to come.

Anwi travelled with her son, Benri, and daughter-in-law, Silla. Also her uncle, a very old grey-haired Puri man called Paatan, who was once head of his tribe but had been deposed for bad behaviour. He scowled a lot, Rae noticed, and she could understand why, living with the shame. She had not the heart to ask what behaviour had caused him to lose his leadership. In addition, there were four young male cousins, Leni, Arvi, Olin and Karp, who appeared to be aged from thirteen to about twenty. They often talked to each other as they rode, wondering about the delights of Silverdale.

"We will have our pick of its fruit," one would say and the rest would laugh. After a few days of this Rae realised that there was something more to what they were saying than raiding orchards, particularly when she noticed Anwi frown and shake her head.

When she tried to catch Anwi's eye, the woman drew her robe about her and strode ahead. Rae had to wait for her moment, when they stopped again in the evening. That night, she realised they must be closer to Silverdale. The landscape was changing, becoming greener with vegetation as they travelled. Ahead was a narrow cutting between the foothills of the Fortitude Ranges that rose up behind the Upper Plateau. The cutting was narrow, but quite short. As they rode through it she realised that it was part natural, eroded by many years of wind and rain, and some of it had been excavated. Piles of rock lay scattered and she could see that some of the edges had tool marks. This surprised her because the Puri did not like to shape the earth. With her heart plummeting low in her belly, she knew the Argenterrans would not have stood a chance: they must have been overrun before they even knew who was attacking them.

How could Hanal have been party to this plan? It was not honourable. Had he issued a formal writ of war or even a list of demands or attempted to negotiate? She doubted it. Umri had been working on him, hooking into his weaknesses, flattering him. The seer's influence had been growing—look at what the seer had done to Sophy. Rae shook her head; she had no idea what the woman expected to gain from this venture. Greater access to the *given* perhaps. For one such as she, more power to fuel her gifts could be a motive. Rae could not understand her; she was certain Umri did not care particularly for Hanal. Or was she just jealous of the other woman? Rae thought not; she pitied Umri now. Thoughts of Hanal made her heart ache. He had such potential to be a great leader, to have his deeds spoken of along with those of his worthy ancestors. A jerk of her horse jolted her out of her reverie and brought the baby awake with a squeal. "There now. It is all right now," she soothed the child as she followed along.

Once through the cutting, they were heading into Argenterra proper. Tall trees grew on the sloped foothills. Water ran in streams. With the water so plentiful, they could use the *given* to summon it through the ground. Anwi danced about when she tried to call water and it came easily, bubbling up clean and pure into her cooking pot. For one of the Puri, to experience the *given* like this was a rare treat.

Food grew aplenty and was gratefully gathered up. Also, they met other Puri on their way to Silverdale. Due to her nursing the baby, they travelled slower than the other groups, making camp earlier and watching them pass. As they were making camp and Anwi was setting her pots, Rae caught the young men muttering and sending her annoyed glances. "I am sorry for holding you up."

Anwi told her not to worry about it as they would all get there eventually. "It is better to be well fed and well rested before entering that place. In case we do not like it and want to leave."

Leni's jaw dropped. "Not like it? It will be like paradise. Food in abundance, women and fine clothes, and houses to live in."

Anwi folded her arms and glared at the four boys who complained about the delay. "Why you expect satisfaction from food and riches unearned I do not understand. I fear you will find that Silverdale, and Argenterra for that matter, are not what you expect."

"But we will miss the best of the crop if we linger here," Leni replied. His cousins added their complaints.

"Enough of that talk," Anwi scolded them. "You shame your families by speaking that way."

When Leni tried to argue she picked up a strip of dried rush she had put by for later weaving and hit him across the head. "No more lip from you. You are still a boy child."

Leni continued to sulk the evening away, chewing solemnly on a piece of dried meat, while glaring at his aunt and cousins. By nightfall he had recovered his good humour and could be seen kicking a cloth ball around with his cousins near their camp.

Rae was so well, she was able to set up her borrowed tent and wash out her baby's swaddling rags in no time at all. She worked fast so she could catch Anwi at the cooking pot. Once her chores were done and the baby was put down for a nap, she made her way over.

The old woman greeted her with a smile as she cut dried meat and some scrounged green vegetables into a pot. Spices already swirled within the stew and wafted on the moist evening air to tease Rae's taste buds. In the coals were toffel tubers. "May I help you, Anwi?"

"Nothing to do now. Everything is fine."

She stirred the pot, her gaze roaming around the camp, her teeth chewing on her inner cheek. Something bothered the older woman. Rae followed the direction of the other woman's gaze but saw nothing there other than the encroaching night.

"May I sit with you then?"

Anwi nodded, looked into her pot. "We are running low on supplies. Thankfully there seems to be plenty of food for the gathering in this land."

"I can help you find more toffel plants tomorrow. As well as being delicious when roasted they are good for extending a stew because they take on the taste of the meat and the spices."

Anwi smiled at her and poked the tubers in the coals, turning them over. "I did not think to look for them until you mentioned it when we made camp. They do not grow in the wastes. Not enough water." Her eyes closed in memory. "Tasted some once, long ago. I think it was Kushlan who brought some to us. It was made into a sweet, dripping with syrup."

Rae smiled too. Kushlan was a good man. He tried to bridge the gap between the Puri and the Argenterrans. It was so sad that his efforts had failed. "We picked a few today. There will be more the closer we get to Silverdale I expect. There is plenty of water here and they like the moisture. I will check along the banks of the stream over there in the morning."

"Mind you do not overdo it with the gathering. You must keep your strength for that babe of yours. Rest and good food is the best for producing milk. I fear you do not get enough of either."

"I am well rested, I thank you." She paused, meeting the older woman's eyes. "Anwi, what is the fruit that the boys speak of, that they fear missing out on? I know Silverdale has orchards but they are not famous for their fruit."

The old woman looked away. "I do not like to speak of it."

Rae let out a pent-up breath. "I want to know. Please."

Anwi stirred the pot savagely, her lips tight. Then she sighed. "Very well, but you will not like the tale. Indeed, it makes me ashamed." She knelt and turned the toffel in the coals. She was so quiet and contemplative that Rae thought she was not going to talk after all and then she began. "I heard the stories before we set out. Everyone was talking of it." Anwi glanced at her, bit her lip then looked away, looked to the night. "Puri men taking the fat, white-skinned girls of Argenterra. Taking them from their families and shaming them."

"Shaming them?" Rae could not admit the thought that was in her mind, the suspicion that had been growing from a shadow to a storm cloud.

"Yes, by not offering them oaths or marriage in return for bedding them."

Rae sucked in a breath. "Surely they are not forcing them?"

Anwi let out a wail. "I do not know! Perhaps the girls, these women, offer themselves to save their families. The men do not fight. Cannot. They missed their chance. But I do not...Oh do not judge me by others' actions. I know your heart is in Argenterra. You will feel this insult all the more because of that."

Rae could hardly speak. "So that is why the men do not fight? Because the Puri have stolen their daughters, sisters? The ones who are not bound by oaths?"

"That is the story. Although the Argenterrans were caught unaware and so lost their chance to fight before our men came and took their women." Anwi sniffed and wiped at a tear that slid down her cheek. "The Puri use the women of Argenterra to shield themselves from harm and they harm the Argenterrans by their actions. They use threats against the women to bend the men to their will. Many have been conquered that way. It is said that the Puri do not keep to their bargains. When they say they will return the women to their men, they do not. When the men have surrendered their homes, their farms, their arms for their women's return, our young men laugh and take what they want. They have filled these women with children and sworn no oaths."

Rae's mouth fell open. Hanal could not have condoned this. But then she remembered how he had treated Sophy. At first he had starved her, but when that did not weaken her, he tried humiliation, stripping her naked and tying her up, then when that did not work he let Umri beat her and cut off her hair. It was Umri that offered to drug Sophy, to urge Hanal to slip beneath Sophy's oathbond to Oakheart that barred his way to the power within. Was he now so lost to everything but ambition that he would rape women to gain his ends, or turn a blind eye to rape in his name? She could not believe it. Dared not believe it, because then he would not be worthy of her love. Her chest grew so tight she could hardly breathe.

When she could finally form words, she asked, "Could Hanal truly support such tactics? Surely it is only a few who do such things?"

The old woman banged her spoon on the edge of the pot. "I wish that were so. I am ashamed to be Puri, to travel with young men bent on rape and dishonour. We can speak no more of this. We must eat." Anwi called out to the rest of their group that the meal was ready.

Panaat came out of the darkness and had obviously been listening. "Shut up, old woman. What do you know? In Argenterra I can father pale-skin sons and raise fat horses to sell. No more scraping a living off the land."

Rae stood back as the old woman surged to her feet, spoon waving in her angry hand. "You should talk. You who shamed your name and that of your kin. I do not forget what you did. How you treated the young children in your care. I will petition Hanal to have you sent home. There will be no reward for you."

Panaat lunged, batting the spoon from Anwi's hand and sending it spinning. Rae stood there, not sure how to act. So that was why he had been deposed. He had tried to harm children. A certain unease passed over her when she looked at him. Then he lashed out, backhanding Anwi and sending her flying.

"Do not hurt her!" she cried out.

Panaat spat at her. "Shut up, you whore!"

Anwi rolled on the ground, stunned. Ignoring Panaat, Rae dashed over to her, relieved to find that the woman was shaken but suffering no serious hurt. Rae helped Anwi to her feet. With all the noise the young men had come, standing speechless, and her son came too.

"What is going on here?" Benri asked. Rae could see he looked ready to strike out at his great-uncle.

The old woman climbed to her feet to stand beside Rae. "Panaat is overly sensitive. Think nothing of it."

"Mother, let me come to your defence."

"It is too late for that." Anwi turned and glared at Panaat. "The harm he did me happened long ago. Nothing you do now can fix it. Let us eat."

Picking up her spoon and wiping it on her apron, she went to the pot. Bowls appeared, brought out from people's robes or baggage. Anwi filled them using her retrieved spoon. The tension dissipated but Rae could not forget: the pieces had been put together. She found that she was keen to see Hanal again, but not in the way she had first envisaged. She was angry and would speak her mind.

Rae went to find her plate. She needed to eat, even though her stomach churned with anxiety and anger. For the first time she found herself not proud of her blood. She worried for those nameless women, young girls, who were taken by Puri men and bedded. It made her own actions pale in comparison. She had lain with Hanal freely without an oath. How could that compare to this?

# IN DEFENCE OF HOME

While lying on his bunk in the early morning, Oakheart analysed the situation. It was time he got up and readied himself for the next leg of their journey. But he lingered, wanting to imagine Sophy coming up with some cute saying to describe his not-so-silent war of wills with his mother. The he remembered that Maralain was like a mother to her, too. Would Sophy have taken sides against him? Or would her loyalties be divided? His eyebrows furrowed. That was too painful to even contemplate.

He ached when he thought of Sophy. Was she safe and happy in her own world, as his mother attested to daily? Or was she fighting for her life and soul at the hands of Rufus? The nothingness where their oath had been was an empty, dull ache. When they had been separated before, there had been her thoughts, feelings and dreams touching on his own, letting him know she lived and still loved him. Being adrift like this did not improve his mood. He thought of the love she spoke about. How for her it was stronger than oaths. Perhaps she was right. He wanted her back and there was no longer any oath to bind him to her.

Despite the angst, the negotiation had been successful. Dellbright had ordered four hundred men to travel to defend Silverdale, with the promise of one hundred more after he had secured the Valley. That was what Aria's sacrifice had brought them—hope. He picked up the small talkstone, one of two that the retreat had prepared, and it warmed to his touch.

"Lianal?"

There was a dull glow in the crystal but nothing more for a few moments. Then a face appeared, one of Lianal's assistants. "He has been summoned, excellency."

A few minutes later Lianal's face appeared. "Oakheart? All is well, I trust?"

"Yes, from this end. We have had a good response to our call. Women as well as men seek to defend Argenterra from our invaders. Do you have news for me?"

Lianal lowered his head for a moment then glanced up again. "Progress, but not the answer you seek. When we know we are on the right track I will contact you. Then you can make your way back here in anticipation."

Oakheart jerked upright, nearly dropping the talkstone. "You have found something?"

"I hesitate to confirm that at this stage, but we have found something promising. Trust me, Oakheart, when I can confirm what we suspect I will contact you straight away."

Oakheart's chest grew tight. "By the *given*, can this be true? Thank you, Lianal. I will await your call."

They had mustered two hundred and fifty more men and women from around fifty settlements. It was all these communities could spare without undermining their own viability. Each community had to have some fighting force to defend them from raids. Fern had been dispatched to Gilton Forest, hot on the trail of Lillia, Mellow and their son, Brook, to seek the forest queen's aid. Would his friends heed Silverdale's entreaty? They had been deeply scarred by what had occurred at the retreat. He hoped they did not brand all of the overlanders, as they called non forest-folk, as betrayers and deceivers after their dealings with the adepts. He could not blame them if they did. His own regard of the retreat had been severely lessened. Also, he feared Lillia would not venture out again, being so close to childbirth, but perhaps others would come and in time to be of use.

He finished his breakfast alone in his tent. It was better that way, he mused, and was just putting his boots on when the other talkstone chimed as it did at this time every day. His father held conferences with him, seeking updates and providing his own.

"Oakheart?"

Oakheart knelt in front of the stool to better see into the talkstone. "High king?" He bowed his head in salute.

"We have lost access to the river. They severed the pipes, we believe. We are relying on the town wells now, although with rationing we will survive. Food is getting critical, though. We have been stripping the orchards with the *given* but they are depleted now. To risk more will drain the life from the trees and they will die. Luckily, we had a bumper crop of toffel, enough for two years in normal circumstances. We have started in on those supplies now. Flynt estimates that even as a sole source of food, they will last for two to four months. It is time."

"You wish us to come to you now?"

"Yes. You must break this siege. I know 'tis difficult with them attacking from the north. They have taken the By-way too."

Oakheart could understand the sore point. Attack always had been anticipated from beyond Brightfalls, hence the lookout usually placed there. Although no peoples had been sighted in the Unknown Lands, that did not mean they did not exist. All the defences had been staged around the usual road that climbed up to the Upper Plateau.

"And our strategy?" Oakheart asked.

"You can come up to the Upper Plateau via the By-way. Their forces are split. We can make a foray at the rear of the city, drawing their forces to us there, which should distract them enough for you to break through. Once on the Upper Plateau you will be able to fight the forces on that side of Silverdale directly. Hanal may have more men but they are unruly, unskilled."

Oakheart kept his doubts to himself. "Very well, I will draw up some detailed plans for you to consider. I caution you, though, that a full-on attack will be difficult. They have our defences to protect them. It could be stealth might better serve us."

"You have no need to caution me, Oakheart. I have the man holding a torch to our city and threatening to tear down our walls. You must break this siege."

"Have you tried negotiation? Has he offered terms?"

"Terms? Surrender or lose Silverdale to the flames? They are not terms, but the threats of a bully."

Oakheart bit his bottom lip as he considered his next words. "Perhaps you could offer a counter proposal, even to delay him acting on his threats. We are too far away to provide immediate relief. I fear Hanal will not wait to carry out his threats."

Veld wiped at his eyes. He looked fatigued beyond measure. "You speak true. I can but hope at this stage. Any word from Gilton Forest? From Fern?"

"Not yet. I suspect it is too soon." Oakheart bit his lip. Seven weeks was ample time, surely, but he dared not add to his father's worries.

"Are you ready, Oakheart?" his mother called from outside the tent. "We are waiting." She pushed through the tent flap. Veld's eyebrows lowered, and abruptly the talkstone went blank. Veld had not yet spoken with his wife, for which Oakheart did not blame him. The talkstone was a useful tool, but was no substitute for meeting in person.

"Is all well?" Maralain asked.

Oakheart shook his head. "They have lost access to their main water supply. With only the wells left, they cannot last long. We must now head towards Silverdale. We have run out of time to gather more soldiers."

She nodded. "And Veld. Did he speak of me?"

Ahh...Oakheart prevaricated. "In general...yes."

*Maralain's eyelashes lowered over her green eyes. Not deceived,* thought Oakheart. "Interesting." She lifted the tent flap to allow him to exit. "How long before we reach Silverdale? We have covered half the ground already even with all our riding about in sideways directions to press the towns for volunteers."

"We have time to cross the Argent Flow." By full summer it would be impassable, but in spring the thaw had not yet swelled the river to make the weir dangerous to cross.

"Oh yes. Is it still passable?"

Oakheart squinted as he cast his gaze around the camp and took in the number of tents in the process of being taken down, some already rolled for packing into carts. "It is but less than a day to reach there. Are all assembled?"

"Nearly, Falen is just finishing up with the morning training sessions." They walked together towards Falen's tent. "I must say we have some very good female archers."

Oakheart smiled. "Excellent. We must leave now then. I will draw up plans—"

"We," Maralain interrupted, putting a gloved hand on his forearm. "We will draw up plans this evening. Old man Barkly, although retired, appears to have some strategic capability. Rush also. We should include them."

The older veteran was a good find. The village of Mistletoe had yielded some well-trained young people as well. Rush from nearby Willowood had also spent time in Silverdale in the King's Guard. "Dangler," Oakheart added. "He is also well-trained and knows the layout of Silverdale."

"The tailor?" His mother gasped. "Surely not."

"Yes," Oakheart said. "He was a tailor but he also travelled a lot and had needs to look to his defence, at least be prepared for it. Also, he has a certain way of looking at things."

"Good. Five heads are better than one. Not that I doubt your abilities."

Oakheart laughed. "Not that you have cause to, but I thank you for the thought. Shall we?"

Maralain led the way. Oakheart turned back and saw his aide dart into his tent to ready his things for travel. Not that Oakheart had much with him. His once finely tailored clothes were now wearing thin in places. He was the poorest looking royal, next to his mother who wore only borrowed robes from the retreat.

"Falen?" Maralain said as she entered the commander's tent.

COOKING FIRES WERE PUT OUT AND THE LAST OF BREAKFAST consumed as Oakheart looked out over their gathered force. His quartermaster, Filken, an adept purloined from the retreat, came up to him.

"We need to gather more food or we will starve before we reach the Upper Plateau. It is likely the Puri have stripped the bounty that grows there."

"Yes, I have concerns too. Ideas?"

Filken drew a paper from inside his travel-stained adept's robes. The once white fabric was now grey with darker smears of brown mud along the hem. "We must gather the available bounty as well as tax what food we can through the *given*. We should dispatch three groups for that purpose. Triversmeet is a centre of trade. Send a squad to procure what they can from there, then have it follow along."

Oakheart rubbed at his chin as he listened. Filken was a sensible man and he wondered what his role was at the retreat. He did not appear particularly gifted with the *given* but had good administrative skills. He supposed the retreat needed good organisation to operate so he could not begrudge them. "Good, but they will need protection and they will need to be quick or we will be cut off by a swollen Argent Flow. Send two squads, but mix them up, some experienced with the inexperienced. The Puri could well be this far south. I will write you some warrants for the merchants in Triversmeet so the goods can be placed on Silverdale's account."

Filken nodded and folded up his paper. "It will be as you command, excellency." Then he bowed briefly and strode off, calling out orders as he went.

Oakheart was alone but a moment before Barkly strode up to him.. The old man's leather was well polished from his boots to his belt. Oakheart passed on the news from Silverdale and primed him for the planning session scheduled for the end of the day. "Let Rush and Dangler know about the meeting, will you? I want an assessment of our troops. What skills we possess. What our weaknesses are. And possible plans of attack."

"Yes, your excellency. It shall be as you command. I have a number of scenarios to place before you."

"Good. Thank you." Oakheart let his shoulders relax. It was good to have someone else to contribute to their strategy. His own understanding of the situation left him in no doubt of the difficulties they faced.

There were too few horses for everyone to be mounted. Almost one hundred people were on foot. Although Oakheart had commandeered all the carts and carriages he could find, there was not enough to transport everybody. That meant progress was slower than he liked. His mother was now a good rider, regaining her skills after twenty years of not being on a horse. He mentally calculated the feed that would be required for the horses that they had and turned white. Too much. He went off to catch Filken before he left for Triversmeet to make sure he obtained sufficient grain for the horses.

The main force set off towards the Argent Flow. The place threw up painful memories of Sophy and the attack on her life. Afterwards, she had been so ill that he had used the *given* in a dangerous way to save her life. Even now he did not know what the consequences of that oath were. That evening, before the planning meeting, Maralain walked up to him. "My son, would you care to join me for a meal?"

Oakheart smiled lightly. "Thank you for asking. Anything special on the menu?"

Maralain paused and looked sideways before a smile lit her lips. "Why, surely roasted toffel is your favourite. I even found some gady root."

His eyebrow quirked. "Gady root? Truly? You remember how to make it?"

Maralain let out a scoff. "What? Of course I remember. It's your favourite. Not that I actually made it for you as a child. Vola was the one who enjoyed cooking. But I had a sketchy recollection of the method and as I've been cooking these last twenty years, I coped. It may not be as good as your aunt's but I was hoping you would at least try it and let me know."

Oakheart flushed. He was struck that his mother had made a particular effort to coax him into a better relationship. An effort he had stopped making for at least two weeks. He was ashamed of himself. "I would be delighted," he said at first. Then believing he should proffer more of a peace offering, said, "I am very touched that you have put such an effort into a meal for us to share."

Maralain's eyes widened but then a twinkle grew in her eyes. "When you're ready then. It's done, just warming by the fire."

He took her hand gently and placed it in the crook of his elbow. "My lady queen, let me escort you to dinner."

Maralain laughed. "Thank you, Oakheart." She squeezed his upper arm with her free hand. "You are a comfort to me. Have you heard news of Aria?"

Oakheart shook his head. "No. Sadly I have not." His thoughts took a darker turn. What was happening in Valley Keep? What was happening in Silverdale? What was happening to Sophy?

# TO THE VICTOR THE SPOILS

The gates were shut tight against Hanal. His easy victory had been thwarted. All was not lost though. He still had the upper hand.

Tarkel rode up. "They had warning. The gates are barred. The walls are manned with armed men."

"Are any of our men killed, injured?"

"Some were injured by arrows, Hanal. None are dead, although one young man fell from his horse and has not regained consciousness."

"Are there any messages from Veld?"

Tarkel shook his head. "Will you make demands on him?"

"Yes." Hanal dismounted. Ahead was a house, its former contents strewn across the street. "I will write them down." He walked through the door of the house, flinching because he did not like houses, did not like constructed things. Yet if he was to rule he would have to get used to it. In Argenterra they expected palaces and displays of obvious wealth.

He was provided with paper and a pen and he wrote with a flourish:

*Veld, surrender to me or I will tear Silverdale to the ground.*
*Hanal of Puri.*

"Deliver this to the gate."

Tarkel took the note and passed it on to a messenger. "What orders to you have?" Tarkel asked once the messenger had departed at a run. "With surprise on our side, the way forwards has been swift and sharp edged. Now we have a siege to deal with."

Hanal righted a chair and sat on it, looking out at the debris on the street. Someone had lived here. Those were their belongings. He swallowed. He must go on as he intended. Tarkel searched about him and found a table and scraped the legs along the floor as he put it between them.

He drew out a map from the inside of his robe and spread it out. He swirled his finger around the town of Silverdale. "We have the surrounding land. They are cut off from food, supplies and people." Tarkel pointed to the river. "They need the water from the river to survive."

Hanal agreed. "Find their water supply and shut it off. They have some kind of pipe, I believe."

"Food?"

Hanal bit his bottom lip as he considered. "There is a storehouse. It is likely they have supplies but without water they will not last." He tried to recall the resources inside the walls. The palace itself had a well. Not sufficient to keep them all watered though. "Veld will not surrender until he is desperate. I must make him desperate."

Tarkel sat back and studied him. "Will you really tear down the walls and burn the town?"

Hanal tilted his head, considering. "Yes. If I am forced to."

Tarkel's dark eyes glittered as he thought things through. "Veld will not risk the town. Vorn built parts of this place. The palace, in particular. Would you really destroy something so revered?"

"Not if I can help it. I, too, care about our heritage. But I care not for their finery—their fine houses, their furniture and clothes. Veld will surrender. He has no choice. He values it all."

"The people most of all."

Hanal stroked his chin and nodded. "Yes. The people most of all."

The patter of arrows landing on the cobbles drew Hanal out of the house. From cover, his men fired back at the wall from whence the attack came. A few Argenterrans caught arrows and fell back inside the walls. One fell off the wall and out onto their side. He was rolling on the ground moaning, trying to staunch the blood. A broken arrow protruded from a wound on his thigh. Two of Hanal's men went to retrieve the man, under cover of the rest of that squad. No arrows flew when his men gathered up the stricken Argenterran. It appeared they would not risk their fallen comrade even to strike at his Puri men.

For Hanal the *given* was strong in Silverdale. He could detect the tremor of it beneath his feet, and it sank into him every time he inhaled. *It will not let us take life. It will not stop us taking property or hostages or women.* "The *given* will not protect Veld for long," he said to no one in particular.

"Hanal?"

He turned back to Tarkel, who was watching him from the shadowed interior of the Silverdale town house. "The *given* is strong here, brother. We will find it hard to kill, I suspect. We must use other means."

Tarkel's eyes widened. "*Your* gift? You can tell?"

Hanal inclined his head. "Yes. The biggest prize of all is the *given* that few of us can fully appreciate or understand." He thought of Sophy and the power in her. Did the outlander maid even now strengthen his enemies with her vast store of power?

Tarkel drew his attention to the map. "About the other access points, what is your command?"

Hanal studied the map. He could not rely on the Glasshiver warriors. They waited in Silverdale to be paid. Hanal still had a use for them. Holding the town once they had taken it, and all access to it, was Hanal's role. "Deploy men to the By-way. We must secure it. It is the only other way up to the Upper Plateau. Once we hold that, then Veld has nothing. No chance of reprieve. Anyone coming up has to go through us, and we will have the tactical advantage."

"That is where the army will come, if they can raise one."

"I know." Hanal nodded thoughtfully. Veld might have gotten word out through his talkstone but any help was a long way off.

Tarkel's finger slid along the edge of the Upper Plateau. "Brightfalls? There is a garrison there."

"Ah yes, they were still building it when I was last here. Send Welin and Juri's clan to secure it. The Argenterrans have had no sign of anyone from the Unknown Lands. They will be fat and lazy and not expecting us."

Tarkel stood and bowed. "As you command."

Shortly, Tarkel's voice issuing commands outside reached him. Hanal shrugged and looked around the dishevelled room. He did not feel comfortable there. He emerged into the street, finding even more rubble on the ground. From not far off came the sounds of breakages and screams as his men ransacked the town that remained outside the walls. Let Veld feast on that, he thought, as he strode down the street seeking his tent.

*With that music in his ears, Veld is likely to crumple by nightfall.*

⚜

AROUND MIDNIGHT, HANAL RECEIVED WORD THAT HIS MEN HAD been dispatched as ordered. No signs of any reinforcement had been spotted either from the By-way, Brightfalls, or behind them through the ranges. He had done it! He had taken Veld by surprise. Tarkel reported that the water had successfully been cut off from the city.

"Put in place a transport system for us. We need water and having a plentiful supply will boost our people's spirits. Send word that the rest of our clans can now join us."

Tarkel did a double-take. "You mean to make this place our home?"

Hanal straightened his shoulders. "Of course. What do you think I am doing here? Playing?"

Tarkel bowed his head. "No, of course not. I just did not think we would abandon our homeland."

"We are not. We are expanding our notion of our homeland."

Over the next week, Hanal secured the By-way, captured the garrison at Brightfalls, and had Silverdale at his mercy. Still Veld would not yield. The weeks continued on. Hanal bided his time. His people joined him, swelling his numbers. He formulated plans and made speeches to his people. After nearly eight weeks, Hanal had had enough. His respect for Veld had grown. He had considered the old king weak and a fool, but his fortitude in resisting the siege was to be commended. Sadly, Hanal would have to break him completely.

Before the gates, Hanal stood out of arrow shot range. "Veld, time has run out!" he called in a loud voice. Faces appeared, looking over the wall. He heard the voices, the sound of running feet as messengers were dispatched. Veld would be summoned by this new activity. Hanal had his prime troops dressed in fine robes arrayed behind him. For this, he wanted to present a show, a strong spirit to crush the weaker foe. Veld and his people were near to collapse.

Tarkel nodded to his second and a show was made with his elite guard brandishing their weapons and marching in formation. Hanal called out, "Veld! I offer you one last chance. Surrender or I will tear down your walls and burn your town."

There was no immediate answer. Hanal waited for a reasonable time and still there was nothing. He signalled to his men and they brought stacks of wood and bales of hay and rested them against the houses that abutted the walls.

The houses would burn easily. They had been cleared of their owners so Hanal would not be risking life. Without water, Silverdale would burn. By rights, Veld should have yielded already. If the *given* held true, he would not light this fire. Or, as the *given* worked in mysterious ways, if he was able to light the fire, the people now holed up inside would be able to flee.

"Bring Rexford's man," he called. "We will bring down the walls, just there. Be ready, those houses will burn first."

The gates could have been attacked, but knowing Veld he would be prepared for that. A successful attack on the stone walls though, he would not expect.

The Glasshiver man came with his pouch, his assistant ready to strike the flame. For this work, the traditional feathers were absent and he wore leather belts across his torso and a skirt in blue fabric to just above the knees. A few feathers fell limply from a head band. Hanal's eyelids narrowed as the man placed wads of something into the gaps between the stone. Hanal wanted only a small demonstration of his power over Veld and Silverdale. He did not want to bring it all down. His heart beat a frantic time as he considered the power of Glasshiver's weapon. For that is what these 'explosives' were.

Rexford's man lifted his head, waiting for Hanal's signal.

"Last chance," Hanal cried. "Veld, hear me. Your walls will crumble and your city will burn if you do not surrender now."

There was no response and Hanal gestured with his hand. The flame was lit. Rexford's man retreated and so did Hanal and his Puri guards.

He held his breath wondering what would happen to that tiny flame. The concussion threw him backwards and stole his breath. Stunned for a few moments, Hanal lay there looking at the sky, hearing nothing. His ears were throbbing and felt dead to noise.

Hands came to help him up and sound slowly leaked in. Cries. Screams. Fear all around him. His own breathing was too fast and hard for calm. Flames licked the houses they had primed, smoke and dust billowed in clouds obscuring the view. Rock that had been part of the wall lay in shattered pieces. A short section lay in ruins. Hanal gaped, appalled.

With a whoosh the flame caught and smoke started to billow up in small white clouds, which grew bigger and darker. The scent of burning filled the air, and was soon at the back of his throat. Screams started from the other side of the town wall. Still no sign of Veld.

The flames grew, and soon they licked up over the lip of the wall, leaping over the top to be visible from the castle. Hanal stood poised, ready to send his men through the breach, ready to defend if Veld's city guards attacked.

His men moved away from the flames as they expanded and the heat intensified. Soon, scorched beams of wood could be seen and particles of ash floated over the walls and fell like black snow. There was the sound of many feet coming closer.

Tarkel gave a signal. His men were ready for a counter-offensive. Swords glinted in the sun. With a grunt and a groan, the bolt to the main gates was pulled back. The gate opened and Veld stood there. He ambled out, his age and girth making him no longer agile. His eyes met Hanal's.

Veld stood still then lowered himself to his knees. The flames behind the kneeling high king wafted and beat in time to Hanal's heartbeat. No guards accompanied the high king. Hanal's heart beat faster. He had won. No one could look more dejected than the high king. Hanal flicked his outer robe over his shoulders and strode forwards.

"Veld?" he said.

Veld looked up at him, tears in his eyes. "Hanal of Puri, I surrender Silverdale to you. Have mercy on my people."

Hanal jerked up his hand in silent command. His men rushed to put out the fire, hurling buckets of water that had been hidden behind his arrayed troops. A quick glance revealed that a house or two on the other side had caught fire and tongues of flame already licked the eaves. His men poured through the gates, some to put out the fire, the rest to secure the palace and other key strategic points about the town. Hanal was proud. His people had not been lax while they waited for Silverdale to fall. They had learnt a lot. They were not perfect, of course, but they could hold Silverdale and hold it long.

"Thank you, Veld. You will be my guest."

His escort formed up around the deposed king. Hanal strode through the gates of Silverdale to take possession, with Veld trailing along behind, a prisoner.

✤ 13 ✤

# TO THINE OWN SELF BE TRUE

Dela led Gilly away by the hand. Aria chewed the inside of her cheek as she watched them. There was something wrong with the child. She had underestimated Dellbright's deception—life at Valley Keep was not normal. It was nothing like when she had first come to Argenterra. Although the stain of Aurore's murder had been cleaned from the keep, it was a sad place. Sadder now as Dela closed the door. That Dela and Willow were in on the deception wounded her. They had no loyalty to her nor respect for her as Gilly's mother.

"My lady, you look troubled." Leyla was packing up the tea things and placing the cups and the pot on the tray. Her guise as a lady-in-waiting was still holding.

To all intents and purposes, Dellbright had been a gentleman. He had gathered up the last one hundred men just that morning and sent them after Oakheart for the defence of Silverdale.

He had ostensibly provided access to her son. And now that the troops were dispatched, he expected no less than she should share his bed. Aria tightened her fist and clenched her teeth at his audacity.

"My lady?" Leyla asked again after handing the tray to a servant in the corridor. "What is it?"

Aria unclenched her hand and ceased rubbing at her jaw trying to ease the tension there. "I'm heartsick."

"I am sure you must be, but you have a particular concern do you not, rather than a general one?"

"That child is not my son."

Leyla blinked, then bit her bottom lip. "Are you sure? You have been separated for a number of months. Children grow and change quickly."

Aria's eyes watered and she wiped at them, trying to control her emotions. "At first I thought as you did. That I had grown distant to my child, but then I began to consider and compare. Today I know for certain he is not my son."

"How?"

Aria strode to the window and stood looking out over the bailey and the valley beyond. How she had loved this place, this view. Now it was all tainted. "I'm not sure you will understand, but I think you might. He has not got the same vibration. There are some physical characteristics too that I've been able to check on the sly. A birth mark not in the right place. The shape of his feet when his shoes are removed. The way he smiles and the shape of his forehead. Subtle things, I know."

"Vibration? Do you perhaps mean his saturation in the *given*?"

Aria swung round in surprise. "Yes. That's exactly what I mean."

"Then you have much greater ability than I thought."

"Oakheart said I was strong and that I needed to learn more skill."

Leyla inclined her head. "But tonight is it not..." She left off saying what Aria had been dreading since she returned with Dellbright. But if he had not kept to the whole of the bargain, why should she be expected to live up to hers? The troops so newly sent could easily be called back. She bet her life that Dellbright had a rider ready to do so when she refused him. Or would he retrieve the men anyway and take what he wanted from her? She shivered at the darkness that inhabited her husband. How had she ever trusted him?

Despairing, she decided that Fern, too, had been a disappointment. In the end it was all about him and his needs. No consideration for her and her needs, her duty. She felt relieved they'd decided at the retreat that their relationship was over. Convinced it wouldn't take him long to take up with another woman, she steeled herself for news of his betrothal. The thought wounded her, but more her pride and the acknowledgement of her own stupidity.

Where men were concerned she had no brain. She was attracted to superficial things like looks and flowery words and professions of undying love. What an idiot she was. She deserved what she got—heartbreak—for all her mistakes. Oh, and what about Sophy! She had abandoned her best friend for Dellbright and had taken up with Fern who had been cruel to Sophy.

"My lady?" Leyla broke into her thoughts.

Aria sniffed and met her gaze. "I'm sorry. Just some morose thinking. Now you've been teaching me more about using the *given*, how am I to defend myself tonight?"

"My lady, I think you are ready to take the next step. We will need quiet for this." She took a chair to the door and wedged it under the handle so it couldn't be opened. "We will meditate and practise touching the *given* that is present on the surface of the skin."

The adept lowered herself to the floor and with a wave of her hand invited Aria to join her. "Now, my lady, empty your mind of your cares. That is good. First, seek the vibration of the *given* within you. Yes, that's right. Now invite the *given* also outside of you to within you."

Aria could sense the *given* in herself. Much emanated from the walls of the keep and then Leyla herself yet she felt too overwhelmed to take in more. "But I can't..."

"Think of yourself as the spider in the centre of the web. Concentrate, and soon you will detect the threads and you can touch them, draw them closer to you. The *given* will not cause you harm, but will strengthen the connections."

Aria had no idea how long they sat and meditated on the *given*. A banging on the door interrupted them, and just as she thought she had drawn the threads of the *given* into herself they all collapsed and faded away.

"Open this door!" It was Dellbright.

Her heart thudded. Leyla shot to her feet and helped Aria up. Before Leyla went to the door, Aria raced to a work basket and drew fibre fluff from within and strewed it over the floor. Next, she picked up a drop spindle that lay on the basket and sat in a chair, giving Leyla a nod.

The chair was removed and Dellbright thumped on the door as it was opened. He stood on the threshold, face red with rage and hands balled into fists. His gaze fell on the fluff and Aria's handful that she was spinning into thread. "Oh. I did not know you worked with the fibres in the rough. I thought you only worked with the fabric once woven."

Aria placed the fluff in her lap and gazed up at him. "I seek to learn the whole process of making fabric. Perhaps I can come up with an innovation."

"Your maid helps you, I see." He signalled to Leyla. "Go fetch your mistress some seed cake. It has just come from the oven."

Leyla surreptitiously glanced Aria's way. Aria lowered her eyelids, not daring to nod. Leyla curtseyed. "Yes, your highness." Without a backward glance she left the room.

Dellbright stood watching Aria closely. She returned his stare, lifting an eyebrow in query. He lunged for her, grabbing her arm and hauling her from the chair. His face was close to hers. "You remember our agreement?"

"Yes," she replied steadily. "Every word of it. Your part, and mine."

He continued to glare at her, breathing hard through his nostrils.

"Please, let go. You're hurting me and that's not part of our arrangement."

He released her, shoving her backwards, his lips compressed. He made no move towards her. Wary, Aria said and did nothing more. The door opened and Leyla returned with a tray. Her gaze flicked towards them as she set out the cups. She'd brought enough so Dellbright could join with them.

"I'll pour," Aria said and then Leyla bent to pick up all the fibre fluff and drop spindles and packed them into the basket.

"You were very quick," Dellbright said, watching the maid while she worked.

Aria sighed. Leyla must have performed a feat of magical proportions to get back to the room so quickly. Aria could not relax, but she could be polite. She poured tea for Dellbright, which he took. "How did you find Gilly?" he asked.

Aria poured her own cup, not ready to challenge him. Once she did, she would have to leave and it was better to prepare properly.

"I found the boy well," she said, not giving in to the illusion that it was Gilly, that it was her child. "He is tall for his age."

As Dellbright studied her she kept her face neutral.

"I was tall for my age."

Aria lifted her lips, not quite a smile. "I'm not surprised."

He continued studying her as he toyed with his cup. He waved away the piece of seedcake that Leyla offered him.

Aria flirted with danger. "I'm surprised, though, that he doesn't have more of your colouring. I thought his complexion would be a little olive and his hair curlier." She fingered her own twirling locks and smiled slightly.

Dellbright, sipping from his cup, straightened his back and then lowered the cup to peer at her. "I have just as much of Vorn's blood as you," he said flatly. "So there is no need to wonder that he has skin as fair as yours."

Aria put her head on one side. "That is true. I expect he will take after Oakheart, strong, blond and handsome."

His cup dropped to the floor, shattering. He didn't even blink at the sound. "Think what you like," he growled. "I will escort you to our bedchamber after the eve-tide meal. Your lady-in-waiting will take herself elsewhere. I am advised that Willow has need of her services this evening."

Keeping her expression bland, Aria nodded. Her heart thudded, but she did her best to hide her fear. "How thoughtful of you, although I assure you I am quite capable of finding my way upstairs and into the correct room. I don't need your escort."

Dellbright glared at her and Aria breathed through it: she *could* do this. Suddenly, Leyla moved towards the tea tray. Dellbright turned and glared at her before stalking from the room. The door snapped shut behind him.

"Dear lord!" Aria lifted her shaking hands and looked at them. She had pulled it off, but at what price to her sanity?

Leaving the tea things, Leyla came across and hugged her tight. "We will be ready. We have some time to practise. You are very close. "

To save time, she barred the door again and dispersed the fibre, pulling from her apron a drop spindle with quite a lot of thread wound around it. It would give the impression that they had been spinning instead of doing something else.

⁂

While the eve-tide meal had been interminable, Aria hadn't been able to get away before Dellbright cornered her. "Not so fast," he said, cutting her off at the end of the table. People milled around. Dela cast her a look before directing servants to remove the dirtied dishes and leftover food.

He drew her close to him, mouthing pretend admiration for her looks. "You look beautiful as ever." A servant passing by nodded and smiled, loaded down with a tray of empty goblets.

Aria threw up a fake smile. Aria's clothing was poor and she had not bothered trying to look good for him. "Thank you for the compliment."

Dellbright checked his surroundings and just then the hall was empty but for one person wiping down the tables and Leyla who had risen with her. He tugged her towards the doorway and she went with him out of the hall.

Willow met them, sweeping a bow to Dellbright. Dellbright acknowledged his chamberlain with a nod. Willow surged behind Aria, blocking Leyla from accompanying her. "I have need of you in my office, young maid," he said in a loud voice.

Aria surreptitiously shook her head: they had planned for this. Leyla bowed her head and followed Willow out of the hall.

Dellbright held Aria's upper arm tightly as he half-dragged her up the stairs.

"You will give me a bruise. Please ease your hold. I am quite capable of walking up the stairs unassisted."

He sniggered at her. "Forgive me. I did not want to lose you on the way...you might misplace your way in another excuse to avoid your duty to me."

Her face was close to his. "Why do you say that? We have a bargain, do we not? Have I not kept to it? Have you?"

Almost nose-to-nose with her, he said, "It remains to be seen whether you will keep to it. I have certainly been patient and true to my word."

They reached the landing and Aria pulled her arm back. After a moment of resistance Dellbright released his hold.

"Oh yes, the Prince of Valley Keep has so much honour and would never dare to stoop to subterfuge when his word is pledged. It is his bond. His *honour*."

He grabbed for her again, shoving her along the corridor. "You dare mock me to my face?" He pushed open the bedchamber door and flung her through. "I will teach you to respect me."

Aria laughed, even though she knew she was playing with fire. "Respect? Hardly. I can barely keep my derision in check."

The blow sent her flying backwards—she had misjudged, and not expected him to lash out so quickly. Was he now going to bash and rape her? Would he so callously go against his word and shred their agreement? She knew in her gut that he would. "Is this foreplay?" she said.

"Shut up, you insolent whore."

"You attempt to woo me to your bed with blows?"

He raised his hand again and she flinched, not ready yet to reveal her hand.

"You dare to break your word to your high king, to Oakheart, to me?"

He lowered his arm, relaxed his fist. "My love," he said with vinegared spite. "I would have sold my soul to the Ancient Evil to have you back in my power again. I want to taste your sweet flesh, delve into your sex until you cry my name and beg me to stop. Now take off your clothes, or do you need help with that?"

Aria moved away from the bed. "You expect me to sleep with you after this?" She gestured to her throbbing cheek. "You're even crazier than I thought."

He lunged. Aria stood still, sought the thread of *given* and focussed on her skin. Her gown tore at the shoulder and his hand grabbed her hair and wrenched her head back. She tried to keep focus, but it wasn't working. His mouth came down hard on her neck and he bit her. She screamed and tried to keep the threads of her concentration together. He tore her dress and underclothes as he immobilised her with his bite. She hit out at him, yanked on his hair. He punished her breasts with a clawed hand and she cried out.

Then she calmed herself, made herself go limp. His bite eased and he took her by the hair and thrust her onto the bed, climbing on top of her. He reared over her and tore the remaining shreds of her clothes away, leaving her breasts and upper body bare. "How I have waited for this moment."

A knocking on the door momentarily drew his attention. "My lady?" came Leyla's voice. The door rattled. Dellbright must have locked it.

He reached down to grab her breasts, laughing derisively.

Aria closed her eyes, letting that calm place inside her channel the *given*. Dellbright shook, screamed and then his weight was gone. A loud thump sounded as he hit the floor. Half-crying, Aria sat up and crawled across the bed to view him.

He convulsed, heels kicking against the floor, his jaw stretched in a rictus. Moans leaked out of his mouth and drool dripped down his cheek to puddle on the floor. "You will never touch me again. Never!"

Turning away, she looked down at herself, giggling hysterically, trying to order her thoughts and losing. A hectic pounding on the door alerted her to Leyla's frantic attempt to aid her.

Slanting her head, she looked at Dellbright. He had no control of his body and the spasms that wracked him looked painful. Whether he could hear her or not, she didn't know or care, but the words had to be spoken. "You have no power over me, Dellbright. I gave it to you once, but never again."

The pounding on the door grew more desperate. She scrabbled for something to cover herself, got up and let Leyla in.

"My lady?" Leyla burst in, gaping at Aria draped in a sheet. "By the *given*, you are hurt!"

"I'm okay." She nodded in the direction of Dellbright who lay on the carpet with his arms and legs twitching, eyes staring at the ceiling. White froth was gathering between his taut lips. "I'm not sure about him."

Leyla spared Dellbright a glance and a smile lit her lips. "My lady! You did it. Come, I will tend you in your rooms." She grabbed Aria's hand and tugged her out the door.

In the corridor Willow stood there, his face severe. "My lady?" He no longer called her princess even though she had told him she was Veld's daughter and wasn't beholden to Dellbright for her titles. His gaze flicked nervously between her and the bedroom.

"I believe Dellbright has had an accident. You might want to help him into bed so he can be more comfortable." Willow gaped at her stupidly. "I'm sure he'll be fine in the morning." Her voice was light, cheery even.

Willow brushed past her and dove into the room. She heard him crying, "My prince, my prince!"

Supported by Leyla, Aria made her way towards her own room. "We must prepare," she whispered to Leyla. "My time has run out."

"Yes, my lady."

Just then, Dela rushed along the corridor, wringing her hands. Willow's wife glanced nervously from Leyla to Aria. "My lady, are you well? Has something happened?"

Aria touched her cheek where pain throbbed. "Nothing of note, Dela. I am going to bed now. Your husband is tending to Dellbright. There is nothing for you to do here."

Aria took a step away from the woman, who rushed ahead and curtseyed hurriedly. "Very well, my lady. Shall I bring Gilly to you in the morning?"

Aria paused and considered the woman. Why couldn't she say what she wanted to say? Because it wasn't time or the place. "That would please me greatly. I would love to see...my...son." She suspected Dela knew of the subterfuge and a slight greying of the other woman's upturned face confirmed it.

Aria did her best to hold onto her anger, to check her hate. This woman had abetted Dellbright in starving her, taking her child, and stayed quiet when he beat and raped her. What kind of hold did Dellbright have over her? Surely he must have some for her to acquiesce to all that went on in this keep. Perhaps Willow and Dela were caught up in the taint. Good lord, how was it possible? They had treated Sophy so badly, and she had defended their behaviour. Poor Sophy! She had betrayed her best friend, in so many ways.

"Come, my lady. Come away." Leyla guided her along the corridor to her room, talking soothingly. Aria realised she was shaking in anger more than fear, although regret had its claws in her as well.

Shortly, as Aria soaked in a hot bath, soothed by the herbs Leyla had added, she spoke to Leyla through the open door. "I have sworn off men."

Leyla tilted her head. "I have not found much to like in men myself. Not in that way, I mean. I respect the male adepts, but I could not be intimate with one of them."

Aria tilted her head. "Do you mean you haven't had the opportunity?"

"No, I have had plenty of opportunity and invitations, just not the inclination."

"Oh." Aria frowned, a sudden thought occurring. "Do you prefer women?"

Leyla laughed softly and entered the bathroom. Aria blushed at her own nakedness and the bruises on her breasts and arms. "I..." Leyla paused, a frown marring her brow. "I have not had the opportunity to discover that. They are certainly more appealing than the male of the species both in form and in turn of mind. Your experience has only confirmed for me that men are the lesser species."

"So you don't want to marry. Be a mother?"

"No, I have never desired it. I have always wanted to study the *given* at the retreat. That is what I was doing before I was requested to serve you. Many female adepts never marry. It depends on the individual, I suppose."

Aria lay back and closed her eyes. That might have been her fate if she had been born in Argenterra—studying at the retreat. Aria considered sex. Not all her experiences had been good, or bad. At its best it had been good with Dellbright—and at its worst, terrifying.

Fern had pleasured her within the limits of her vow. She had liked that, and had liked pleasuring him in return. Fern confused her: she was angry at him, angry at his selfishness. She could not be with him and he did not have the patience to work things through. How could she decide whether she liked sex or not? The unresolved sexual frustration Fern had evoked in her made her want to scream. She was attracted to men. But she'd sworn off them just now. What did that mean for her?

It was so confusing. The future was so murky. It was enough that she could stay alive and escape. What was she to do about Gilly? She doubted he was even at Valley Keep. A tear slid down her cheek. She was never going to see Gilly again. She stood up in the bath, letting the hot water fall from her body. Leyla handed her a towel and helped her out of the tub.

"Let me dry you off," Leyla said.

And Aria agreed.

$$\text{❧ } 14 \text{ ❧}$$

## CURIOSITY'S KILLER

Illuminated by the afternoon gloom, the ruins were sheathed in a yellow-stained mist. Nothing moved within the city. Sophy picked her way clear of the ridge and the last tunnel, and then made a bee line for the edge of the ruins, hoping to take Rufus by surprise. Rufus had not come to investigate the collapse of the ridge and she bet he never thought she would come looking for him.

Her fingers tingled while she walked, the aftertaste of power on them. That made her thoughtful. Hopefully, there would be no more tremors to disturb her excursion. Glancing up at walls that appeared to be standing only by the grace of god, she decided she didn't fancy one of them falling on her, or the ground opening up and letting an aged sewer swallow her. Things were complicated enough.

Sophy shivered. Clumps of debris were unrecognisable, twisted and dull grey. Thankfully there were no bodies. That would have made her run. Whatever catastrophe had happened here was a long time ago.

The harsh wind was thwarted by the ruins, diverted and softened to a breeze that hurled the lighter debris down the roads, or bent metal sheeting with spine-chilling ease. She found it hard to picture the people who might have lived here. None of the structures seemed familiar; these were all too decayed, too distorted to make out. The artefacts she'd found were the only type of things she actually understood, all household items, except for the sword. That was not an everyday item where she hailed from. She stood stock-still. Was that a memory? Instead of struggling to remember, she let her mind relax, let the images float and linger, convinced that if she forced them they would flee from her grasp. Then she recollected cars, planes, buildings made of steel and glass. People, lots of people. She tried to shut off the images when they began to cascade and reel through her mind too quickly. Home, familiarity, but there was no cohesion, no story. She still did not know where she was and why.

The fairly intact building she had spied before stood in what seemed to be the centre of the town. There was no noise, no voices or machinery working. She couldn't tell if Rufus was still there or had gone elsewhere. She faced the building but held back. Helplessly, she looked at the junk around her feet and kicked at it. She'd thought it would help her, but it was all meaningless. None of it, the destruction, the proximity to Rufus, made her remember anything of importance. She hesitated. He knew. He could tell her everything, even the nameless fear that stalked her. Should she go inside, spy on him, hope he dropped a hint? There was a sound behind her. It was not the wind. Her heart went flip, flop. Why had she been standing there stupidly in the open? *Fool!* Slowly she turned around, her mouth so dry her throat closed up. She couldn't even swallow her fear.

There he was. The creature. Larger, uglier than she remembered. Remembered? She screwed up her face. She remembered something.

Then it spoke. "You are so filthy, little one, I could smell you as soon as you entered the town. Tell me, do you like my home? Pretty, isn't it?"

Sophy glanced left and right looking for a way out. The reality of Rufus was more than she'd expected, and a fear so great took hold of her. The debris behind blocked her escape. She had inadvertently caged herself in, walking steadily forwards without realising that a frame of debris on one side and a pile of sharp, rusted spikes on the other cut off her escape route. She stepped back, running through the options as the back of her knees touched a lump of compacted concrete and metal.

Her gaze left Rufus, darting left and right. She could throw something at him, hurt him, distract him, and she could make a run for it. Now if the ugreals could dig a hole beneath her and carry her away then maybe she could escape. But there was no hole opening up to save her. She'd walked into this.

Her chest hurt as she struggled to breathe through her fear. Rufus moved again; the way his ungainly limbs bent made her stomach clench. Something was not right with him. "You do not cringe as you used to. Nor do you look as hungry and as cowed as you should. How is it that you survived all these weeks without food?"

He turned his head to the side and sniffed. "I smell nothing but you. Interesting." His eyes reflected red as he studied her. "Come with me quietly and I'll let you wash that grunge away."

He put out a clawed hand towards her. Was it meant to comfort her? She thought not. "Why would my being clean have anything to do with you? You mean to hurt me."

She wanted to recoil from the force of his gaze.

"Hurt you? No. I want to worship you. You used to like me once."

Sophy gaped at him. "I did?" She sensed a truth to his words, but there was confusion too. No clear memory of what they were to each other; too many unanswered questions. "Why am I here? Where is this place?" She wanted to ask who am I, who is Sophy meant to be, but that would reveal too much ignorance. She couldn't afford to be in a weaker position than she already was.

"I brought you here with me, my sweet. But somehow the transfer went wrong and I lost you. I worried for you, called to you, but you would not come. Come with me now." Clawed fingers stretched towards her, the filmy membranes at his wrist flapping in the breeze.

Her stomach heaved. "I don't trust you. Where are we?"

Rufus turned his head to take in the ruined city, his scrutiny lasting a long time. She saw many emotions flit over his features. Turning back, he smiled at her. "This is Vorn's homeworld—Yulandir, the inhabitants called it. Before he left here he named it the Deadlands. Rather apt, don't you think?"

Sophy scrunched up her face. "Vorn? What or who is Vorn?"

Rufus studied her, a slow grin spreading across his whiskered snout. "You don't remember?"

Her silence was her confession.

His smile broadened. "Any of it?"

Still she didn't answer.

His eyes glowed red around his grinning visage. "You don't remember him?"

"Who?"

"No one of importance. Not knowing is much better for you. Come now, little one. Unesta wants to talk to you."

"Unesta? Look, I'm not going anywhere." A burst of wind rattled metal and pounded against another object. Startled by the sound, she looked right, trying to see what it was. Too late she heard the whir, before wire bit into her flesh around her ribs and upper arms. Rufus hooted as he tightened his hold, pulled hard so that she toppled over, hands locked tight against her sides. She must have blacked out, because the next thing she knew he was dragging her along the ground, the soft dirt giving way easily as he tugged her along in rhythmic bursts.

She screamed in outrage, in fear. He stopped and leant down to swipe his hand across the top of her head.

"Shut up."

Worse, he covered her head with a torn piece of his own dirty robe. She gagged when he cut off her vision, making choking sounds. She hoped to make him feel it necessary to free her but he did nothing. Just went back to his wire and pulled. And it hurt. The wire cut into her soft flesh. The more she tried to struggle the tighter the wire pulled, cutting into her flesh, cutting off her circulation. Her hands were going numb. Her chest was a hot flare of pain. She had no choice but to let him drag her.

Of the ugreals there was no sign. They had tried to warn her. She'd brought the situation to crisis, and there was no one to help her. She tried to picture Vorn. Did she know him? All this destruction looked old. If he had been alive when it happened then she couldn't know him. He'd have to be dead. But the name was familiar, there was a resonance. All she could understand was that it was all linked and important. Then the wire bit deep again and she cried with more than just self-pity. It was agony.

Thrown to the floor, Sophy struggled up to a sitting position as Rufus lifted the cloth from her head. A green light drew her attention. Rufus lowered to the ground, genuflecting—grovelling more like it. "Mistress!'

A woman appeared, her form alternating from young, to older to old hag and back again. Shades of green covered her skin. "You have found her finally."

"Yes, mistress."

"Stand her up. I want to see."

Rufus grabbed Sophy by the scruff of the neck and hoisted her. Sophy cried out, near stumbled.

The woman approached, sniffed. "Not as much power as I was expecting."

"She drew much into herself. Argenterra is weaker now."

"Not weak enough! I want it dead. I want it all."

Rufus recoiled. "We can drain her. The power will be yours."

The woman nodded, her many faces all displaying a scowl. "Yes. It will."

"Who are you? What are you talking about?" squeaked Sophy.

The woman sneered. "I am Unesta. Your friends call me the Ancient Evil, but you don't need to listen to them. I am only taking back what is mine. He stole it from me, stranded me here. I'm taking it back."

"What?"

"Power."

Sophy swallowed and the woman disappeared. Rufus picked her up like a sack of vegetables. The wire cut into her again and she screamed.

## 𝄞 15 𝄞

# LOVE, HONOUR AND CHOICES

The waters in the Argent Flow were swirling quite docilely. Oakheart's group had made it before the spring thaw swelled the river. Maralain at his side, Oakheart watched while the troop they had gathered performed a drill, worked hard by Falen. Originally one of Dellbright's men, Falen had offered to put some shine into the variously gathered people. Maralain did not look impressed.

"Why aren't you distributing these new recruits amongst the more experienced ones, like Dellbright's force?" Maralain asked.

"We thought it best to keep them separate for now as we train them up. Later, once we get closer to the plateau, we will make new assignments, add the inexperienced to the experienced," Oakheart replied reasonably.

"But why do we linger here? Surely they can train in the mornings before we march?"

Oakheart looked sideways at her. "I was hoping to hear from Fern and the forest folk. I was hoping to get a glimpse of them before we set off."

Maralain nodded. "I see." Her mouth narrowed as she observed the troops then she switched her gaze to Oakheart. "Fern and Aria are no longer an item. I can't say that I'm sorry about that. I knew Fern's mother. We did not get on."

"I know. Aria bore it well. It is for the best, I'm sure, although I worry about her with Dellbright."

"He will make it right with her." With a quick incline of her head, Maralain walked away.

Oakheart's fists clenched. He could not let that comment ride. "There is no making it right, mother. Dellbright is beyond help."

Maralain swung back to face him. "Just when I thought we had an accord between us. Why are you so bent on destroying his character?"

"He has done that himself. Look, I have no wish to quarrel with you. We will leave in the morning, whether Fern shows up or not."

A group of female archers took their places for their exercise. Maralain's mouth moved as if she was going to say more, then she paused to watch. "Those girls make good archers, don't they?"

Amongst the trees, female archers were shooting targets that peeped out from tree trunks and then disappeared. A better fit for battle than shooting at static targets. It kept them nimble.

"Yes." His gaze fell on some new recruits. There was not much in the way of weapons to give these men. Some had made staffs out of their garden tools and made savage displays against their opponents. Oakheart was secretly impressed. Others made staves, the sharpened ends puncturing sacks stuffed with straw. Personally, he thought the staff was a better weapon. It could put someone out of action without causing the flesh to be punctured.

"Why are you grinning?" his mother asked.

He lifted an eyebrow and regarded her. "Those men with the staffs. I like their weapon."

"Perhaps you should practise with them."

With an elegant bow, Oakheart decided to do just that. He could use some loosening up.

His opponent was taller and broader than he was. A backwoods farmhand who could wrestle stampeding horses. Oakheart ducked the sweep of the staff that flew harmlessly over his head and shoved the pointy end into the man's undefended gut. Except he was no longer there. Surprisingly agile for his size, the man had sidestepped and brought his staff...*thunk* across Oakheart's shoulder. Oakheart came down to his knees and dropped his weapon, his arm stunned from the blow. His opponent stood at ease, his weapon end on the ground. There was applause from the onlookers.

"Very well done," Oakheart said as he rubbed at his upper arm. "What is your name?"

"Sky, your excellency. Sky Thunder." He bobbed his head and grinned at Oakheart.

"Well, Sky, do you think you could teach a few of these men your technique? I know you are taller and have better reach, but you have some swift moves that might help the others. Teach some of the women, too."

"Women, sir? Me..."

"Yes, why not?"

"It is just that women are usually scared of me." He glanced down as his body. "Being so big and all."

"Think nothing of it. I will have Falen assign a few to you for training."

He returned to his mother. "Did you enjoy the display?"

Her lips lifted in a sly grin. "I did. Are you hurt?"

"Not permanently. But young Sky put me in my place. I will train with him again later. The staff is not a weapon I have used much."

Her gaze raked over the camp with its occupants all training at some kind of weapon or general fitness. "You haven't had the need before. Not really." She shook her head. "I can't believe Veld let the situation develop to this."

They had discussed the reasons for the current crisis many times on their journey. Oakheart found it hard to criticise his father, whereas Maralain had no such compunction. He had thought more than once that if Maralain had not left her husband then things would have been different. But it was too unkind a thought to voice. He had placed enough blame on her and she, he knew, took plenty on herself. Aria's plight had wounded her, even though she often tried to console herself that Dellbright was a good man like his father.

IT WAS A WEARY OAKHEART WHO SAT AROUND THE CAMPFIRE THAT night, shovelling a bowl of toffelporridge into his mouth. If he did not eat fast enough he was likely to collapse. He was bruised and aching from three more sessions with Sky, the new staff master. The young man was indefatigable. Oakheart put down his bowl and looked around. A few others were limping and one young woman was holding her side as she hobbled to her tent. Yet, Oakheart was pleased to have been put through his paces. He had picked up a few new moves and was much more confident with the staff than previously, although his preference remained for his bow and arrow and his sword.

Maralain walked over to him, tilting her head as she regarded him. "Could I be of assistance?"

He glanced up at her. "What do you propose?"

"I believe you could do with a massage, son. Some liniment and some hot towels to those bruises. We will be riding out tomorrow and I fear you will feel today's exploits even more than you do now." She pulled a jar of ointment out from her robes.

"Most definitely I will feel it." He nodded. "Your ministrations would be most welcome, mother. My tent or yours?"

"Yours will do."

Oakheart passed his bowl to his aide to be cleaned and then went into his tent, not without looking to the direction that he hoped Fern would come from. There was no sign, so he dropped the tent flap and took off his doublet and shirt. His mother told him to lie down on his bunk, which he did. His aide positioned a kettle on the fire. Maralain poured hot water onto the towels and wrung them out before placing them on his skin. He sighed as the heat softened his muscles and eased his aches. Next, she applied the ointment and began to smooth it into his skin. This brought back memories of Sophy's ministrations— memories that made his eyes water. He let his eyelids lower and enjoyed the strong fingers his mother brought to bear on the knots in his shoulders and back.

"Thank you," he said when she sat back. "That was very good."

"Feeling better?"

"Yes. I will sleep well now." He rolled on his back, stifled a yawn and looked at her. "Do you mind if I ask you something?"

"What?" she asked as she piled up the towels.

"What do you feel for my father? What future do you envisage with him?"

He did not mistake her intake of breath. She had not expected such a question. Indeed, for many weeks he'd thought it none of his business and then considered it most definitely was and then changed his mind, over and over again.

"I...well...I'm not sure. I came looking for Aria and Sophy. I didn't come back for Veld. But now...with everything...I have a sense of duty to protect Silverdale, to act as a queen should. I won't know how I feel until I see Veld, speak to him."

Oakheart recalled that Veld had never spoken to his wife on the talkstone. Was he too waiting for a face-to-face meeting? Oakheart tried to think what he would feel in the same circumstance and failed.

"And if it does not go well?"

She harrumphed. "I have a daughter that I can live with, and a grandchild too. I will have sufficient to keep me entertained."

"By agreement, Aria is to remain at Valley Keep. Will you live there?"

"Agreement? I'm sure Dellbright will be reasoned with. He cannot deny me my daughter. Then I have to find you a wife."

Oakheart stiffened. "I have a wife."

"But Sophy isn't here. Your bond is broken. What if she never comes back? Surely you have considered it?"

He sat up. "No, I have not considered it. Even now, the retreat is close to finding the means to control the Crystal Gate. When the word comes I will go there, use the gate, and I will find Sophy."

"But what if she is happy in her world? Will you stay there with her?"

"Only if she has no desire to return will I leave her there. My home is here, mother."

Maralain nodded. "I see. Well, if you end up having no wife then I will find one for you."

"Mother, I can do very well without your assistance."

"But..."

"Please, let us not discuss it further. I find that my temper will fray. Good night."

Picking up her towels and her jar of ointment, Maralain took her leave, wishing him a good rest.

Oakheart lay back on his bunk and pledged to the night. "Sophy, I am coming for you. Please believe it."

He thought on Fern's absence. If only his cousin would turn up. He would feel better knowing he could turn command over to Fern. His cousin was a much better commander and then he could have a much clearer conscience about returning to the retreat to find Sophy. Surely Fern would come, even if he could not enlist any forest folk to help them.

Oakheart's sleep was troubled and it was with a certain weariness that he heard the sounds of the camp being broken down before dawn for their continued journey. During the night his tortured muscles had tightened and he sat up with a groan. His aide came in with hot water and a clean shirt. Oakheart thanked the man and drew himself to his feet. Before washing and getting dressed, he went through a series of stretches, hoping to ease the tension from his body. When his muscles were moving smoothly, he washed and dressed.

His aide came back. "Any sign of Lord Fern?" Oakheart asked the man.

"No, excellency. None so far. The high queen asks if she should start moving people across the Argent Flow."

"Tell her, yes. I will see the last across."

After their conversation of the previous night, Oakheart was quite sanguine about his mother wanting to give orders. If Fern did not arrive, he would have to leave their troops to her care. At least Falen and Barkly would be suitable advisers.

He checked the talkstone but his father did not call him as usual. Oakheart frowned . What did that mean?

As he travelled light, Oakheart did not have much to organise and in short order his aide had packed his saddle bags and put his tent and bedding in the cart. He walked to the edge of the Argent Flow and saw that his mother and their commanders already had about half their people over the river. The stragglers were still breaking down tents and tying equipment onto carts.

Sky walked up to him. "I hope you are not feeling too poorly this morning, excellency."

Oakheart straightened, denying any debilitating aches and pains. He did feel much better than he had on waking. "I am mostly recovered. You?"

Sky rubbed at his shoulder. "My shoulder is aching something fine."

Oakheart laughed. "Good to know." And he refrained from pounding the other man on the back, no matter how sorely tempted. It was good to know the young lad was not impervious to injury.

A shout drew his attention. He said to Sky, "Go! Tell the high queen that someone approaches."

Oakheart bolted off to the edge of the camp. Could it be Fern at last? Yet, he could not discount that the Puri had come this far. "Ware the watch? What do you see?"

"Riders, sir." A guard put up a hand to halt Oakheart's forward movement. Not recognising the man, Oakheart guessed he must be one of Dellbright's men. The man was receiving signals from the outlying guards as they were relayed to the camp.

"Ours?" Oakheart asked impatiently.

The dark-haired man, shorter than Oakheart, shook his head. "I cannot tell yet, excellency. Please stay back. Telno is on the perimeter."

Oakheart waited. He did not know the name but suspected Telno was another of Dellbright's men. He calmed himself, slowing each breath. Still he could not relax as he clenched his fist, not sure whether to race ahead to attack raiders or prepare to make merry with Fern's arrival.

A whistle sounded and was repeated. The guard who had stopped him spoke. "It appears all clear, sir. Must be ours."

Ten riders came into view, followed by about forty on foot. Some limped and the horses, Oakheart could see, were ill-used. His gaze raked the riders and he discerned Fern, his shoulder bound in a blood-stained bandage. The party had been attacked.

Oakheart spoke to the guard. "What is your name, man?"

He bowed his head slightly. "Quill, of Oftenbe, your excellency." Not Dellbright's then.

"Double our guards along the perimeter and send out scouts in pairs up to two miles out. There are likely to be Puri raiders about. Send the word to the other side of the river. I want the same orders in place there. Also, tell Falen I said to place a guard around the high queen."

The man bowed and ran off. Oakheart walked to meet his cousin and caught his hand as he dismounted. "Fern!"

They embraced. Fern reeked as if he hadn't bathed for nearly a month. His clothes were travel stained. Oakheart urged him back so he could look at him. "Serious?" He nodded towards Fern's shoulder.

"Flesh wound. An arrow took a piece out of the top of my arm. No healing bark handy."

Oakheart frowned. "We have some, so report to the camp medic." Fern nodded and waved at the group behind him. "I have brought the forest folk volunteers as you requested. Also some volunteers from Overland and Salty Cove. We also picked up some stragglers from Juniper Steading and one from as far as GadyGady who had been trading for horses in the steading."

Oakheart inspected the assortment of road-weary people, impressed by how far they had travelled. He had only been to Juniper Steading three times in his life and his pride breeding stock had come from there.

"I fear we are worse for wear as it has been a hard road," Fern continued. "We were attacked a week ago and two weeks before that, before we'd even left the outskirts of the Gilton Forest. If it was not for the assistance of some of the inhabitants of Overland we might be trussed up and in the custody of our Puri invaders. As it is, I have about twenty more Overlanders still marching behind us. They should catch us up in two days."

"Well done," Oakheart said, distracted as he looked to the other riders. He acknowledged a salute from Illart and a smile and a nod from Raven. The two were companions from their previous journey to rescue Gilly. Oakheart noted that Mellow and Lillia were not amongst them. He had not expected them to be, but still he had hoped. "How are my friends, Lillia and Mellow?" he called to his forest friends.

Illart dropped to the ground, a better rider now that he had been on a horse so long. "Well delivered of a girl child. Lillia has named the child Sophy. She asked me to seek your permission to use the name and hoped it did not offend."

Oakheart nodded. "I am touched, and I am sure Sophy will be too. They reached Queenstown then. Brooke, too?"

"Yes." Illart's expression changed to a frown, at once looking so like Mellow that Oakheart did a double take. "The news from the retreat was not good. However, there was much to celebrate with the return of Brooke. He will serve our heart tree so the queen was pleased."

Oakheart smiled and then opened his arms as Raven stepped into a hug, slapping him roundly on the back.

"It is good to see you again," she said, pulling away only to slap his chest with one hand. She narrowed her gaze. "Have you lost weight?"

"No! Of course not," Oakheart replied, chuckling at her teasing. "By the *given* you are a welcome sight."

Raven swung her hair over her shoulder and grinned cheekily. "It is good to see you too. I wish the circumstances were different." She sported several bruises around her neck and a black eye.

Oakheart frowned as he studied her face. "I hope your opponent looks worse than you do."

Raven grinned. "He does. We brought our prisoners. The overlanders bring them in a cart. We caught seven Puri men."

"Good." To Fern he asked, "And did they tell you about Hanal's plans?"

Fern shook his head. "These were not part of the main force attacking Silverdale. These were other Puri, raiding through Panal's Pass. They had been driven south by Dellbright's cleansing of the Valley so they strayed into our path near Gilton Forest."

Oakheart narrowed his gaze. "You said you were attacked twice? Not screavers?" With Rufus gone, Oakheart hoped that his minions would wane in power and number.

Fern absently pressed the wound on his shoulder as if it pained him. "No. Nasheen himself, trying to recapture his lost kin. I am afraid

Raven's arrow caught him in the shoulder. His men secured him and dragged him away. We broke off the fight to make our way here. I did not pursue them, knowing you would be expecting word of me and I was already so late. I think Nasheen was persuaded to leave us be since he did not follow after us."

Oakheart considered it strange that Nasheen was not with Hanal in Silverdale. He was a wily old man. Perhaps the clan leader had had a falling out with his leader. "Yes," Oakheart said as he focussed on Fern again. "I fretted at your delay, my friend. As you see, we have started the crossing. Another week and it would be too late. Already the water is rising. Your company should rest now, the wounded should seek treatment. Do your crew need feeding? I can order the food cart to stay here and a meal prepared."

Fern shook his head. "We ate earlier and will feel more comfortable on the other side of the river." He turned and gave orders for the wounded to find the camp medic.

Oakheart looked across the river. "There are likely to be more Puri on the other side. We do not know how far south the Silverdale attackers have raided."

Fern snickered. "Let them come. I am ready for a fight. Our numbers are greater and I like the sense of security of being surrounded by friends rather than foe. Too many nights have I been exposed."

Oakheart patted Fern on his good shoulder. "Very well, report to Falen after you have had your wounds tended. He will organise for you and your men to be transported across. I will meet with you on the other side. We have much to discuss." Oakheart made to move away.

Fern put out his good hand and stopped him with a touch on his forearm. "Silverdale?"

"No news this morning. Yesterday they lost access to the dam. Veld is beside himself with worry. He said they had enough food, but the loss of the dam means that they will have to call water from the ground. There's not much unpaved ground there."

"And...Aria?" His cousin's storm-grey eyes raked Oakheart.

He shook his head. "No word from her, either. Not for weeks. I did hear through the retreat that they had arrived safely though."

"I see." Fern's mouth grew thin and he stalked away without another word to Oakheart and barked orders to those accompanying him.

Oakheart motioned for Quill to approach. He had just returned from conveying his orders to Falen. "There are more men on foot coming along and we will need to wait for them as they will join our fighting force. They have Puri prisoners, who we will need to guard. Send word to the other side to make camp not too far along the road. Have some men dig a ditch big enough to hold seven men and line it to prevent escape. Have others fashion a grate to cover it. I think it is the best way to secure the prisoners. I will think of the best place to leave them. There are a few settlements along our trail that should be able to accommodate them. We will leave directions for them to be collected. To do otherwise is to risk them being rescued or getting free on their own. I fear it will be late before we have everyone that is here now across. Double check the guards and the scouts. We cannot take our safety for granted."

"I will send word, excellency." Quill bolted away.

Oakheart gazed down the road Fern had just come along. He did not like waiting for the stragglers, but he could not leave them behind. His heart was lifted at the thought that overlanders joined them. Part forest folk and part Argenterran, they were a hardy lot, but normally kept to themselves. Fern must have been convincing when he went recruiting. He made a mental note to recommend rewards for these communities that had offered members to aid Silverdale.

His thoughts strayed to the retreat, and he hoped it would not be long before they sent him word that they had discovered the gate's secrets. Rolling his shoulders, he headed back to the river. He needed to fetch his talkstone, just in case Veld called.

# 16

# POWER FOR THE TAKING

Rae and the party she was with continued to linger on the outskirts of Silverdale town. Anwi ordered the rest of the party to hunt for game and gather food. The young men complained about the delay, but soon sauntered off to do as they were bid. Except Benri, who remained and talked softly to his mother, but Anwi shook her head. Rae concluded that whatever they were discussing, Anwi did not agree.

Lots of the Puri people appeared to be congregating in the fertile lands between the forest and the town of Silverdale, hunting or just lying around being fat and lazy like they previously had thought the Argenterrans were. Rae gritted her teeth as the occasional scream sounded from the denser part of the forest—screams presumably from young Argenterran women. Her fists clenched as she imagined what was happening. Her stomach churned with anger as all the supposition and stories gelled into truth. How could Hanal let this happen?

Early the next morning, Anwi's party started once more along the road to Silverdale. Their pack horses were tied with bags of food—toffel, greens and salted meat. The sun rose bright and yellow and a chill wind blew down from the mountains, letting them know it was not quite summer yet. More Puri family groups passed them, an eager bounce in their steps now they were close to their goal.

Rae bit her lips as she observed the farms and homesteads close to the road showed signs of ransacking. In the meadow in front of one house she saw a Puri man lounging on a blanket while an Argenterran worked the fields. A tent stood in front of the farm house, where the Puri man obviously lived. Rae shook her head, wondering what was going on and why. If the Puri did not want the houses or to work the land, then why did they take them?

Houses were situated closer together and Rae could see the town arrayed up ahead. Pale strands of smoke lingered above the closely packed roofs. To her eyes it was a large place, a city even. Never had she thought she would come to Silverdale thus. Her dreams had been full of fun and laughter, with pretty dresses and dancing. Not that such frivolous activities attracted her now, but the contrast was nevertheless potent.

Puri warriors patrolled the perimeter of Silverdale in evidence of the full-scale invasion. Hanal had called all the clans to come into Argenterra: no battles or negotiations. The Puri had just come and by sheer force of numbers taken whatever they wanted.

As they passed into the town of Silverdale proper, houses crammed in around the streets. After so many days in the desert she felt penned in by the buildings and overwhelmed by the activity. The palace towers loomed over them as they passed by. Was Hanal already inside? Was he now in charge of this town? What of the high king, Veld?

Rae looked around and shuddered. It was as if the sunlight avoided the place altogether. There were no Argenterrans going about their business. No normal sounds like children laughing and squealing or hawkers selling. Dark eyes watched them as they passed. Only Puri men were in the streets, lounging against door frames, weapons visible.

They turned a corner, heading ever deeper towards the centre of town, and Rae noticed a haze hung over the rooftops, a residue of fire. Then a trail of Argenterrans streamed towards them, heading out of the town and squeezing past them along the road. Most were men and older women. Young children sprinted amongst them, seemingly making a game out of the exodus. Crude push carts with belongings and food was all they had. Rae counted the young women and there were not many. Those she saw looked to be with husbands. Her eyebrows drew together: this was not a good sign. Generally, there were roughly equal numbers of Puri men and women. What would this influx of Argenterran women do to the balance of things with the Puri?

More and more Puri lined the streets the further inwards they travelled. This was not a town under siege. It was too quiet and calm for that. Panaat sought directions to Hanal's quarters. From the response received Rae gathered that he was in the palace—as she had feared, Silverdale had fallen.

Anwi and her family accompanied Rae as she made her way to the gates of the walled part of the town. Anwi led her horse and sent her nervous smiles. Rae acknowledged the older woman's attempts to reassure her but Rae was worried and grave. She scanned the streets, the walls up ahead, seeing the scorch marks where the houses had been torched and the signs of recent repair to the stone walls. The houses were unnaturally quiet and Rae shivered as she passed the open doors leading to empty houses with their contents strewn about. What had happened to the occupants?

Six Puri warriors stood guard at the gates. She scanned their faces, looking for anyone she might know. Being recognised would provide for quick access to Hanal. The faces that looked back at her were hard and angry and not familiar at all. She squeezed her baby close to her chest as they approached the gates.

Looking back over her shoulder, she hoped to see someone she knew amongst the Puri camped in front of town houses. While they were all strangers, she thought they looked out of place and bored. Along the street young men played games with stones or just lay back against a wall, watching the happenings around them.

At the gate they stopped and Panaat bowed and greeted the lead warrior. Panaat indicated Rae sitting on the horse with his right hand, his robe fluttering in the breeze. "Tu Raenal, daughter of Kushlan, requests an audience with Hanal."

The warrior scowled as he looked them over, barely looking at Rae as she sat in the saddle holding the baby. "He is busy. Tell her to go away."

Panaat turned to her and shrugged. Anwi rubbed at her chin and shared a look of dismay with Rae.

"I will dismount," Rae said.

Panaat came over to help her down, taking the baby and handing it to Anwi while Rae climbed down. Taking the baby and holding it close to her body, she confronted the lead man. She did not know him and was too angry to care. Of the same height, she met the guard's gaze. She unwrapped her daughter from her swaddling cloths and held her out.

"I am Tu Raenal, formerly of Hanal's household. This is Hanal's child. Do you keep it from him?"

The guard blanched and lowered his head. At first she thought he might spit on her, but then she saw him swallow. "I will send your request to him." He turned to the guard behind him and spoke quickly and quietly. "Wait here," he said, turning back to her. "We will hear what the will of Hanal is." The other guard raced off, presumably to deliver the news that Rae had arrived.

Rae rewrapped the child, her heart filling with dread. What if Hanal spurned her, called her a traitor and left her in the street, without even seeing the child? That would mean the end for her. Her knees shook and she fought her fear. She had to keep her countenance calm, her chin raised with pride. It was perhaps the hardest thing she had ever done. Many faces came to peer at her and she heard them whispering. She wondered if they knew of her betrayal.

Anwi touched her lightly on the shoulder. "Rae, we will go to find our allotted place within the clan. If it does not work out for you, come and find us. You will be welcome to share our tents."

"Oh, you have done so much for me already." Rae hugged the older woman and then stood back. "Thank you for everything. I will send word to you if I can."

Anwi nodded and stepped away. "I fear for you, Rae. Hanal is a proud man with a long memory. He does not forgive easily."

Rae tried to smile, chilled that her own thoughts dwelt on the same thing. "I will be well."

"May your waters always flow with the *given*."

Rae waved to Anwi as she walked away, tears threatening to fall.

Anwi had braved much for her. She locked down her emotion. She was about to face Hanal and tears were no use to her. As she peered through the gate, to the Puri that gathered in the forecourt, trampling on the gardens and destroying fountains and statues to the jeers of others, fear coursed through her. Did she know her people at all? Everyone and everything seemed so changed.

Clutching her warm, small daughter to her, she hoped the baby would sleep a little longer. She did not feel comfortable at the thought of feeding the baby here, standing in the street.

Shortly, a runner came darting across the lawn up to the gate and whispered urgently to the guard. The man's dark eyes rested on her and widened. He yelled to two other men: "Escort this traitor to the honourable Hanal, leader of all Puri, future king of Argenterra."

Rae's exclamation of surprise was cut off when one of the guards grabbed her arm and dragged her forwards.

She nearly lost hold of her baby. "Do not touch me! I have come here freely. I have walked far and have suffered much."

The other guard pushed her from behind. "Shut up and get walking." Luckily, she had the baby clutched tight in her arms or she would have dropped her.

She turned around and glared. "You dare treat a woman so, and a child?"

The man sneered. "You are a traitor. You deserve no respect. Hanal has decreed it. Now move, you slut."

Her eyes widened at his insult and a chill rippled down her spine. She squared her shoulders, turned and walked briskly. Hanal may not forgive her, she had to accept that, but she would give him the opportunity to see and name his *daughter*. His daughter! Not the son that Umri had prophesied.

The guards marched her briskly through long and ornate halls. Some of the tapestries had been ripped and rubbish and food scraps were strewn in the corridors. She grew ashamed of the Puri lounging around in the rooms, and of their behaviour. *So this is war, this is how the Puri visit their anger on others. What have they achieved here? Possession of a jewel they do not know how to use?*

As they approached the main throne room, two large doors were flung open. Firesticks threw light from their sconces. Crammed full of Puri warriors, the room was disorienting and hot. It took her a while to pick out Hanal, seated on the throne atop a dais. A little dart of pleasure at the sight of him so hale ran through her. It was short-lived as standing next to him was the tall, dark form of Umri, dressed in the most opulent robes Rae had ever seen adorning a Puri woman. Their eyes met and Umri lifted a painted eyebrow, a smile drawing a snide line up her face. Her expression was all challenge.

Rae swallowed and quaked on the inside. Had she miscalculated? Was Umri even more powerful than before? What had happened to Hanal after he was left unconscious from that explosion of power? She had thought, perhaps, he would be incapacitated for days, but that had proved to be wrong. Had he been injured in such a way to bend his reason? Surely he would have blamed Umri for the damage as it was she who had planned that last assault on Sophy. That did not seem to be the case.

Thinking back, Rae realised that even when he had had Sophy, Hanal's plans were already in motion and the clans had already gathered. Sophy was an edge he had been seeking, but his plans had not revolved around her. When he could not possess Sophy's power, he had sprung into action. Rae herself had helped trigger the plans into motion, plans she was not aware of.

As she looked around the throne room of Veld, she realised that Hanal had succeeded. Hanal was victorious, but what kind of victory? Where did it take him? He was the leader of the Puri. Nothing had changed. He did not have respect and recognition from the Argenterrans and never would—not like this.

People moved out of her way as she walked towards Hanal, flanked by his guards. The expressions on their faces scared her—mouths tight, or with lips twisted into sneers. All with hard eyes seeing nothing but a traitor. She lifted the baby higher, placing its small head on her shoulder. Her gaze lifted to meet Hanal's. She quaked: there was nothing in his glittering, pale eyes. No emotion. No warmth. Nothing. She did not exist in his heart.

She took a few more steps, then shakily lowered herself before him. With nervous hands, she placed her little daughter on the floor next to her knee and bowed and waited, heart thudding loudly in her ears.

"You dare come before me?" Hanal bellowed over her head. "The thorn has been plucked from my chest and stabbed into my back."

Rae swallowed but did not lift her head.

"Well, traitor, grovel! Seek my forgiveness. Attempt to worm your way back into my household."

Rae gritted her teeth. She could not be weak; too much depended on her actions. She pushed back up into a kneeling position and looked him full in the face. "You should ask me to explain my actions before you label me a traitor."

"There is no other word for what you have done."

Rae inclined her head. "There are many words to explain my deeds." She placed her hands on her lap and feigned calm. "I come here of my own free will to seek a private audience." Her voice was clear and not loud. She fixed her gaze on him and resisted the temptation to glance to her baby.

Words and murmurs swirled around her. She could cope with the humiliation. Had not she lived with it for months when she went to Hanal's bed without an oath? She could bear it now. If only she could speak with him alone; he would listen to her, she was sure.

He broke off his gaze, the silent war of wills, and his eyes rested on the baby. "What have you brought with you, traitorous Argenterran wench?"

Rae lifted her chin a notch. She was not ashamed of her love. "Your child. The one that grew in my belly." The last was delivered with a challenge. Let him deny it. Let him see if he could.

Hanal grunted and nodded to Umri. "Fetch the child to me. You said she would birth me a son."

Rae tensed. Her eyes never left Umri as she came in close, her scent spilling over her as she took the baby into her arms. Taking the bundle to Hanal, Umri unwrapped the child. His eyes lingered on the baby. "This is a girl child." He looked out to the audience. "Therefore it is not mine." Then he directed his gaze back to her. "What have you done with my son?"

Rae frowned, her gaze shifting from Hanal to Umri. Something was not right. Blood drained from her face. She was sick to the stomach and could not deny her shock. "A girl child was in me," she said steadily. "Your seer was mistaken in her foretelling."

"Liar!" Umri hissed.

Hanal inclined his head a degree. "My seer sees true. You seek to deceive me."

"I do not."

"Traitor!" Umri snarled, body clenched as if ready to pounce.

Rae's eyes widened and her pulse pounded loud in her ears. Hanal's behaviour was unexpected. Her gaze flicked to Umri and she saw the glint in the other woman's dark eyes. Was he drugged? Deranged? Rae had lost—not only her place in Hanal's household and in his heart, she had lost her place in his reason. "This is the child I bore alone on the wastelands as I walked to find you. I suffered deprivation and pain to bring her to you."

Hanal exploded up from the throne. "Where is my rightful son? Why do you seek to foist this girl child on me?"

Rae lowered her gaze, her world crashing down, the final threads of Hanal's' glamour falling from her eyes. He was laid bare. Clearly, he was not worthy of her love. She was alone in the world with her child. So be it.

A tear crept down her cheek. She did not care if he saw it. She no longer cared what he thought. "I speak true. Deny your rights as father if you choose. I was going to ask you to give her a name. Your behaviour denies you that right so I now claim this child as my own." She glanced around, raising her voice so all could hear. "I name her Lien of the Wastes. Her name is taken from Goslien of the Valley, for she has the eyes of Goslien, passed down to her through her true father."

The room went quiet. Umri jerked at her words and the baby woke with a loud cry. Rae's breast tingled. Milk began to leak, dampening her tunic.

Her gaze shifted to the other woman. "Please give my baby to me. Lien is hungry."

Umri hesitated and after a nod from Hanal she brought her back. Discreetly as possible Rae fed the child, wishing for privacy, which was denied. Hanal descended from the dais and walked slowly in her direction. Finally, he stepped close, curiosity winning over his indignation. Lien opened her eyes and held his gaze. Rae heard Hanal's sharp intake of breath, and the swish of his robe as he turned away.

Despite seeing the evidence he still denied her. Rae's sorrow knew no bounds—her hero was just an ordinary man, with an ordinary man's weakness of pride and vanity and violence.

Rae fed the baby until she was sated, wondering all the while what Hanal would now do. Everyone would see the eyes and know the child was his. Denying his fatherhood would mean he had no claim on either of them. He could hold her for being a traitor, but he would still have no right to take her child from her.

Giving him one last look, she still could not help but wish that she could have some time alone with him, that she might yet convince him. Not of his paternity, for that was proven, but of this folly, this invasion of Argenterra and the crimes his people were committing in his name. If only she could speak to his heart.

She waited for him to make some form of declaration. He sat on the throne, staring into space with a pout on his mouth. Umri looked uncertain. Had she, too, seen the eyes that were undeniable? How could she deny the paternity when she was complicit in the child's conception? Umri had placed Hanal's seed inside her and had confessed it.

Hanal sat forwards. "The child is my own."

Rae's head jerked up, her heart thudding. Would he claim them both?

"Let her be known as Lien, daughter of Hanal." He paused, his brilliant gaze sweeping over her. He pursed his lips and then said, "The mother will be held for trial for treason against me. Let her be taken below with the other prisoners."

Hanal would not look into her pleading eyes. Rae disengaged the baby from her breast and covered herself quickly. "Please, Hanal, let me speak to you in private." Her gaze flew to the men coming for her. "Let me explain myself to you. Give me that one thing and I will make no more claims on you."

Hanal waved his hand dismissively. The guards hauled her to her feet, gently though, because she held Hanal's child.

"Make sure no harm comes to my daughter. Care for her well," he said and Rae checked a sob.

The men marched her through many corridors, so many that she lost her sense of direction. Down stairs they continued until the weight of the building hovered over her. Hanal was placing her in the ground, in the dungeons, if Silverdale had any. Her heart beat triple time as she hugged the baby to her. Even when a wall of fear seemed to spring up around her, she had hope. He had acknowledged his child. He would then want to see Lien. Then she had time to work on him, speak to him in private. She had to make sure that everything she said and did was correct. Their future and the future of the Puri depended on it.

## 17

# THE KNOWLEDGE OF PAIN

When Sophy next came awake she was trussed up on some kind of contraption. Her legs were splayed and appeared to be connected to wires that were wound around wheel cogs suspended from the ceiling. Her arms were anchored somewhere below her. She tried turning her head to see if they were also connected to a mechanism that could pull and stretch her, but could not see. Supported by a metal plank, she was thrust up, exposing her partially clad body.

Already she hurt. The tendons in her inner thighs and underarms ached painfully. Her neck muscles had spasms. Above her head was the metal point of something that could have been a funnel. Her vision blurred and she gave up trying to make it out. The sounds of chains rattling echoed around her as the contraption moved, whirling wheels and gears. That must have been what woke her.

"Awake now, my lovely?" a voice hissed in the air around her. The machinery jerked to life. Her body rotated, her legs seeming to bend in impossible angles as Rufus manipulated her body like a puppet, flipped her over and lowered her. The device took up the whole space, which was a cavernous warehouse-type building. Next breath she was nose-to-nose to Rufus, inhaling his putrid breath.

In the strained position she was in, she couldn't talk. He continued to contort her body. All she could feel was pain. The squeezing of her lungs meant a slow gurgling groan was forced out of her. "The mistress wants you clean. She wants nothing between her and access to your power. You stink."

He smacked her in the face with a wet cloth and water dribbled down the side of her face, a little finding its way into her mouth. Although the water was cold and smelt dank, she swallowed what she could. She had no idea when she'd get the chance to eat or drink again. Rufus plopped the cloth into a bucket at his feet, swished it around and flung it back to slap against the skin of her back.

He rubbed at her. She could do nothing to fight it or complain about his rough handling. He manipulated the machinery, using his wiry arms to haul on chains. The board she was strapped on continued to descend. Using his claw to guide her, he angled her head down while lowering her into the rusty metal bucket. Sophy sucked in a painful breath before he dunked her head in the water. His nails raked down her back like hot spikes. Panic burned through her mind and she fought her bonds. She couldn't hold her breath. She swallowed water, and at that moment she thought: I am going to die—and then he moved her up and out of the bucket. With bone wracking sobs, she spat and choked the water all over him, as her oxygen-starved body struggled for breath.

Time stretched out as she fought for air and for her body to relax. A blow to the face, a blinding pain before it all went dark.

When next she could see, she was dangling flaccid, her mouth aching from the blow. Queasiness filled her. Her eyes wouldn't focus.

"Filthy bitch. So you will not let me bathe you. Never mind, I can deal with that." He grabbed a handful of her hair and groped at his waist for a knife. She saw the blade held high before he sawed at the chunk of hair, pulling on her scalp. It hurt. It brought back memories. Her hair had been hacked before. Before when?

Whimpers leaked out of her mouth. Her scalp stung like he was peeling it off and tears fell unchecked down her face. It was not the loss of her hair, but the pain and the knowledge that this was just the beginning. There was worse to come and she could do nothing to stop it.

After he had denuded her scalp, Rufus cut away the rest of her clothing, taking no care so that her skin began to bleed from tiny nicks. When he was cleaning her private places he pressed hard, and dug his fingers in until she cried out. Then, leaning in close he sniffed exaggeratingly. "Never get these holes clean," he muttered before pushing the cloth inside of her, pushing and probing and hurting.

Utter terror swamped her and while she screamed and writhed he just laughed at her. There was no limit to how much he wanted to hurt and humiliate her. She did not understand. Finally, after there was not a spot on her that did not ache or throb or itch, he tipped the remains of the bucket over her and flung it to the side where it bounced with a dull gong and rolled away on its side.

His skinny arms pulled on the chains again, the cogs turned and dizzily the board she was on thrust upwards. The manipulations flipped her over, dragging her legs and arms down, exposing her navel to the tip of the funnel. She could barely breathe and her spine felt as if it would snap. A low hum surrounded her. She looked this way and that, but could see nothing but chains and wheels and cogs.

Then Rufus went away, leaving her naked and suspended in that uncomfortable position, grumbling to himself as he disappeared from the room. Tears fell as she moaned. Why ever had she thought she should approach Rufus? There was no way out. The ugreals were far too afraid of Rufus to dare enter the city.

Time wore on. There was nothing but the funnel and the hum. Exhaustion overwhelmed her; despite the pain, her hold on consciousness slipped away.

When next she was aware, her eyelids fluttered open and she found her body was in a different position. She had been lowered to the ground again. A pungent, putrid smell wafted over her as she found herself folded over, buttocks high in the air suspended over the edge of the board that supported her body. The wires on her arms and legs were taut, giving her no leverage to move. The edge of the board dug into the bones in her hips. Then it dawned on her what he was trying to do. She froze, her heart thumping hard in her chest. Rufus's claws clutched at her, grasping her thighs, puncturing her flesh as he secured himself above and behind her.

She struggled, jerked her head so that the contraption swung suddenly. It wasn't much, but it was enough to startle him. She heard him curse as he lurched to the side and grasped onto a chain for support. He dragged himself back towards her.

"Rufus?" A scratchy, slightly feminine voice pierced the air. It sounded like a saw cutting through wood. *Unesta!*

Rufus stilled, his claws clenching her waist, breaking through the skin. "Mistress?"

"But do not fornicate with her, Rufus. My spell of rending is not binding here. You are sufficiently human to impregnate her. A child conceived before I drain her will complicate matters and lessen the power that I can draw."

Rufus whined like a dog denied a bone. "Aw...mistress. I have waited so long." He climbed down off her, cursing under his breath.

Sophy swallowed. Spared from that horror at least. What was Unesta saying about a rending spell?

"Later, when I am done you can do what you like with her. She will be fit for nothing except food. I will be free, finally. I will be free to destroy his well-laid plans. Vorn's world will be undone, free to plunder..."

Unable to move her head properly due to her position and bindings, Sophy couldn't see Unesta. The voice itself was all around her, not coming from any fixed position. Was the Unesta she had seen a conjuring of some kind?

Rufus reached the floor and half crawled to a rectangular container. She couldn't tell if it was a box with the lid open or an open dish or urn. It glowed slightly with orange-tinged light. He stroked it. "I will wait, mistress. Your leavings will be the more heavenly for the waiting."

Sophy was imagining things or was that a communication device? A storage device?

"You are a good servant, Rufus. You must not touch her now. Later you can have your fill."

"What is your wish, mistress?"

"I need more suffering! Her defences must be lowered. Start the machine. I need her weak before we complete the drain. That first draining was hardly worth the effort as hardly any power came through."

Rufus pulled on the chains. Sophy groaned as she was hoisted higher, her limbs contorted.

The voice continued. "She is full of power. I must have it, have maximum drain. I need that power, Rufus."

"Yes, yes. I am working as hard as I can." Rufus sounded annoyed.

"I did not risk everything to drain the magic from Argenterra for such a paltry harvest. I need sufficient to break free."

"Yes, mistress." Rufus's voice receded. "Misstresss."

The thrum of power surrounded her and the clink of chain rattled in her ears as the machine churned faster. Then her body moved and twisted. If it was physically possible to scream she would have, but she had no voice.

She circled down to the ground. Rufus poked her with a metal prod. It hurt and tears fell. Then with a clang he sent her spinning and swaying and up again and around and around. The machine spun her, faster and faster. Colours whirled and converged; dizziness rose until she lost her hold on reality. Her head was ready to explode—her vomit sprayed out in an arc and then a massive burst of pain preceded darkness.

When next she became aware, pain radiated around and through her. Her scalp throbbed. Rufus was nearby again, hands touching her. *Sick bastard!* That voice had told him to leave her alone. She tried to shut him out, ignore what he was doing.

Then the voice issued from the atmosphere again. "Start the machine. I got a better yield, but there must be more. Again."

Rufus started the machine, his claws snagging against her battered skin, and then her body flipped over and surged up towards the end of the funnel. She was one extreme ache. Machine noise filled her ears. The tip of the funnel glowed and gave off heat. A beam shot out, centring on her chest. As more white hot pain ripped through every fibre of her being, she shook. It was as if her life was being sucked away. "Nooooo." Her yell was drowned out by the noise around her.

Sophy fought back. She struggled to hold onto the life force within her, otherwise this contraption would kill her, would take away something important. Images crushed into her skull, tearing through her memories...a beautiful land unfolded, green and abundant.

Out of the dark of her mind rushed the memories—she heard laughter—hers. Then she recollected happiness, remembered making love, remembered a smile and green eyes that danced with merriment and burned with desire. *Oakheart!*

The strength of the memories froze her body. Everything was there. Her life. Her journey to Argenterra. Her love for Oakheart. His love for her. Silently, she mourned for Oakheart as the memories came sailing back—his strength and nobility, his smile, his wonder when they made love. He was her husband.

All the pieces of her past glued themselves together. Rufus, Vorn, Argenterra, Aria!

The assault of memory allowed her to forget where she was briefly and the fear and pain ebbed. A kind of euphoria oozed through her at knowing that this moment was not her whole existence. If she fought hard, she could have her life back.

Doubt entered. Why hadn't Oakheart come for her? Why hadn't he saved her when Rufus dragged her through the gate? Did he not love her? Was he not bound to her through an oath? Didn't oaths have power?

Groping for that invisible thread that existed between them, the one that had grown steadily stronger and tangible to her, she couldn't sense it. Oakheart had even told her about it, what he could feel and sense of her. It hadn't been her imagination; the bond had been real. Panic surged as now the bond was gone.

Pain lurked, her nerves tingled, but she resisted and forced her mind to dwell on the oathbond. Think! Oaths were only binding in Argenterra. Now that she was no longer in Argenterra, did that mean there was no oath? Would he not come for her now? Then she remembered: he believed in oaths and not love.

Her heart stuttered. No. He loved her too. She had to believe that. Surely he didn't think she'd left him willingly. *I could never leave him.*

"Please, Oakheart, help me," she whispered in the dark place of her mind. Louder, she said it until she thought she was screaming it.

The machine went on and on and the funnel sucked at the power within her, she could feel the pull of it and the burn of it. Oakheart couldn't help her. But the thought of him gave her strength and her memories gave her wholeness. She would fight. She just had to figure out how.

The will to live was all she had. She wanted to see Oakheart again. The hum of the machine filled her ears, reverberated through her mind. The pain notched back up to excruciating, as if she was being dismembered. Her consciousness was yanked away.

Her nose itched. She sneezed and dust blew back into her face. She was now lower, practically nose to the ground. The machine was quiet and all she heard was Rufus's nasal rasping breath. The chains rattled and her limbs moved again, sending shafts of pain through her. Rufus rubbed himself against her and she dry-retched. He ran his hands over her body as if he had the right. There would be no stopping him once Unesta got what she wanted. Murderous rage swelled up inside her: she would kill him. She just had to figure out how.

In the dark spaces of her mind, her fears grew. Why hadn't Oakheart come to save her? He should have come. He could have prevented this. She had been there for weeks, maybe months, and he had not followed her. Had not saved her. She would have come for him. Most definitely she would have died trying to save him.

Now it was too late. Harm was done and could not be undone.

Then Unesta's voice came again, stronger, more vivid. "Put her on the machine again. Rufus, come on. Stop playing with her. You can have all of her when I am done. I'll leave some life in her for you to quench."

Rufus grunted. Then she was again contorted and hoisted high into the air. The machinery whirled to life around her, energy vibrating through her. The heat began again and before the fear could take over, she fought. This time she used her anger and her rage to guard her life force. She focussed inwards, trying to hide what she could, imagining filling up her cells with power. The machine whirred harder, straining to pull her life out of her. She resisted as long as she could, but as she lost consciousness something stirred inside of her, a small life. She centred her mind on that, sent one last heave of her life into it and then went limp.

⁂

THIS TIME WHEN SHE WOKE SHE WAS CRUMPLED ON THE FLOOR OF A cell, barely big enough for her to lie straight in. Her neck was bent, her head newly bruised and her legs kinked. Gingerly, she moved her limbs and gasped at the shafts of pain that came from everywhere. Slowly, she worked out the stiffness, stretching and bending her legs before placing them at more natural angles. Her knees ached so she rubbed at them, massaging the strain from tendons stretched too far. She doubted she'd be able to run again, walk or ride. Biting her lip, she resisted crying out at the pain. She bent her arms and massaged her neck. Everything worked, albeit painfully. At least she was alive. Unesta could easily have snuffed her out. No, that evil being had had to leave some crumbs for her awful minion.

Naked and cold, she shivered and was unable to sleep because her body ached too much. Moving hurt. So she held herself as still as possible and thought through her limited options. Staying put would mean she would end up dead, after much more suffering. She thought back to her treatment at Umri's hands. That had been nasty, painful and nowhere near as bad as this. How on earth had she survived? At least she had remembered who she was and what had happened. A painful bonus, but a bonus for sure.

Thoughts of Oakheart swelled up. The thought that he had deliberately forsaken her made her want to cry. He should have come. How could he abandon her to Rufus?

And why was she alone here in Vorn's homeworld? It had to be that place—the dead world. Unesta was stuck here. The power sword was buried in the maze. That had to be Vorn's, or at least a relic of that time. Could she free herself? If she did, could she find her way back to Argenterra? Her heart leapt. What of Aria? Maralain? She tried to remember more but it hurt too much to think.

Eyeing her surrounds, looking for even the slightest possible means

170

of escape, the thought of why she was off the machine intruded. Did that mean Unesta had taken all the power that she could? Did Rufus have permission do what he wanted with her at his leisure?

Sophy wished she could sense the power within her. Was anything left? Through no fault of her own she had sucked the *given* magic out of Argenterra, a place she had come to love, even though it was inaccessible to her. She was a like a talisman, a thing that held power but was inert and unable to use it.

She had let Argenterra down and relinquished all the power to Unesta. It was terrible. What would that mean for everyone she now remembered she cared for?

At a noise in the corridor she held her breath and waited. Was that Rufus? Her hand rested lightly on her abdomen and the fluttering she'd detected when she had tried to hide the power in herself came again. Unesta didn't want Rufus to impregnate her. Rufus couldn't, anyway, because she was already pregnant with Oakheart's child. Was that why the machine was having trouble draining her power? She looked down at her body, marvelling. She'd pushed what power she could into the unborn child. Despite everything, her suffering, her pain, she'd beaten Unesta. If she could get back to Argenterra, she would still have some of the *given*. All was not lost.

Unesta's words came back to her clearly. The Ancient Evil had put a curse on her when she had entered Argenterra. That would explain the violent spontaneous abortion she had suffered in Gilton Forest. Between Unesta and Rufus, they had aborted her baby. Even though at that time, she had not been prepared to be a mother or even married, that loss had stayed with her. A child with Oakheart was something special. He would have been a great father.

A scraping sound drew closer, then breathing. Sophy turned around, knelt and pressed her face against the bars of her prison. All she could see were shadows flickering against the wall. Something was in the corridor beyond her sight.

*Oh Oakheart! How I wish I was with you instead of here. If you were here with me now I'd forgive you for abandoning me in this frightful place.*

Alone and afraid, she could only think that he had betrayed her, betrayed their love. She could find no way around it. Nothing should have stopped him from coming for her and rescuing her.

Their love should have been strong enough for him to understand that.

The scratching sound continued. Rufus trying to scare her? Something worse?

# 18

# POWER PLAY

It was several days before Aria saw Dellbright again. She'd put her plans in motion, but she needed to play for time. Those one hundred men needed to get farther on their way to the aid of Silverdale before she fled from Valley Keep. Aria had kept up the ruse by playing with the little boy Dellbright was passing off as her son. She had no issue with the child—the boy knew nothing. Dela played with "Gilly" and fed him and brought him to Aria at the appointed time, meaning that Aria was never alone with the child. So much for Dellbright's promise that she could bring Gilly up. He had manipulated an oath to get her back with him. What would he do now that she had defended herself against him?

With each passing day, she grew more worried about where the real Gilly was. How was she to get him back? Would he know her after so long apart? Aria kept up the usual keep routine, except she didn't enquire after Dellbright's health but rather enjoyed his absence. Walks in the garden were a pleasure and, with the gift of sunlight, lifted her mood. There at least she was unwatched and could freely discuss escape plans with her adept companion.

On the morning of the fourth day since the bedroom incident, Aria and Leyla were at breakfast in the great hall when Dellbright swanned in as if nothing had happened between them. He'd been indisposed all that time. Aria was surprised how powerful a weapon the *given* had become. Now that he was up and about, Aria couldn't help but be wary of him striking back at her in some way. He was clever and vindictive. Her defence must have been a shock.

"Good morn to you, wife." He spoke coolly and his expression betrayed nothing. Very few people were in the great hall. Nothing like the number of visitors that used to gather there back in her first days at the keep. Those days that had been filled with laughter and adventure. Aria tried not to get morose in her thinking. Those days were gone and she must look ahead.

"Good morn to you," she replied. "I trust you are well." She sipped at her cup of water, fingering the stem as she kept a wary eye on her husband.

His smile was faint and his eyelids were hooded. "Perfectly well, I assure you." He sat down opposite her and served himself some porridge and hacked at the cheese. He took a drink of watered wine and lowered his mug. "A courier brought word from Silverdale."

Aria's brows rose as she was surprised that the courier network was still operational. "How goes the war?"

"Almost over, if you ask my opinion." He paused to study her. "Not that you value my opinion. Hanal has not only laid siege to Silverdale lands, he has taken the entire town and palace. If the cutthroat had any sense he would have killed Veld and all the rest straight away."

The water hit the back of her throat and she almost choked. When she finally could speak, she croaked out, "Hanal holds Silverdale?"

"Yes." Dellbright's eyes glittered with mirth.

Aria wanted to throw her cup of water over him. She stood up from the table and paced a few steps before turning back. "Surely it's not too late."

Dellbright lounged back in his chair, a satisfied smirk marring his handsome features. "Silverdale was not able to repulse the Puri raiders. Not like me. Our valley is near empty of the swine. I have kept enough men to keep it that way. And now that Silverdale has fallen I am sure the men I pledged will return soon."

Sudden anger at his complacent attitude erupted. Coming closer, she leant over him. "The Puri struck without warning. It's no wonder Silverdale had weak defences. They were at peace, whereas you are always fighting with the Puri. You wouldn't fare so well if Hanal came with all his horde and without warning."

He pushed back his chair and bolted up from his seat. Aria was forced to step back so as to not bang heads with him. He kept coming until he was leaning over her. "You would like that," he said sneering into her face.

Aria took a step back, creating a space between them. She closed her mouth and kept eye contact. She was not going to back down.

He threw out his arm to gesture at the room. "Yes. You would like Valley Keep and all those I hold dear laid waste."

Aria shook her head. "No such thing. It's just that you seem to find it amusing that Silverdale is overrun."

People stood still, watching them. Dellbright let out a breath and cast his eye around the room and smiled. "Not at all. Silverdale is a beacon to us all." Here he spoke to the whole room rather than her. Her gaze shifted sideways and people began to go about their business once more. Dellbright's men sat down to eat. Servants brought food. Other people carried this and bundled up that. Her attention once again fixed on Dellbright.

He took his seat. Aria looked to hers and with a nod from Leyla she sat back down too. Leyla had stayed perfectly calm through the exchange, though Aria knew she was ready to spring to her defence.

Dellbright broke some bread. "I am sorry for Silverdale's predicament but in some ways it is only just desserts for Veld not helping us. Remember, I am heir now. My son shall rule one day." He flashed her a fake smile.

Aria lifted her chin, pressing her fingernails into her palms. "One of the heirs. You forget Oakheart may have a child who would be ahead of Gilly." She hesitated to say more. Dellbright's expression had lost its fake amiability and what remained was unfriendly to say the least.

"I forget nothing," he hissed at her. He bit into the bread and after chewing swallowed more wine. Sitting there with him after what had happened between then was unnerving. She shared a look with Leyla and the adept gracefully filled their cups with more water. Aria could only wish to be as calm as Leyla made herself out to be.

After he had polished off the last of his breakfast, Dellbright placed his elbows on the table and rested his chin on his linked hands to stare at her. Aria put down her cup and tilted her head in query.

"When you have finished your repast, would you be so kind as to step into my sunroom? I have something I wish to discuss with you." His gaze shifted to Leyla. "Alone." He stood up, ripped some more bread from the loaf on the table and stalked away.

"I will attend you shortly."

To Leyla she whispered, "Make sure we are ready to go."

Leyla put her hand over hers. "You do not have to go to him," she said in low but urgent tones. "We could just leave now."

Aria shook her head. "I have to give those men more time to reach Oakheart. I'm sure all is not lost. My brother will not give up on Silverdale. He would not let our father suffer."

Leyla gripped her hand. "Then, I should wait by the door."

"No." Aria soothed Leyla's wrist. "I will be fine. Go now and if you don't hear from me in, say, ten minutes, come to find me."

Leyla pushed her long plait over her shoulder and cast a wary glance around the room. "But it would take a second to hurt you."

"No. You have shown me how to protect myself."

Leyla nodded. "Well then, I will do as you bid." The adept hurried from the room.

Aria looked around her, nodding to a number of house guards who stood by the wall. She was not going to rush to Dellbright's bidding so she took her time. Not quite able to eat, she sipped her water slowly. A kitchen hand came out and cleared away the mess.

The time was right. Aria rose with all the calm she could muster, arranged her skirts, and went to speak to Dellbright.

The door to the sunroom was shut so she knocked. Not without a flashback of memory to her early days at the keep with Dellbright, did she enter the room. She froze.

An unconscious Leyla sprawled on one of the easy chairs. A red lump rose on her forehead where she'd been hit. Dellbright had the adept's head over his leg and a knife resting on her throat.

"Dellbright! What are you doing?"

He grinned up at her, not with boyish charm but with a glint of evil in his eye and a twisted turn to his mouth. "What does it look like I am doing? I am threatening the life of your maid. But as you were able to use the *given* in some twisted way against me, I suspect she is not a maid but a retreat spy."

Aria's gaze swept over Leyla. A dark bruise was forming around the lump on her forehead and blood leaked from her nose.

"You have no respect. You have hurt her badly."

He laughed. "I intend to hurt her a lot worse. Take off your clothes."

"What?"

"Take off your clothes."

"You can't be serious."

"Deadly serious." He moved the knife and Aria flinched.

"But you cannot kill her. You can't."

"I can maim her." He moved the knife to just below Leyla's left eye. "Cut her here. Make her ugly."

"Leave her alone."

"I said, take off your clothes."

Aria looked down at her dress and slipped off her shoes. Leyla had taught her to strike with the *given* from a distance, but she had not yet practised on any one. She couldn't risk striking Leyla and incapacitating her any further. Damn Dellbright. Just when she thought she had the upper hand.

She grabbed her dress by the hem and drew it over her head so she was standing in a petticoat. Her hands shook but she didn't know if it was with fear or rage.

"More," he said.

Aria stripped off her petticoat and was left in a pale shift and an Argenterran bra. "All of it."

Chewing her lips, Aria undid the bra and drew it off. Leyla moaned and Aria stilled. If Leyla was conscious they had a chance of overpowering Dellbright.

Even as she thought this, Dellbright grabbed Leyla by her hair and wrenched her to feet, shifting the knife back to her throat and drawing blood. It seemed Leyla could not stand unaided. He had hurt her badly.

"I am waiting."

Aria had to make a stand. Closing her eyes, she took in a calming breath and then fixed him with a hard stare. "Look, you had your chance and you wasted it. I told you that you will not touch me again without my agreement."

"I think we are in agreement. You have taken off your clothes. We are halfway there. Take the rest off!" He yelled the last.

Casting a worried glance at Leyla, who still hung limply in Dellbright's arms, Aria stripped off her shift, leaving her skin bare.

"Still so beautiful to the eye. Pity your heart is dark. Perhaps I should have wooed Sophy instead. She was meant to be the one for me. The *real* Gift of Crystal Tree Woods. I saw her real face at the retreat, and, to be honest, she was far more beautiful than you."

He wanted to hurt her pride but she was beyond that. "Sophy saw through you from the start. She would never have married you. And because you are so superficial, you would have let the enchantment that hid her from your eyes sway you into letting her go."

"Enough! Lie on the carpet."

"No." Aria picked up her shift and slipped it on. Then she reached for the bra.

"I said take it off!"

"No." She slipped the bra on and did it up.

Dellbright's eyes widened and he shook his head as if he couldn't quite believe what she was doing. "You barter your maid's life for your modesty?"

Aria stilled, a small grin her only indication that something was about to happen.

Leyla moved quickly. She wrenched Dellbright's knife hand up, nearly cutting his face in the process. Then she twisted his wrist and he dropped it. "Now," she urged, giving Dellbright a shove as she moved out of the way.

Aria struck, hitting Dellbright in the chest. He flew back, his buttocks hitting his desk before he flipped and landed on top of it, scattering pens and papers everywhere. From there he fell limply to the floor. Aria winced when she heard the thump. He might have broken something in the fall. He didn't move after that. Aria put on her clothes hurriedly.

"Well done," Leyla said as she stood, a tad dizzily. Leyla sat down on one of the chairs and touched the lump on her forehead carefully, making "ouch" noises. "They were waiting for me when I left the hall. It happened so quickly I had no time to defend. I am so sorry."

Aria righted her clothes. "Don't be sorry. I'm just glad you are alive. But it does teach us a lesson. We can't use the *given* when we are out cold."

"Indeed."

Willow burst in. "What in the *given*'s name is going on?"

"Dellbright had a bit of an accident."

Willow did a double take. "Another one…but?" He rushed forwards and put his fingers against the prince's neck looking for a pulse. Dellbright was out cold.

"We are retiring to my rooms. When Dellbright is well enough please tell him I seek a conference with him. You and Dela should also attend."

Leyla's complexion greyed and she wavered when she gained her feet. Without waiting for Willow's response, Aria put her arm around Leyla and supported the adept as they left the sunroom and climbed the stairs together.

"That was close," Aria commented. "We cannot stay here any longer."

"My thought also," Leyla commented and then licked her lips. "The troops?"

Aria shared a look with her and placed a lock of Leyla's hair behind her ear. "I forgot he has couriers. He can do as he wishes. I think you and I would be better off joining the fight for Silverdale. Do you think you are able to travel?"

Leyla drew back. "Yes. I can apply some healing bark and will be well enough to leave. You do not wish to return to the retreat? You would be safer there."

Aria frowned. "No. I do not want to go to the retreat and be safe. I want to go to Silverdale and fight for my father's freedom. I want to join Oakheart and my mother. You will come with me, won't you?"

"Nothing…" the adept said before her knees sagged. Aria propped her up. "…Nothing I would like better."

To her relief, Aria found that Leyla's injuries were not too bad. A spot of healing bark on her neck and her temple eased her hurts somewhat. Aria was shaken by Dellbright's effrontery in attacking her through the adept.

"I wish I could put healing bark on his heart. He is so full of hate and anger, so tainted by it."

Leyla sat back and nodded. "I know. Pity that healing bark is not such a wonder as that."

"Have you been able to gather supplies for our trip?"

"Yes. Not everything but enough. Just under the bed here."

Aria climbed to the floor and found two packs partially filled with supplies and drew them out. "Just clothes to go in. Pity I don't have many of those."

Leyla pulled herself out of bed and together they sorted clothes and packed them.

"A pity about Dellbright," Aria said as she rolled up a blanket. "He had so much potential."

"Do not blame yourself for his misdeeds."

Aria's head shot up. "I'm not." Her eyebrows furrowed. "Am I?"

"If you think he is worth saving, perhaps you should try using the *given* on him. I heard a tale at the retreat that you and Oakheart cleansed the fabric of this keep from a terrible taint. Could you not try it with Dellbright?"

Aria stared at Leyla, opening and shutting her mouth as she thought through her answer. "Has such a thing been done before?" If only she could use the *given* to sever her oath to him. She thought that might entail using the *given* against itself—a contradiction she could not unravel at this stage.

"Not to my knowledge, but neither had anyone cleansed the keep before. Nor any building. We live in strange times and these reveal strange talents. You have much talent for the *given*."

"He would not suffer such a treatment from me willingly. If he wanted help we could try it. If Sophy were here, perhaps she would be able to help because she has so much power. But as it stands I can't see him wanting my help or any help." Aria paused before she drew tight the strings of her pack. "I am not responsible for him. I have to remember that."

Leyla smiled. "I am glad you realise that."

"While I'm meeting with Dellbright I want you to saddle some horses for us and one to carry our supplies. It is a long road to Silverdale. If anyone tries to stop you, you have my permission to use force."

"Yes, my lady."

Once their packs were full, Leyla took them and headed out to go to the stables. Aria sat down on the bed, casting her gaze around the room. So much had happened here. So much beauty and wonder turned to pain. Getting up, she placed a hand against the keep's wall, and detected the *given* there. It was less now than what it had been but still throbbed like a heartbeat and fluttered against her skin like butterfly wings. Another layer tasted like sugar on the back of her tongue. She hadn't detected that before. Was it her growth in sensitivity? She thought about the *given* in the bonding chamber. The pond had contained a store of the *given* that Oakheart had tapped into before they cleansed the keep of Rufus's murderous taint. The essence of Vorn existed there. Perhaps she could draw some of that into herself. Deciding that she would visit the chamber before her final conference with Dellbright, she picked up her skirts and hurried along the corridor to the stairs.

The bonding chamber was dark and neglected. Dust rode the light rays that spilled from her firestick. A lump formed in her throat. Had this once beauteous and happy keep come to this...to the neglect of its heart? She spoke the flame into more firesticks until the room glowed with golden light. With a deep sigh, she decided that she could not bear to see the baskets full of dead flowers and threw them out. Then she found a broom to sweep up the dust. Her efforts made little dent in the neglect of the place. Memories of her bonding ceremony and of Adage presiding over them threatened to move to the forefront of her mind so she shoved them into a tight little ball and buried them in her mind. Then thoughts of her visit to the chamber with Oakheart came to her. Although these recollections were fraught with pain, they were bearable. She replayed the moment when Oakheart summoned the crystal tree and the spirit of Vorn. Slowly, she stepped up to the bonding pool and knelt in one of the niches. Breathing deep, she steadied her nerve. Oakheart had put his hand in the water. Almost unwittingly, her hand touched the surface. The liquid rippled and was so cold she nearly snatched her fingers out again. Not knowing the whole ritual to summon the tree, she readied her mind and her heart to receive the *given*. Without the tree the pond oozed with the *given*.

A frigid sensation seeped into her skin and climbed up her arm. Her heart thudded. "Please share the *given* with me!" she said, recalling part of Oakheart's words. The chill in her flesh intensified, seeming to make her bones ice. She wanted to pull her hand out, but gritted her teeth and held on. The tip of one branch of the crystal tree appeared. Her heart lurched and the coldness spread through her chest and lungs so that her breath misted. A current of the *given* tickled her mind as it was drawn inside her.

Slowly, she eased her hand from the water and the branch dropped back beneath the dark surface. Aria sagged and pushed away from the niche. Her gut throbbed and her mind was electrified. Kneeling on the floor, she sobbed at the ache in her breast and the wonder. She really was part of this land. She had known it intellectually, but now she encompassed it in body and spirit too. After a short rest, she climbed to her feet: it was time to face Dellbright.

Dellbright, Willow and Dela were waiting for her in the sunroom when Aria entered. Willow stood still but his gown flowed about him as he fidgeted. Dela sat on the easy chair, her fingers worrying at each other. Dellbright leant against his desk, arms folded and glowering at her. He appeared unharmed from her attack. She swallowed, not liking to admit even to herself she was disappointed he had taken no harm. He had injured Leyla and threatened more besides.

"You dare come before me," Dellbright said thunderously. "You dare compel me to speak to you?"

Aria smiled a fake smile. "Yes, I dare. Please take a seat, Willow. You and Dela will be our witnesses."

Dellbright sneered. "Witness to you weaselling out of your promises to me?" He cast Willow a triumphant smile. Willow kept his expression neutral but inclined his head to acknowledge the point.

She threw back her shoulders, raised her chin and glared at them. "As you have done to me."

Dellbright sat back, rubbed his chin before answering. Leaning once more on the desk, he opened his palm. "I have let you be mistress again at the keep." He lifted his eyes to hers. "I have let you see your son."

She opened her mouth to respond but he kept talking.

"Yet you deny me the getting of more children. No brothers or sisters for Gilly. Your word is nothing."

Aria suspected it was pointless to argue, but she wanted to state her piece in front of witnesses. "We both know that I have no say in the running of the keep."

Dellbright turned away and waved a hand negligently. "You lack the interest and the experience."

Aria held her temper at his arrogant dismissal of her complaints.

Once again he faced her, dared her to make him a liar. "You have your son, or does he not mean anything to you now?" His eyebrows rose in mockery. "Is your lust for Fern Ripplebark so great that you cannot commit to your child?"

Don't bite, she told herself. "The child I see each day is not Gilly. You know it." She pointed accusingly at Willow and Dela. "They know it."

Dellbright spluttered. "Nonsense. Your mind is addled."

"It is not. I know my son and how his essence feels. I think you know by now that I am strong in the *given*. Although I have not seen Gilly for many months, I know what he feels like. I know his resonance. The child you bring to me, sweet as he is, is not my child. No matter how much he looked like Gilly early on when you chose him, each day he changes and grows less like our son."

"Hysterical female!" Dellbright spat at her. "Your wits are deranged." She could taste Dellbright's anger and malice from where she stood. His reaction only confirmed that she was right. Not that she doubted herself, but he needed to acknowledge it.

"I am in my right mine. I have other evidence that the boy is not my son."

"What evidence?" he replied, forehead furrowed. "You lie."

"No more lies, Dellbright," she replied calmly. "Perhaps you can tell me why you never see your son. Not once in a day since I've been here."

Dela gasped and Dellbright's face reddened. "I have seen my son." Yet his protest was weak and Aria knew she was right, her own observations confirmed by Dela's reaction.

"No, you haven't."

"How would you know?"

"Because I do. You slipped up."

"Rubbish!" He fumed and paced in front of her. "You are delusional." He stood in front of her, feet planted. "Weak."

Aria lifted her chin. He was no longer able to rattle her. "Your words don't hurt me anymore, Dellbright. Don't you want to be free of this anger and hate inside you? Don't you want to laugh again?"

His eyes kindled and for a moment there was the old Dellbright. She tried reaching through her bond with the *given*, tried to feel her way to cure him. She had such a store of the *given* inside her that it could work. The sensation of lurking malice was so like the taint that had been cleansed from the fabric of the keep she nearly gagged. Yet, she did not shy away.

"What are you doing?" Dellbright asked, backpedalling.

Gasping at the filth that assaulted her senses when she reached out, Aria put her hand on the nearest chair for support. The taint was so much a part of Dellbright that she could not see where he ended, where it began. She pushed some *given* into him.

He screamed and fell to his knees.

"My prince!" Willow cried as he dove to help his master. "What is it?"

"Her!" He pointed a clawed finger at her. "She is trying to kill me."

Sweat trickling down her back, Aria retreated a step. Dellbright fought back; the evil inside him surged towards her. She withdrew from him. "No! Dellbright. I was trying to help you."

Dellbright held clenched fists in front of him at chin height. Her glared at her over the top of his knuckles. "I want no help from you."

Aria straightened her shoulders, and mentally let her concern fall away. She was done. "Very well. I have come to tell you that I am leaving you for good. You have proven to me that you have not changed. You cannot be trusted by word or deed. Even the *given* cannot restore you."

"I need no curative. I am the best I have ever been."

Inclining her head, she curved her lips up, not quite a smile. "You have it in you to cure yourself, Dellbright. You have to want to."

She turned to go.

"But my men fight with Oakheart. You cannot leave. I kept my bargain. Oakheart will have to be bound by his oath. He cannot come to get you."

Turning her head to look over her shoulder, Aria smiled sweetly. "He doesn't need to come for me. I go by myself."

"No. I forbid you to leave." His voice was a savage hiss.

Aria looked him up and down scathingly, wondering what she'd ever seen in him. "You have no say over me."

Dellbright's fists tightened but Aria ignored him. To Willow and Dela she said, "You must find where he has hidden Gilly. He is the true heir of Valley Keep and in line for the throne in Silverdale. You best send word to every village seeking my true son. I have no rewards to offer you but I expect it of your decency, such as that is. Just let it be known that whoever Dellbright gave him to will be thanked for his return. This is Gilly's home and he deserves to be brought up here."

Willow and Dela gaped at her. Aria stared back until Dela dropped her gaze with a meek nod. Willow cast a look at Dellbright and swallowed.

She turned to the door. "Goodbye."

Dellbright lunged for her. "You are mine." She was expecting his attack and detected the movement in the air as soon as he dove. Spinning, she struck him full in the chest with the weight of the *given* scrounged from the bonding chamber. He screamed and fell to the floor, his face an expression of surprise in an unmoving body.

Out the doors, she strode purposefully through the hall and out to the bailey. Willow's excited exclamations followed in her wake. Waiting for her in the courtyard by the stables was Leyla, three guards lying unconscious behind her. Two horses stood tacked up with bridles and saddles; the third was laden with supplies just as she had instructed.

Leyla grinned when she saw Aria. "I was about to come get you."

"No need. I had it under control. Let's go," Aria said as she took the reins to the finer of the two saddled mounts, a kind-looking grey.

"As you command, my lady." Leyla bowed low. "You are leaking so much *given*, my teeth ache."

Aria climbed onto her horse and tried to quench the power that squirmed with life inside her. The grey nickered and shifted from foot to foot, as if detecting the energy. Aria focussed her mind while Leyla climbed up on the chestnut mare, kicked her mount and tugged at the supply horse's lead rope.

At a brisk cloppety walk, they soon reached the main gate and directed the horses out onto the road. Aria didn't know the way to Silverdale, but she knew which direction Oakheart had taken Sophy, so she pointed them in that direction.

## 19

# THE REALITY OF SEEING

Oakheart wiped dust from his eyes with his sleeve. Eyes watering, he turned his head and noticed his mother watching him.

"I don't remember it being so dry here before?" Maralain commented before raising her eyes to the Upper Plateau in the distance. "Has there been some issue with the climate, recently?"

"'Tis not normally so dry." He chewed on his lip as he patted the last of the dust off his face. The wind rose again and the horses shied at the mini eddies of dust swirling amongst their hooves.

Oakheart's mount nickered nervously, and he detected a hint of smoke in the breeze, mingled with the dust. His gut twisted with unease. "Father has not called for days now. I fear the worst."

"He is not dead," Maralain said flatly.

Oakheart inclined his head in acknowledgement. As her oath held true, she could feel Veld's life force.

"Not that you meant that. You meant he is captured? That Silverdale is no longer under siege but in the hands of the invaders?"

They shared a look and he did not need to confirm her fears. Maralain let out a sigh. "I'd forgotten how long it takes to get anywhere in this place. It's so frustrating. Rivers, hills, forests and no proper roads, except in the towns. Tedious carts slowing us down." She gazed around. "So many people on foot to consider."

While horses were one of Oakheart's passions, they were not in such good supply for everyone to have a mount to ride. His mother inhaled loudly and her head jerked up. "Is that smoke coming from Silverdale? Surely they haven't razed the town?"

Oakheart's eyebrows lowered over troubled eyes. The uncertainty was eating at him. Surely the Puri would not destroy everything? The change in the weather was more likely due to the loss of *given* and disruption to the farming caused by the war. Lands normally tended were not being farmed and were progressively turning to dust. The evidence was all around them of farms abandoned for a month or more, fields fallow and bare of crops even though spring was well advanced. Is this what Hanal had planned? Misery for them all? The ramifications would extend well beyond the next month or two.

Oakheart settled his prancing mount; they could not afford to waste such energy. To be fair, it was not Hanal who had caused the *given* to be drawn off and oaths to wane. Hanal's grievances were longstanding and were ones that Oakheart understood. He had no sympathy for the man's methods, though.

A shout from one of the sentries alerted him to the approach of a scout. His horse continued to fret and fidget until the breathless man stopped just before the horse, his face begrimed with dirt and patches of sweat. "Excellency! Puri raiders not far to the east of us." He took in a couple of breaths. "Twenty or so are weighed down with stolen goods. And...a number of Argenterran prisoners."

"Good," Oakheart said. He turned to the nearest man. "Send word to Barkly that we will need two squads for a pincer attack. We are going to attack this party before they harm anyone else. Also, we must rout them all out as we go. We do not want any Puri harrying us from behind."

The man ran off further up the line.

Oakheart twisted in his saddle. "Mother, you should continue on. I will catch up with you."

Maralain's brows shot together and she pushed her long braid over her shoulders. "Why are you going on this raid? Surely you are too important to risk."

"I need to test a theory, and I need some action. As you say, travelling in Argenterra can be tedious."

"You're risking yourself because you're bored? I thought better of you."

Oakheart grinned. "You did? That is truly remarkable."

Maralain scoffed. "You are joking with me." She rolled her eyes. "Really."

"Will you continue on, mother?"

She glared at him. "Very well. But be careful."

He bowed his head. "Of course."

Shouts sounded and Oakheart dismounted, leaving his mother to walk her horse further on and keep her place in the line.

Fern rode up, his forehead creased. "What is it?"

"Keep the column moving. There's a party of Puri raiders to the east. We are going to attack. I am about to assemble two squads."

"I am coming with you." Fern made to dismount.

"No. Keep the column moving. My squads will catch you up when we are done." Oakheart considered his cousin's frown. "You will need to reinforce the rear. The stragglers are vulnerable. Surround them with mounted men, with swords and spears. Some archers, too. Rest the weary by rotating them to horses or available cart space."

Fern looked away down the column of men and horses and carts and chewed his lip. "You are right, of course. The mounted are too bunched up. Let me select some archers to accompany you."

Oakheart smiled. "That would be nice. Barkly will bring a few fighting men. If you see him tell him I am waiting here. We must talk strategy before we leave."

Fern saluted and then kicked his mount, which spun on its hindquarters and bounded stiff-legged towards the rear of the column. Oakheart sighed. Fern would follow his orders, and probably better them.

Barkly approached him on foot, a squad of eight wizened warriors at his shoulder. Those men might have seen better days but they looked fierce and capable.

"Barkly, thank you." Oakheart nodded to the men. At a brisk pace, another squad of six women marched double time and then joined them, bows and quivers on their backs. Next, Sky came up with four men with quarterstaffs in tow.

"Now that you are all here, this is what we are going to do." He told them there was to be no killing or unnecessary maiming, that they were to incapacitate and capture the Puri. Liberate the stolen supplies and the prisoners.

"Are you saying we should not attack them?" Barkly asked.

"No. I am saying that when we attack we take care to minimise harm. The binding oath is weakened. I will not have us do anything to break it completely, you understand?" He eyed the gathered men. "There may be deadly intent in your heart but you will hold it back."

"But," Barkly spluttered, "what if our own lives are at stake? Do we to let them run us through?"

Oakheart blinked and regarded the older general. "If you must kill to save your life, then that is a decision you must make. But if you cherish Argenterra and the *given* in your lives, you will consider and honour my words."

"But they have attacked us, invaded us!" Barkly's fingers gripped his sword.

"That is so. But as far as I know they have not killed us."

There was general grumbling at his words. He looked at each fighter in turn. "If you cannot keep to this plan then step away. There will be other opportunities for battle."

None turned away, but they still grumbled. *Oakheart has gone soft. What sort of war is it when you have to stay your hand? I want to smash their grinning faces in. Yeah, me too.*

Oakheart ignored the undertones. He needed to test his theory and had been thinking long on it. Waging war without killing had to be the most difficult of martial arts.

THE TERRAIN WAS MILDLY HILLY WITH STONY OUTCROPS THAT GAVE Oakheart's group cover. They had ridden hard to catch up with the

Puri and had stashed their mounts in a copse for later retrieval. The Puri were spread out over a long line and moving slowly. It was nearing sunset and soon they would stop for the night. Oakheart wanted to attack before then, before the Puri were organised with sentries and could protect their inner circle.

"They are heading to that farmstead in the distance. It will have water for their horses and a place to store their booty. If we hurry we can attack from behind as well as at their flanks. See where the prisoners are grouped?"

Barkly nodded. "I will take my men and charge them from behind. Archers should initiate the attack when I give the signal."

Oakheart nodded. "Let us get to it, then."

Oakheart's squad used mainly quarterstaffs, but he had also brought his bow and his sword. His group attacked the line midway, where the Argenterran prisoners were being held. As he galloped up close he could see five young women, with an older weary-looking one being half-supported by the girl next to her. His first arrow brought down one of the Puri men guarding the women. When the man fell to the ground clutching his thigh, a shout went up from the nearby Puri. The women huddled into themselves. Oakheart launched another arrow at a guard who grabbed the long, dark hair of one young woman, but the arrow thunked into his arm. The girl pulled away and hunkered with the other women, crouching as low as possible. Another young Puri man let out a cry. Oakheart had no choice but to hit him in the shoulder. He went down with a strangled sound.

When more Puri ran back down the line and joined the fight, Oakheart's men joined the fray. Bilt, the youngest of Oakheart's crew, smashed his staff across the neck of one man, who dropped and then writhed. Another, Cave, engaged with a Puri man who used a spear against his staff. Cave ducked the spearhead successfully three times before he was able to sweep the man off his feet. Then he walloped him and the man dropped like a stone.

Seeing that all his men were engaged, Oakheart dismounted and ran up to the women. "Easy," he said as they eyed him warily. "I will undo your bonds." This he did quickly using his knife. The skirmish continued in full force and yells echoed around him.

"See that set of rocks over there? Run to there and wait for us. Do not wander off."

"But…the Puri…" said the girl with the long, dark hair.

"Go now. Talk later!"

A yell alerted him to an attack. He pivoted, bringing up his staff end first into the Puri man's chest. His assailant was thrown back while his limbs were still in forwards motion. Another sweep of the stunned man's legs and he was down.

He turned back and the women were still there. "Move!"

The women jerked into action and loped away from the Puri line. He watched for a few minutes until he saw they were not pursued and were doing as instructed.

Relieved they were out of the way, he brandished his quarterstaff and engaged the nearest Puri. A spear thrust close to him and he deflected it and kicked the wielder. The man was hardy and came at him again with a wild cry. Oakheart sidestepped then knocked him out with the butt of his staff. Shouts from the other end of the line reached him. Panting, he paused to take stock. The fighting had eased and dropped bundles lay strewn on the ground. Groaning Puri cradled heads and arms and legs. Others huddled over clutching at their sides with possible broken ribs. With a glance up the line in both directions, he could see they had won.

"Secure them all. Then distribute the goods. The Puri can carry them. It will keep them out of mischief."

Barkly approached, a satisfied smile on his face. "Any injuries?"

Oakheart thought not. "None reported. The surprise attack worked."

Barkly grunted then spat on the ground. "They attacked us sneakily when there was peace. They crushed all our hasty resistance. Now they will know we are not so weak as to let them dominate us."

Oakheart surveyed the Puri who were being bundled up and bound. "These are not Hanal's prime fighters. They are just ordinary folk by the looks of them. Less than fifty." He slapped Barkly on the back. "I agree it is good to have a victory on our side, no matter how small. Will you be able to manage this lot and rejoin our column? A few looked injured so will not be able to do a forced march. I want to escort those captive women either home or to our line."

Barkly chuckled. "Of course I can handle this lot. We should rejoin the column by tomorrow morning. I will keep this lot walking now. Better to keep them exhausted."

"You will need to treat the injured first."

Barkly ground his teeth. "If you insist. I was planning to have the fit carry the wounded."

Oakheart looked at him square-on. "We have made our point. They are captured, wounded. Let that stand."

"It will never repay what they have done, Oakheart. Most of us feel this way."

Oakheart nodded. "I know how you feel, but think to the future. How will we live if we do not resolve this conflict for good? Do you wish to live out your days in conflict, in death?"

Barkly's eyes widened. "You think it will come to that?"

"I do not know. I only work so that our future will be full of peace and that we will abide in the *given*. If your heart is full of murderous intent, I beg you not to act on it. For we will lose the *given* as surely as if it never existed in our lives."

Barkly's gaze considered him a few moments longer. "I see that you believe what you say. I have yet to have such a feeling in my breast. Anger, yes, but I have no killer lust in me. Perhaps our oaths still bind us."

"I hope that is so. I will meet you back at the column. I leave these men in your charge."

Oakheart took Bilt and Cave with him to help the group of women. He feared the women would be severely taxed by another long march on top of their recent traumas. His own group of people were strung out over a mile as they headed to Silverdale. The skirmish had ended quickly, so he thought that they might reach the tail end of the Argenterran force in a few hours. If they hurried. The horses they had tethered were sufficient to take the women, doubled up, over a short distance.

He spoke to the women, who were introduced to him: Wren, Sade,

Mari, Eve, Silver and the older woman Lilly. "I am Oakheart, the high king's ambassador. I would like to return you to your families."

"But...the Puri..." said the girl with the long, dark hair. Wren was her name.

"But our homes are taken. There is nothing left!" sobbed Silver.

Oakheart paused. "Do you mean your families were killed?"

The women shook their heads. Oakheart now noticed their bruises and ripped dresses. He blinked. A sense of severe wrong clung to the women, just as it had to Aria. He swallowed, momentarily at a loss at how to deal with these women. "I am sure all will be well. The Puri cannot harm you now."

They followed him to where they had left the horses and then Bilt and Cave helped the women to mount. Lilly had a horse to herself. She was older than the others but not much more than forty. The others ranged from fourteen to twenty. When they were all mounted up, he urged his horse forwards into a quick walk, turning around to make sure all was fine with his charges. The woman clung to the mounts and only Lilly looked comfortable.

"Has the high king defeated the Puri?" Wren asked as she tossed her dark hair over her shoulder. She lifted her chin indicating the Puri line. "Those said that Hanal was king in Silverdale and that all the free Argenterran women belong to the Puri. We were their reward for service."

Oakheart's gut twisted as he saw their hopeful expressions in turn. "The high king has not defeated the Puri as yet. I am part of a force sent to lift the siege in Silverdale. You have not been offered as reward to anyone. What has been done to you is a crime." He gripped his reins and his horse danced beneath him, his rage communicated to his mount.

Some of the women looked away, Wren clenched her jaw and nodded. Lilly shook her head slightly.

Wren told him the general direction of their homesteads as the five young women had been near neighbours. It was dark now and although the moons were casting some light on the terrain, with scudding cloud and the haze from the fires, Oakheart knew they would have to camp before long. He needed to put some distance between their skirmish and the women. Thoughts of the women grew large in his mind. He did not like that they had been held captive.

Near midnight, he called a halt. Bilt and Cave helped set up the camp while Oakheart scouted around, checking for signs of pursuit and for other Puri nearby.

Bread and cheese served as their meal for he would risk no camp fire.

As it was late no one appeared interested in talking. The women paired up and slunk into their allotted tents without a word. Wren reached up over her head and stretched her back and groaned. "I do not believe any of us have ridden a horse so far before."

Oakheart bowed his head. "I apologise for your hurts."

Wren's head jerked up. "Forgive me. I meant no complaint. We are grateful for your rescue."

"I took no offence, Wren. I sincerely wish there was another way to get you to safety."

Wren nodded, then, picking up a blanket, she pushed through the flap of her tent and disappeared inside.

"I will wish you good night." Oakheart watched the silent tents for a few minutes before setting Bilt on the first watch.

Once all was arranged to his satisfaction, Oakheart rolled himself into his cloak and settled himself in the dirt in front of the row of women's tents. Cave slept close by. Although his mind was troubled, and the ground hard, Oakheart soon fell into a deep sleep.

A pain in his stomach woke him, along with the need to draw air. He woke up to a grey dawn haloing a Puri man, with the point of his sword jabbing into Oakheart's throat. He stayed very still, trying his make his breathing shallow. Across from him lay the unconscious form of Bilt, an angry red welt on his forehead.

"Stay where you are, Argenterran scum. You took something that belongs to me." He lifted his head in the direction of the tents. "Lilly! Come out."

The older woman's head peeped out of the tent, her eyes ringed with dark circles. "Daya?" she said in a hoarse voice.

"Lilly?" His head jerked up and a light kindled his eye. "Praise the *given* I found you."

Lilly emerged from the tent, a blanket wrapped around her and stood still. "Daya, please."

Oakheart realised he could hear whimpering from within the tent. He cautiously slid his glance to each side. Another Puri man was tying Cave's hands. The man looked down the blade of his sword into Oakheart's eyes. "I have no quarrel with you, Argenterran. I just want my wife back."

"Your wife?"

"Lilly is my oathbound wife."

Oakheart lowered his eyelids. "The others?"

Daya shook his head. "No concern of mine."

"Let me up and we can discuss this rationally."

Daya's dark eyes glittered. "Nothing you can say will dissuade me. You forget that I have the upper hand."

"Yes, for the present you do. But if you are acting in good faith you should treat me fairly."

Daya's gaze shifted to Lilly and back to Oakheart. "I do not trust you."

Oakheart tensed. "I am only anxious for the others in my care."

When Daya's sword point did not budge he added, "I give you my word, my oath in the *given*, that if Lilly is willing to go with you then I will not attempt to dissuade her."

Daya considered a moment, then withdrew his sword. Oakheart kicked out, catching the Puri in the ankles and toppling the man. Then he rolled on top of him. In his peripheral vision he could see Cave fighting with the other Puri man. Oakheart caught Daya across the chin with a fist, but the man was hardy and returned the blow. They wrestled this way and that.

Lilly screamed. "Stop please! My lord, please do not hurt him!"

There was a sting as Daya's knife blade cut the tip of Oakheart's chin. Both of them were panting. "I said I only want Lilly. Can you be trusted to keep your peace?"

"Please, Oakheart," Lilly said. "Listen to my story."

Daya rolled off Oakheart and allowed him to sit up. Then Oakheart stood and went to Lilly, touching her hand fleetingly before checking her over for harm. "Is he your oathbound?" he asked softly.

Lilly's eyes moved to his. "Yes."

"Tell me, was your oath pledged freely?"

Her dark eyes met his. "Most willingly."

Oakheart's eyes narrowed. "I do not understand."

"I have known Daya for many years. We met when I lived in the upper reaches of the Valley. My family disapproved of our relationship and forbade me to see Daya. Then they sent me to Netherfold, to my cousins. I was miserable but they would not let me return to my family. They would not let me take Daya for my husband. They hated the Puri as much as my own parents and brothers. Daya came looking for me. To take me away."

"Then you are not a spoil of war?" Oakheart watched her face but he could see no fear or lie in her countenance.

Lilly shook her head. "Those others are, I think. I had not met them prior to meeting in the column. Not me, though. We want no part of this war but became caught up in it by accident. We were travelling when we met the larger band of Puri. We could not avoid travelling with them. We just want to be together without interference. Without hate."

"Without hate," Oakheart repeated under his breath. He wiped at the blood on his chin and turned to face the Puri man.

Daya met his challenging stare. "I will not interfere with your rescue of these women. I have no argument with you about your treatment of my kin. As Lilly says, we want no part of this war. Hanal's war. I just want to take my wife home."

The other women had come out of the tent and now huddled together, their eyes round with fear. The rising sun bathed them in a golden glow, the sky lightening to a pale blue behind them. Oakheart nodded, hoping to reassure them. To Daya he said, "I cannot stop you taking your wife if that is what she wants."

Lilly came forwards and took her husband's hand. Daya smiled at her and his eyes gleamed. He planted a kiss on her forehead and she embraced him. Oakheart sensed that their affection was genuine. "I hope you will not be harmed in this war, excellency," Lilly said. "I cannot see how this will all end. Why is there so much hate on both sides? They are not so different from us."

Bilt groaned loudly and moved a hand to his head. Oakheart cast up a fleeting smile, relieved that Bilt was not as seriously injured as he thought. He turned his attention once again to Lilly. "I also do not think the hate is justified. If we tried but a little, we could live in peace. Go now, and be careful. Prince Dellbright has patrols in the Valley."

The other Puri man joined them, leaving Cave on the ground still wrestling with his semi-tied bonds. "This is my brother. He means you no harm either."

Oakheart waited, lest the man try to take another of the women, but both men bowed in the Puri way before turning and walking away. One of the women helped Cave untie his bonds.

A drop of blood dropped from his chin and landed on his hand. He gazed down at it. "As we are all awake now we should leave. It is not far to your homes."

He reached down and helped Bilt to his feet. The man staggered and blood drained from his face. "Are you hale?" Oakheart asked him.

The other man nodded then winced. "I can ride."

"Good. Let's go then."

Oakheart wanted to get this job done as he had a burning need to meet up with his cavalcade. The evening was a long way off, which was when he expected to be with his army once more and to see if there had been any word from Veld or Silverdale. He hoped Falen was well prepared. Oakheart's stomach lurched at the terrifying thought that his army might have been attacked while he went skirmishing.

$$\maltese \quad 20 \quad \maltese$$

## THE WORD COMES

It was a tired Oakheart that caught up with the column late in the evening two days after the skirmish. A mind loaded down with worry made it hard to return greetings from his troops with any outwards sign of joy. The families of the women had been most grateful for their return, despite some hesitation from the women. Silver and Eve in particular complained of the shame of being defiled by the Puri. All Oakheart could do at this time was hope that time and maybe a hard-won peace would help them recover. To his eye the families were sincere in their gratitude and joy when reunited with their stolen women folk.

Yet something niggled in Oakheart's chest—the Puri may not be killing in this war, but they were taking the unbonded women. The five women were lucky to have been returned to their families, but at what cost? He had not had time to assess their level of harm. What if this was a widespread Puri tactic? As the Valley was in close proximity to Panal's Pass, such incidences were sometimes reported, but on a large scale? They might not be slitting people's throats but they were doing harm to these women.

He passed off his horse to be rubbed down. A task he did not normally delegate but he needed to catch up with events. After sending word to his commanders advising them of his return, he strode purposefully to his tent, which had been set up in his absence.

"What took you so long? The others have been back more than a day," his mother enquired as she pushed the tent flap aside and followed him inside. His aide had already prepared hot water and a meal for him. Oakheart looked longingly at the canvas bath with steaming water and turned to greet his mother.

"I had to restore some women to their families. It took a bit longer than expected."

Maralain's gaze passed over the tub. "Women?"

"Yes. As well as goods, the Puri it seems now prize Argenterran women who are unprotected by oaths."

Maralain paled. "I see. We'll talk later. After you have had your bath and eaten. There has been no word from Silverdale, so Falen concludes that Veld is prisoner."

Oakheart nodded as he undid his sword belt and unhooked his other weapons and placed them on his travelling chest. "That was my thought as well." He bowed to his mother, who turned, hand lifting the hem of her borrowed adept's robes, and left his tent. His aide went outside to guard his privacy and Oakheart stripped off his travel-stained clothes and lowered himself into the water.

"What are you doing, Hanal of Puri? Have you lost all sense of decency?" He spoke to the tent walls what had been churning in his mind.

Later, as he finished dressing in clean clothes, he heard the chime of one of his talkstones. He uncovered it and held it aloft. "Lianal?"

The adept's face appeared within the facets of the crystal. "Your excellency. I tried calling you yesterday but received no answer."

"You have found something?"

"Yes. I estimate that we will have it all deciphered before you arrive. Will you be coming soon?"

Oakheart stared at the crystal, his heart thumping. This was the moment where his loyalties divided. His mother would argue, and although Veld had allowed him leave to find Sophy, it would be exceptionally difficult to abandon his fighting force before they had engaged in the fight for Silverdale. He bit his lip. Sophy. He could not abandon her as she had no one but him. Even in her own world the only mother she knew now was here in Argenterra. He could not imagine what it would be like to live in a world with no kin. Sophy was his kin. His centre. "I will leave in the morning. I have much to arrange here before I depart."

"Very well. We will expect you."

Lianal faded from view. Oakheart wrapped the talkstone again and placed it on his chest. He picked up the other one. Veld's stone. It was cold and dark. *Father, forgive me. I will come as soon as I can.* The message could not be communicated but it soothed his heart to think his father would understand.

❧

MARALAIN PURSUED OAKHEART AS HE STRODE THROUGH THE CAMP, robes floating behind, her hands clenched into fists. Even with her auburn hair in a simple single brain, she managed to look regal. "You're leaving! What, just like that?"

He paused and shifted so he could face her. "Yes. I did warn you how it would be, mother." He rested his hand on his sword pommel and decided to go to his tent.

Maralain followed close behind, even as he took long strides. "But I...I don't understand. Sophy is bound to be safe in her own world. Surely, you can go for her later."

Oakheart sighed heavily and turned back, holding the tent flap open so she could pass through. "We have discussed this at length. I must go to Sophy. I *will* go to Sophy, and as my king has agreed nothing you can say will sway me. You were as a mother to Sophy. Do you not worry about her welfare?"

Maralain's eyes widened. "Of course I do. I just don't believe she is in any danger. The Crystal Gate was set to her home..."

Dropping the tent flap, Oakheart swung around, put his face close to hers. "Mother! I am her home."

She arched back and then bit her lip. Her complexion reddened and he thought he detected tears in her lashes.

"Mother you told me you do not understand the workings of the

Crystal Gate. Why are you so certain? Is there something you are not telling me?"

Maralain's eyes flashed. "No. I really don't know about the workings of the gate. I assumed it to be so...logic, I thought...."

Oakheart stepped back, inclined his head, trying to act reasonably. "Forgive my outburst. I try to believe you mean well."

"I do. I want you safe and happy."

Oakheart inclined his head and smiled faintly. He had to understand that Maralain was out of place here, trying to find her way while dealing with the loss of Daken. "I leave the command of these warriors in your hands. Falen will serve you well, and you are well supplied with other experienced commanders. You have a decent force ready to aid Silverdale."

"But you are their commander. They need you."

He shook his head. "Sophy has no one. You will do well until I return."

Her forehead crinkled, marring its marble beauty. "But it will take ages. You can't possibly be back in time."

He inclined his head. "I will do my best. Support me in this. Take command."

"Of course I will."

"Very well, I must prepare. Excuse me. "

Oakheart rolled up his blanket and shoved it in a bag. Next, he found a shirt and shoved it in. Looking around, he saw his aide had already packed most of his gear. He turned to his mother, a grimace on his face. "I will try to catch up to you in Silverdale. If there is still a siege it may take some time to break. If Hanal is already nesting in the castle, then it will be hard work to dislodge him. Diplomacy will be the best option. You are best to handle that."

Oakheart tossed one of his packs out through the tent flap to his aide. Maralain gaped at him, shaking her head, and exclaimed, "You are really going? I can't believe it."

"Believe, mother. I am going."

Mara stamped her foot and rolled her eyes. "Oakheart, be reasonable."

He frowned as he scanned the tent, thinking of a few last-minute things. "Quiet now. My mind is made up and I need to tell you things."

She let out a sound of frustration. "Oh very well. Tell me."

Oakheart found a map poking out from under a chest and dived on it. He would need that. He tucked it in his pack and straightened up. "You do not know Hanal of Puri, so I must tell you about him. He is proud and clever and he feels that Veld has denied him justice, denied his people access to the *given* amongst other real and imagined slights. You understand? He is not here for a game or for a show of strength or to even conquer. He feels that he has no other option."

"What does the man want? The bloody crown?"

A fleeting grin crossed his features. "Almost, mother. He wants Puri to be seen, to be treated as equal. For himself, he is sick of being looked down upon, being undervalued. He has Vorn's blood in him."

Maralain looked askance. "What? Not that hogwash about Goslien?"

"Exactly so. He has the eyes—you will see, if you meet him. Do not underestimate him. He had Sophy tortured to gain her power. He successfully brought all his tribes together and swarmed into Argenterra."

"What does he want then? He has everything already. What will make him leave?"

Oakheart pursed his lips and then let out a slow breath as the memories flashed into his mind. "At first he wanted a royal alliance, but father said no. This comes after many years of Dellbright chasing the Puri from the Valley, where for many years they have had free passage through Panal's Pass to the fertile plains and the uncultivated lands along the River Argent."

"So some land in Argenterra then?" She whistled. "That will be interesting."

"You forget he has Silverdale. The question is: does he want to keep it?"

"I see. What about the royal alliance? You are not free. Aria is not free."

"Fern. He is willing to marry. Hanal has a sister called Lyant. He may want more, such as future betrothals of our children."

Maralain's green eyes washed over him. "Oh my, that is serious. Are you sure you want me to be this negotiator?"

"You can speak to Veld and to Hanal."

She winced. "Veld? I do not…"

"What were you expecting if you went to Silverdale? You must at least see Veld…I thought you might have wanted to."

Her eyes lifted to his once again, this time tinged with tears. "I haven't thought it through. I seized upon this campaign to avoid thinking of grief and the future. Now I see that it was stupid to do that. In the next week, I may face all my fears at once." A tear slid down her cheek.

"'Tis not easy, mother," he said, clasping her upper arm and giving it a squeeze. "None of this has been easy for any of us."

Nodding, she opened her arms to him and he embraced her and kissed her cheek. "Go with the *given*, mother. We will see each other again."

# FACING UP TO THE FACTS

Three full days had passed while Rae sat in her cell. She knew this by the passage of light and dark out the tiny window, and the morning and evening meals that were provided. At least she was fed, and so the baby continued to thrive. She had no cause for complaint, except for the huge disappointment in Hanal and the Puri. Despair was hard to swallow. She had no idea of her fate. Would Hanal banish her and take the child? She looked down at Lien and stroked her chin. Lien snuggled into her finger then opened her mouth to feed. Rae's smile was laced with tears.

Her own actions had brought her to this point, and she must be prepared to accept the consequences, although she could still mourn for her loss. Lien cried for food and Rae set about feeding her, staring morosely at the walls of the small room. Her cell. Her prison.

Her legs cramped and she found she missed the outdoors, missed taking long strides. The cell had hardly any light and very little fresh air. She paced back and forth the three steps it took to cross the room, patting Lien on the back as she propped her up over her shoulder. Lien gave a satisfying belch and Rae continued to soothe her. Locked in a cell, she had little to do to pass the time except feed her baby, sleep and think. She slept when the baby slept and ate whatever food was delivered to her. She had not expected this treatment. Indignant on behalf of Lien, she fumed silently. Puri did not like to shape the earth. To lock one of them, particularly a blameless child, below ground was cruel and an awful insult.

Having been raised in Argenterra, Rae found she could bear the cell quite well but the treatment still angered her. Why had he not come to talk to her, to hear from her own lips the reasons for her actions? Was Umri's hold so great? Was his love for her so shallow?

Hanal was an honourable man, she reminded herself. He had only temporarily misplaced his sense of honour. Surely he would find it soon and come to his senses. If he did not, she vowed she would not let him know his child or speak his name to Lien. He would be dead to them both. As that thought crystallised, she fell to her knees and sobbed brokenly. It was an empty threat. There was no one to come and stop her tears. No words whispered to her that would restore her hope.

The small shutter in the door opened. Lifting up her head, she scrambled over to it. "Please, I ask to see Hanal." There was no answer. "If he will not see me, then please let me out of here for some exercise. I will not escape. I will await his justice." A bowl was placed into the chute. Rae took it and then leant closer. "Please tell him it is not good to be so closed in. I will sicken and the baby will die. Please ask him to release us from this room."

The person who handed her the food said nothing. The shutter closed and it was quiet again. Hopefully the guard would have some compassion for a mother and a child and pass on her message. She took the food, knowing she was eating the stores of the true owners of Silverdale. Yet that was not her fault. The boiled toffelbread was tasteless and without spice or sweetness, blander than the blandest porridge of her childhood. As she ate she thought of what was going on outside the castle. *This is not honourable, Hanal*, she thought. *I love you more than life but this is not your true heart and mind. You have been warped and I can guess who by.*

Later, the sound of the door opening roused her from a nap. The child, snuggled tightly in her clothes, slept deeply. One of Hanal's guards stood there. "You are free to walk within the lower level but no further."

"He will not speak with me?"

The man bowed his head. "He did not say. Only that you are to be allowed some exercise for certain periods during the day. You will be confined at night, though."

He stepped backwards and then turned away, leaving the door sitting ajar. Rae stared at it, blinking at the haze of light that hurt her eyes.

Climbing to her feet, she stepped through the door hesitantly. She was free to walk around. Her eyes adjusted to the brightness. Soft, yellow light spilled in, inviting and warm. Her cell had been mostly dark. Cradling Lien carefully, she stepped into the room beyond. Firesticks lined the corridor that glowed golden.

No one else appeared to be about. She walked tentatively down to the left and turned into the corridor. It was so good to be walking again. So she was free to walk around and she had best take advantage of that. No telling when such a privilege would be revoked.

She continued walking, thinking to do a circuit back to her cell. The corridor opened into a large suite, richly furnished and with triple firesticks in separate sconces. At first she was confused because it looked out of place in the dungeon. Through a door a large bed dominated one room and in the main room there was a table with bench chairs tucked into it. An old woman sat there sewing under the light. She looked up as Rae entered.

"Well hello. Come in. *Given* be praised." She smiled invitingly. Then turning her head slightly, she called out, "Company, Veld."

Rae gasped at the name. She could not mean High King Veld. Surely Hanal had not imprisoned him. Then she realised of course he must have. He could not kill the king for such an act would sever the binding oath. Banish him perhaps, but then Veld would be able to raise an army and there would be full-scale war. War such as Vorn and the First Comers had fled from.

She bit her lip.

"What is it, Vola?" The high king came out of an alcove where he had been seated at a desk. He lurched in her direction. Rae took another step and faltered. The king's white hair frizzed out around his face. Rae blinked. He was a large man, with a portly stomach and bright blue eyes. Should she bow?

"Oh, visitors. Come in, come in. Do not be shy. Vola, some spring wine for our guest."

The old woman glared at the king and leant under the table to bring out a small cask. She pulled a goblet over, wiped it with a cloth and poured some wine out. Then she placed it next to her on the table. "Come on, dear. Sit down." She patted the seat of the chair next to her and smiled warmly. "We have not been introduced. You are?"

Rae smiled and moved slowly forwards, changing her hold on her child. She had not had the pleasure that other mothers had of showing off their child. Only Anwi and her family and then Hanal had seen baby Lien.

"Ohh, who have you got there?" the old lady said. The high king came closer too, a big grin on his face; his eyes sparkled.

"My daughter, Lien, named after Goslien of the Valley. She has her eyes."

"May I?" The old woman held out her arms. Rae placed Lien in the cradle of the old woman's embrace. "Oh, it has been so long since I held a baby. What a dear, dear thing."

Vola opened the coverings and stroked Lien's chin. Lien stretched and yawned, opening her startling blue eyes, and blew a bubble of milk.

Veld leant in too, letting the baby grab his large finger. He looked across the baby at Rae.

"You are right about the eyes. Why are you here, a prisoner like us? A mother, and a Puri, too."

Rae glanced down and played with her fingers in her lap. "I offended Hanal of Puri greatly. I await his judgement for...for betrayal."

"This is his daughter, is it not? She has his eyes." Vola's eyes were narrowed, missing nothing.

Rae nodded.

"Then why? What could have you done to offend him?" The older woman shared a look with the high king.

Rae looked at them in turn, not sure where to start.

"It is all right, my dear," Veld said. "We are not going anywhere. Why not start at the beginning? Vola will make tea."

The older woman glared at him. "I will not make tea. If you want tea, you put the kettle on. I am holding the baby."

Veld laughed. "I can surely do that. Tea will warm us better than wine and it is a mite chilly in here."

He put the kettle on the stove and came back to sit with them, playing with the baby's fingers. He glanced up at Rae and nodded.

Rae took a breath and began. "I was born in the North Valley. I am Rae, daughter of Kushlan. The Puri know him as Silvertongue."

"Him I knew…" Veld's eyes clouded over as some reminiscence took him. "Long ago." Then he nodded. "Go on."

"We are descended from the children of Panal and Goslien of the Valley. We are kin to Aurore of Valley Keep. As well as having kin amongst the Puri."

Rae lowered her head and flexed her fingers nervously. Suddenly, not having the weight of the child in her arms made her feel empty. She took a breath, lifted her head and continued her tale. "I went to live with the Puri after the Gifts of Crystal Tree Woods came to live in Valley Keep. Dellbright, who had been my intended, turned aside my hand. There was nothing for me in the Valley so I dreamt of marrying Hanal of Puri. I thought him honourable and brave. Aurore bartered the marriage for me and I had the blessing of my father."

"And?"

"I went to live as kin in Hanal's clan. I am related to him as well, but not too close so that marriage was a problem of the blood. But he was not interested in marrying me. I was told I had nothing to offer him. No great alliance, and me not being a beautiful, light-skinned maiden of Argenterra. At first I did not believe it. My heart was so set on it and I had built up Hanal in my mind. He told me my eyes were blinded by tales of the First Comers and the other greats from our past. Yet I would not believe him. I did not want to believe him to be less than I thought he was. I did not give up. Umri, his seer, suggested a way for me to get Hanal. I conspired to…to…" She lowered her head, afraid of what they might think of her. Both of their blue gazes studied her and occasionally Vola would gurgle to the baby.

"Pray continue…" Veld said gently.

Taking her eyes from their faces, she started talking again, laying it all out in her mind—her bad deeds and the good. "I planned to take Hanal to my bed. Umri taught me the art of seduction. I cannot blame her. It was a passion in me to have Hanal any way I could. I thought he might soften and give me an oath but...he would not. Then I tricked him. Using Umri's art we stole his seed and made a child in me. I loved him and I thought that he loved me, though I was no use to him politically. I wanted him so badly that I believed as Umri said that a son would deliver Hanal to me. Umri, his seer, aided me, guided me, perhaps persuaded me. Although, I must admit I cannot blame her for my actions. I knew they were wrong. I loved him and wanted him above all others."

"For this he has banished you to live with us, his prisoners?" Vola asked, her face full of wonder and concern.

"No, there is more." She straightened her shoulders and looked Veld in the eye. "One day Sophy, Gift of Crystal Tree Woods, was brought to us by Nasheen."

"Sophy! I heard that Nasheen betrayed Oakheart and snatched her from his side. His oathbound wife. I like it not to hear of such deeds." The high king's fists clenched until his knuckles were white.

"Yes, Nasheen brought her to Hanal. But Sophy was proud and tried to negotiate on her own terms. She agreed to let Hanal try to take the *given* she had stored inside her. A great power it was. But nothing he did seemed to work. Then Umri advised him to let her try. She tortured Sophy, drugged her. Hanal was desperate." She shook her head. "I do not know, but something had to be done."

"Then what did he do?"

Rae bit her lip. "He tried to touch Sophy's power, when she was weakened and drugged."

"So what did you do then?" Veld asked her quietly, absently touching his lower lip with a forefinger.

Rae stood up and took a few steps away, not able to look at them. She had had time to think about her actions and her motivations. "I decided to help Sophy escape. It was difficult at first because she was guarded and Hanal was always close. Then an opportunity came."

Veld sat forwards, his mouth slightly agape.

"Hanal touched her power briefly—"

"He did?" He glanced to Vola and then riveted Rae with his bright gaze. "And then what happened?"

Rae shook her head. "They were injured. Hanal and Umri. It was like a big wave of air pushed them over, except they were singed, like there had been fire."

"And Sophy? Was she hurt?"

Rae tilted her head and considered. Sophy had been hurt for days, but did the actual explosion harm her? "No, not more hurt than she already was. I believe the power did not touch her."

Veld exclaimed, "Praise the *given*!"

"Oh, do tell us what happened then?" This was from Vola.

Rae looked at them. Either her story was very interesting or they were very bored. Maybe it was more than that. Perhaps they sought information that might help them. Rae bit her lip. "While Hanal and Umri were unconscious I took my chance. I released Sophy from her bonds and snuck her out of camp. I disguised Sophy as a Puri woman, you see. I had prepared some supplies for our journey. We took to the wastelands with just one horse. The way was long and Sophy was not well after all her trials. I took her in the direction of the retreat."

"You delivered her to the retreat?" Veld asked.

"I...er," Rae looked away as her cheeks warmed. "I stopped at N'Brell's Chasm and left her there."

"The chasm? Did you tell her the secret of the maze beyond the bridge?"

Rae's chin rose up a notch. "No, for I do not know of it. I was lucky that Kushlan had told me of the bridge over the chasm."

Veld exhaled and seemed to grow smaller. He lowered his gaze, his eagerness diminished.

"I know not if she survived," Rae went on. "My heart tells me she did because she is strong in ways that I am not."

"Ah, you saved Sophy." Veld nodded to himself. "She did survive, although at present her fate is not known."

"She made it? I am glad. She has a strong character."

"If not for you, for your strength, she would not have made it. You are strong too...in mind and in body. For that, I thank you."

Rae grew defensive and angry too. She did not want honour and glory. Not for separating Sophy from Hanal. "I did not do it for her," she said with vehemence.

"Why did you help her then?" Vola asked in a soft voice.

"It was to get her away from him." Her voice broke. "I was jealous, you see." She covered her mouth with her hand, holding back a sob. Taking a few deep breaths, she added, "I could not bear that all his attention was on her. When he took me to bed he was thinking of her. It had to stop."

Veld leant back and considered her. "Are you sure that is all? You did not condone his treatment of her. You were moved by her plight."

"Yes, some. But, you see, I am not noble at all. Just a desperate woman in love."

"Which has cost you everything. Your freedom," he said.

"Yes." Her voice was chill. Hanal had forsaken her.

"He has spurned you. I take it you have no oath still, even though you have a child?"

Tears stung her eyes. She fought them and that cost her the ability to speak. She nodded instead, swaying slightly on her feet.

"You love him still?" Vola asked.

Again, Rae nodded, and then she broke down, standing there crying into her hands. She felt movement and warmth as the old woman embraced her. "Cry now, tears will wash it away for a while. We all make mistakes in life. Make bad choices. It is how you live with the consequences that matters."

Her hands soothed along Rae's back and the wise words penetrated her mind.

"You have a beautiful child, one that will make you proud and happy. If that Hanal had any goodness in him he would recognise you, give you an oath and make you a family with your daughter."

"He will not," she said brokenly, possessed by more tears. She had played a game for his heart and lost.

"You cannot control his decisions. You are not the first to give yourself to a man without an oath." Vola sighed, a sigh imbued with memory.

"Vola!" Veld said, his exasperation evident. He held Lien and he soothed her because his outburst had startled her.

This outburst made Rae lift her head and study them both. "What is it?"

Vola cast her a quick smile then turned her head to her brother. "Hush now, you old git, and take care of that baby properly. Support its head." Veld adjusted his hold. "That is right. Now, where was I?"

She turned back to Rae, held her close and rocked her gently. "I loved a man once, a man I was not allowed to marry. I went to him in secret many times. Veld knew and kept quiet about it. That is why he does not want you to know the story. He kept quiet and things went bad. My parents found out and the man was banished. They tried to force me to marry another man of their choice. I refused. I could not bind myself to an oath without my heart being engaged. We could never agree. I refused to marry at all and so I never did and have no family of my own. That is the part that saddens me most. No children of my own. You were blessed."

"But I have never heard this tale." Rae blinked, not daring to believe.

"Veld kept it quiet all these years because of his love for me."

Rae lifted her head and gazed at the woman in wonder, wiping the tears with the back of her hands. "Truly. You do not say this just to gladden my heart?"

Vola's eyes narrowed. She straightened, dropped her hands and left Rae standing there. Rae gaped as the old woman went back to the table and picked up her sewing. "Of course I made it up." She snorted. "One tells shocking tales that will ruin my reputation and tarnish that of the throne for fun." She lifted her head and scoffed. "In jest, if you please."

Rae swallowed and blinked. "I see. It was true then. I am sorry for your pain. Did you miss him, the man who was banished?"

Vola looked up from her sewing, her eyes moist. "Every day."

"Do you know what became of him?"

Vola nodded. "He sent word with some Glasshiver merchants. That was where he was banished to. Glasshiver, a strange and distant place. He met and married a woman there. That was the last thing I heard."

"I am so sorry." Rae stared at the old couple. Veld still held the baby, mouthing words to it animatedly. Rae was confused. There were worse possible outcomes for her. She knew that. She may have to stand by while Hanal married another. He may take the child and thwart the Puri laws in this respect.

The baby wriggled and cried. Veld stood up and passed the baby back to Rae. "She is hungry, I expect." He backed away as she moved to sit where he indicated. "Tell me why you think Hanal is honourable?"

They were interrupted by the guard entering the room and demanding that Rae return to her cell.

BACK IN HER CELL, RAE PONDERED HER MEETING WITH VELD AND Vola. Why did she feel that Hanal was honourable when his treatment of her could be deemed dishonourable? His treatment of Sophy would certainly be considered dishonourable. He had hurt her and allowed an unarmed woman to be abased. If Sophy had not had an oath to protect her virtue, would he have raped her? Or would he have wooed her to a willing oath? She thought it would have been the latter. Had he not desired her when they first met, despite some kind of spell that marred her good looks? Yes, Hanal would have sworn an oath to Sophy, for desire, for her body and for what she represented. Whereas she, Rae, represented nothing. Just another part-Puri woman who joined his clan. But what if all that motivated him was his love of his people, his desire to better their position, to make them equal with all others? For that, she could forgive a lot. Was she gullible to believe he cared for her, that he loved her? Her heart told her that he did love and care for her. She fed Lien and wrapped her up for the night. She could hear Sophy's voice telling her how deluded she was for believing Hanal cared. She could imagine Umri's derisive laugh and sharp words of mockery.

LATE IN THE NIGHT A SOUND WOKE RAE FROM HER SLEEP. SHE WAS instantly awake as she tried to identify the sound that had disturbed her. While she lay there listening, the lock turned. The door swung open as she sat up wearily and peered into the bright light of a fire stick. Shading her eyes with an upraised hand, she asked, "What is it?"

A familiar spicy aroma teased her nostrils. Hanal! He had finally come to her.

"Rae?" he said softly.

She closed her eyes, inhaled the scent of him. "Hanal," she whispered in return. Shame tinged her longing and her love of him. How could she greet him as though nothing stood between them? As she grew more aware, she grew wary. Why was he here? What did he want?

He stepped through the door. He was in his sleeping clothes covered by a robe that lay parted over his chest. Rae felt the full heat of him as he entered her cell. "This small room is not very comfortable, is it?"

Try as she might, she could not decipher his mood. Rae shrugged, trying to disguise her excitement and her longing for him. "It is adequate. I am more comfortable now I can walk around to keep fit during the daylight hours."

His eyes studied her. She was in no position to criticise his treatment of her.

"But you have cause to be angry with me and to punish me. I have no right to ask for better."

He sighed, a sad sound to her ears. "I agree. You have no right."

Rae studied him. She could not make him out. He seemed uncertain and that was not what she remembered about Hanal. He did not appear angry, just thoughtful and tired.

"I am sorry I left you when you were injured. I hoped that you would be well."

"You hoped? You offered no aid."

"There was no time."

He let out a chuckle. The sound did not cheer her for there was no warmth in it. "You took Sophy and fled. You betrayed me. After all that I have done for you, for my people, you betrayed me." His body was still, but his voice was low and angry.

Rae squeezed fingers into a fist, but looked up at him when he stood over her. "I knew you would see it as betrayal. That was not what I intended. I did it for you."

His eyes widened and his nostrils flared. "For me? Tell me how you did it for me? What warped logic is in that brain of yours?"

"Please sit and I will tell you anything you want to know."

Hanal placed the firestick in a brace and searched the small space for somewhere to sit. He spied Lien and his mouth parted and his eyes widened. Rae repressed her joy. He was not immune to his child. He sat down and crossed his legs. "Go on. Tell me, Tu Raenal of the Valley, how you saved me from myself."

Rae sat up straighter, facing him across the sleeping form of their child. "Sophy's power would have killed you."

"What do you know?" He threw his head back, his long braids swinging along the flesh of his waist.

"I know just a small part of that power nearly killed you. It killed Umri's child."

Hanal glared at her. He lifted an eyebrow. "And? There are more of your powerful observations, I can tell."

Rae disliked his sarcasm but she was prepared to work with what she had. "What you were doing to her was wrong. That is not the way of an honourable man."

"So it comes to this. Your belief in the old tales of glory and honour. You place too much at my feet, young Rae. Your notion of honour does not stand well in reality. I am a man, with a man's faults, a man's desires. Let go these dreams you have of me and my motivations."

"I see you, Hanal. I know your motives are good. You seek to better the lives of the Puri, to fight against perceived injustices."

"Perceived?" He scoffed, throwing his head back in disdain. Then looking at her square in the eye, he said, "The injustices are real."

"I did not say there were not." Rae looked around her, to where they were sitting in the basements of the castle in Silverdale. He did not mistake her meaning.

"I suppose you have some moral pronouncement about my conquering of Silverdale." He watched her, the light catching the crystal clear blue of his eyes.

"Yes."

"Pray tell me, what does Rae of the Valley have to say about my methods, about my deeds?"

"They are wrong," she said firmly. "All of it is wrong." She gestured to the building around her. "Puri do not belong here in this town, in buildings such as these."

"They can adjust. They are smart and will learn to live as the Argenterrans."

Rae narrowed her gaze. "Are you so blind? The Argenterran women do not deserve to be stolen away from their homes and raped by our young men. That is not right. Not honourable!"

He surged to his feet, fists clenched at his sides, the tendons in his neck rigid. "You do not know what you are talking about! Only willing women are permitted to go with the men. Only the deserving are offered oaths."

Rae surged to her feet, her fists also clenched at her sides, and leant closer to him, chin raised. "Was that your decree?" His eyelids lowered as he glared at her. "Was it?"

"Yes!"

"Hah!" she exclaimed, throwing up her hands and all caution to the winds. "Then your people do not follow your words."

"You dare mock me?" He loomed over her, rage deepening the colour of his skin. "To my face?"

"Mock you?" Shocked, she turned to him. "I did not come here to mock you. I came to remind you of your honour. I came to save you from yourself."

"My honour!" he snarled. "Enough harping about my honour. You place too much emphasis on it. And I am well satisfied with my accomplishments." His lips turned into a sneer. "I do not need your counsel, or your good will, or your opinions."

Rae reached out a hand to his forearm but he moved it away. "I have seen with my own eyes what has happened here," she continued, relentless now; this was her one chance. "You may have made a decree. That may have been your intention to honourably take the women of Argenterra to use for breeding or..." she shrugged. "But it has been warped. Of the refugees leaving Silverdale none are young women free to go about their lives. No! They are taken, stolen. You can hear their screams in the Forest of Galen on the way here through Glass Cutting Canyon. You can hear the men laughing and rubbing their hands as they come here seeking women to rape and goods to steal. There is nothing honourable in what your men are doing. You are complicit in the shaming of the Puri."

"You lie. I have not claimed you, so you hit back at me."

Rae stilled, breathed deeply. Raising her face to his, she took in his beloved countenance, now distorted in anger and fear. Her words had hit him hard. "I love you more than my life, Hanal of Puri."

His eyes widened. Perhaps he was surprised that she would still speak her heart to him.

"I honour you where you do not honour yourself. You have not claimed me or our child. So be it. I will not take you, now, even if you beg."

He cut the air with his hand. "Your words mean nothing." He stopped to draw breath before adding, "I did not say I will not claim my child. Have I not called her Lien, daughter of Hanal?"

Rae scooped up Lien and held her to her shoulder. "You lost your chance. You cannot have her. I claim sole parenthood over her."

His lips curled into a snarl. "You are a deceitful, vengeful woman. You will be judged for treason. Then you will have no rights over my daughter. They will be forfeit."

Rae's chin lifted and her eyes narrowed. "Find out for yourself what your men do in your name. I dare you. I dare you to face the truth."

Hanal turned to the door, snatching the firestick from its holder. "You lie. You seek to shape me into some hero of old. I am just me. Just myself."

Rae lowered her head and spoke quietly. "I have faith that you will see the true way in the end. My heart is yours till I die. I sacrificed myself for love of you. If that is a crime then punish me, if you will."

Hanal's expression closed in, as if he could not bear to show her his anger. "No more! I have heard enough of this treachery that comes out of your mouth."

He gathered his robe about himself and left. The lock clicked shut behind him. Lien wailed, woken by harsh words and hunger.

❧ 22 ❧

# A PRISON OF DESPAIR

A biting thirst roused Sophy from her doze. Wiping the dust from her lips with the back of her hand, she lifted her head off the ground. There was dirt, bricks and cell bars and an all-encompassing rankness. Blinking a few times didn't improve the view. Sniffing didn't improve the smell. She tried to imagine what the source of the smell was but that only made her eyes widen. Best not to think what was decaying down there with her. The light was dim, coming from some unseen source. A window around the corner, down the hall? As her head ached, she didn't mind the absence of light that much.

Listening hard, she realised the beasts, or whatever they were, had gone. For the moment at least. Sleep had helped her gain some strength.

Groggily, Sophy looked around her. The cell had no furnishings. She lurched to her feet and looked down—she'd been wrapped in some kind of filthy grey-brown cloth. She undid the material and other rags fell to the ground. Those must have been the remains of her clothes; but for the wrapping cloth she was naked. Fingering the material she realised it wouldn't keep her warm, but it might cover her nudity. The cloth was worn thin in places. It wasn't much but she should be able to fashion something to wear.

Again her thirst bit at her, nearly making her throat close over. She tried licking her lips and swallowing but that made it worse. There was no moisture in her mouth. Her thoughts went back to the water cavern where the ugreals had kept her when she first came to this place; if only she could have some of that water now. If only she hadn't gone charging off into danger.

Her body ached as she tied the rags into a semblance of underwear and then ripped the cloth to make a wrap skirt, which she secured with torn strips. Another wrap of fabric covered her breasts. She shook her head. Time was running out. She had to get out of this place, away from Rufus.

She examined the brickwork of the walls of the cell carefully, starting low to the ground and then up the walls as far as she could reach. In a place this old, there must be some loose stonework, some way out. She shook her head. Ridiculous to even try. Gritting her teeth, she swept her fingers along the mortar joins, pushing and shoving at bricks that looked suspect. A dry cough scoured her throat, reminding her of the lack of water. It took a few moments for her chest to settle, for her breathing to ease. Feeling desperate, she wondered if there was some moisture she could lick off the walls. On closer inspection it was dry as a bone. She thumped the brickwork. There was little hope of escape that way.

Turning away, she focussed on the cell bars. Thick, rusty bars. She grabbed a pair and pulled and shoved but they didn't budge. Twisting and groaning, she gave up when there wasn't even a squeak to reward her efforts. Sucking on her smarting palms, her gaze swept the cell again. A low sigh full of defeat escape her. This first assessment of her situation wasn't going so well in the optimism stakes.

The cell was too small for a decent pace. Soon after she started pacing, she realised she needed to pee badly too, but there was no bucket. She would have to do it in the corner and hope that she did not foul the rank cell even further. Undoing the cloth that she'd only just secured, she made a shallow impression in the dirt and squatted. That done, she refastened her clothing and continued to scan the cell.

Although none of the stones were loose, she leant in closer and scraped at the mortar with a fingernail. Higher up, her fingers yielded nothing. Yet farther down, some came away at her scraping. The mortar between some of the bricks was soft. She scrambled amongst the debris on the floor, searching for something, a twig, a stone, anything that she could grind the mortar out with and loosen the bricks. She didn't want to think about what would happen after that, or even before that. She had to try. It was a long shot. She had no idea what was on the other side of the wall. It was all hope and focus. She'd go crazy if she didn't try something. There had to be a tunnel around there somewhere. Had to be.

If she could make it out of the cell and into a tunnel she had a chance. She was good with tunnels now, she could dig her way out. Would she survive that long without food? Already she was weak, drained. The machine took more than Argenterra's power from her, it drained her energy too. Clenching her jaw, she decided she wasn't going to let Rufus win.

The child growing inside her needed nutrients to survive. That meant she had to eat to live. She might survive without food for a couple of days but her unborn child would suffer. She would have to ask for food, beg even. Closing her eyes, she denied the vision of her begging Rufus for anything.

In the sand on the floor she found a chip of brick and hid it in the corner. It wasn't much but it would work. Then she went up to the bars and pressed her face through. "Hello! Helloooo. Food. You have to give me food. Water too."

There was no response. She waited and listened and there was nothing. No sound of man or beast. She was alone. Just to make sure, she repeated her yell. When there was no response, she started working on the mortar. She chose three or four bricks that were at waist height, with mortar that when scratched became more crumbly. It was imperative that her work went undiscovered. She could lean against these to hide them if someone came to look at her in her cell. Hopefully, if they took her out of the cell, they wouldn't notice what she was up to. The dirty, sandy ground absorbed the ground-up mortar without a trace.

The chip of brick she used dug into the grooves between the bricks, peeling off mortar in thin layers. While the mortar appeared to come away quite easily, it was going to take time. While she etched the edge of the brick into the mortar, she used her feet to sweep away the grey dust and mingle it with the other dirt fragment and debris that littered the floor. Every now and then she paused, listening for signs of Rufus.

Then when her arms ached, and her back pained her, she paused to inspect her work. She'd been at it for what seemed like hours but hardly anything had changed. There was less mortar but the bricks stayed firm. She'd have to work longer and harder to loosen even one of them.

Sliding down the wall, she sat in the dirt. What if Unesta and Rufus were both gone now? What if they had left her there to die? Tears started in her eyes. No. No. That couldn't be right. Crawling over to the bars, she yelled again. Not that she wanted to see Rufus but she did not want to be left abandoned to die a useless death, either. With a bar in each hand she shook the grill. After a number of pulls, the bars started to rattle noisily in the metal frame. She looked up at the joins. There didn't seem to be a possibility that she could loosen them. A few flecks of rust dropped down onto her face.

She shouted and rattled the bars again. That might get someone's attention. She continued to holler and shake the bars until her ears hurt. Then she stopped again and, as her ears adjusted, she heard movement down the corridor.

Soon, Rufus turned the corner and came shuffling up the corridor. A sigh escaped her. She was not alone. But she was still in danger, still caught in a trap. Rufus looked even more decrepit in the daylight. Yet she should not underestimate him. No matter that he appeared fragile, he could use magic and his thin muscles had unexpected strength. Had he not thrown down trees in the wood when he was looking for her? He was capable of mulling her mind if he chose to, or was she now immune to that magic? She remembered how she had desired him when he had placed a glamour on her causing her to see a fake angel form. Either she was resistant or he didn't need to bother to try anymore.

She peered out through the rusty bars. He rammed his face close to hers. She held herself unflinchingly to the bars, willing herself not to draw back as his fetid breath washed over her. She breathed through her mouth, hoping to fake it out. "Feed me. I want food."

"Why should I feed you? I prefer you weak and close to death."

"I will be cooperative if you feed me."

"Cooperative. How?" Those rat eyes of his drifted down her body, wreathed in cloth. "Take off those rags and show me your body."

For the first time she caught a glimpse of his humanness. Desire glowed in his dark eyes, the red luminosity dimmed. He had been human once. Had his mistress changed him, or was that something he did to himself? Was the corruption within now etched on the exterior?

"I could make it worth your while..." Sophy did her best to appear seductive, which was quite difficult as she wanted to vomit. She moved a hand to the ties on her skirt.

"I like it when you try to fight, try to sway me. Makes your pain... your despair more...tasty."

Sophy glared at him, fighting to keep her impotent rage in check. She put her hands back on the bars, her clothing still intact. "Did you like hurting people when you were human too?"

His gaze that had been roving over her body snapped to meet hers. "Shut up."

Sophy tilted her head as she considered him. "Sore spot is it? Were you as ugly then as you are now? Is this rodent form an improvement on the evil man that was?"

A clawed hand encircled the bar close to her face. "You shut up. You cannot know what it was like then. What happened here."

Sophy drew back, then stepped away as she turned to inspect the cell casually. "I have plenty of time, nowhere to go, and I am willing to listen."

His laughter was like a hammer on her spine. "You mock me." He stood up taller. "You think you can trick me by pretending you are interested in my history?" His flimsy wings flapped behind him, giving him more space to control. "Hahaha...I've eaten young things like you for breakfast and sucked on their bones in the evening. Don't even try to match wits with me."

He moved to turn away. "No, wait!" she called out involuntarily.

Rushing forwards, she pressed herself against the bars. "Please, I need some food and clean water."

He was still turned away from her. "And that interests me how?"

"Please, I beg you. Some mercy. Some food and water. That's all I ask."

He paused, looked over his shoulders, coarse hairs standing up on the top of his otherwise bald head. "Begging? Already? You have not even begun to suffer yet."

"Please, water then. Just a small amount. I'm so thirsty."

He chuckled as he walked away. As soon as he was out of sight, she raced back to the wall and continued to grind away at the mortar, tears bathing her cheeks. Everywhere hurt, but she couldn't give up. She had to get out of there or die.

It would take a while before she could loosen the brick she was working on. It would take days, weeks, to loosen enough to escape. But anything was better than sitting here waiting, waiting for it to end.

Not long after Rufus left, a clank sounded. She paused and waited. It was coming closer. Was he bringing her food? Could it have been that easy? She raced back to the front of the cell, wiping the dust off her hands and the grey rags she was wearing.

A warren beast lurched into view. She recoiled, heart thudding. It prowled along the corridor. Then it sniffed once, turned its overlarge head in her direction and leapt. Surprised, Sophy fell back and landed on her rear. The warren beast threw itself at the bars repeatedly, slavering away. Sophy looked at the frame, watching the mortar holding the frame fragment and fall. She half-hoped it would cave in on the beast. At least then she would have a fighting chance, provided she knew where to attack the beast to render it unconscious or kill it. She clenched and unclenched her hands. Could she fight it? Could Rufus have planned this? Had he let more of the beasts into these ruins? She would not put it past him. A sick game to taunt her with hope and then watch her will to live fail. Well, she was happy to play. Hope was the only dice available.

Other noises confirmed her suspicions that more of the beasts were roaming in the corridor beyond. That pushed up the stakes. The beast continued to snarl and snap at the grate, trying to force its head between the bars. Sophy crouched and snarled savagely in return, approximating a territorial challenge. Inching forwards on her toes, she made loud whooping noises and waved her arms. Look bigger. Sound scarier. That was what was in her mind. A bellow that came from deep inside her filled the space.

The snarls broke off suddenly and the small piggy eyes peeking around the enormous mouth widened. Following up, Sophy stomped her feet and lunged aggressively at the bars, mimicking being savage and out of control. It wasn't far from how she felt.

The warren beast paused, all motion halted. Sophy kept up her aggressive stance, watching the beast. A breath puffed out of its nostrils. A muscle on its back quivered, but it stood its ground. A snarl showed so many teeth she became uneasy. At least it had stopped attacking the grate. Another head peered around the corner—a second warren beast drawn by the commotion.

As Sophy considered the situation, she wondered if she had done the right thing. Perhaps it would have been better to encourage the beast to keep lunging at the grate, thereby loosening it in its frame. Her gaze studied the warren beast in front of her and the other as it came up behind. Now she had twice the problem. The escape route, besides the grate itself, was complicated by feral creatures. She had tested the frame and did not think it would give easily. Her gaze shot up and what she saw confirmed her suspicions. Even with the pounding it had received and the positive signs of crumbling mortar, she could see the frame had long prongs of metal that continued up into the fabric of the building overhead.

Maybe ten warren beasts could shift it, or explosives. She doubted she'd survive either of those. Once her stance relaxed, the warren beast moved to snuffle and sniff at the door again, worrying it with its sharp teeth. Keeping the beast in her sights, she stepped back to the wall. It tracked her with its beady eyes, showing signs of awareness. She was hoping it was not intelligent enough to understand what she was doing with the bricks. The other warren beast lost interest now they were both quiet. He lumbered back around the corner and out of sight.

Ignoring the remaining warren beast, she knelt to continue rubbing the stone at the mortar. She thought she was going to get away with it, but the little beast started to howl and attacked the door anew. Pausing, she lifted the gaze to the beast. It wasn't about to break through. Its grandstanding was annoying but not actually going to harm her.

A clang sounded, slightly muted as if it was several rooms away, and the warren beast turned its head and paused, as if listening. Another sound, like a chain rattling, then it bunched its muscles and bounded off down the corridor, its claws rasping on the stone floor.

Not quite certain what was going to happen next, Sophy worked furiously and then stopped, holding still and listening for short intervals. It was not long before she heard the lumbering footsteps of Rufus. Quick as she could, she dusted the mortar off her hands and her clothes and used her foot to smear the rest underneath the rotting mess of debris already covering the floor. She smeared some of the ground dirt onto the wall, smiling to herself when some of it actually stuck.

From the middle of the cell, she swung around when she heard his nasal breathing. At the bars, Rufus stood with a bucket in his hand. With her back to the wall, her gaze fell immediately to the bucket. She could almost feel its cool moisture on her face and skin. Water. Her lips were a mess of cracks and her tongue felt thick.

A rat-faced grin greeted her when she looked up from the bucket. "Come here, if you want a drink."

"What do I have to do for it?" Sophy held her fear in check. There was nowhere to run and she was desperate.

"Come closer and find out."

She had to have that water. She stepped forwards using small, hesitant steps, keeping her eyes riveted on him, watching in case he made a grab for her. She wanted to do this on her own terms. Rufus smiled, not a pretty sight, she thought as she studied the deep creases in the skin of his face, searching for the traces of humanness. The knowledge that he was once human sent a surge of fear into her gut. She did not want to lose her sense of self, her humanness. Death would be preferable to ending up like him.

His gaze lingered on the water, passed over her and then went down the corridor in the direction the warren beast had gone. She paused, waiting for his next move. She did not realise that her eyes had drifted in the direction of the bucket again. The water looked clear. She began to imagine what it would taste like as it dribbled down her throat. The spell broke when he spoke, making her start. Body tense, she focussed on him.

"Did you meet my pets, Xyl and Flix?"

Sophy assumed he meant the warren beasts. She nodded, feeling surreal in the moment.

"I want them to get used to your scent. You smell pungent. They like that. When I go I will let them back in. It will drive them crazy wanting to get at you. Then when I am ready for some entertainment I will let them at you. Xyl likes females. He likes to rut while he rips their throats out. Very enjoyable. Flix likes to watch and nibble on the leftovers."

Sophy wasn't sure she believed him. "At least," she said, knowing she shouldn't bait him, "they are better looking and more intelligent than you are."

He made to move away, bucket in hand, and she realised her mistake. She threw herself at the bars. "I am sorry. Please, I need the water. Don't leave."

He paused and looked behind him. "On your knees."

Sophy lowered herself to the ground, whimpering. She did not have to pretend. "Some water first. Just a sip, please." She could see his erection, knew what he wanted from her. She began to dry-retch and tried to cover it up, making herself shake so he would think it was fear and not revulsion. She had to remind herself that whatever he looked like, he was a man underneath. A corrupted man, but a man and not an animal.

She lifted her face. He draped himself over her face through the bars. Reaching into the bucket with his hand, he dribbled some water from his fingers. Then he lowered his fingers into her mouth and she sucked on them. He gave her another drizzle and she was in heaven. Her mouth tasted water. "No more. Until you are done working on me."

Sophy closed her eyes, shut her mind away, almost reaching out to touch him. With a burst of revulsion, she pulled away. "Water now, and food. The exchange is not equal."

"You want equal? Crazy bitch. Whatever I give you is more than you deserve."

He laughed as he picked up the bucket and tossed it over her head.

She sucked in as much water as she could and then threw herself to the ground to lap up the dregs before it drained away. She didn't care what it tasted like and didn't care how desperate she looked grovelling like an animal. All that mattered was getting some moisture inside. She managed a few mouthfuls, enough to keep her going for a little while longer. Soon she would be too weak to fight and he would take what he wanted and then feed her to his pets.

Before he left, Rufus chucked a hunk of dried bread in through the bars. It hit her in the head. "You need practice. Obviously, Oakheart was a terrible lover if that's the best you can do. Cringe and whine. I guess your heart wasn't in it. Let's see if you can do better next time."

Then he lumbered away down the corridor. No sooner had he gone than Xyl was back, sniffing and whining like a dog at the bars. The sound of its companion echoed down the corridor. Two warren beasts. Inside the cell, next to the chunk of bread, was a piece of cloth. She reached for them. The fistful of bread was dry and hard and the cloth looked like a piece of her old clothing. When she lifted it, Xyl jumped at the bars and started snarling, spraying spit all over her. Edging back, she kept her eyes on the creature and lifted the cloth to her nose. She realised then that the creature had been baited with her scent. Instinctively, she was revolted and went to toss it through the grate, then stopped herself. It might come in useful later. She placed the cloth away from the bars and let the creature tire itself out.

Ignoring the warren beast the best she could, she returned to gouging the mortar from between the bricks. Whenever she paused she would gnaw on the hard, musty bread. There was a quality to her work that marked desperation and anger. Time was running out and that made her anger boil. If she got out of this alive and saw Oakheart again, she would give him a serve that would send him rolling head over heels through any theoretical barriers into her world.

Then she heard the gong again and the warren beast lifted its head and yelped. Sophy sat down with her back to the wall, covering her excavation work with her body. The beast started gnashing its teeth again, but did not leave the door. It did not sound like Rufus was coming back. Curiosity got the better of her and she inched along. Two larger beasts bounded around the corner. By god, no. Not screavers! The sight of them sent her mind back to the Gilton Forest and their flight from the beasts. The sound of them rending the forest, rending people, gave her chills. She remembered the sight of Oakheart being attacked and his awful wounds. What chance did she have now?

Angry tears bled from her eyes. "You bastard!" she said, thinking of Rufus, thinking of the things she wanted to do to him. Let him offer his soft, vulnerable parts to her. She'd give him a treat he'd never expect.

The screavers leapt at her as soon as she reached the bars, their sharp teeth not a foot from her face as they growled and slashed. She jerked backwards. Not only did they strain to get at her, they jostled each other for a place in front of the cell. Xyl cowered out of the way, blood leaking from a rent in its fur. Rufus had been playing her. She could have defeated a warren beast, maybe two, with her bare hands, but not screavers. Not those sharp-toothed, slavering maws.

Sophy turned her back on the furore outside her cell and went back to work. She wasn't going to give in to Rufus. "Not in this life time. Never. Ever," she said as she put more effort into the bricks.

⁂

HANAL SLAMMED INTO HIS CHAMBERS AND STALKED UP AND DOWN the room. Long windows opened out into the courtyard and let in dull afternoon light. By rights he should be happy but he was not. Rae! Rae and her words cut into him. He wasn't honourable. Worse, his men were not honourable. His men were rapists. Despoilers of women. Even the young men, unblooded, untried, came to Silverdale with rape on their minds. He closed his eyes and thumped the wall. He didn't want to believe it, but could not shake the truth. This had not been his order. Somehow it had been warped.

Umri wafted in. "You sent for me, Hanal." She bowed from the waist, apparently no longer willing to abase herself on the carpet. She had risen high, Umri had.

"Tell me, Umri, what was the order you gave to my men?"

Puzzled, Umri shook her head. "What order, Hanal?"

"The one from my lips that you took to the men. The one regarding the Argenterran women."

Umri walked around the room, touching a statue, picking up a box, kicking a cushion negligently out of the way. "You have been speaking to Rae." She laughed softly. "You know you should not have done that."

"Yes. I've been speaking to Rae. I'm waiting for an answer, Umri."

Umri flicked her head back, not quite meeting his eye. "I can't remember the exact wording. Something about Argenterran women being their reward."

Hanal faced her, fist clenched. "I included conditions, did I not?"

Umri screwed up her mouth. "Did you? I don't recall."

A growl escaped him. "It's true, then. You told them to rape whoever they could."

Umri's chin came up, her dark eyes like wine. "I wouldn't go that far."

"They did, Umri. My men are raping innocent women. Vows?" He threw his arm to the side. "Vows are nothing. You have allowed them to become less than they should be."

"It has nothing to do with me. Is it my fault that their true nature has shown itself? Men are weak, creatures of lust and desire."

Hanal's eyebrow rose. He caught sight of Tarkel, who darkened the doorway, silent and patient as ever. "And do you see me as a weak fool, too, Umri? Am I a creature of lust and desire?"

Umri chuckled. "Possibly."

"You tread on dangerous ground."

"I don't believe so. You need me. Without me, you are nothing."

Hanal lifted his hand to stay Tarkel. Umri was unaware her husband listened in to their conversation. "Umri, I believe you have a gift. One that you misuse. You will leave Silverdale tonight."

Umri gasped. "You can't send me away."

Hanal smiled, but there was nothing nice in the expression. "I can and I will. Tarkel will take you with him. He will start a new clan. You will give him many sons and never enter my tent again."

Umri stood shocked to immobility, her eyes wide. "You can't be serious."

Tarkel entered the room. "Wife, pack our things. We are leaving."

Umri turned to him. "You can't make me. I'm not leaving. Not now. Not when we will win everything."

Hanal lowered his head, his chin almost touching his chest. This is what he'd been afraid of. That Umri would lead him astray. She didn't have to do much, for he was halfway there already. Rae was right: he had dishonoured himself. Now he had to see if he could restore his honour. First thing was to clean his house. Umri knew his weaknesses and exploited them. He could not blame her for that as they were his weaknesses, after all. But now his eyes were opened. Now he must negotiate a different path.

Tarkel grabbed Umri's arm, but she shook him off and threw herself at Hanal's feet. "Please let me stay, let me guide you. The Argenterrans are nothing, not compared to us. You will rule. You will have many sons who will rule after you. I can make this happen. You must listen to me."

He nudged her away with his foot. "I can only enjoy victory if I am worthy of it. Leave me, and never come back."

She looked up and met his gaze. "Weak fool. Rae has twisted your mind with her bastard child."

'The child is mine."

"Pah! You know nothing."

Tarkel secured her arm and lifted her. "Come, wife, we will leave my brother in peace."

"No. I won't go. He was my lover, did you know? How does that feel to know he passed you used goods?"

Tarkel's jaw clenched but he shook his head. "You think I didn't know? I cared not. I wanted you, used or not."

Umri no longer fought. She gaped at her husband. "You knew. All this time, you knew?"

Hanal nodded to his brother. "Farewell, brother. Thank you for your service to me. May you build a strong clan. I will send others to join you as befit your station."

Tarkel dragged Umri out of the door. "Thank you for returning my wife to me. We will be at peace now...in time."

And they were gone.

⁂

Sophy's next period of wakefulness coincided with a vengeful thirst that eclipsed her hunger. She had eaten the bread the previous night and there had been no more sign of Rufus in the corridor.

Being seen as food by beasts with mouths and teeth like these was intimidating. The warren beasts had double rows of teeth and horns too, but their bodies were no bigger than a medium-sized dog. Their fur was short and striped in blacks, whites and greys, with a hint of ginger. When they weren't slavering after her flesh they could be cute.

The screavers, though. She'd only ever seen them in the distance. Up close, they were grotesque. They had the same double rows of teeth, but included six vicious-looking fangs. They could stand on their hind feet and were nearly as tall as a man. Their claws were long and sharp and they had barbs on their elbows so that they could stab backwards. Her eyes dropped to their feet. They were like the hands, able to climb and with the same sharp claws. Their fur was not as rich as the warren beasts'. She could see pale flesh under the cloak of hair. They had large genitals. She looked away. There was no point in dwelling on it.

No point in waiting. She knelt down and began to rock the loosened brick back and forth. She sucked at her fingers, the skin already worn off. She tried thumping one end with her palm. The brick moved. She tried the other end, wiggling it slowly. It was a tease. It rocked so far then stopped. So she tried another one. It, too, moved slightly. After promising much, the movement in the bricks petered out. After about an hour of trying to budge them she gave up. They moved but she could not lever or pry them out. For that she needed tools. A depression draped itself over her mood. She was hungry, tired and thirsty. Weakening by the hour. What if she had wasted all her energy on nothing at all?

Again she lay down facing the wall, tracing her fingers over the lattice of brick joins, with her head resting on her outstretched arm. Very soon, her eyelids closed. She dreamt she was working on the bricks, she dreamt she was getting somewhere. She dreamt there was a tunnel on the other side. With that thought she snapped awake and sat up. Immediately the warren beasts and the screavers started fighting. After fending off their rivals, the screavers began snarling at the bars, straining to get in and managing to flick hot saliva all over her.

While she was distracted, her foot touched something. She leapt to her feet with a screech, thinking it was a snake or something else that slithered. When she had calmed enough, she prodded the object with her toe and it rolled. It was a root.

She hadn't seen it before. A root? A root like the ugreals had brought her. She pounced on it, sniffed it, broke a piece off and licked it. It did appear to be an edible root, like the ones she'd eaten before. She started gnawing hungrily. Half-way through eating, when her hunger had abated somewhat, she allowed herself to think about where it had come from. Her gaze flicked around. The bricks she had been labouring on were still in place. That part had definitely been a dream. Her gaze searched out the cell, concentrating on the ceiling, sometimes turning to the bars of her cell and considering that one of the ugreals had snuck past the warren beasts and screavers and tossed it to her. That didn't seem likely. That meant that the little beasties had found her, or at least had a way in. A flash of hope lifted her spirits. She tried to pin it down, to stop it over-exciting her, and couldn't.

Even after eating some more of the root, she was still very thirsty and swallowing had been difficult. After an interval she felt invigorated despite her thirst. The root was nutritious, something she would not guess looking at it. It was a root, after all. The lack of water was unpleasant and she worried about what dehydration would do to her body and the baby.

Then she had the idea that the warren beasts needed to drink too, surely. She approached the bars slowly, ignoring the increase in growls and snarls from the four beasts. They went crazy when she edged closer. She could feel their hot breaths as they slavered over the bars trying to get their heads through to get at her. After a few failures and not flinching, she was able to brave it out long enough to peer to the side. There, perhaps an arm's length away, was a tub of water. She didn't recall it being there before but she wasn't surprised that Rufus had put it there while she slept. Then the thought that it was Rufus after all who had thrown her the root to eat, and not the ugreals, returned. She shook her head. It just did not fit with her assessment of him. She didn't want to relinquish hope.

All she had were her hands. Putting them outside the bars meant they would be savaged, chewed off, eaten, unless she could distract the beasts. Then she remembered the cloth. Would it work if she threw it to them? She moved closer to the bars and looked sideways. Then she sidestepped, ignoring the beasts as they jumped up and tried to claw her. Then she checked again. She was not one hundred per cent certain that her arm could reach the water container but she had no other choice.

Stepping back from the grate, she breathed slowly, calming the racing of her heart. Anxiety nearly crippled her. She had no choice. She had to try to get at the water. She searched near where she slept for the remnant of her old clothes. She rolled the grubby cloth in her hand, considered it, wondering whether to tear it in half. Then she opened it out. It would make two fairly reasonable pieces. If she divided it, she would have something up her sleeve, something to fall back on. So she tore it. Then to make extra certain that they would go crazy she sponged the cloth between her legs, making sure it had her scent, as pungent as it was at that moment. Then she balled the cloth up into her fist and stood there waiting, waiting, waiting...

"Right there, one, two, three," Sophy counted, then she darted for the bars, ignoring the warren beasts but holding the cloth low, making sure she trailed it near their snouts and tossed it over their heads. She stepped back and stood still. Would they go for it? One beast stared at her, mouth open, teeth splayed. The other three sniffed and went for the cloth.

"Move, you little bastard," she said under her breath.

She stood still, hoping, praying, waiting. Then she decided to move anyway and took a step, hoping she would survive putting her arms out of the bars. The sound of fighting rolled over her. The remaining warren beast, Flix, held his pose. Silent and still. She paused, eyes locked with the beast. Then with a slight sniff, it turned and jumped on the backs of the other three beasts as they grovelled for the cloth.

Sophy dropped to her knees, close to the corner of the bars. She put her arm out, her gaze shifting from the tub to the beasts, who were chasing the flimsy rag around the corridor. In her first few attempts her hand met with empty air, batted the wall or the floor, and she could not touch the tub.

Then she pressed herself harder to the bars, pushing her shoulder out, almost jamming it tight between the bars. Now not able to see, as her face was squashed tight between the bars, she patted around blindly with her hand. Then she touched it. The damp surface of the water container. She tried again, touched it, then carefully walked her fingers to the lip of the tub. She almost moaned in pain. The tub was heavy, too heavy to move. Yet she had to move it to survive. She stifled the noise she was making, worrying in case she alerted the animals to her efforts.

They were still engaged in the fight but that could not continue for much longer. There was always going to be a time limit on how long she had to reach the tub. She was tempted to pull with all her might and spill it. She might be able to get a few mouthfuls before she ran out of water and time.

Then the beasts' argument died down. One of them had the cloth and was chewing it, slewing its head from side to side. Another two looked worse for wear. Blood leaked on one's foot and the other looked like it had damaged its mouth. Yet they had let up their attack. As one the others joined in to attack the one with the rag again. This was it: the last chance.

Then she found the lip and drew the tub forwards gently. There was a slight give. She repeated the exercise, changing position now that it was slightly closer. Facing it, she was able to draw it closer steadily and deliberately, though not very far. Taking a big breath she tried putting her hand inside. Water kissed her fingertips. She tried for one more tug, cupped her hand and carefully drew it out. With her lips pressed through the bars she sucked the water from her palm. She managed three handfuls before the beasts noticed and leapt for her. She ducked back in behind the bars, smiling. She'd done it. There would be other opportunities when the beasts slept. She tried not to think about how good it would feel to dip her head in the tub and drink and drink. She had to be satisfied with what she had done.

Perhaps it was the confidence of beating Rufus and his beasts that brought her another small victory. This time, when she manipulated the brick it moved freely. With a gasp, she dropped it, barely missing her toes. Gaping, she knelt before the wall, unable to grasp that she had managed to get a brick out. Dropping lower, she peered into the hole and made out that there was some kind of rubble behind it. Not soft soil as she had hoped, and not bricks as she had feared. Yips and yowls at the bars to her cell distracted her. She glanced over, suddenly tired by all her exertions. The team was back in its usual position. There was no sign of the rag. She slid the brick back into place and lay down to rest.

One down, five more to go.

❦ 23 ❦

# SECRETS REVEALED

Oakheart strode along the retreat's main corridor on his way to Lianal's office. He had acquired an escort of two adepts, who had introduced themselves as Leoff and Rye. They were young, not far from being new recruits as far as Oakheart could tell. The retreat was relatively empty of adepts, a goodly portion having gone to fight the Puri at Silverdale with his own men. Oakheart thought he should be sorry for this lessening of the retreat but he was not. Too much had happened to destroy his confidence in the power and the knowledge that rested there. He wondered if his faith in the adepts and their abilities could ever be restored. It came from believing blindly and then discovering the truth was not what you thought. Perhaps the adepts were too far removed from the people of Argenterra, and maybe that would have to change. Oakheart's feelings and thoughts were conflicted on the matter. Finding a way to reach Sophy would help restore his faith.

When they reached Lianal's office, Leoff knocked and when a voice responded with an invitation to enter, opened the door. Rye stood aside and bowed. Oakheart squared his shoulders and entered.

"Well met, Oakheart," Lianal said, rising from his desk. "You made good time." His gaze dropped to Oakheart's travel-stained clothing.

He had rarely stopped to wash or change his clothes or rest himself. Even with two horses, he had to match his pace to his mounts.

Oakheart bowed. "Well met, Lianal. Forgive my attire for I have had little time to waste. Have you made progress?"

Lianal inclined his head. "I believe we have. Leoff will take you to Adept River. He will be able to explain it to you. I believe he has some further research to conduct, then we shall begin the summoning of the Crystal Gate. But perhaps, Oakheart, you might wish to refresh yourself. We are by no means ready to begin so take your time, take your ease."

Oakheart nodded, relaxing a little. Fatigue pulled at his muscles and he was hungry and thirsty. "I will take up your kind offer, then, if Leoff does not mind the wait."

Leoff smiled and gave a short bow. "I am at your service, excellency. I will happily be of assistance."

Oakheart regarded the head adept. "Have you word from my father? From Silverdale?"

Lianal frowned. "I fear not. We have had no word for weeks."

Oakheart had not dared hope but it was worth the asking. "Very well, Leoff. If you would be so kind as to show me the way to some quarters I will avail myself of the retreat's amenities."

"If you will follow me, your usual quarters are as you left them."

As they walked through the crystal corridors, Oakheart saw that night was drawing close as the fabric of the retreat developed dark contours and shadowy recesses.

Leoff opened the door to Oakheart's usual suite. "I will return early in the morning. I will speak to Adept River now."

"Thank you," Oakheart said. "I will take advantage of a soft bed and a good meal. See you then."

Leoff bowed and walked back down the corridor.

Oakheart stood on the threshold of his old quarters, overwhelmed by memories. So much of his life was spent here in the aftermath of emotional upheaval. His mother leaving with Daken through the Crystal Gate, years of grieving for his loss, then finding Sophy wounded, used, abused, and their short reunion before she was snatched away. He inhaled, hoping to catch the light perfume of her, but there was nothing left. He closed his eyes, trying to capture her, the sound of her laugh, the saucy way she had of speaking to him. Closing the door behind him, he went to run a bath. First things first: wash the road dust off himself. His saddle bags were sitting on the bed and a tray of food sat on the table. He took a glass of spring wine, sipping while his bath filled.

The warm water soothed his aches and, once in, he thought it would be hard to leave, but his mind was too active to relax. The hot water seemed to draw all his fatigue to the surface. So long on the road, worry, fear...His heart leapt at the thought of traversing the Crystal Gate, of leaving his home. He was not as brave as Sophy. He recollected how well she had adjusted to the new surroundings of Argenterra. While she did not have a good time at first, she rarely complained or talked of her home with any regret.

He knew that bringing Sophy back was not going to solve most of the problems in his life, but it would seal the wound of his heart, knowing she was safe either in her world or back here with him. Not that Argenterra was the same anymore. Would Sophy notice? He closed his eyes and opened himself to the world. The *given* was so much less, but it was not gone completely. That surprised him. He had thought it would run out of the land like the water in his tub when he pulled the plug. But it had not. Not yet. Perhaps there was hope, after all.

After towelling dry, he picked at the food on the tray. Salted meat and toffelbread baked with honey, and fresh fruit and cheese. It was better than the fare on the road, but still did not overly tempt his appetite. He ate because he had to. If tomorrow brought him the summoning of the Crystal Gate and Sophy, then he needed his strength—emotional and physical.

In some ways he wondered if this was a test. Vorn had been tested, and he and the First Comers had sworn the binding oath. Perhaps the people of Argenterra were being tested again. Their ease in the *given* had been withdrawn. The Puri had invaded, taking all they wished for. But the Puri had never been rich in the *given*. Oakheart considered the why of that, for surely it was not accidental. The forest folk had their heart tree, a gift from Vorn. Why did the Puri not have the equivalent?

Why did they live in the wastelands, where water and food were scarce? He did not think the issue was with Vorn—he could see no fault in Argenterra's founding king. But how about Adage? He had lived from those early times. Had there been some age-old grudge? It made his chest ache just thinking about it. He had revered Adage; to think him the cause of what they were suffering now was painful. And he had not the time nor the means now to research and discover further.

He chewed his bottom lip as he thought things through. No Puri were adepts, nor did they even study at the retreat to become one. That made little sense to him now that he thought about it. Things had to change and the retreat was part of the answer. Maybe he should confirm that now...The bed looked comfortable. Maybe he could broach the subject with Lianal before he left. Best to do it then, for what if he did not return? Then the thought would be lost. He should be more positive, but that stomach-churning fear of leaving his home still roiled within him.

His dreams were full of Sophy. Sometimes filled with them making love. Then the images would shift and Sophy was calling his name. Danger pierced the images of her. Nothing he could do would clear his mind, shift the dream, ameliorate his despair.

Near morning, his dreams settled somewhat and he was able to direct them to a more pleasant course: Sophy's warm body up close, safe by his side. Just when he was getting cosy with this dream, a knock at the door made him sit up. "Come."

Leoff opened the door a fraction and spoke through the gap. "If you desire it, I have ordered some breakfast for you. I have alerted River to our intended visit to the library so we have time for you to eat and get ready. River is himself only just waking up after a late night in study."

"Thank you."

After Leoff closed the door, Oakheart got up and dug in his pack for fresh clothes. Despite the dreams, he was well rested. He pulled on breeches, shirt and then a leather vest. He would put on the rest of his apparel before he left. His sword remained in its scabbard as he did not need it for the visit to Adept River.

A delivery of hot bread rolls, sweet jam and toffelporridge filled out his hollow belly. All too soon Leoff appeared at the door: it was time. He took a deep breath, not quite believing how soon he might see the gate and go looking for Sophy.

Down the stairs they walked into the lower levels of the retreat to the library. A few adepts were in there, quietly copying out of books or reading. An old man with long silver hair and a beard to match came forwards and bowed. "You must be Oakheart."

Oakheart bowed. "Yes, I am. Pleased to meet you. I do not think we have met." He peered at River, who was perhaps the oldest man he had seen. Adage did not count due to his young appearance.

"No, I have been gone from the retreat for many years. I was living in Glasshiver, searching for..." He shrugged and grimaced. "Knowledge is probably the best word, and have only recently returned."

Oakheart nodded, noting the man had an accent, the gift perhaps of living in a far-off place. At any other time he would have been fascinated by the adept's adventures and would have quizzed him. He had not ventured to Glasshiver himself but he had met representatives from that land. Their involvement in Argenterra's present troubles worried him greatly.

"I understand you have found instruction on how to summon the Crystal Gate?" Oakheart said, corralling back conversation to his main purpose.

The older man's long silver hair fluttered with his movement. He acknowledged Adept Leoff with a smile full of warmth. Walking back to his desk, he reached down to a large, heavy book. "I studied with Adage when I was younger. When I returned to the retreat and Lianal asked for assistance, I remembered this book." He flipped open a few pages. "See here."

Oakheart had followed him and now leant over and saw drawings of the Crystal Gate. The base was constructed of two small boxes on either side of the arch. The arch itself looked like light and crystal together, with tiny fractures and cracks like a deformed glass construction. "That's the Crystal Gate," Oakheart said. "Is there more?" He narrowed his gaze, looking at the handwriting. Although it was hard to read, he recognised the style of Vorn's writing, his words. A gasp escaped him. "Vorn wrote this!"

The old man peered up and Oakheart's face. "Yes, Vorn wrote of the gate. It was how he brought the First Comers here. It appears he had knowledge of the mechanism before he fled Yulandir."

"It is well known that Vorn used the gate to come here, although there is nothing written about his prior knowledge of the gate. What I want to know is, did he leave instructions on how to summon it?" Oakheart was brusque.

The old adept lifted his face, shock leaving his mouth open.

Oakheart swiped a lock of hair from his forehead. "Forgive my rudeness," he said as he squared his shoulders, fighting for calm. Adept Leoff tilted his head to the side, but nodded to Oakheart with a reassuring smile. "Much is at stake. I need to act quickly if I am to assist my father in Silverdale and I am desperate to use the gate to find my wife. I have come a long way, risked much. Time is short. All I want to know is: can you help me?"

The old man's mouth closed and he nodded. "I believe so." He ran his finger down the page. "I have one more paragraph to translate then I think the instructions will be complete."

"You think? You mean you do not know for certain?"

The old man gaped at Oakheart. "Nothing is certain in this world. In all the worlds, if you must know. I am confident that we will succeed. You will have to trust me. The gate will either answer the summons, or it won't."

Oakheart clenched his fist. He did not want to hit the old adept but he felt like striking something. "How long before we know?"

River lifted his shoulder. "This afternoon, perhaps. If I am left alone to translate. Vorn's writing can be difficult and these terms are difficult to understand. I have to consult the old dictionaries, you understand." He smiled at Oakheart. "You have time to take your ease and prepare for your journey. Once begun, the summoning does not take long."

"Truly? How do you know that?"

"From what it says here." River pointed to a paragraph and some scrawled notes he had made on a loose leaf. "Vorn left it operational...I think he says automatic...so that it comes at certain intervals without being called. That is why it comes now and then. I have not charted it myself, but it appears from the records to be at regular intervals. However, the intervals are not aligned with Argenterran time, which is why the gate appears less predictable."

"And Daken was able to summon it."

"No, just predict its arrival. I found some of his notes in the back of this volume." River tapped the book. "Vorn set it as a precaution so that people trapped between worlds could come here. You see, he speaks of the animals and the plants and the birds that came through the gate. Some with the First Comers, and some on their own."

Oakheart looked down at the page. There were drawings of animals, some familiar to him. "Horses." He outlined the drawing with a finger. "Sophy said there were horses on her world too." It touched him to know that they had that small sliver of connection.

Adept River bowed his head. "Vorn speaks of many wonders."

"I am sure he does."

"In these days it would be best to stop the Crystal Gate from coming of its own volition, this 'automatic', Vorn speaks of. Then we can use the gate when required, if say, we were ever required to flee these lands."

Oakheart's gut clenched and his reply was rather abrupt. "I pray that it will never come to that!" *Flee Argenterra, my home?* It did not bear thinking about. "You say we can summon it and I can leave. Are you sure I will be able to come back again?"

River considered him, pulling his bottom lip with a finger as he considered his answer. "Yes, I believe that is what it describes in this last paragraph. How to control the gate at the other side, how to hold it there." He tapped the book. "Go now and rest. Tomorrow we will begin."

Oakheart touched the elder adept's arm. "Thank you. I will ready myself."

Oakheart found it very hard to rest, to take his mind off his pending journey. He had packed and unpacked his knapsack. He had dressed his arms in leather vambraces and taken his sword to the grinder to be sharpened. He had performed gentle exercises to ease the stiffness from his travel-sore body. He had visited his horses and set the two men who followed him to practise their battle skills, urging them to be ready for his return. Books that had been favourites of his held no appeal; he was unable to relax enough to engage with the words. Time flowed so slowly as he waited for Adept River to complete his translation.

Lunch did not tempt him either beyond keeping hunger pains away. Eating had become a mechanical action, rather than something he enjoyed. His thoughts were centred solely on Sophy. Some thoughts were dire. What if she was happy in her home world and did not want him anymore? Closing his eyes, he knew he would simply have to accept that. What if she was dead, killed by Rufus? His heart lurched just contemplating that. What if her danger was still present? It had been so long. Would she understand, and forgive, his delay?

Leoff approached his table in the nearly deserted refectory and Oakheart leapt to his feet. "Is it time? Do you have news?"

Leoff smiled fleetingly. "No on both counts. Do you mind if I join you?"

"What is it?" Oakheart did not think the adept chose his company for pleasure.

"There has been some news from Silverdale."

Oakheart's fists clenched. "And?" He kept his gaze fixed on the younger man.

"Your father is alive but captive. We had this news from Hanal himself."

"Hanal used the talkstone?"

Leoff nodded, his face held a sombre expression. "There's more: Hanal demands your presence."

Oakheart sat up straighter. "Hanal wants me in Silverdale? But I am here..."

"Yes. Soon to leave us. Hanal wants confirmation that you are on your way to Silverdale."

Oakheart chewed his bottom lip. "By the *given*, how did he know I was here? 'Tis like being caught in a vice." Oakheart chewed his lip as he gripped his hands together. "Any more information?"

"From what we know, your force has made it to the By-way leading to the Upper Plateau. They have not managed to climb it. There have been a few," he shrugged as he decided on a word, "altercations."

"My mother?"

Leoff grinned. "Is holding a tight rein on your forces. But I believe only your presence will provide them what they need to ascend. If you gather my meaning."

Oakheart nodded. "If I am with them, Hanal will allow me up the By-way. He wants hostages, leverage, someone to use against my father. I wonder if he knows my mother leads the forces. Possibly he cannot credit it as she has been absent for so long."

"Yes. Lianal suggested as much." Leoff lowered his head and breathed deeply. Lifting his head, he met Oakheart's gaze. "Unless there is another way to break the impasse."

"Or stall for time. Mother will need to send an envoy to Hanal. Not herself, but someone with connections to the high king. Please tell her I suggest she sends Fern Ripplebark. She already knows our preferred bargaining position regarding Fern."

Leoff nodded. "I will pass your words onto Lianal. What shall we tell them about your movements...your intentions..."

"Does Hanal actually know I am here? Did Lianal confirm my presence?"

Leoff shook his head. "He just said he would pass on the message."

Oakheart stood up and walked away, thinking hard. "So I have some time, some time to manoeuvre."

Leoff stood also. "What time do you have, your excellency?"

Oakheart considered. "More time than I thought I had." When Leoff's expression grew puzzled, he added, "If he does not know I am here yet, then I have some leeway."

Leoff's eyes widened as understanding blossomed. "I see."

"Ask Lianal to speak again to Hanal after I pass through. He is to advise Hanal that I am not here but as soon as I arrive he will pass on my message. That way he will speak true in case there are spies here."

Leoff let out a pent-up breath. "That is by far a better plan. None at the retreat would betray you to the Puri." He bowed. "I will leave you to your noon-tide meal." His eyes drifted to the plate with half-eaten food arrayed on it. "Is the food not to your liking?"

Oakheart shrugged. "The food is fine. It is my appetite that is not good."

"You should try to eat more, Oakheart. Who knows how long your trip will take and what supplies there will be." He lifted a hand. "I know. I will have some food packed for you. Just in case."

Oakheart smiled. "Thank you for the thought." His gut clenched again. He was hoping to go through the gate and come back in a very short time, an hour, maybe two. The thought of leaving Argenterra for longer than that filled him with terror. It was as if he would lose his connection to his home if he left it. Why did he think that? Maralain. Yes, that was what was on his mind. She came back different: disconnected, a stranger. Even her speech was affected. She sounded so much like Sophy it hurt.

Not long after, before he had sunk himself into even more morose thoughts, Leoff came back at a run. "It is time."

Oakheart surged to his feet. "Adept River?"

"Yes."

Oakheart followed the young adept down to the library, walking so fast he nearly trod on the man's flowing robes. When they entered, Adept River was seated as his desk, chewing on a pencil as he studied Vorn's writings. He pursed his lips and did not look up at their approach.

"Adept River?" Oakheart said softly, not wanting to startle a man so deep in thought.

Silver eyebrows rose and dark eyes fixed on him. "Ah, you are here." He tapped the page. "It is done. Now you must see if it makes sense to you."

Oakheart dropped into the seat Leoff procured for him and drew the book towards him. "See here. This is the summoning. It should work easily enough. Holding the gate in place when you are through requires Vorn, or should I say Vorn's blood. You, I understand, are well favoured in this regard."

Oakheart looked up. "'Tis tied to the blood?"

"Yes." Adept River did not hold Oakheart's gaze and looked down. "Vorn speaks of it being linked. The terms he uses are arcane and have no meaning to us in this day. But yes, the gate is tied to his blood."

A terrible thought occurred to Oakheart. Something his mother had said about breeding. Was he, and Aria too, the result of some machinations of the retreat for this purpose? To use Vorn's technology?

He studied the old man, looking for signs of knowing or guilt. A flush to the old man's cheeks gave him pause. "Is this...Is this deliberate?"

River's head jerked up. "Is what deliberate?"

"The amount of Vorn's blood in me. My kinship to the first high king?"

The old man pursed his lips and studied him. "I cannot say. The link to Vorn, as you know, has always been prized. Many are his descendants. It would be expected the royal house would have more blood passed on than any other. Is that not so?"

Oakheart nodded, but he could not wipe away that feeling, that knowing. Was his mother right? Did Adage have ulterior motives? It was hard to believe, as Adage was Vorn's grandson. That meant he had a quarter of Vorn's blood in him. Oakheart did a quick reckoning. He himself had nearly half, perhaps more. Vorn's blood mixed over time, his pedigree strengthened, perhaps his outlander grandmother had diluted the mix. Outlander blood was prized as new blood.

He shook himself. Now was not the time to repine for what was past. He was what he was. "No matter how it came about, I am glad my blood is to be useful."

"With it you should be able to control the gate."

"You say 'should' be able to hold the gate in place? It worries me that you do not know for certain. What if I cannot? Will I be able to summon it again?"

River wiped some sweat from his brow as he reread his notes, nodding and whispering to himself. "I think...I believe so."

A chill wormed into Oakheart's chest. Fear, clear and true. "By the *given*, am I to sacrifice everything to retrieve Sophy?" He said this to himself, forgetting for the moment he had an audience. Adept River did not respond. Staring into space, Oakheart grappled with his greatest fear—losing his home, his connection to Argenterra—and lost track of time.

"Oakheart? Oakheart..." Leoff was shaking him by the shoulder.

Oakheart refocussed. "Forgive me. I was lost in thought. What you say, though, is not good enough. The risk of failure is too much to bear. If you cannot be sure that I can control the gate from the other side, we need a back-up plan."

Adept River, who had been studying him, inclined his head. "Certainly...although I am fairly sure..."

"Spare me your guesses. I am grateful for your help, but pray do not gamble with my life and my tenure in Argenterra. My father needs me. Our people need me."

Leoff interjected, "Could we not control the gate from here, if you fail to return? Or could you send another person through in your place?"

Oakheart grimaced. "If you can control the gate from here, this would be a good failsafe. I would just need to be in the vicinity on the far side when you sent the gate to me. Alas, for the other suggestion, I can send no other in my stead. Sophy is my oathbound wife. My responsibility...and..." He looked away for a moment. "I have to know for myself if she is safe and if she wishes to return with me. Please understand."

Leoff nodded. "I can see that it is important to you."

They both turned to stare at the old adept expectantly.

Adept River was deeply engrossed in his study of Vorn's document. Oakheart cleared his throat when the old man did not look at them. "If, say, I am not back within a day, can you summon the gate and send it to me?"

The old adept looked up suddenly, his eyes widened. "Send the gate to wherever you are?" His face screwed up in thought while he ran through his notes, mumbling away. At last he looked up, face still lined with the effort of concentration. "We can summon the gate to come here. That much is certain. But you would need to call it from wherever you are." He rummaged on the desk and found a slip of parchment. "See," he said tapping on it. "You use this incantation."

Oakheart tore off a piece of paper and scribbled down the words.

They did not mean anything to him so they were going to be hard to memorise. "You think this will work? Surely you can send it to me."

"No. You would have to wait for the cycle to bring the gate to you. From what I understand, your blood link to the gate will allow it to answer your summons from anywhere in these realms." He shoved a map in front of him. "This is where we are now. This is a link to Sophy's world, where Daken took your mother. The gate regularly travels between these places. He did not need Vorn's blood to summon the gate. He had only to wait for its next appearance. Judging by these notes that he made, he had calculated when that was."

"So when my mother returned it was with the regular appearance of the Crystal Gate. That is why they took so long."

Adept River grimaced and then cocked his head, apparently thinking. Then after a pause he said, "I imagine if Daken knew he could have summoned it with your mother's blood, he would have done so as soon as your sister disappeared."

Oakheart agreed. His mother had said she knew nothing of the workings of the gate and Adept River had swept any lingering doubt away. He pointed at another place on the map. "And what is that place?"

"That is Yulandir. Vorn's homeworld."

"And these others?"

"They are not mentioned by name. From what I can gather they were never visited by Vorn but he believed others who joined him here came from those worlds."

"So I have two choices. How do I make the gate go to the place I require?"

"After you say the words, you add this to your incantation for Sophy's homeworld: Verdanterra. For Yulandir, you say the name Yulandir."

"And to return?"

"If you are in contact with the gate, say Argenterra."

Oakheart nodded. It seemed straightforward enough.

"How do I hold the gate in place?"

Adept River smiled. "You ask it to stay." He pointed at the

incantation that Oakheart had written down. "Use those words without a destination and it will stay put."

Oakheart swallowed a great gulp of fear. This was it.

"Where will you go first?" Leoff asked him.

Oakheart looked up. Maralain had told him of Verdanterra. It was full of people, and if Sophy was not near the gate, it would take days, maybe weeks to locate her. Even though he had her instructions on how to get to Sophy's home town, it would take precious time. Yulandir, however, was a dead world, and therefore uninhabited. Finding Sophy should be more straightforward. If Sophy was not there, then he would know that she had gone home to her world. "Yulandir."

Adept River sucked in a breath, his eyes wide. "You choose to go to Vorn's homeworld—the Deadlands? Even Vorn never ventured there after establishing Argenterra."

"Do you mean he went to Verdanterra?"

"Apparently, he did. He brought things back with him. People maybe, animals and seeds perhaps. The record is not clear. Although it was not stated clearly, it was implied that he created the wanderer, the passageway between worlds that brings women to Crystal Tree Woods."

Oakheart's heart leapt. If Vorn could travel between worlds, so could he. Then his mind turned to what else Adept River said. If Vorn created the wanderer then Sophy coming to Argenterra was part of his plan. Did Vorn's vision extend that far? He put those thoughts aside. He had to think about retrieving Sophy. "We should begin now. I want to leave right away."

Adept River pushed up from his feet and Leoff went to aid him, for the old man moved carefully and slowly. When he was standing, he looked hard at Oakheart. "Then get your things and I will meet you at the place where the gate appears."

Leoff bowed. "I offer my arm with pleasure."

Oakheart squeezed the man's bony shoulder gently. "Thank you. I owe you for all your hard labour. If there is anything I can do for you then please ask."

Adept River smiled feebly at Leoff. "I will need your assistance to make it to the place where the gate appears." Then the old adept placed his hand over Oakheart's. "Just tell me all that you see. I will write it down. It will add much to our knowledge of Yulandir. And if perchance Sophy is not there and you must go to Verdanterra, the same applies. All that you see and hear. Remember?

"I will."

❧ 24 ❧

## ON THE LINE

**A**ria did not have time to get caught. Many times, they had hidden in the scrub along the trail, trying to avoid wandering Puri. Some of these were large family groups with women and children, others were bands of armed men. Right now, she was hiding again and it annoyed her. She hitched her arm up higher in the sling. She'd been hit by an arrow two days before. A flesh wound, but it hurt like hell and there was no healing bark in their packs. Their supply had been used when Leyla had gashed her leg in the woods when they were making a run from a band of Puri two weeks ago.

Leyla came up behind her. "You see anything?"

"No, but that doesn't mean there isn't anyone there."

Leyla peered through the leaves obscuring their path. "I will go around and whistle an all-clear. You stay here."

Aria nodded as she bit her bottom lip. She wished they still had their horses, but out of the Valley and on the road they were too conspicuous. That had been their first mistake, going too fast and blundering into their first entanglement with Puri raiders. It was only their use of the *given* as a weapon that had saved them. Aria had been afraid. The way the men had tried to drag Leyla off and the things they said to each other made her stomach clench. This did not match the tales Rae had told of the Puri people. Their behaviour was certainly not honourable.

Aria hunkered down and listened to the wind rustling the leaves and branches around her, masking the sound of Leyla making her way. Aria's gaze flicked here and there as she hitched her pack onto her good shoulder.

Soon, a whistle sounded. It was the signal Leyla had devised. Aria rose and, hunched over to keep below the line of the bushes, she pushed through the undergrowth. *At this rate we will never make Silverdale.*

A thump behind made her turn. In surprise, she fell backwards, tripping on her own feet. Hands dragged at her. She tried to call out, struggled against those who tried to subdue her. It happened so fast. Hitting, kicking, biting. Before she could summon the *given*, a sharp pain in her head made everything go black.

❧

ARIA WOKE IN A TENT. SENSING SHE WAS NOT ALONE, SHE OPENED her eyes to just slits and saw there was a figure next to her. She repositioned herself as her arm pained her and realised that her hands were unbound. *Not a prisoner?* She sat up suddenly.

"Aria?" It was Leyla. "Vorn's blood! I was so worried. They said you struggled and were accidentally knocked out."

Aria grabbed her hand. "That was no accident." She rubbed the spot on her head. It was sore to the touch. "Where are we? Who has us?"

"One of Oakheart's patrols."

*Oakheart!* She let out a **whoosh**. Before she could ask more questions, Leyla went on. "They took us quickly and a little brutally because we were walking into a trap. You have been out for a whole day and night." Leyla frowned. "I have been beside myself with worry. Are you sure you are all right? Do you want to eat?"

Aria lay back down. "Oakheart's patrol? Then we are there. I gather Oakheart is not with them?" Her newly discovered brother would have been there for her on waking, she was sure. A wave of dizziness washed over her and she put a hand to her head. A sharp pain and a thudding headache.

"Not quite there. This is a rear patrol. I am not sure exactly where we are, but we are two or three days behind the main force." Leyla poured some broth that was simmering on a small stove into a bowl and passed it to her. "You better drink this. You look so pale."

Aria struggled to sit up again and closed her eyes as the tent spun. Leyla waited patiently until Aria took the bowl and sipped from the rim. After a few sips, her stomach settled and she felt refreshed. She drank off the rest then handed back the near-empty bowl. "I need to use the bathroom."

Leyla got up. "I will show you the way and introduce you to the commander."

Aria climbed to her feet with the assistance of Leyla and then tried to tame her unruly and very dirty curls. She realised there was dried blood in her hair. Leyla glanced at her as she fingered her hair.

"I do not think the facilities in this camp extend to a bath. But perhaps when we join the main camp? They have carts full of equipment. I cannot imagine your mother going without a bath."

Aria winced as she sniffed. The tent concentrated her body odour. She sniffed again and realised Leyla was a bit ripe too. "Privy first. Then we'll deal with cleanliness. They should at least be able to find a basin of hot water."

THAT NIGHT THEY HUDDLED UNDER BLANKETS IN THE TENT SHE'D woken in. With Leyla and Kern, the commander of this squad of men, for company, they sat facing each other. It was too risky for a fire outside in the night. "Princess," Kern said. "I am so relieved you are finally awake. Believe me when I say your injury was accidental. I am so glad we have found you."

Aria fingered the lump on her head. "Did it have to be so hard?"

He gestured towards her head. "I apologise—the need for quiet, you see."

Aria grimaced. So much for accidental, but there was no use in recriminations. She was not permanently damaged. At least, she hoped not. Her thought processes appeared to be rational and her body functional. "No need to apologise. I completely understand. How soon can you get us to the main camp? To Oakheart and my mother?"

"The Argent Flow is nigh on impossible to cross. It is risky for one such as yourself..."

Her eyes widened.

Seeing her expression, he cleared his throat before continuing. "We have established guidelines and a pulley system. People can cross. Some supplies. But not larger items, such as carts or horses."

Aria sat back. "Are you saying that because I am a woman?"

Kern was very blond with deep-set blue eyes, almost always in the shadow of his prominent brow. He gaped at her and then glanced to Leyla, almost leaping out of his seat. "No, my lady, it is because of who you are. A valuable person...em...important...If anything happened to you, well I..."

"Oh, that's okay." She waved a hand and he settled down. "I take it the alternative will add more time to our journey?"

"Yes, the Lake of Reflections. We think the barge that is used for crossing the lake is in Puri hands, anyway."

"Then we have no choice. You must get me across the Argent Flow."

"Could you not wait on this side of the river, my lady? We could take you to one of the well-guarded towns, like Mistletoe or Triversmeet. Until the battle is won."

"What? No! I'm not waiting it out here. I am going to do my bit with my mother and my brother." She nodded to Leyla, who gave an acknowledging nod.

Kern's cheeks reddened. "As you wish. If the way is clear, we will leave in the morning." He stood up, bending his head because of the tent roof. There were voices outside. "If you will excuse me, my patrol has returned. Sleep well." He bowed his head to her and swept open the tent flap to leave.

Aria stared at the exit for a moment and bit her lip. Turning to Leyla, she asked, "That is all right with you, isn't it? Crossing the Argent Flow? I'm sorry I forgot to ask you first."

Leyla laughed softly. "Yes, my lady. I will go where you go. Although I hear the water is chillingly cold. If we were to fall..."

It took a day and a half to reach the Argent Flow. There was a rudimentary camp established on the river banks, with a perimeter of guards to protect the only access to the upper lands and the supply route for Oakheart's and her mother's forces.

Aria paled when she eyed the contraption for crossing the river. The water surged and churned menacingly close to where the drooping ropes allowed people to reach the other side.

"It is better than it looks," Kern advised with a grin. "We use horses to pull the ropes taut. You may get wet feet, but that is all."

Leyla stood with arms crossed. She wore trousers and a borrowed tunic that hung limply around her thighs. Aria also wore borrowed clothes. She felt dowdy and a little cold.

Kern signalled to the other bank and ropes were attached to horses. He addressed them. "Who will go first?"

Aria detected a challenge in his tone. "I will."

"My lady, perhaps I should go first." Leyla frowned at the water, the foam bubbling like a cauldron.

"No. I can do this. Besides, I might chicken out if I have to watch you do it first."

The horse on their side of the bank was led away from the river at a walking pace. The pulley squeaked and the ropes purred as they ran through the contraption. Kern and one of the men who managed the crossing assisted Aria into the harness. It wasn't really a harness, more like a place to rope her hands to that she couldn't let go.

"How long does it take to cross?" she asked, pulling on the harness to test it. Being dangled by the arms was going to hurt. A lot.

"Not too long." Kern said as he inspected her grip. "Hold on as long as you can. It will make things easier on you."

Aria managed a smile. Already she could feel the rope pull against her weight. "Thank you for the advice. Are you joining us?"

Kern shook his head. "Once you and the adept are across the river we will return to our patrol."

"Oh! Well thank youuuu...." The pulley jerked her up and away. In the next minute her feet were dangling above the water. Splashes wet her trouser legs and soon her boots were soaking wet and her toes grew numb. Another jerk and she was drawn farther out over the water. Her muscles pulled, her shoulder ached. The wound in her arm tore open. Feeling the blood trickle down, she bit down on a moan. She had to prove she was up to this: no screaming allowed. Letting go wasn't an option, nor was begging to be let off the thing. She thought about Sophy who would have thought nothing of swinging on a line to cross a river. She clenched her teeth and bore through the pain. She had to be made of sterner stuff. These people looked up to her. She had to be brave. As brave as Oakheart and his men. Braver even, because she was a woman.

For the last few minutes she kept her eyes closed as the transfer played out. She knew it wouldn't be long but the pain was terrible. It felt as if it was never going to end. Next thing she knew hands grabbed for her and took her weight. Her shoulders and her upper arms throbbed and pain snaked up into her jaw. Tears welled in her eyes. Then she was free of the pulley, huddled on the ground while they sent it back for Leyla. Aria saw nothing, curved around herself, curved around her pain, waiting in silence for it to lessen, waiting to join the rest of those gathered. Her predicament went unnoticed and she wanted to wait it out until she could ride over the pain and regain her composure. Those around her were caught up in transporting Leyla across and by the time the young adept joined her on the ground, Aria was more in control of herself. Her shoulder still hurt, but the bleeding had lessened with the benefit of her hand clasped tight over it.

A young man knelt beside her. "My lady? There is blood on your sleeve."

Aria glanced up at him. His hair was red like hers and his face was covered in freckles. He had wide brown eyes. "I had an injury. It opened up while I was crossing the Argent Flow."

"My name is Filbert. I will fetch the physic. It should be bound up again." His eyes were round with concern.

"Thank you. Maybe a drink of water, too, if you please. For me and my maid."

Filbert nodded and ran off.

Leyla and one of the armsmen, who had helped them cross, carried Aria to a tent where she was placed on a pallet.

The water and the physic, Holbrook, arrived at the same time. The slash of light into the tent as the door flap opened made Aria's eyes hurt. The physician set about attending to her. Aria sat with her mouth closed tight as the wound was stitched. It stung, and the needle tugged, and all she could think about was that it would be over soon. She just had to hold on: it would be over. Healing bark was not available at the rear of Oakheart's column. It was up front, closer to the battle lines. Aria would have some soon.

Panting and trying not to cry out, Aria bore up until Leyla fetched her some strong wine. After sipping some wine she lay down, suddenly faint.

"We should rest here until you feel better," Leyla said as she drew a blanket over Aria.

"I don't think I'm ever going to feel better."

"Surely it was not that bad. Your wound will heal."

"I meant this war business and the loss of the *given* and poor Sophy. The whole situation is making hope leak out of my heart."

"And anger?"

"Anger?"

"Yes, anger for all that has been done to you, to the land, to your friend."

Aria sat back and stared at the ceiling of the tent. She did feel anger, but it was buried so deep inside her she couldn't touch it. A lifetime of suppressing anger. Just the same as suppressing tears. Why was that so? Why was it wrong for a woman to express these feelings?

"I'm angry, Leyla. When the time comes I'll be ready to direct it in the right quarter." She opened her eyes and gazed at the adept. "Except I don't know what the right quarter is."

Leyla lowered her gaze. "I see your dilemma. Usually we think of the Ancient Evil as the focus of our anger, but Argenterra has blessed us so that we let that anger slip through our fingers. The Puri, though, they have kept hold of theirs. They have nursed it like a child at the breast, a slowly roasting rage. They understand anger more than any Argenterran can. They are here to teach us the meaning of it. To let us know anger, fear, frustration and, most of all, sorrow."

Aria pulled at her bottom lip. "You sound sympathetic to the Puri."

Leyla shrugged and looked away.

"Why?" Aria persisted.

Leyla turned back, eyes ablaze. "At the retreat we live so close to the Puri, but I wondered why there were no Puri amongst the adepts. They can use the *given* like us. Surely one of them wants to study."

"And?"

"I asked." She looked down her fingers absently. "I was told that they were not welcome. Not now. Not ever."

Aria crinkled her forehead. "And in the past?"

Leyla shook her head. "Not a one."

Aria considered this. She'd only had Dellbright's point of view and he hated the Puri. But the retreat, too? Hints and clues slid into place. The Puri were the hated other. Her heart faltered at the thought. Just like her own world, or the world she was born into. Argenterra was meant to be her home, after all, but even it wasn't perfect, despite the potential to be so. Why was there always someone that a community or group of people despised? Had the Puri not been amongst the First Comers? Surely they had moved beyond history. Those living in the present were not being held accountable for actions of those in the past?

"It is part of the history of this place, isn't it? Something that seems like it has always been so but it was some act, some decision way back when that has just been repeated over and over and now no one knows why."

Leyla pursed her lips and nodded. "Yes. I fear it is so."

"Then we must do something about this before something more dreadful happens."

Leyla smiled. "I had a feeling you would say that. Shall I prepare some supplies?"

"Yes, we shall leave in the morning to catch up to the lead group."

Aria lay back down, suddenly exhausted. "First we must speak to Oakheart and my mother. Then we will take steps."

Leyla smiled. "Oakheart and your mother are on our way. No detours involved."

"Good." Aria closed her eyes and let sleep take her.

❧

Aria made the lead group in good time. The physician there had had treated her arm with healing bark and she had the opportunity for food and rest before she saw anybody. Lucky for her she had taken the time to see to her needs. Right then, she stood with arms folded across her chest as she faced her mother in her tent, her chin held proudly.

Maralain turned around, the long skirt of her robes in a swirl about her. "What do you mean you left Dellbright?"

Aria's jaw clenched. "He did not keep his bargain."

"He sent us men. He let you see the child."

"The child I saw was not my son." She lifted her chin higher and met her mother's angry gaze. "He tried to rape me."

Maralain scoffed. "What of your maid? She was dispatched to keep you safe."

Aria shook her head. "Mother, Leyla did what she could. He did not injure me, but there was no reason to stay, not when I can help here."

"But he's Jeff's son."

Aria shook her head, tears welling. She understood that her mother wanted to believe the man she had loved was born again in his son. But it was not so. Her actions had changed Dellbright forever. Rufus had twisted him. There could be no resurrecting their marriage.

"...but he's not Jeff."

Tears rolled down Maralain's cheeks and the sight of them twisted Aria's heart. But she wasn't going back to Dellbright and she wasn't going to be made to feel guilty about that decision.

"But you chose him. No one forced you to marry him."

"I know. I should've listened to Sophy."

"Sophy? What does she know about love and marriage? Her parents were a mess. Her mother abandoned her."

"Exactly. She could see more clearly than I."

"But, Dellbright..."

"Mother! There is no way of making the relationship work. Your arranged marriage didn't work for you. You had twenty years with Daken. You were lucky, not everyone has that. A love match will not always work out either."

Her mother sat down. "It seemed like a perfect idea. So handsome..."

"Let it go. Let Dellbright go. I want to help here."

"Help?" Maralain swiped at her cheek, swatting at the tears. She turned an angry eye on Aria. "What can you do?"

Aria exhaled slowly, her chest aching as she hadn't realised she had been holding her breath. She was prepared to be sympathetic to her mother, but she wasn't going to be squashed into someone else's expectation of her. She'd grown up a lot since she lived with Maralain on Earth. Her mother wasn't wise to this yet; it wasn't going to be easy for her. Not with everything else going on, but Aria couldn't afford to wait for a better time to show her steel. She took a deep breath, letting her own anger wane. Obviously, there was something going on here. Her mother was not usually so obtuse as to argue and throw barbs of spite.

"Where's Oakheart?" Aria took a seat on a stool, now noticing that her mother's tent was less than neat. It spoke of a disordered mind.

Maralain growled. "He has gone after Sophy and left me in charge of his fighting force." She paced back and forth. "He wouldn't listen to reason. He said he'd come back but he hasn't yet. Why would he not believe that Sophy is safe and well at home?"

"Because he can't believe she'd leave him. She loves him and he her. Is that so strange to understand?"

Maralain paused and glanced at her. "Perhaps not so strange, but the Puri...the invasion."

"Are less important than him finding Sophy."

"Nonsense. Sophy can wait, but this situation can't. Hanal has responded to my request for parley. He wants Oakheart or me to go in person. Both of us if he can get us. My advisers are against that. I will be held hostage and our forces will be left leaderless."

"Then I'll go."

"You? You can't be serious." Her mother's face was full of surprise, mouth gaping, eyes wide. Her whole posture radiated disbelief.

"Deadly serious. I'm sick of sitting around, pretending to be a good wife when I can do much more than that. Let me negotiate with Hanal."

"But he will make you hostage."

"Let him. I am Veld's child, the same as Oakheart. I'm sure he must know this by now. Let me go to my true father and be a comfort to him. Let me take your terms. Hanal will listen to me. He must."

Maralain wrung her hands, her mouth tight with concern. "If only Oakheart were here." She started pacing again in the large tent.

Aria put herself in her mother's way, making sure she couldn't avoid looking at her. "I am here. Use me. Trust me. We came this far to help. Don't stop me now."

"I can't let you."

"Then don't let me." Aria turned and stormed out of the tent. "Just don't try to stop me."

Leyla followed close behind. "My lady?"

"We're going. Now."

Leyla nodded and went to get their horses and supplies.

"Wait," Maralain called as she came out of her tent. "I will tell you the agreed bargaining position. Then you can go with my blessing. Do me proud, Daughter."

Maralain was alone. Totally alone. Oakheart was off rescuing Sophy and Aria was off to bargain for Argenterra. It was what she deserved. She blinked away her tears as she walked back to her tent. *Oh Jeff, I never knew it would be like this. I didn't think. I didn't anticipate. My decision ended you, ended us.*

Maralain had been young, in love and her passion was everything. The handsome prince had not been her husband but he had filled her with desire and longing. His kisses had tantalised her. His mouth could do wonderful things. Things her husband didn't know or understand. Veld had intercourse with her, but he wasn't a lover, not like Jeff had been—totally devoted to her and her pleasure.

Veld was her husband, her duty. She was angry with him. Angry that she had married Veld before she met Jeff. Before then, she hadn't known what true love was. Because of Argenterra, because of the *given* and its unbreakable vows, she suffered.

Her love for Jeff had grown indifference in her heart for Veld. She saw him as oafish, and stupid and clumsy. Her son, though, had been the light of her life.

She sobbed into her blankets as the memories swamped her. She could never repair the damage. Oakheart was what he was because of her, because of what she had done to him.

And now Aria. Also a light of her life, so similar to her in many ways, denied her true heritage because of Maralain's decisions. Her choice, her lack of fortitude.

She'd had a great life with Jeff. A life filled with love and happiness. But the price, dear god, the price! The land she loved and cherished ripped apart.

Now, her eyes were open. She could see how her support could have strengthened Veld's reign and how her ideas could have moderated his. The what-ifs that Aria didn't want to talk about loomed large in her mind.

The troops deferred to her as queen and she cringed inwardly. It was a respect she didn't deserve. By the *given* she was going to do her best to deserve it.

Maralain may be flawed but she was going to do her best to put things right. And she would accept any punishment Veld saw fit. She deserved it.

✼ 25 ✼

# THE TRUTH BE TOLD

Rae had not heard from Hanal for two weeks. Nor had anyone come to take her for punishment, or take her child. It was strange. Food still arrived at regular intervals and every second day she was allowed out to walk the halls. Once or twice she encountered the high king and his sister.

"I cannot believe how well she looks, so rounded, so cuddly. May I?" Vola asked. She lifted Lien into her embrace. "My, how heavy she is. This little girl must have a healthy appetite."

Rae smiled, only slightly for her heart was heavy. The conversation with these prisoners was a highlight of her week, but she could not stop herself hoping and wishing that Hanal would come to see her, that he would tell her she was right. She was afraid he was too proud for that.

Veld looked down at the baby. "I wish I had seen my daughter when she was a baby." Lines of worry had carved themselves into his cheeks and his frame had lost some of its plumpness.

"I did not know you had a daughter," Rae said as she shook her daughter's little fist. Lien's eyes opened and she smiled at the older woman holding her.

"I did not know either until recently. You might have met her."

"Me?" Rae sat back, puzzled.

"Yes, she was thought to be one of the Gifts of Crystal Tree Woods. Aria is really my daughter. Imagine that. After all this time."

Rae frowned as her memories and thoughts rearranged. She recalled a discussion when Umri had said that Aria was an Argenterran. "But Aria did not know. Surely she would have said."

The old king looked at her and wiped his mouth with a kerchief. "She did not know. Not until her mother returned. Queen Mara is once again in Argenterra."

Rae's pulse raced. "Surely these are glad tidings. They are certainly profound."

Veld nodded and winked at her. "Certainly are."

"That means it is Sophy who is the Gift of Crystal Tree Woods. Although she is certainly the strangest one that I have ever heard tell of."

Veld nodded. "Strange girl with strange powers."

"Powers? Why, she has none...well, none that she can use. She is like a talisman. A tool for others to wield."

After a cough to clear his throat, Veld grimaced. "The poor girl has had a bad time, that is for certain." He looked around him and then back at Rae. "Then, none of us are having a merry time, either."

Rae nodded. Veld offered her watered wine and she drank it down, suddenly nervous. Did Hanal know about Aria? About Queen Mara being here? She thought he must by now. Lien began to cry and started sucking her fist.

"Time to feed her. Forgive me."

The royal siblings waved her away, with Vola giving her a cloth with still-warm griddle cakes inside. Nodding her thanks, Rae went back to her cell and fed her child.

What was she going to do? Should she seek another audience with Hanal? Did this news affect his position? As Lien suckled, she closed her eyes, willing her heart to cease its erratic beat. Should she? Dare she? There were risks. Reminding him of her presence could precipitate a punishment for treason. Or he might ignore her. Could she cope with that? If he did come, would he believe her? With her head back against the wall, the cool brick soothing her heated skin, she struggled with her options. She had to do it. She had to tell him.

If he already knew then well and good. No harm done.

When the guard came to deliver her next meal, she sent a request for Hanal to speak to her. The guard grunted.

"Please, just let him know I have some news for him. That is all. No pleas for favours or forgiveness. It is important."

The man shrugged his way out of her cell.

She had done it. Her ragged heart beat was distracting. Yet she had time to calm herself. He might not come. She had to accept that. Had no choice in the matter.

A SOFT LIGHT WOKE HER IN THE DARK OF NIGHT. RAE WAS NOT YET accustomed to being woken frequently to feed her child. Most of the time she was hung-over with sleep deprivation so it took her a few moments to digest the situation. The glare of the light, the fragrance of him, the soft shaking of her arm by his hot hands. Between half-dreaming and half-waking, she imagined his hot skin brushing against her back, her flanks, her face, and she groaned. Then snapped awake.

"Hanal?"

He rose from a crouch and backed out of the room, beckoning for her to follow. She hastily checked that Lien was comfortable and fast asleep and left her there on the mattress.

A small room was well lit against the night and she followed him there. He sat at a table, a pot of hot tea sending wisps of steam into the night. With a wave of his hand he indicated she should take a seat. It stuck her as strange that he was using Argenterran ways. Why were they using a table rather than a mat and cushions on the floor? What strange things were going on in his mind?

"You asked to see me." He poured tea for them.

Again, Rae was surprised. Perhaps he thought she would use the teapot as a weapon, hurl it at his head. Then she calmed her mind and tried to think. There was something else going on.

"Yes. I have news for you."

Hanal's head shot up and he gazed at her with his bright eyes, which glittered with reflected light. "News? From your cell? Pray has my daughter cut a first tooth already? Or has the texture of her motions changed? Is she ill, perchance? Do you require a physic?"

Appalled, Rae blanched at his mocking tone. "It has nothing to do with my daughter. She is no concern of yours."

Hanal took a sip of tea, appearing to be calm, but not succeeding. "You harp on as if you have some power here. You have none."

"I do not harp. Nor do I want power...only power over myself and my child. That is all I crave."

"You seek to chastise me. I warn you my patience grows thin. Tell me what news you have or I will have you returned to your cell."

Rae lifted her cup and took a sip. It was a good brew, smoky and strong—a Puri blend that reminded her of the wastes and camp fires. "Let me finish this excellent tea first before you send me away."

She opened her eyes to find him staring at her, a faint smile on his face. She blinked and then all trace of indulgence was gone from his face.

"Aria," she began, "...it appears that she is the high king's daughter. This is why she bears the mark of the binding oath. Why she can use the *given*."

"Curious..." He sat back and rubbed his chin with a thumb and forefinger.

"You already know?"

He shrugged and shook his head and then lifted his gaze to hers. "Not exactly. There is an Aria at the barrier to the By-way who claims to be Princess Aria, daughter to Veld. She wishes to parley with me in lieu of her brother Oakheart."

"The high king told me she was his daughter."

He shook his head at the ceiling. "You are so gullible. Veld tells you something and you believe it. Do you think they do not know you tell me everything? That you are my spy?"

Rae closed her eyes and clenched her lips tight. "I am not your spy. This is the first time I have told you anything. I thought it useful information."

He faced her. "You seek to bargain?"

"No." Appalled, she plunged on. "I seek to help you." Hanal turned away from her. "Tell me," she said, hand reaching for him, but finding only air. "Did you investigate my claims? Was I right?"

The expression on his face grew harsh, all trace of humour gone. He stood up suddenly and the table shook violently, spilling their tea and knocking over Rae's cup.

"Well?" Rae asked, certain that he had found the truth.

"All those who wish to have been returned to their families. Oaths were offered to the others."

"And did many take up these offers of oaths?"

Hanal pierced her with his gaze. "A few."

"And those that are carrying children?"

His nostrils flared. "They are in a minority. Argenterra's *given* is not so weak as we are led to believe. The *given* keeps many barren. Only two are with child."

Relief washed through Rae. She had only half believed the tale that the *given* limited the number of births in Argenterra, but it appeared to be true. Would that suit the Puri who valued large families, strong sons to support the tribe and daughters to create alliances through marriage?

Hanal stood facing the wall, his back to her.

She stood up. "I will leave you, then. It seems I have nothing of value for your ears."

"I did not tell you that you could leave yet." His tone was clipped.

Rae paused and looked back at him. Nothing could be deciphered from his back. "You will be with me when I grant Aria an audience."

"Me?"

He turned around, his face chiselled into hard lines, his eyelids narrowed. "You know this woman. You will know if they have sent another to pretend to be her."

"You cannot have her. She is married to Dellbright."

He snorted. "I have enough troubles with women in my life as it is. I do not seek this woman for my bed."

"You will change your mind when you see her. Her beauty is her curse."

He turned to face her, the muscles in his jaw bunching. "You will offer her friendship," he bit out. "You will do this or I will take the child from you."

With clenched fists, she faced him. "You do not need to threaten me. I am friends with Aria so I will be pleased to see her. You will not take my child from me. You have no rights."

"Go!' he hissed. "You are wrong about my rights." He chuckled then. "Believe what you will. You will not stop me."

Rae ran from the room, across the hall and back into her cell. Sitting cross-legged on her mattress, she fought back tears. Lien stirred and let out a small mewling sound. Rae's milk came in and she sighed, rubbing at her tired eyes. *Kushlan, have I a tale for you.*

# VORN'S SWORD

In the night something heavy landed on Sophy's knee. She sat up and hollered, then hugged the wounded limb to her chest until the smarting sting eased. Immediately, the beasts raised hell outside her cell, a cacophony of growls and scratching and slavering. Flicks of saliva hit the skin of her legs and she could feel the heat from their damp breaths. It didn't pay to have an imagination.

It was dark; she had no means to tell what was going on. Was it her yell that disturbed them or something else? She blinked a few times, her eyes adjusting to the low light levels. Instead of just a wall of black, there were lighter shades of grey. She could make out the blackness of the wall.

Thumping the dirt around her, she detected a hard shape not far from her. Assessing the outline and its heft, she knew what it was. A brick must have fallen out of the wall. Thinking crazily, she tried to picture how she had left it. Had she loosened the bricks enough for one to fall out? Then she slapped the ground around her again, searching for more items, and came across another shape. She lifted it and detected its hazy outline. Another brick was on the ground. She blinked. Two bricks? It took a while for her brain to kick in.

Definitely, only one brick had been fully freed from its mortar and she had put that back. It was possible that she had accidentally loosened another one, as she had been working on them consistently. Between the howls and growls of the excited warren beasts outside the cell, she thought she heard a sound. It was like a brick grating against another one. Another brick was being worked free.

Excited, she stood up and patted along the wall to the place where she'd been working. A brick pushed out into her palm. She gripped it with her fingers and worked it out. Once it was free she lowered it to the ground.

The ugreals! Her heart leapt at the thought. She edged back and then carefully padded her fingers around the widening hole in the wall. All four bricks were out and she could hear dirt hiss to the floor.

Another brick fell, and another, pushed out by the force behind it. Then rubble pattered to the floor like hail. Sophy could not believe it. She squeaked with excitement. The ugreals had come to help her. Gnawing on her fist, she glanced outside her cell. The beasts were going crazy now. High-pitched squeals from the warren beasts that nearly deafened her. Lower pitched growls from the screavers vibrated in the air. Would this cacophony in the night rouse Rufus, make him investigate? It would be such bad luck if he did. Silently, she begged the ugreals to hurry. She heard a noise, the grinding of metal on metal as if someone was coming through a series of grated doors. She wasn't sure if she imagined it or not. She didn't care.

"Hurry, he's coming," she hissed urgently to the ugreals who were feverishly burrowing a tunnel big enough to take her. It was all she could do not to thrust herself in there head first. She did not want to meet Rufus again. Death was written in the script of that meeting.

There was a shift in the opening of the tunnel. A liquid movement in the black and grey that filled her sight as several shapes plopped onto the floor. She heard more than saw them. The snarling beasts went mad, throwing themselves against the bars, hooting and scratching at the door as their fangs tried to rip at her.

Sophy flinched: the moist heat of the beasts' breaths was suffocating. It occurred to her that the ugreals would be in danger if the beasts got in the cell or were sent after them. *The rag!* She knelt on the ground and patted her hands on the grimy floor, seeking the last piece. She heard the urgent clicking of the ugreals. Then her fingers met the small piece of cloth and she closed her fingers tightly over it.

The clicking of the ugreals sounded over-loud in her ears. She didn't know what they wanted so she had to guess. They were faster if she was carried. The hole didn't appear big enough for her to crawl through. She lay down on the floor and made her body relax. More clicking, louder, surrounding her, momentarily drowning out the rage of the beasts trying to get at her. Then many tiny hands touched her skin and never had anything felt so good, so comforting. The ugreals lifted her, swung her around and drew her feet first into the hole. She closed her eyes and prayed for them to hurry. He was coming. *He was coming.*

*The thought of Rufus was more than she could bear. Please hurry, she prayed to the dark. Just get me out of here!*

She wished she could communicate with them and tell them to cover the hole up, disguise her escape route. There was no time. Escape first. Worry later. He would know when he saw the hole. He would send his critters after them. She tried to think about the size of the tunnel and whether the beasts were limber enough to force their way through. She did not think they were built for digging, but they were called warren beasts so that implied they lived in warrens, which were holes in the ground. They certainly had the claws. Definitely they were going to be able to come after her. The screavers were less likely to follow that way.

The tunnel grew narrow and her passage slowed. The ugreals stopped. There was movement, the sounds of digging and chirping. Then they moved her again, tugging her along with their tiny hands, turning her as they bent her body around a particularly difficult corner. Her body was floppy, malleable. It was the only way she knew how to help them. She made her mind blank and tried not to let the terror of enclosed spaces or the fear of Rufus surface. They had moved her through tunnels before and she'd been safe. They could do it again.

A brush of something touched the skin of her stomach, a steel support or something similar. Then a firmer encounter as it grazed against the bony tip of her hip. Being tense, she had to let go of her muscles one by one. She slowed her breathing, letting her body relax with each dirt-scented breath, making herself flaccid and easier to manoeuvre through the narrow passageway. They were going to make it. She was pressed so much she had to hold her breath.

The tight section continued and Sophy was near to losing her sanity. Another girder blocked them. They stuffed and pushed and squeezed her around it. Contorted, hurting, she held onto her scream. Then the pressure eased somewhat. She sucked in a breath, and another. It smelt dank in the tunnel. A cough teased the back of her throat so she tried to think of something else, something that would take her mind off where she was and the closeness of the dirt and the lack of air. The ugreals had never let her down. She knew she could cope. Then she was through and the ugreals sped up again. She tried to estimate how far they had got. On the one hand, she hoped they were clear of the ruins and, on the other, she feared they hadn't even cleared the underground cells. There was no way of knowing.

The time it took to travel through the tunnels drove her crazy. She kept thinking she heard the growl of the warren beasts behind her. At times the air was so hot and fetid she thought it was Rufus breathing on her. A wave of soft clicking washed over her. She sensed the ugreals communicating. Then there was light and she was thrust out into the open. She sat up, drew in large chunks of air, coughed and heaved until she took in her surroundings.

The sky was the light grey of approaching dawn. The scene was flat and grey, her perception distorted from the lack of light and shadow. It was the ridge. She sat in the space where the land had subsided, carving out a bowl in the earth. As she wiped dirt from her face and cleared her vision, she saw the dark shapes of ugreals darting into holes in the wall of the depression. Staggering to her feet, she peered over the edge of the ditch to the ruins. There were no obvious signs of pursuit but it was coming. It was inevitable.

As she checked her surroundings, she wondered where to next. Back into the tunnels and the water cavern, or would they proceed on foot? Then she caught a glimpse of something silver in the tumbled, grey soil. It was the sword, the one she had touched before. She looked at her hand, remembering the sting of power when she had touched it the first time. Then the second time, when nothing happened. A sword would be useful for hacking at warren beasts. It would look good stuck in Rufus, too. She hobbled over to it, stretching the kinks from her back and flexing her knees. It would be heavy.

The ground was soft, dangerously so from the recent upheaval. The ugreals clicked and swarmed around her, shovelling the dirt away to reveal more of the sword. The hilt jutted out. There were markings on it, like the outline of a machine, a circuit board or some such pattern. It was technology, but not something she was familiar with. Something in those markings made her chest ache. Putting her hand there just below the breast bone, she remembered the crystal leaf, buried there so long ago. It had made her able to understand the Argenterrans. It had drawn the *given* from the land, when she'd been transformed. It was her burden, a millstone around her neck, or actually buried within her flesh.

She knelt down to examine the hilt. There were characters written on it: Vorn's name. She didn't know the language but she'd seen this name before, in the library at the retreat. This had been his sword, must have been. Had he hidden in this place when the end of the world came? Lost it in some battle as he fought his way free of his enemies, protecting the refugees who fled with him? Was it here that Vorn gathered the First Comers and struck out for the Crystal Gate? Was it here that he fought the final battle to free them from Unesta's forces?

That meant the portal must be here, close by. A jolt of hope shook her to the core. If she could find it, then she could find her way back to Argenterra, to Oakheart. Her lips tightened in anger. Oakheart had not come for her. She wanted to smack him one for that. How dare he abandon her to her fate. First things first. She had to get to Argenterra first, before she could reckon with her oathbound husband.

Determined that she too would fight her way clear if anything got in her way, she reached for the hilt. This time there was no explosion of power or rending electrocution at her touch. She pulled on the hilt and the blade slid free from the earth. It vibrated with a gentle hum; not a simple sword but a product of technology. She swung it experimentally, making sure she didn't lop off important parts of herself. It was not too heavy. Not as heavy as it should be, judging by its size and heft. She could swing it, perhaps wound with it. Maybe the technology allowed it to be lighter. She hoped it was as deadly as the sharpest sword though, for she meant to use it.

As she had no clothes or belt she would have to run along holding it. A low rumble filled the air. The earth moved beneath her feet and she stumbled. The sides of the ditch started caving in, pouring earth like mini waterfalls. It was another quake. Ugreals clicked ominously and scrambled up the sides and into their little holes. Panicked, she leapt at the sides of the ditch, clawing her way out with her feet and one hand while the other kept a tight grip on the sword. She punched her feet into the walls, the softer earth giving her a precarious purchase. With effort she was able to scramble up and out.

The ridge was unstable. She needed to find solid ground, rock instead of these softer mounds of earth, half pulverised, like the remains of some ancient building. The tremor continued. Her instinct was to run. Run from the city ruins, as fast and as far as she could. She took a step and then heard a great roar and looked back to the city. The ground appeared to ripple and great sections of buildings swayed, then with a sickening screech crumbled. Her jaw ached with the noise and vibrations of the tortured earth. With her heart thumping painfully in her chest, she had to decide what to do and where to go.

*Click, clicking* of the ugreals drew her forwards. Ahead were some rocks so she scampered over to them, believing that they provided better support than the soft earth. The tremors meant something. It wasn't Rufus. Then she remembered clearly being at the retreat, the quakes and the tremors that preceded the arrival of the Crystal Gate. Could it mean that the gate was coming? That she could escape back to her own world or Argenterra? Hope leapt in her heart. A smile lit her features and froze.

Over the sound of the groaning earth came the growls of the screavers. Ugreals paused, their dark eyes wide, then as one they disappeared when a long drawn-out growl reached them. Her head jerked in their direction and her heartbeat thumped hard. The terrifying yowls drew closer. Time was running out. More than three of the beasts approached, by her guess. The less-sharp yips sounded like the warren beasts. Rufus didn't have a use for her now. He didn't care if his pets tore her to shreds.

Looking down, she saw that she still had the cloth, tucked into the waist of her rag-wrapped skirt. It would be good to have a diversion and she considered using one of the ugreals to take it and head off in the other direction. That would be unfair, though, because it would put them in danger. She suspected their rescue had already done that.

Rufus had been unaware of their existence but he would have deduced by now that something had aided her previously and had then rescued her. He would send the warren beasts after them. Squeezing her eyes shut, she tried to block images of the warren beasts shredding through the tunnels, ripping and tearing at the ugreals. How defenceless would they be? She did not want to see them harmed. It was not her fault that she had been brought here. She felt guilt all the same. But she had not summoned them. They had come of their own accord. She knew not how to control them. With a frown, she let her guilt slide away. *No use fretting over what you can't control.*

Scrambling up the wall and over the side, she jumped down onto a pathway. She ran up it and over the rise to join the main path. She could see that it cut along the top of the ridge like a spine. The scrape of claws over rocks sounded behind her and she realised it was too late for more thinking. Turning, she brought the sword up and placed her feet a shoulder width apart. Without warning, a warren beast rounded the bend and leapt for her. She swiped at it, putting her weight behind the arc of her arms. As the blade stuck in its body, it squirmed and yowled. She fought to free her sword because another beast was coming. She put her foot on the beast, just behind its enormous jaw, and pushed it off her blade. She caught the second one with the reverse pull of the blade, which bounced off the bony head. The beast paused, shook itself and then leapt again.

The first one rolled around on the ground, screaming in pain and flinging hot blood in all directions. It tripped the second one, which dropped just shy of her sword. That allowed her to stab straight into its back. It let out a scream of pain and bucked. Sophy tried to keep a hold of the blade. The first warren beast was calming down, getting ready to attack her again. She had to get the blade out as she could not afford to lose it. Larger beasts were coming. Fear nearly closed her throat. The screavers were bigger and more deadly. Panic wet and hot almost defeated her.

The thuds of many feet approached her. Still she wrestled with the blade, trying to free it from the unfortunately bony back of the second warren beast. The other beast tried to bite her as she passed close to it while wrestling with the other one. She took a second to kick it in the side, sending it whining off in pain. Then the first of the screavers turned the corner. Looking down, she had only the ragged remains of clothing on her, strips dangling. She tossed a piece of her clothing. Without momentum, it fluttered in the breeze not quite sure where it was heading. It floated and wafted and came down in the middle of the new bunch of beasts. She groaned in disappointment. The two beasts she was already struggling with took no notice. However, the cloth did set the other beasts fighting amongst themselves.

Her sword came free, staggering the second warren beast. She quickly stuck it in its throat before it could gather itself. Then she jerked the blade free and finished off the other one, its teeth barely missing her arm. Her mind went back to the warren beast attack in the forest. There she had fought to save Oakheart with only a knife. She killed them, bashed them and stomped on them in a blind rage. She could do it again.

Hot breath on the back of her leg made her turn sharply. Sword swinging crazily, she whipped it around, casually slicing the head off the warren beast who hadn't quite died. She blinked, amazed by her prowess, until another dived from above her head, bringing her down. She was covered in fur and teeth snapped near her face. The sword was lying half in the ground. A scream ripped from her throat.

Then she heard something else. The beast she wrestled with kept on unabated but the others shifted as if there was something else there with them. At least that left her free to fight this one. It was all she could do to prevent it from taking chunks out of her. She got her feet underneath its weight and pushed. Teeth caught on her arm as it went flying, slicing down her right forearm. It hurt like hell yet she grabbed for the sword. The beast picked itself up and she jabbed the blade straight through its chest.

She heard desperate clicking and realised the ugreals had come to her aid. She ran a few steps down the path and saw the first body. A bloody dark mess on the ground. Then she heard desperate clicks and the body of an ugreal flew through the air and landed against the side of the path with a splat.

"No, no," she moaned desperately. They were defenceless against the warren beasts. She doubted the warren beasts were native to this planet; they had the potential to wipe the ugreals out. Having no idea how to make the ugreals stop joining the fight, she ran, screaming and waving the sword, hoping to scatter everyone. The ugreals disappeared into holes and burrows. A few of the warren beasts savaged the entries to the holes. One came away with a struggling and clicking ugreal. With horror, she watched the beast flick the ugreal up into the air and catch it in enormous jaws. Sword out, she leapt, slicing the beast in two. She was getting the hang of the sword. This time she freed the sword easily and swung again. She heard a grunt and the slunch of a blade hacking flesh. Not her fighting. She looked behind. There, backing towards her, was a large man with blond hair slicing a path through the screavers. No wonder they hadn't started attacking her.

A wave of anger swept over her. *Oakheart. Now he comes.* Too late to save her from all that had happened. She ground her teeth and sliced and cut and stabbed. Soon the warren beasts' bodies mounted up, impairing the remaining ones' ability to get at her.

"Oakheart?" she called.

He looked over his shoulder, stared at her and then turned back to kick a wounded warren beast in the head. A screaver loomed.

"Watch out!" she shouted.

He turned and stepped to the side as the screaver struck downwards. He lunged with his sword, cutting off its head. Blood splattered over him and the ground.

The warren beasts were thinning out. Sophy knew they had to get out of there before Rufus came, or Unesta herself. She ran up the path to him.

"The gate?" she cried, before turning to swipe at a warren beast yipping at her heels.

Their eyes met and he squinted. "Sophy?"

That sent her rocking backwards. He had not recognised her. She looked down at her body, mostly naked, thin and smeared with dirt, and her hair short, filthy spikes. She was a mess.

More screams and cries erupted behind them. A second wave was coming.

"Who bloody else would it be?" she yelled over the din.

He grinned. "This way," he said. He booted a furry mass out of his way.

One more swipe of her sword and she killed another beast. She was getting better at this. Then she leapt up and scrambled over the bodies to get close to him.

Oakheart paused. There was something blocking the path ahead. With a groan, Sophy turned back to the mass of beasts coming up behind them.

Back to back, they faced off the beasts while slowly stepping along the path. Two lunged and she struck, taking both with one cut. Oakheart was grunting as he stabbed, thrust and kicked. Sophy had to be careful she didn't slice into Oakheart. That made fighting harder. She wanted to slash and slice and maim and scream until they were all dead. Instead, she had to prod and chop and wade through blood and gore. They were making very slow progress. What was it all for? Then she remembered.

"Can you call the gate?" she rasped. Exhaustion was pulling at her muscles.

"Yes, it is not far," he said with effort. "Are you all right?" Thrust, kick, squeal.

She grimaced. How was she going to answer that? "I am alive, Oakheart." She sliced and kicked, taking out another two beasts. Thank god she didn't have the screavers for Oakheart had scored these. Yet she couldn't repress her anger and disappointment. She growled out, "You took your time." She turned slightly, gritting her teeth as he stabbed his sword into an oncoming beast.

"I know. 'Tis complicated. I will explain later." He spoke without sparing her a look.

The warren beasts thinned considerably. The last four or five suddenly bounded off, as if they had been summoned. Sophy shivered. What was coming now? Rufus?

"Come on," Oakheart called and sprinted along the path. Sophy leapt over a warren beast's body and took off after him. She was tired, afraid, and darned angry. How dare he show up just when she was about to win free all by herself? He should have come months ago before she was hurt and had suffered. A deep resentment filled her. She didn't know if she could ever let it go.

At the base of the path where the ridge expired, Oakheart disappeared from view. As angry as she was, she did not want to be left behind. She put on a final burst of speed and reached the bottom of the path. Then she saw him standing not far off. She took off in his direction, looking behind her occasionally to see if anyone or anything was pursuing them. Nothing. She thought that strange.

The ground trembled, sharp and hard and sudden. The gate was coming. She could feel the vibration in the air, caught some words that Oakheart was repeating. The sword in her hand tingled as if it resonated with power. The baby she carried fluttered. It was moving. How strange.

The gate materialised, large and bright, sending out a luminous rainbow of colour. Squinting against the sudden light, she could make out the outline. It was a construction. At its base was a box and the arch of the gate appeared crystalline, shooting light that split into a full spectrum of colour. That much she could see. The ground trembled slightly as the weight of the gate settled. Oakheart faced her, then his eyes widened.

Sophy sensed a presence behind her. She turned slowly, afraid. There was Rufus, holding a chest with the lid open. Within was a green glow. Unesta!

"Stop." Unesta's voice echoed around them. "The gate is mine. I forbid you to use it, child of Vorn."

Oakheart's gaze burned. "Ancient Evil!"

Catching her attention, he gestured for Sophy to move his direction. Sophy hesitated. Unesta had all that power. She would come after them. They had to do something.

"Sophy, come now. Please," Oakheart called, unable to disguise his desperation.

Rufus continued to close on them. He held a chest reverently in front of him, muttering quietly under his breath. He did not seem to notice them at all. Sophy was sure that Unesta would strike, possibly killing them if they chose to use the gate. She could not risk it. The child had to live. Sophy yelled suddenly and ran at Rufus.

He kept walking, concentrating on the aged container holding his mistress. Her sword aimed true, ready to strike him in the heart. His eyes glowed red then widened when he finally realised her attack. He lifted the chest in defence and the sword struck it. Sophy was knocked backwards as power struck the sword and her. From the ground, she saw the chest erupt in green flame. Free of its container, Unesta's essence arced through the air and centred on the gate. Rufus, too, was thrown back by the explosive discharge of power.

"Oakheart!" Sophy warned. She saw him gesture quickly. With an implosion of air the gate shut. Too late to stop Unesta. The Ancient Evil had made it through with an eerie screech of triumph.

Sophy sat on the ground, winded and shaking her head. "No!"

Rufus didn't move, but he was breathing. They had to get out of there.

Oakheart shook his head. He glanced at Sophy.

"Call it again, quickly." Sophy climbed to her feet, clinging to the sword. "We have to go after her." Her eyes never left the form of Rufus, scared that he would rise up before they won free. His foot twitched; his hand opened.

Oakheart called the gate again, using the same words of summoning. The ground trembled and lurched. Sophy struggled to stand. Oakheart came to her, and he grabbed her outstretched hand. "Come on!"

The gate materialised again. Together they limped to the gate and then lunged through it. The last thing she heard in the Deadlands was Rufus's screech of frustration. Then her vision went white.

THE PATHWAY BETWEEN THE WORLDS WAS A NO-SPACE, A SORT OF narrow, colourless corridor. Oakheart was close behind her. "Sophy, wait. Let me go first."

"No. She's here, waiting."

"Let me get ahead of you." He touched her shoulder and she jumped. Turning back to him, she shook her head.

He gasped. "Sophy, your skin is glowing."

Sophy looked down. A bluish radiance emanated from within her body. Like the time Adage had brought forth the crystal leaf that had been growing within her, except now it glowed throughout all of her.

She cocked her head as she locked gazes with Oakheart, her mouth open, nothing to say.

A presence behind her left shoulder made her turn. Green light, a coalescing form. Unesta barred their way. Sophy rounded, set her feet, raised the sword. This entity—this thing—had caused her harm. Sophy was no longer afraid. She was beyond afraid and into reckless. Unesta embodied hate and lusted only for power and destruction.

Unesta took form, one that alternated between young and old, immaculate and diseased. It made Sophy think: virgin, goddess, crone. A legend of Earth.

"Sophy," Oakheart whispered urgently. "Let me."

Again Sophy shook her head. "I've got this. Back me up, would you?"

A growl of frustration was his reply.

Eyes like green fire faced Sophy. Unesta couldn't move ahead. The way to Argenterra was barred. Sophy lifted the sword, knees flexed, ready to strike.

"You dare threaten me?" Unesta's voice rasped through the air, seeming to grate against the skin, the eyes, the brain.

Sophy acknowledged the question with a tilt of the head, mouth closed tight. This creature had harmed her, had caused her so much angst. All the spells and manipulation that had made her life a misery when she first went to Argenterra were because of this woman, this being. Sophy wondered now if it had been the crystal leaf that had preserved her against all that threatened her. Argenterra had tried to protect her, and thus protect itself. It had been a gamble. Sophy had lost some of the *given* power, but not all.

With a piercing scream, Unesta unleashed a force at Sophy. Sophy blinked and then stumbled back as it hit. The blade drew the power in, light forking like electricity through the air. As the sword glowed brighter, Sophy's arms throbbed and her hands tingled painfully. Yet she kept hold of the hilt, held the sword in front of her, protecting both herself and Oakheart from the strike.

"Thank you for giving back the power you stole." Sophy grinned and lifted a challenging eyebrow.

Unesta screeched and then lunged. Sophy stepped back instinctively but not far enough. Unesta had a grip on her forearm and tried to shake the sword loose. Oakheart yelled but there was nothing Sophy could do. Unesta's grip burned her skin and Sophy screamed but she didn't let go. Nose to nose, they turned around each other in the small space.

"Give that power to me." Unesta's essence was rank. Pungent, she nearly overwhelmed Sophy.

Sophy clung to bravado. "No. The power stays with me."

"No! It's mine!"

Sophy shook her head. "I'm afraid not. It's coming back with me to Argenterra."

The face that phased through its various perspectives—young, old, beautiful, ugly, pure, diseased—sneered. The face grew in proportion, nose jutting out, teeth elongating, eyes sunken dark holes. Sophy had had enough; had endured enough. She slammed her forehead against Unesta's nose. Unesta recoiled, dazed. Power thrummed against Sophy's skin. Forks of power leapt between her sword and Unesta, who screamed as she slowly turned to vapour. Dirty, green smoke dissipated.

Sophy clawed at the smoky wisps, trying to catch them. Oakheart too tried to capture the essence of the Ancient Evil, but she slipped through their fingers and was gone.

In the way between worlds Sophy didn't know what would happen to Unesta, but she had no time to wonder. The Crystal Gate opened up for them: a blinding, brilliant light.

The land beyond beckoned her. Oakheart let out a cry. "Go!" he said in a triumphant voice and, with his hand on her back, he shoved.

Euphoric, Sophy surged forwards. She had done it. She'd beaten Unesta—the Ancient Evil. For once, she had done something right. She held the sword high and its glow outshone the Crystal Gate as they emerged back into Argenterra.

## ❧ 27 ❧

# THE AFTERTASTE OF HATE

Aria rode in silence. Her oathbond to Dellbright gave her trouble. She hated knowing he was on the other end of it. Most of the time she could sublimate it, sublimate him. Knowing she could never be free of him was more than she could bear.

"You have something on your mind, my lady," Leyla said with reins held casually in her hands. Their walking pace allowed for conversation.

"It's Dellbright and my oathbond." She looked at the adept. "Has no one ever broken an oathbond?"

Leyla screwed up her mouth as she thought. "Not to my knowledge."

"I thought so."

"But that does not mean it cannot be done. We live in interesting times."

"What do you mean?"

"The *given* is weaker yet you are strong. If anyone was to break an oathbond, it would be you. You have a genuine reason. You have been harmed and Dellbright is warped beyond saving. You must look to what binds you to him and undo those bonds, then I think the oathbond will shatter."

"But what if it doesn't? What if I fail?"

Leyla shifted her gaze to Aria's face. "You lose nothing. You will still have your bond."

Aria shook her head. Leyla was right. The barriers to her breaking her bond lay within herself. Loyalty, the promise she had made, the fear of being branded unfaithful or an oathbreaker, the fear of being less than she should be. If she could dismiss those perceptions then maybe she could see the anchor of her bonds and thus think of a way to undo them. Dellbright clung to their bond, used it to shovel his malice at her. He was not an adept but he didn't need to be, not with that much hate inside him, twisted, evil hate.

As they rode along, she untwisted the cords to her side of the oath, swept away her loyalty, the remnants of her love, the desire for him. She slammed the door on the fears: what people would say, what they did say. She threw away the pitying glances, the comments behind the hands, the sneers. Instead of thinking herself less, she thought of herself as more, rising above the hurt and the blame and the shame. She had done nothing to deserve his treatment of her. It was all Dellbright. It was his actions and choices that had affected her.

Here, amid the *given*, her oathbond was stripped bare. She saw its component parts and isolated the wall of self-hatred that was Dellbright. He was trapped in that, clinging to their bond as if his life depended on it. Perhaps it did. Then she applied her concentration, bent her psyche, and called out to him, drew his attention, told him what she was doing. He fought her. He drew their bond tight and clung desperately to keep control over her.

Then she severed it.

Her sudden gasp drew Leyla's attention. "My lady?"

Aria breathed, tears rolling gently down her face. "I did it, Leyla." She turned to the adept, wonder and awe in her voice. "I did it!"

Leyla's eyebrows drew together. "What? What did you do?"

Aria gripped her reins, drew in a breath and lifted her chin. "I broke the oathbond. I am free."

Leyla gasped, then shut her mouth, turned to face the direction they were riding, a smile playing around her lips. "You are amazing, my lady. My princess. You have done what no other has."

Aria nodded. Her heart wouldn't relax its heavy beat. She had done it but it scared her. "No one must know."

"For now, my lady. For now."

❧

DELLBRIGHT WALKED ALONG THE LANE TO THE TWO-STOREY HOUSE. After checking that no one was watching, he knocked on the door. After a few moments the woman came, scarf over her head, white apron covering up the skirts of the russet dress.

"Good sir! You have returned. Come in." She stepped back, opening the door to him.

Dellbright stepped through. "I have come to see the child."

The woman curtseyed. "He is well. I will take you to him. He should be waking from his nap soon. He is growing well. Such a character, so full of life. Chatters away with his nonsense words. And those curls! Lovely red curls."

"Stop your prattle, woman. I came to see the child. Time is short."

It annoyed him that the woman treated him like some backwoods farmer as he had kept his identity hidden from her. He had no idea what she supposed about him and he did not really care. Gilly was hidden away where none would find him. He could not risk bringing the boy back to the Valley, where others could lay claim to him. That Aria had seen through the ruse with the other Gillcress infuriated him. Time had separated mother and child, and yet she knew his decoy was false. Her influence on his son was not to be tolerated.

The ceiling was low in the little parlour, but the window was tall and wide, leading to a small balcony that looked over the large yard, groomed with trim garden beds full of vegetables and ringed with fruit trees. He glimpsed the land beyond the closely tended yard, a terraced field with sharp stones delineating grain from toffel plants. The old woman worked hard to maintain her home.

Touching the blade at his belt, he was reassured by its presence. If he could not have his son, no one else would. *She* would never have him. Hate for her filled him up. So too did the visions of what he was going to do to her son. Then he sensed her, strong and powerful. She was in the oathbond. He shook his head, reading her intent. *No.*

Yes! she whispered back through their bond. I *will be free of you and your hate. You will never harm me again. You will never have a chance to touch me, beat me, rape me.*

*You cannot be free. We are bound in the given.*

I can. I can undo our bond with the *given.* I have learnt how. Watch!

A sudden pain in his chest, his head, like some vital organ was being ripped out. Then there was nothing—an aching empty throbbing. She was gone. He reached for her, for their bond. There was nothing. *No!*

His gaze fell upon Gilly, lying quietly in a small truckle bed set against one wall. The child stirred, his ginger curls a vivid drawing on the white of the pillow. Large green eyes blinked at him in confusion. Despair sliced through him. He could barely stand. She had escaped from him. It was unthinkable. Unimaginable. The slut was free to rut with whomever she chose. That could not be. She was his. Only his.

The old woman went to Gilly, ruffling his curls and squeezing his shoulder as she helped him to sit up. "Now there, Pert. Your da has come to visit you."

"Da. Da." A bright smile lit his face. His body shook with repressed energy. The woman placed the boy's feet on the floor.

"Make your da a nice bow now, child. Show him yer manners."

The child bent his legs at bit unsteadily and dipped his head. Dellbright's heart melted. He dropped to his knees in front of the boy and hugged him close, weeping suddenly as if the ties on his emotions had snapped. This child was his only link to Aria, his only hold on her.

"Dear sir. Is all well with ya? Perhaps I should bring some wine. To calm yer nerves." The woman was clutching at her apron.

Dellbright nodded. "Thank you." He sniffed and used a fist to wipe the tears that dropped off his chin.

He wanted the woman to go.

She brought a jug of wine and a cup.

"Leave us," he growled.

Backing away, she fled the room, her dark eyes wide with fright.

Dellbright grunted and wiped his face with his sleeve. Letting out his breath, he stood Gilly at arm's length. "You are grown tall, my boy."

The boy smiled at him and lifted onto his toes to show his height to greater advantage. "Big. Dada, big."

Dellbright stood and ruffled the boy's hair. "Do you like it here? Is Mistress Dooley good to you?"

Gilly smiled. "Doodoo. Good." Then the boy bounced about, picking up a wooden block and placing it by his feet. "More?"

Dellbright smiled at the boy's obvious delight. His heart was breaking. It had been so perfect. She had been so perfect. Now, so flawed. So free of him. He pulled out a box that was tucked in the corner and handed his son another block. Gilly carefully, with much concentration, placed it on the first. "More?"

Visions arose in his mind as he played with Gilly. Aria, her beauty, all his. His home, his keep, the days light and bright. Marred only by that outlander, Sophy. The woman with a heart of evil. Then it all turned to ash. Aria changed, faulty. His mother killed. No longer his to hold. His son. Taken! Days of darkness so deep that no light entered inside his soul. It got so that he did not recall the source of the darkness, only the knowledge that he was part of it. He was darkness.

Losing interest in the blocks, Gilly began to fidget, going after a ball that sat in a box. "Ball...ball."

"Come here, child."

Gilly hesitated, looking between the ball and his Da. He was Gillcress no more, but Pertwee Rye. Son of Dalton Rye, the name Dellbright provided to Mistress Dooley to explain who he was. A nameless town; a nameless child; a nameless future. Gillcress deserved more than that. His future was stolen from him. Betrayed by his own mother. Now he must live in the shadows, never knowing who he truly was.

But Dellbright did not need to worry any longer about discovery or shame. There was a new plan: a better plan. Now that Aria was irretrievably gone, he understood that she was more powerful than him. Her use of the *given* to injure him was an insult to him, to all men who allowed their women folk too much freedom. It was against the natural order of things. She would never be his again. The promise that was the beginning of their love was extinguished. Her heart was as stone where her husband and child were concerned.

The knife blade glistened in the light streaming through the window. "Mine?" the boy asked, his eyes bright with excitement. Gilly licked his lips and put out his chubby hand.

"Yes, my son. This blade is for you." He held it out point first, his palm sweaty.

Their eyes met. Dark to bright, innocent green. The boy licked his lips, eager for the gift.

A crash at the door made Dellbright jump. The blade caught the boy's cheek and a red stripe grew there. A red line of accusation turning to a ripple of red dripping off the boy's chin. The boy cried out, put his hand to his cheek and backed away.

The accusation in his hurt look tore at Dellbright. He was caught in it.

"No. Stop. Ya beast!" Mistress Dooley rushed forwards.

Dellbright jerked up and around in surprise. He raised his hands and stepped back. The woman barrelled into him, shoving with great force. Before he knew it he was on the balcony, the cool breeze rippling his curls, throwing strands of his hair into his eyes. Instinctively, he shoved the woman back, clouted her across the head. She stumbled to her knees, dazed.

Gilly's cries were like maggots in his ears. "Doodoo! No." His young voice was full of terror. "Bad. Bad da!" The boy grabbed him around the knees. Dellbright shoved him away and the boy was flung back into the room and sprawled onto the rug. The woman grabbed for Gilly, caught him up and curled her body around him as she choked out sobs.

Dellbright lowered his arm and stared at the knife in his hand, glistening with his son's blood. "What have I become?" Horror rose up from his gut and threatened to strangle him. All the deeds he had performed arrayed themselves in his mind: Cruelty. Pain. Dishonour. Abuse of others. Those deeds had become him, and he was defined by them.

Turning slowly, he saw the mountains in the distance and the plains swathed in green running before them. Sunlight threw down shafts between pregnant clouds of grey. White fluffs of mist hung low over the upper valley, hiding the cleft that led to Panal's Pass.

My beautiful land! Tears welled in his eyes and his throat clogged with emotion. Looking down, he saw the garden, really saw it, the sharp points of stone guarding the lush plants, and knew what he must do. Before he could swing around, Mistress Dooley barrelled into him again, shoving with two strong arms. His breath whooshed out of him. He lost his balance, arms flailing, the knife flipping and turning in an arc. He made a grab for it and toppled over the balcony rail.

He had some time to think as he fell. It was going to hurt but the fall would not kill him. Then he remembered—the knife! It had grabbed it with his hand. *Thunk*!

The knife was in him. Pain, darkness, stillness.

Wide, green eyes watched him. Aria had been caught up in his last moments, drawn to thoughts of her son. She detected Dellbright's death and the vision of the mountains in the distance.

## ❦ 28 ❦

## SOPHY RETURNS

Sophy landed with a grunt, then fell to her knees, keeping hold of the sword. Oakheart stumbled and wearily rolled clear. The Crystal Gate loomed over them, so hauntingly beautiful that Sophy was lost for words. Argenterra impinged upon her notice bit by bit.

Dazzling light flowed over them, blinding her to her surroundings, but she was aware of small rocks poking into her knees and feet. Blinking and shielding her eyes, she made out the stony outcrop not far from the retreat. Blue sky provided a canopy overhead. Craning her neck, she saw the rocky path to the Crystal Mountain Retreat. They'd made it. Thank god for that. They were really back.

Her heart thumped like she was going to expire from a heart attack. Sweat and weakness swept over her as if she was in shock. Taking calming breaths she tried to focus her thoughts, tried to get used to being free.

Unesta! She'd beaten the Ancient Evil! With Vorn's sword. She looked down at the blade, clutched so tightly in her hand her palm felt warm. She, Sophy, had achieved the unachievable.

Beside her, Oakheart climbed unsteadily to his feet. He mumbled a few words and the gate thrummed, seemingly glowing brighter before it snapped closed. Sounds drew her attention and Sophy could make out figures nearby, people running, exclaiming in surprise. It was a relief to make out the robes of the adepts as they surged ahead to assist them. Part of her had doubted they would make it, wondering if the gate would hurl them to yet another world. She had beaten Unesta and hoped she had seen the end of her.

The same thing must have been on Oakheart's mind. "The Ancient Evil? Did she pass this way?" he asked the adept gate attendants.

"No, the gate opened the once just now, when you returned."

Oakheart stared at them uncomprehendingly, before turning to Sophy. "Then it is done." His green eyes were hooded as he studied her and moved close to touch her, but she shook off his hand.

"Don't."

"Sophy?" He gasped and lowered his head. Adepts ran to assist them and she could no longer see Oakheart. Hands touched her, drew her along. "Don't touch me." Her skin was sensitive.

They gave her space, surrounding her as they walked along.

One adept tried to take the sword, so she shoved him with her free hand and kept the sword out of reach. "It's mine. You can't have it."

"Sophy?" It was Oakheart.

She turned and saw that he was behind her. Sending him a quelling look, she said, "Tell them to leave me alone."

The adepts stepped back. Oakheart lifted wounded eyes to her. He swallowed but didn't speak. Why did he have to look at her like that? He had left her alone in a strange world at the mercy of Unesta and Rufus. She had every right to be pissed. And she was. Looking away from him, she sniffed. Smelt something so foul it nearly rocked her back on her heels. She lifted an arm, sniffed again, and realised it was her.

Giving herself a once over, she remembered that see she was nearly naked and filthy. "I need a bath and some clothes."

Oakheart lurched in her direction. He shook off the adepts who were trying to impede his getting close to her. "Sophy?"

"What?" Her tone was not too friendly.

"You are angry with me."

Her chin rose and she clenched the sword tighter. "You bet I am.

You left me to rot. You left me at Rufus's mercy. You let her drain the power out of me."

"You have to let me explain. Here is not the place."

The adepts backed away. Maybe it was the place. She laid the sword down on the ground and glared at the adepts near her, letting them know she would hurt them if they tried to take it. Then she faced Oakheart but didn't look at him, didn't want to see his contrite expression, the words burning in him for release.

No, she was going to focus her anger because she had tasted nothing but fear for so long she needed something different. A dessert to clear her palate. She ran at him, fist held high and ready to pound. She landed one, right on his chest. Oakheart fell back. He didn't try to stop her. She landed another fist. It smacked against his breast plate so hard it hurt her hand. She hit him again and a sob escaped. "You bastard! You abandoned me!"

Her fists fell faster, rapid, harmless taps, like the tears falling from her eyes.

"I am so sorry, Sophy." Oakheart spoke softly.

"Sorry," she said in a low voice and glared into his face. "Sorry doesn't cut it." She was angry as a cat facing off with a dog: she wanted to spit and howl and rage at him.

"Give me a chance to explain," he said softly.

She shook her head, a savage denial. More tears threatened to spill and she was mortified. She did not want to cry in front of him or bare her soul. Once, they had shared something special. Now she couldn't even feel him. There was too much hurt in the way.

"Sophy, please..." He didn't try to defend himself. It was his voice and his eyes that undid her.

She hit him again, tears falling unchecked down her cheek, dripping off her chin. "You left me!"

"I know."

She stepped back from him and scowled into his face, her vision blurry from tears. She slapped him across the cheek. Then hands dragged her off.

"Let me go!" She struggled as the adepts wrestled with her. "I can't hurt him. He is impervious."

"You must not assault his excellency," one of the adepts said in her ear.

"Calm down, please," another adept said as they dragged her away from Oakheart.

"Sophy?"

She flashed her gaze at Oakheart and covered her eyes with her forearm. "I'm not in the mood to deal with this right now."

"I know, but 'tis not as clear cut as you think."

In the aftermath of her rage, the weakness in her limbs grew and the empty space in her gut demanded attention. She'd been running on adrenaline. She shook her head, trying to think clear thoughts except there was nothing there but anger, venom planted by Rufus and Unesta.

"It is time for you to rest," Oakheart said. "Your injuries need treating. You need good food, peace and quiet to recover. Go with the adepts. Let them help you."

She ceased struggling and the adepts that held her let her go. His words got through to her. Just the quiet voice of a strong man, which penetrated the wall in her mind. "Truce," he suggested.

She wavered, then reached down to collect the sword and clutch it to her chest.

An adept stepped up to her and wrapped her in his outer robe. Calmer now, more in control, she murmured thanks to the young adept. Breathing deeply, she relished the air of freedom, of Argenterra, a place she thought was lost to her forever.

"Be careful of her," Oakheart said. "She is the hero of Argenterra. She has fought the Ancient Evil and won."

Had she won? Unesta had still drained the *given* from Argenterra. Sophy had let Unesta drain it from her. Yet the sword had some of it, she was sure, although in Argenterra her sense of the *given* was blinded.

Oakheart's words sent ripples of excitement around the adepts. 'Truly? The Ancient Evil is defeated?" There was awe in the voices now.

Sophy wasn't quite sure how to respond. Previously, she felt like she had to apologise for her presence, for being in the way and faulty because she couldn't use the *given*. Now, because she had the sword and had fought Unesta, she had a certain amount of cachet.

The absence of fear was a new sensation. Could she get used it? She'd been geared up for so long that she didn't think she'd ever be able to relax again. Thinking more rationally, she acknowledged that Oakheart had a tale to tell. What was going on in Argenterra? Memories came flooding back. Maralain had stood there, having come through the gate, and Oakheart had called her mother. And where was Aria?

*Oh shit!* She shook her head in bewilderment and studied Oakheart while other adepts assisted him along the rocky path to the retreat. He had some small wounds, bite marks on his arms and legs. A scratch on his cheek. Not from her, she hoped. She could not meet his eyes. Her body was heavy, like it was drugged. Her knees refused to lock and when an adept held her under the elbow, she didn't fight him off.

"Come, my lady, we will take you to the retreat." Her guide assisted her up the steps to continue up the path.

She walked in front of Oakheart. Catching a glimpse of him over her shoulder, his stance told her he was hurt by her attitude but also accepting. He would blame himself, would be full of guilt and pain. She couldn't face him, wasn't ready, couldn't bank her anger.

The steps were uneven and it took some climbing to make the path that would lead to the retreat. By the time they were walking across the forecourt into the retreat, Sophy's body felt full of lead. Each step was harder than the last.

Once inside the cool corridors, she relaxed some. Rufus couldn't get her here. Along the hallway, the crystal facets of the ceiling and floors seemed other-worldly after dirt-filled tunnels, prison cells, warren beasts and screavers. Still, joy or relief were distant, not embraced. Safety was something alien. Oakheart used to make her feel safe. Now she was not sure. He hadn't come when she needed him. Although, he had come eventually, just when she had won free. *Yeah, big deal. Thanks for nothing.*

The Crystal Gate? He had controlled it. That was something new. Maybe she should cut him a break. She screwed up her nose and held the sword to her chest. Maybe not.

As she walked along the corridors, other sensations made themselves known. The oathbond between her and Oakheart hummed to life again. Vibrant. Thrilling. Much more real than she remembered. She could sense the warmth of his essence at the end of it.

There was a certain comfort in the connection. Although, it was like wearing a cashmere jumper, soft and warm but a bit scratchy. It was not entirely comfortable after her experiences of being so alone. Now her life was not her own. She was bound to Oakheart. That hadn't seemed too bad before. Now, her feelings were so overwrought and confused, the knowledge of her oathbond didn't sit comfortably.

The adept was leading her to a familiar place—Lianal's office. She stopped dead as more memories washed up on the shore of her mind. The *given*. Now was the moment of truth. They would see that she had failed them; that Argenterra's power had been stripped away and she was a useless sack of soiled flesh, not worth saving.

Oakheart would know it too. He wouldn't want her either, even if she wanted him. The adept leading her paused and looked back at her, eyebrows raised in query. It would have been better if she'd been able to get washed, dressed and fed before this interview, but obviously everyone was in a hurry. She nodded and marched on, sword held in a tight embrace.

As soon as she approached Lianal the look on the older man's face made her freeze. She knew directly that he could tell the power was gone. He sat down on his chair as if she had punched him in the gut.

With a shrug of her shoulders, she said, "I'm sorry. It is gone."

His gaze focussed behind her and she jumped when Oakheart placed his hands on her shoulders. She hadn't noticed him following her. After giving a shrug, he removed them quickly. She kept her head down, not wanting to see the look in his eyes when he saw her failure and heard about how worthless she was to him.

"Sophy needs to rest and have a healer attend to her. You can talk with her later if she cares to."

"It is gone," Lianal said.

"Most of it, yes. Sophy has been dwelling in Yulandir."

Lianal's eyes widened and his gaze shifted between Oakheart and Sophy. "Yulandir? Vorn's world?"

Sophy nodded, too tongue-tied to speak.

"I suspect Unesta bled the power from Sophy and used it to get free of her bonds. Sophy fought her in the place between the worlds, and prevented Unesta from reaching Argenterra. She is defeated. Sophy is the hero of Argenterra."

Lianal nodded, taking it in slowly. His eyes narrowed and he raised his face. 'The Ancient Evil is prevented? Yet, the *given* is gone?"

Oakheart pursed his mouth and shook his head slightly. "Most of it, yes. Yet Sophy has retrieved something. Show him, Sophy."

Sophy unclenched the sword from her embrace and held it out. It throbbed in her grip as if it were alive. With a quick glance at Oakheart, she said, "It is Vorn's sword."

Lianal's face filled with wonder. "Vorn's sword? It has power in it? I do not recollect that in the writings."

"It has power," Oakheart said, his voice reflecting his wonder. "This will do much to rally the people."

"It took power from me," Sophy said. "Unesta drained the rest."

Lianal took a step, shifting his gaze from Oakheart to her to the sword. "May I hold it, princess?"

Sophy blinked at the title and fell back a step, bumping into Oakheart. Collecting herself, she lowered the blade and turned it horizontally so Lianal could take it in his hands.

He touched it gently then took its weight from her. "'Tis full of power."

Sophy studied Lianal's face and then nodded to herself. Fighting Unesta was something intangible. These people hadn't seen it. But the sword was something else. It had power. In bringing it back, she had done something right. The control that she held so rigidly inside finally evaporated. Dizziness washed over her and she bit down, not wanting to be sick in this room, right now. The room spun around and then the world tilted.

⚜

Sophy came to in Oakheart's arms. Immediately, she pushed against his hold, trying to get free. She was distinctly uncomfortable as he carried her down the corridor. She did not need his help. "Put me down. I can walk."

"Peace," he said.

"Really, I stink and I'm dirty. Put me down."

"You will be in our quarters soon."

"Our quarters? There is no 'our' quarters." She looked around for an adept so she could request separate rooms, but just when she wanted extra people around of course no one trailed them. She glared at Oakheart, tried to escape his hold, but he held her firmly, his arms like steel bands. Besides, her limbs were weak as water.

This close she could study Oakheart's face. The cut on his cheek was haloed in the blue of a bruise and the blood had dried to dark red. If he was injured, then she must be, too. Looking at her arms and legs she saw the cuts, grazes, claw scrapes. Acknowledging them only made them hurt. She really had been running on the smell of an oily rag. The world whirled about her and her head flopped back. She didn't feel too good.

As he carried her up the stairs, apparently effortlessly, she softened a little. Just a little. It had been months since another human had touched her gently. Instinctively, she reacted with revulsion. Is that what Rufus had done to her: made her despise the touch of a loved one? Or was it just the nausea and the shock. What a terrible thing if she could no longer love Oakheart, bear his touch. Rufus would have won everything then. She had to fight that. She had to win her way back to some semblance of normality.

He was taking her to his room, their room. She remembered what they did in that room so many months ago. He had put a child in her: the child was still in her. Unesta's rending spell had not come to drag its life away. The child nestled safe within her. It was safe. She had won! Don't think that. It's not safe until it's born. The spell was gone now. She hoped it was. Or would it come tomorrow and rip the baby out? She closed her eyes. *No, Unesta is gone. Rufus is wounded, left for dead in the Deadlands.* Although defeated, Sophy suspected the Ancient Evil was still alive, still free to roam in another world, free to grow back her power. Unesta was weakened but for how long—a thousand years? More? Less? At least Unesta wasn't in Argenterra—a small miracle, to be sure. For once, she had done something right, something good. A sense of pride grew in her. This ordeal, all her ordeals, had not been for nothing. What had Oakheart called her? The hero of Argenterra. Really? At least she was a hero in his eyes. Maybe not others'. Once, his respect was all she craved. Now, though, this was mixed with other feelings. Not all of them good.

They had entered the part of the retreat where their quarters were. "Put me down, Oakheart. I can walk." Her voice was surly. She couldn't help it. Didn't want to help it.

"Be quiet." Oakheart sounded unfriendly. "You can barely stand."

She hazarded a glance at him, noting how his face was set in hard lines. She tried to squirm free. He held her tighter. "Really, I am fine. Put...me...down."

They reached the door. He shifted, freeing a hand so he could open it. "No."

Sophy did not like his tone. Why was he angry with her when she had every right to be angry with him? He took long strides then dropped her on the bed. She flopped about and hurriedly propped herself up on her elbows.

"How dare you treat me like that!"

"Treat you like what? Now that is something. I risk everything to come for you and you treat me like I am an annoyance. You have no idea what I have sacrificed. I have turned my back on duty to come for you. How dare you!"

She scrambled to sit up, swinging her legs off the side of the bed. "How dare I? Where were you? Months and months you left me at the mercy of Rufus and then Unesta. At first I didn't even know my own name. I was lost in so many ways."

He blanched at her words and chewed the inside of his cheek as if stopping himself from responding.

"Then Rufus got me. When he hurt me, Oakheart, the memories of you and Argenterra and all of it came with the pain. I called for you, hoped you would come, and you didn't." Hot tears fell on her cheeks. She thumped her chest. "He hurt me, in ways I cannot tell you. Unesta took the power from me, ripped it painfully out of me after torturing me for days, weeks. Rufus. Rufus," she sucked in a breath, anger making her speak all that was inside her. "Rufus he...he...you can hate me all you want. You cannot hate me as much as I hate myself." Then she burst into incoherent sobs and buried her face in the bed clothes. She cried so hard she thought her throat would burst.

His weight depressed the mattress next to her and he drew her into his arms. He wept with her. "I am so sorry, Sophy. I wanted to come after you but no one could operate the gate. I had to wait months for the adepts to find out how to do it, and then there was the war. I had to fight. I had a duty."

Her breathing calmed, her tears subsided. "War? What war?" She hiccupped.

"Hanal has laid siege to Silverdale. He has taken my father hostage."

Her head jerked up. "Hostage?"

"Yes, and there is more. Most of Silverdale's inhabitants have been expelled into the wastelands. The Puri have taken possession of Silverdale."

Sophy stared into his eyes. With a shaking hand she stroked a loose chunk of hair out of his face. "This is terrible. What about Aria?"

He swallowed. "We traded her back to Dellbright for five hundred men."

Fist balled, she sat up. "Are you crazy?"

He shook his head. "Why do you say that?"

"Aria is worth more than five hundred men."

"I admit she is valuable, but not in a fight."

Sophy pulled back, appalled. "She has power, Oakheart. Real power. She could have learnt to use it in the defence of Silverdale."

Oakheart's face flushed. "I was not happy with the arrangement. I did not even think of her potential with the *given*."

"And did I see Maralain just before I was taken by the gate?"

"Yes. She is my mother, the high queen. To think she was your foster mother in another world and that Aria is my true sister. Surely these are amazing times."

"So where is your mother?"

"She is leading the fighting force that attempts to free Silverdale."

"Good god! Maralain?"

"Yes," he said, cheeks growing pink.

"We have to help them."

Oakheart nodded. "We will. You have to get better first. A healer is coming."

He ran his hands over her head, fingertips lingering on the tufts of her hair. "It will grow in time."

Self-consciously she touched the remains of her hair. "I guess it will." Then she sniffed. "A bath before the healer, if you please."

She examined her arm where the warren beast had torn her flesh. It was sore and throbbed. Oakheart studied her too. "Maybe the healer first. Those wounds will smart in the hot water."

"Any healing bark?"

"No," he replied. "All sent with the troops."

"Ahh...well then. I best get these cleaned. The *given* doesn't work on me anyway, remember?"

He nodded and went to prepare the bath for her. Brooding, she sat there. She wanted to tell Oakheart about the baby but couldn't bring herself to do so. Not yet. If he wanted her she wanted it to be for herself and their love, not for a child, no matter how important that child would be. And still she feared that rending spell. How could she raise his hopes and have them dashed when, no, if, the child was torn away?

Oakheart set about finding towels and a clean robe for her.

"I'm still angry with you, Oakheart. I feel like my anger is bottomless, that it will just go on forever."

His eyes were bright as he met her gaze. "I understand. The bath is ready now. Would you like me to assist?"

She shot him a tight smile. "A little privacy, if you don't mind. I have to sort a few things out in my head."

He nodded. "I am glad you are back. Truly. Things will be better now. Your defeat of the Ancient Evil will lift our spirits. Tales will be told, why, I will pen one myself once we have won free."

Sophy walked past him into the bathroom. "Yeah, right." She flinched away from his touch.

"I will find out where that healer has got to."

❧

Later, after a good soak and some treatment, the latter not necessarily pleasant, she lay on Oakheart's bed with her arm bandaged. The stitches she had were few but painful. No such thing as a local anaesthetic for her. Oakheart stood over her while she ate and drank. Then she'd dozed while Oakheart had his wounds treated. She woke up being cuddled by her oathbound husband and was too tired to struggle out of his hold. He was warm and solid and she didn't want to move. Her body needed rest, even if she found it hard to quieten her mind.

Her reflection in the mirror had been her real self, though not a pretty sight. Her cheeks were sunken and dark shadows underscored her eyes. Her scalp was raw in patches. Tears filled her eyes as she remembered what she had been through. Moments of terror. Fear so big it was like it was being rammed down her throat. Soon she was lying there sobbing. Oakheart stroked along her back and spoke soothing words. "I am here now. It's over. I love you."

"It's not over."

"You are back now. Safe." He sounded so reasonable.

"But there is a war. It's never going to be over."

"It will. We will have peace again and things will return to how they were."

She turned her head to look him in the eye. "Things have changed. They will not go back to how they were. The future will be different. Maybe not worse, and maybe not better, but not the same. Consider. Your mother has returned. That changes a lot of things. Aria has power and knows how to use it. Although if she survives being sent back to Dellbright it will be a miracle—"

"Not a miracle. She had a powerful adept who went with her posing as her maid. The adept was also training Aria so Dellbright would not be able to hurt her again."

Sophy studied Oakheart's face. "That's a relief." She propped herself on her elbow. "But how you could even think about letting her go back to him? I don't get it. She's your sister. You love her."

"It was not my decision."

"Really? You had no influence? With Aria. With Veld?"

Oakheart lowered his gaze. "Perhaps I did not exert myself as much as I should have. There was chaos here. You were ripped away, and then there was war, and my unexpected mother and several useless adepts who could not help me get to you."

"It must have been hard to let Aria go. You've always been friends, always clicked." She sat up suddenly. "Aria's a princess, too. A real one. "

"Yes," Oakheart replied, a fleeting smile on his face. "As are you."

Sophy's stomach dropped. "Oh my god. I don't think I'm going to cope. It's impossible."

Suddenly, sobs wracked her body. Oakheart caught her to him, held her against his chest. She didn't fight him; didn't want to. The baby twitched. Not quite a kick but a soft movement, a butterfly sweep of wings. That made her cry more because it was the child that had provided her with the necessary drive to keep on living. If she had not been swept off to the Deadlands, their child would have been ripped out of her like the other one had been. So she'd had to suffer. She had to go to the Deadlands and face the unfaceable to have this child. To have this future. That realisation only confused her.

It was as if it was meant to be. She hated the thought of fate and destiny and not being in control. She had been out of control for so long, ever since she went on that ghost tour. No, even earlier, when her mother left her to run off with her boyfriend. That was the moment that it all fell apart. Or was it? Maralain and Jeff had taken her in. Had provided her with a home and love. But they were linked to Argenterra. Heaven! She was the Gift of Crystal Tree Woods. What a lame one she'd turned out to be. Powerless, then dangerous as she sucked out the magic of the land. Now back, an awkward and unwilling royal.

But that was Oakheart's lot. If she loved him, she had to accept that too. If he were a doctor and worked long hours, would that have made a difference? No. She may not have liked it, but as long as there was love it was worth trying to make it work.

Her tears slowed and she breathed through the anguish that seized her, letting the soft strokes of Oakheart's powerful hand as it drew down her back and the tender sound of his voice soothe her. Her eyelids closed and a lulling sensation overcame her as her grief and rage ebbed. When next she came to, she was folded in Oakheart's embrace, both of them lying on the bed. He had a tight hold, as if he feared losing her.

Her bladder was full and she needed to use the bathroom. She tried lifting his arms, to slip away while he slept, but she was suddenly weak and couldn't budge them.

"Oakheart?" she said, tapping him on the arm. She rocked back and forth. He mumbled something in her ear. "I need to get up. I have to pee. Let me go."

And then he lifted his arm away and she rolled out of the bed. It was strange having him close to her. How fickle was that? One minute she was longing for him and the next it was strange to have him near. She did not like this gyration in her feelings. It made her doubt her sanity. What was it doing to Oakheart?

She went to the bathroom and pondered her options. She realised she would have to talk to him. It was pointless trying to understand how he felt. She was not him. They had to talk. She had to empty her heart to him. It wasn't going to be easy for either of them. She was not looking forward to it.

When she opened the door a smidgeon, Oakheart was sitting bare-chested on the bed waiting for her. She was tempted to shut the door again and hide in the bathroom. Stupid idea. Instead, she took a deep breath and stepped into the room.

An empty feeling enveloped her again. She was with Oakheart alone. He was half undressed. She should have been overwhelmed with desire and love. In fact, she wanted to be filled with those things but she wasn't. What did he feel?

"Oakheart?"

"Yes," he answered straight away, getting off the bed. "Are you hungry? There is food." He stood and went to a tray, to cut cheese and put it on a plate.

"Can we talk?"

He paused and swung around to meet her gaze. "We must."

Sophy nodded and he helped her back into bed. She was afraid. What if he didn't want her any longer? What if she didn't want him?

What if that desire and love were gone forever? What would that mean? Would she have to leave Argenterra so he could marry someone more suitable? Someone who could be a real princess. Someone like Aria?

He offered her cheese and she took a piece, munching slowly as she tried to order her thoughts. They wouldn't keep still. It was so annoying.

Sophy lay back on the pillow and Oakheart propped himself up beside her, head on hand, elbow on the bed. He lay along the length of her. Heat emanated from him, toasty and warm and nice.

Her gaze travelled up his body. "Do you love me still, Oakheart?"

"Yes, more than ever."

She frowned. "More than ever. Why?"

He traced a finger down her profile. "I discovered something important because of you."

"Really? What's that?"

"That love is stronger than any oath."

A grin spread over her face. "That sounds vaguely familiar. I think someone very wise and intelligent said something quite like that once."

"You forgot to add brave, too."

Oakheart angled his head down to capture her lips in a kiss. It was a light kiss. The contact felt strange, not how she remembered.

He watched her face after the kiss, his forefinger brushing her bottom lip. His eyes were intent.

"What do you feel about what happened to me? I worry that..."

"You are not to blame for anything that happened to you," he said with some force. When she pulled back, he let out a long sigh and brushed his finger along her cheek.

"I blame myself for bringing you near to danger," he said softly. His eyes lifted to hers, intensely green. "I berate myself daily for not lunging after you so that I was there in the Deadlands with you.

"The tether of our oath was gone. I was adrift emotionally, physically. My mother reasoned that you had returned to your home world because that was where the gate was pointed when she arrived. She had no knowledge of Rufus. Daily she argued with me, telling me that I was wrong, that you were not in danger. As I said, the adepts could do nothing. All knowledge of the gate had died with Adage and then Daken. Then my father called for my aid." He let out a sigh and brushed his hair off his forehead—a familiar gesture.

"Months of helpless waiting. Not knowing if you were alive or dead. Suspecting that you were suffering, and fearing that I would be too late. You see, I did not forget you, even though our oath was severed."

Sophy traced a hand along his jaw, drinking in the sight of him. Her feelings were still ambiguous. "I didn't know who I was for a long time. I didn't remember my name or Argenterra or how I got there. I didn't remember your name or your face until Rufus captured and tortured me. The memory of you was tainted by pain and suffering. Perhaps Rufus planned it that way." She shook her head, envisioning her time in the Deadlands. "I lived with these small creatures. I called them ugreals. They kept me safe in little tunnels. I ate tree roots to survive."

Oakheart ran his hand over her spiky hair. "Then maybe not remembering helped you survive all that time. I was not so fortunate. Every day, nay, every moment, I was tormented by the loss of you, wondering how you were and knowing with each breath I was letting you down by not coming for you."

Oakheart's touch made her conscious of how ugly she must look. He put his hands over hers. "You look beautiful to me, Sophy. Your hair will grow back. I love you. And that means more to me than our oath."

"Oakheart, I think I love you still. But I have to tell you the truth. I feel strange inside. It's all messed up, like I blame you, blame myself. I feel unworthy and shamed. Surviving like I did took something from me, twisted me. Nothing else I have experienced since meeting you has been as bad as that.

"Nasheen's kidnapping. The torture at Hanal's seer's hand. They were child's play, as agonising as they were. I worry that I will feel this way forever. I worry that I will let you down, particularly if I cannot love you again. What if I'm empty inside forever?"

Oakheart closed his eyes and leant in close, placing his forehead against hers. "Thank you for telling me how you feel, for sharing what is in your heart. You trust me enough to be open with me and that gives me hope. I cannot take those feelings away from you. I cannot make it better or make it go away as if it never happened. I wish that I could. Know that I love you, and that I feel there is no shame. I can understand that Rufus hurt you deeply. I hope in time your wounds will heal. Indeed, although they are not there for all to see, they are real and deep within you."

Sophy let Oakheart stroke her some more. She relaxed and then soon slept, wrapped in his embrace. As she drifted off, she hoped that it was just time that she needed. She had been on her own, not knowing who she was for some time. She needed to get used to Oakheart's presence, get used to the smell and feel of him. She needed to forgive herself and him and then move on.

She needed to tell him about the baby. The news would complicate things. She wasn't ready.

❧

THE SMELL OF HOT PORRIDGE WOKE HER THE NEXT MORNING. "Come on, sleepy head. Time for food or you'll fade away before my eyes."

Sophy sat up and shuffled back so she could rest against the wall. Oakheart placed a tray on her lap. On it was a plate of honeyed toffelporridge and some kind of juice. Before she could even take in what was before her, Oakheart was brandishing a spoon. "I want to feed you."

"Really?" She frowned at him and made a grab for the spoon. He kept it out of reach. "Why?"

"Remember once when I played at being your maid?"

Heated cheeks advertised that she did.

He lifted an eyebrow. "A similar exercise. One in trust. Will you allow me?"

"But I'm not a baby."

He lifted an eyebrow and brandished the spoon. She frowned and then grinned when the loaded utensil hovered close to her mouth. Her gaze met his and she opened her mouth. The food was warm and slid down her throat with ease. She took a sip of juice and then took another mouthful.

While he fed her, Oakheart talked about the political situation and revealed some of his plans. They had to leave straight away. He had to get to Silverdale.

She put a hand up to pause the spoon-feeding. "You're telling me I have to get on a horse now and ride hell for leather to Silverdale?"

His eyebrows rose. "Not today, exactly. Tomorrow, maybe. You are too worn out. But yes, we ride for Silverdale...soon. Although you would be safer if I left you at the retreat, I do not wish to part from you."

"But I'm worn out. Tired." Maybe she should tell him about the baby she was carrying. She bit her lip. She wasn't ready to tell him yet.

The spoon arrowed into her mouth again. After she swallowed, she said, "I can't eat any more right now. I might puke."

The complacent grin on his face disappeared. "Puke? You mean spit up?"

When she nodded he dropped the spoon back into the bowl. "Well, then I will eat. If you will excuse me."

A laugh burst out of her. "Why are you excusing yourself? You've never done that before."

"Because I am hungry and I do not want to surprise you with how much I eat when you have scarcely eaten a thing."

"I've seen you eat before. It is a wonder to behold."

He grinned at her and started by finishing off her bowl, then heaping it full again from the serving dish.

With an indulgent smile, she shook her head as she sat there and watched him eat. In that quiet space with just them, she was able to tell him in more detail about what had happened. Oakheart listened and occasionally asked questions. He was very interested in the ugreals and loved the name she had christened them with. He was fascinated with her description of the ruin of the city. It accorded with some history written down by Vorn when the First Comers settled in Argenterra.

"When this is over and we have the time, you should read some of Vorn's history yourself. He talks in detail of his homeworld and of the final battle before he fled to Argenterra. He even mentions the loss of his sword. The sword you have returned to us."

"That sounds fab, but I'm keeping the sword."

His eyebrow lifted. "You may have trouble prising it from Lianal."

"I don't think so. Possession is nine-tenths of the law. I will get it back. If they behave themselves I may leave the sword to the retreat in my will."

"Your will?"

"Yes, the document that talks about what happens to your things when you die."

"Do not talk of dying." He stood up and tidied their things. "I will speak to Lianal." He turned back to her and grimaced. "Warn him of your intention."

Sophy found her fatigue was still hard to conquer. After eating, she wanted nothing more than to snuggle down in the comfortable bed and sleep. Oakheart went on some errands while she slept. The sound of water spilling into a tub woke her. She lifted her head and saw him leaning against the door frame staring at her. "You taking a bath?" she asked.

He smiled and shook his head. "No, you are."

She quirked an eyebrow. "Do I still smell?"

He shook his head. "No, I want to bathe you. And I have added herbs to the water to help soothe your muscles." Coming for her, he peeled off the blankets, then her light robe, and lifted her. She was too surprised to make a protest.

He lowered her carefully into the bath, his face solemn.

"Why?"

"You forget my ambition to be a lady's maid."

Sophy chuckled at the recollection. It was so long ago, and she was different then. It was hard to recapture that moment. She tried to cooperate as she did not want to spoil Oakheart's valiant attempts to be intimate. "I thought you relived that experience feeding me earlier."

"That was only the warm-up. I do not want to be apart from you, Sophy. Ever."

"Oh?" The water was soft and warm against her skin. A few petals floated on the surface. It reminded her of the luxury of Valley Keep and those days when she and Aria had first arrived in Argenterra.

What a child she had been then, and yet she had considered herself so grown up. What was she now, an old woman?

Oakheart wiped her face and then he unpeeled the bandage on her arm and inspected it. He cleaned her body, ran the cloth over the slight swell of her belly. She watched his hands. Their child was in there. Would he believe it was his? That thought made her eyes widen and her breath hissed in.

"Did I hurt you?"

"No, no...it's just..."

Their gazes locked. Those green eyes of his shone with light and happiness. She could feel now that he was happy to have her there with him. Something as simple as bathing her brought him joy. She didn't have to try to please him or be any different than who she was at that moment.

"What?"

She shook her head. "Nothing."

"Sophy?"

"Just...thank you. Thank you for being you."

He squeezed her hand as he looked deep into her eyes. "Thank you. Thank the *given* you are back with me." She lay back, enjoying the warm water and the slow caress of the wash cloth. Oakheart took his task most seriously and was solicitous and thorough. Soaping up the cloth, he set to cleaning her legs. He asked her to turn over and rubbed her back, careful of any minor cuts and abrasions.

"You mentioned a machine," he commented, gentle hands caressing.

She told him about the contraption: how it was used to debase and hurt her. She told him that Rufus had been a man once.

"The Ancient Evil said that?" he asked.

"Yes. There is more. She had put a curse on me that prevented me from being pregnant. You remember the baby I lost in Gilton Forest?"

"Yes," he said softly, warily.

"That was her. Her curse. You see, that machine she had that drew the *given* out of me? Well, if I was pregnant it wouldn't work effectively. A child in me would draw the power into it, where she couldn't get it."

"Unesta spoke of this?" His eyes narrowed.

"Rufus wanted me. But she forbade him." She looked to the wall, unable to say a word while looking him in the face. What if she saw revulsion? "He was not allowed to impregnate me."

The tension ran out of him. "I see. It is good that she stopped him then."

"Yes," she replied, her eyes returning to study his face. Sophy wanted to tell him about their child then. Knew that it was her cue, but some mean streak held her back. Oakheart loved her, that much she knew. He would blame himself for her suffering. Already did. She didn't want to crush him with guilt. Knowing that he'd risked her and his child with the delay could well be too much for him to bear. He wasn't able to be there for her for very good reasons. She couldn't keep punishing and blaming him. She had to get over herself. Knew she had to, but it was hard.

There was also embarrassment and shame. She also found she didn't want him thinking less of her. She rolled over, sending the bath water in a wave over the end. He was completely soaked.

Looking down at his body, he glanced up at her, a question in his eye. "It appears you have issued an invitation."

"What?"

He peeled off his breeches. "No," she objected. "There's no room."

"Too late," he said with a grin and climbed in. She gaped at him, but raised no objections when he rearranged her body so he could be under the water too. He'd been so nice to her, how could she repay that with unkindness? The view wasn't that bad either. She shivered with the first bit of arousal she'd experienced in ages. The bath was largish, but not a pool. The warm water lapped at their bodies. Sophy noticed that he caressed her still and she could not ignore his pleasing touch. If she had been a kitten, she'd have been in his lap.

Intellectually, she knew he was attempting to get her used to him again. As she liked his approach, she didn't object and acted as if she didn't know there was a strategy in his actions. Lying back in his arms with her eyes closed, she relaxed for the first time in so long. It was like being in heaven. Oakheart added more water and she groaned in appreciation. He was going to have a problem getting her out of there.

A knock at the outer door roused her from a doze.

"One moment," Oakheart called and then leapt out, covered himself in a robe and shut the door to the bathroom while he answered the main door. Sophy looked at her hands and saw the wrinkled skin. It was time to get out.

As the voices penetrated through the closed door, she sighed. Looked like the world had found them again. She ran her fingers through her tufts of hair. All she needed was Aria. Aria would set her to rights. She'd think of some way of making Sophy feel better about her looks. Aria, where are you now?

# 29

# TO THINE OWN HEART BE AWKWARD

In the lead, Aria dismounted first when they made the front line at the base of the Upper Plateau. Up that treacherous By-way lay Silverdale, her father, and Hanal of Puri.

Dellbright was dead. Aria couldn't believe it had happened and had spent the night worrying if in severing the bond she had killed him.

Only yesterday, just after she had severed their oathbond, she'd been drawn into him, into his mind, at the moment of his passing. It was so sudden, so shocking. If not for Leyla she might have fallen off her horse. Their oathbond was severed so she shouldn't have been able to sense his death. Perhaps some part of her had lingered, seeking her son. Some part of the connection had remained. It was possible. No one had severed an oathbond before.

Gilly had been with him. It was the hateful force of Dellbright's intentions that had provided the leverage to undo her oathbond. Thoughts of their son were on his mind at death. Those thoughts hadn't been good; Gilly had been in danger. She remembered the scene, the view of the mountains. She cursed, for it wasn't enough for her to know where Gilly was. Some small town with a view to the Glassy Mountain Range.

He hadn't killed himself. Although, the condition of his mind when she severed the bond led her to believe that he was not long for this world. He couldn't have lived without their oathbond. Her freedom was too much for him to bear; it angered him more than anything else.

The surprise was strong at the moment of death. But nothing else. Not where he was or what he was doing there. One day she'd find that place, find Gilly, or at least a clue to him.

If she grieved it was for the Dellbright who was, who could have been. Her one overwhelming response to his death was relief. Perhaps that was shallow. Leyla had thought not when they discussed it.

The absence of her oathbond was strange. Once it had elated her, then dragged her down, almost suffocating her. Now it was gone. Just like that. She had not expected it. Had not even allowed herself to wish it.

Someone called her name. Swinging round, she came face to face with Fern. A mixture of emotions assailed her. Their sour words at their last parting were fresh in her mind. Her hurt and confusion were still raw. Adjusting her posture, she tensed.

"What are you doing here?" Fern asked peremptorily, a sneer evident in the twist of his mouth.

Aria realised then just how nasty Fern could be. His handsome face was marred by his expression; his mouth readily accommodated a sneer. Was this how he'd treated Sophy? How had she borne it?

Fern was superficial. Denied what he wanted, in this case, her, he'd turned on her. He had not even tried to see her side of things. He said he had been willing to leave Argenterra for her, and she should be grateful for that. She'd fallen for his charm, but it had been a mistake. He was not for her. They both knew it now.

Leaving Argenterra with him would have been her colossal mistake, on top of the one she'd already made by marrying Dellbright.

"I'm the envoy to Hanal of Puri. I am only here to negotiate my passage and perhaps rest a short while before we continue on to Silverdale." She indicated Leyla, who was just dismounting.

"You have got to be out of your mind." He looked around him. "Where's your husband? I thought you ran back to him with open arms."

Aria grimaced. "Not funny, Fern. You knew the situation better than anyone."

"I have had time to think it over. I think you like being treated that way."

Fist clenched, Aria decided to ignore Fern. "We will rest here tonight. Please send word to Hanal's people, and find me two guards to act as escort."

Fern's brow was like a thundercloud. "Just like that? Find you two guards to escort you. You are insane. I will not let you pass."

Aria was tired and cranky. "Look, Lord Fern, I don't need your permission. I can do without the guards if you can't spare them. I don't care." She turned to Leyla. "See if you can find us a tent and a meal. I'll see to the horses."

With that, she took both reins and led their mounts to the stabling yard where the rest of the horses were kept. Fern followed for a short distance, emanating anger, and then strode off when she ignored him. Nice to see you too, she thought at him. Relief flooded through her. What had she ever seen in him? Was she really that bad with men? First Dellbright and then Fern. Would she never learn? What would Lyant make of Fern, if she could secure the marriage between them? Well, that was out of her hands. Hanal had to agree. Apparently, Fern was already in agreement.

Her life was different now, she realised. She was a princess. Princess Aria of Silverdale. She had power...she frowned. Did she? Yes, she had power. Personal power and *given* power. She was also in the service of her people.

A stable girl came running up to her. "I can take those for you, my lady. I will curry them and feed them too."

"Thank you. Umm...what is your name?"

"Ali, my lady. I will take good care of them."

"I am sure you shall." She stood aside as their mounts were led off. Looking around the courtyard, she realised there was quite a number of women there, repairing arrows, practising with swords. Circumstances were certainly different from when she first came to Argenterra. Although, she'd stayed only in Valley Keep and Dellbright held definite ideas about gender roles. She had believed them, too.

Now, though, she wasn't quite convinced. She preferred being valued as a person, for who she was. More like Sophy. And just where was Sophy? Had Oakheart found her? Was she safe?

After asking directions, she found Leyla in their tent. Hot tea steamed in her cup. "Thank you so much." Aria inhaled a waft of steam and took a sip. "Just what I needed."

Leyla spread out their blankets on the camp bed. "I have ordered water for bathing. Have you thought anymore about what you will wear when you meet Hanal?"

Aria sat down on a stool, resting her back on the tent pole and putting her legs up on the crate that served as a table. "No. I didn't bring anything flashy with me. Lordy, I didn't even think of it. Dellbright burned all my beautiful gowns."

Leyla grinned. "Fortunately, your mother came prepared."

Aria frowned. "I can't see how she could do that. She had no clothes of her own. I had none." She gaped as Leyla pulled out an adept's robe. "You want me to wear that?"

Leyla frowned and looked between her and the robe. "Do you not like it? It was the best your mother could arrange. It would be better than smelling of horse, sweat and stained breeches."

"I suppose you're right. I think we will have to camp once we reach the top. Then go on from there."

"I will pack it up then and hope it does not crush any more than it has already." Leyla looked up. "Here is the water."

She opened the tent flap and a small hip bath was carried in by two soldiers. They bowed and left. Aria swallowed the rest of the tea. "Best get serious then."

Leyla helped Aria to strip and then scrubbed her down until her skin was pink.

⚜

"ARIA?" FERN CALLED FROM OUTSIDE THEIR TENT THE NEXT morning.

Aria groaned as she woke, realising she had garnered a few more aches and pains than previously. That last leg had been longer than the rest. "What?" she replied grumpily.

As Leyla was already awake, she went to the tent opening. Fern stepped through. Aria sat up and pushed her ginger curls out of her face. Her fingers tangled in the unruly mess. She was going to look dreadful when presented to Hanal.

Fern carried a pile of clothing, which he dumped on the end of her bed. "I have scrounged around for some suitable clothing. Unfortunately, most of the women here have no gowns with them. Perhaps there is something you can use to your purpose. Although I personally think it best you do not venture to Silverdale."

"So you said." Aria glanced at the pile, which didn't look very promising. "Thank you for the thought. I didn't expect to see a Valley gown here, or ever again."

Leyla went out of the tent with a ewer to fetch fresh water. She gave Aria a small nod as she turned before exiting.

"So you left the Valley?" Fern brooded, his eyes dark in the dim light of the tent.

Aria drew forth the *given*. She didn't think Fern had the perception to see that her oathbond to Dellbright was no more, but she wanted to make sure he didn't get an inkling. "Yes."

"How was Dellbright when you left him?"

Aria's head snapped up, her eyes meeting his. "The same."

She picked up one of the gowns he'd brought and tossed it aside. Some dull, brown rustic dress that was way too small for her. She was in no mood to talk about Dellbright to Fern. Not after what they'd shared and he'd thrown away. All that was left in her heart was anger at her own stupidity. There were reasons she had been susceptible to Fern's charms. After being subject to Dellbright's cruelty, one kind word from another man was enough to sway her. She knew better now. It was up to her and her own actions to direct her life. There was duty and, if she could, she was going to fulfil it.

"Aria, please, rethink this. Oakheart will not forgive me if anything happened to you."

"Really? What do you feel about it?"

He shrugged. "I care not either way." His tanned skin flushed and he could not meet her gaze.

"Have you found me an escort?"

"Yes." His eyes blazed at they met hers. "Though I can ill afford to spare them."

She flashed him a tired smile. "Give me a moment and I will meet them."

Fern gave a short bow and left the tent. She could almost sense the waves of anger he left in his wake.

Leyla came back and put some water on to boil. Together they went through the clothes that Fern had brought and found a few items that might prove useful. None were acceptable on their own, but Leyla reasoned that they could work as underclothes or help them with their own supply of clothing.

Aria changed into clean breeches. They were still damp from washing but she had nothing else suitable. She was not going to see Hanal straight away so there was time to prepare. After they had eaten some porridge and finished sipping their tea, Fern called again.

He stood aside and two guards came in, dressed in fine liveries of white and silver. They were identical twins and looked amazing. Aria stared at them and, with a quick glance at Leyla, she realised the adept was impressed too. Both adepts were handsome in a rough kind of way. Sandy-haired, a spray of freckles across their straight noses, and they had bright blue eyes. Aria figured they were around five foot ten, although one was slightly shorter.

"May I present your escort, Jael and Kael of the White. They were on leave from Silverdale's city guards when it was taken. They know the city well and they are also familiar with the palace. They will guard you well."

Aria stood and Leyla rose behind her. She curtseyed to them. "Thank you for agreeing to come with me. You will make very fine escorts." She straightened and her gaze dropped to their sword scabbards at their sides. Both had knives at their belts. They looked ceremonial but she figured that Fern had provided her with fighting men. "This is Leyla. She is an adept from Glassy Mountain Retreat. If she gives you an order you are to obey her as if it came from me. She is charged with my protection. Her status as my maid is a ruse. She can fight using the *given*. I tell you this so that you will heed her."

Both men bowed. "Yes, my lady." Jael spoke. He was the one that was slightly shorter and, she noted, slightly thinner. "We will have your mounts prepared for departure. Is there anything else we can do to be of service?"

"No. We will meet you at the barrier."

They turned on their heels and left. Fern stood brooding by the tent flap. Aria poked her head out and nodded to him. "Thank you. A very good choice. They will add greatly to my entourage."

Fern shook his head. "They will be good in a fight as well as being decorative, I grant you that. However, I still protest. I have had to double my guards along the perimeter because of your presence here. Why do you think I keep your mother at the base camp? Because I would not trust Hanal. On my life, I cannot. He would take you to force us to capitulate."

Aria's chin rose. "I am sorry my presence has caused you an inconvenience. I will be leaving shortly. I trust Hanal to not coerce me into anything that has not already been agreed as a bargaining position."

Aria withdrew back into the tent. Fern came after her. "I know. I am ready to comply to make peace. There is naught we can do. Army against army. They say the *given* has waned but there is no murderous intent on either side. Negotiation may be our only chance unless we are prepared to leave Argenterra behind. We cannot stay like this forever. Blasted stalemate."

"Exactly so."

Fern bowed again, this time with a flourish that was reminiscent of the courtier he was. The tent flap quivered as he departed, and then stilled. Leyla sighed. "So much potential for anger. I fear he was misnamed."

"What do you mean?"

"Fern implies lushness and coolness. His parents should have named him Storm!"

With a laugh, Aria agreed and finished packing, trying to forget Fern's storm-tossed grey eyes.

THEY ARRIVED ATOP THE UPPER PLATEAU LATE IN THE EVENING after making good time. Jael and Kael were efficient and looked splendid. Aria realised that looking the part of an envoy was as important as being a good one. Their Puri honour guard numbered ten, all dressed in colourful clothes, robes of red, orange, green and blue and trimmed in swirling designs. They wore their costumes with pride as if saying they were in Argenterra but they were not Argenterran.

Smiles flashed in their dark features; most of them were young and eager. Their leader was an older man with grey in his beard. He gave her a grave nod and then ordered them all to dismount.

Her horse was taken and she stood on the plateau looking out over the land with the sun setting in swathes of crimson and gold. The breath stole out of her. She'd come a long way. So this was the land: this was Argenterra. Suddenly she felt old. No longer that young woman who had been overwhelmed by the beauty and the *given* magic of this place. She had matured, suffered, and had been shaped.

"My lady? We are being escorted to our tent." Leyla touched her on the arm, her gaze also flowing out to the scene spread out before them. She drew in a breath. "By the *given*, it is truly a wondrous land. I have never seen a view like this."

Arm in arm, they followed Jael and Kael to their assigned tent. Inside, they were surprised by the splendour. No convenience that was portable was spared. A large tub sat steaming on a rug in the centre of the pavilion. It was too large to be called a tent. A dais contained a mattress big enough for her and Leyla to share. Her eye caught a smaller pallet covered with a bright blanket sewn from scraps of Puri robes.

A low table contained food that was still steaming. Meat, flat breads, fruit. The best food she had seen in ages. Then the tent flap opened and Kael stuck his head in.

"Joval here wants to deliver something. He says it just arrived. A gift for you from Hanal of Puri."

"Oh! Let him in then."

She shared a look with Leyla. Already, she had been provided with ample luxury. What more could Hanal provide? She was touched by his generosity, but was smart enough to know there was an ulterior motive. This was politics, after all. If she had been gullible once in her life, she was not going to be now. With a smile, she realised that she had developed cynicism to match Sophy's.

Joval, the head man who had accompanied them up the trail to the Upper Plateau, entered. He was accompanied by another man, a courier as road-stained as they. He carried a cloth-wrapped bundle.

"Hanal of Puri sends greeting to Aria, Princess of Silverdale. He offers these robes to you as a gift so that you may appear in Silverdale dressed as your station deserves."

Conscious that her hair was an oily, dirty mess, she tried not to pull at it while the Puri were watching. A slight nod of her head and the courier stepped forwards and put the bundle on the bed. Then he bowed in what was the Puri way before withdrawing.

"I send my thanks and my compliments to Hanal of Puri."

Joval waited for her to say more, but she only inclined her head in dismissal. She was currently swimming out of her depth. To say more may give too much away. Best to keep to the essentials.

The courier departed and, with a bow, Joval also made his exit.

Leyla went to the tent flap and spoke to the twins. "Keep people out. We are bathing and resting."

"Yes, my...em...Leyla."

Leyla laughed softly. "You really should not have told them I was an adept. They do not know what to do with me."

"I wanted them to accord you proper respect. Now a bath first, then food, then we'll inspect Hanal's gift. What do you suggest I do with my hair? I fear it is past saving."

Leyla filled a plate. "You can eat while in the bath. Come on. Get in and I will pass you some titbits. No point in letting the food, or the water, get cold."

Aria stripped and lowered herself into the bath. "This is a bit of a luxury. The water is spiced."

"An adaption, I am sure. Water is not so plentiful in the wastes, but the spices are definitely Puri in origin."

She passed Aria a plate of food. Aria lay back and took in the morsels of meat and fruit. "My hair?" she said, around a mouthful.

Leyla frowned at it. "Some oil might help detangle it and restore the curl. You have some hair soap?"

"Yes, I borrowed it from my mother. There is only a little."

Leyla inspected the other items in the tent and opened some vials and sniffed. "Scented oils. That should do. Are you finished eating?"

"Yes," Aria replied, handing back the plate. Then she got serious about washing her hair and the rest of her body.

Wrapped in a large cloth that served as a towel, Aria sat on the edge of the bed as Leyla untied the parcel. Inside was a set of Puri robes. In addition was a high-quality, heavily embroidered cloth, which they weren't sure what was used for. The robes consisted of a lovely burgundy-coloured tunic, with a set of trousers in pale cream with a trim that offset the tunic. Soft slippers matched the cloth.

"He means you to come to him dressed as a Puri woman," Leyla explained as she disrobed, being keen to wash as well.

Aria lifted an eyebrow. "It does appear that way. What am I to do? To ignore this gift will upset the negotiations, but to accept it will be like accepting that he has won, that he has rights over me and all of Argenterra. Yet nothing we have brought matches it for quality or beauty."

Leyla caressed the fabric. "It is the very best that Puri has to offer."

A sigh escaped Aria. "Time to do a stocktake of the other clothes we have brought."

"What are you thinking, my lady?" Leyla lowered herself into the bath water. Her hair was oily and she dipped her head to wet it.

"A compromise. Although how we can make it work is beyond me."

Aria experimented mixing and matching items from Hanal's gift to what they had brought with them. Leyla washed herself and commented on the combinations. Once dried and wrapped in a robe, she arranged the clothes a number of ways, while Aria groaned, sighed or hitched a breath, depending on the combinations. "Perhaps the adept's gown underneath with this cloth worn so, like a sash?" Leyla placed the fabric so. With no mirror, Aria found it hard to judge.

"Maybe. What about the Puri tunic underneath and the outer layer of the adept's robe, then the colourful cloth like a sash around the waist?"

Leyla frowned as they tried it. "If only one of the gowns were presentable. The only decent one is too short for you."

"Oh! I have an idea." She grabbed the gown in question. "If we cut away the front of this and I wear the tunic pants and the sash, then it will look more Argenterran."

"The colour is not quite right, though. Does that matter?"

"No, for I can move the colour around to hide the fading."

"Then that is it."

"Yes!" Together they worked on the gown, Leyla cutting the skirt in the front but leaving the rest to trail down the back. Aria used the *given* on the colour, moving the dye to make a complementary pattern. They decided that the adept's outer cloak could be worn over the outfit to protect it from dust and prying eyes while they rode. Aria was intent on making an entrance and had a few ideas to show her mettle.

Later, Leyla and Aria sat on the big bed. Aria moaned in pleasure as Leyla massaged the oil into her scalp and hair. Carefully, Leyla disentangled her curls and laid them against her back. Aria's eyes closed and she started to drift off.

"Nearly done, my lady. Then we can sleep. Shall I share with you tonight?"

"Yes, I would like that."

# 30

# THE TIME FOR FORGIVENESS

The sound of Oakheart packing up his gear woke Sophy. She didn't want to get up. The bed was warm, comfortable and she was tired. Tired of everything. Being afraid. Being hurt. Most of all, tired of having to go somewhere.

"What are you doing?" she asked him grumpily, failing to keep her annoyance out of her voice. Why couldn't he make noises somewhere else? Why did he disturb her? She just wanted to sleep and sleep and eat and then sleep more.

"Come on, up you get," he said. "Now that you are recovered we must be away."

Frowning, Sophy sat up. "Recovered? Are you crazy? I haven't been back even a day."

"You have been back two days already."

"But I'm tired, sore…have pity."

"There is nothing too serious wrong with you now. Nothing that rest and good food will not heal."

She hugged the pillow to her middle. "Exactly! You said it. Rest. I intend on doing that."

His mouth dropping open; he swung around. "But I must leave. Will you not come with me?"

"You need to leave. I'm not ready yet."

He put his hands on his hips and regarded her. In the early days, he would have bellowed and ordered; now he just gazed at her with sorrowful eyes. "You know I have sacrificed much to save you, but now I must fulfil my duty to my father, to the people of Argenterra."

She lay back down and shut her eyes. Why did he have to be so noble? Perhaps if she didn't look at him, she wouldn't be swayed. She'd had enough of duty. Enough of pain. Enough of it all. If she told him about the baby he'd leave her alone. But that wasn't right. It would really stuff up his sense of duty. He would fall to pieces and never leave her be. She found she didn't like the thought of Oakheart being less than he was.

He had tried to get close to her, not pushing her to have sex or anything, but touching her through the night, soothing her. If only he'd keep that up for another day or week or month...a year? Maybe she'd soften. Maybe she'd have that feeling of love for him again. Actually, she did love him. No doubt about it. Otherwise she wouldn't be there with him. But loving him didn't mean she was willing to go on a quest.

"Sophy?"

She sat up and placed pillows behind her before lying back down. "You want to go to Silverdale? That's too damn far." Folding her arms, she pursed her lips and sent him a militant look.

Oakheart came up the bed. "Sophy, be reasonable."

Reluctantly, she gazed into his face. His mouth was rigid with concern and his eyes held an expression of pain, the bright green irises darkened. "My father has been taken prisoner. Silverdale's townsfolk have been exiled from their homes. Argenterra's forces have been unsuccessful in stopping them. Hanal will soon take the throne of Silverdale. In fact, it is already his by default."

Sophy stiffened. It was that bad already. "What the hell is he doing that for?"

Oakheart clenched his jaw, looking like he had more words in his mind than he could speak. "He has reasons, I suppose."

"He doesn't want Argenterra. I'm sure of it."

"Yet, he has taken it."

She lifted her eyebrows.

Oakheart sighed. "Hanal feels that his people have been treated unjustly by Argenterrans."

"That sounds familiar. Is he justified?"

"I believe there are some grounds for his dissatisfaction with how things are."

Sophy glowered at her bed covers. She was moved by Oakheart's plight, by Argenterra's plight, but why her, why now? "Could this have been prevented, Oakheart?"

Oakheart nodded and stroked her head. "Yes," he replied softly. "You remember how."

Sophy sighed and the memory flared to life. "Oh. Lyant. Marriage. Treaties?"

He nodded. "There is more to it than that. A marriage may not have prevented this. Who is to say?" He brushed his fingers against her chin. "Will you come?"

"Look, I don't particularly want to go anywhere, certainly not across Argenterra in hot pursuit of Puri raiders for weeks and weeks."

Oakheart's mouth lifted in a fleeting smile. "You will not need to do that. We will cross the wastes instead and approach Silverdale from the north as Hanal did. It is somewhat shorter, though we will need extra supplies for there is little water or fodder for the horses. Then we will meet with Hanal of Puri in Silverdale."

Sophy pushed Oakheart and he stood away from her as she drew her legs out of bed. "I don't get it. Why would he take Silverdale?" She reached for a robe and put it on. "What good does it do? The Puri don't even like buildings."

"However, they are there and they have done great harm."

Sophy strode across the room, nodding as she digested Oakheart's information. Turning to him she said, "Okay, say we go to Silverdale. What then?" Oakheart squared his shoulders and cleared his throat, but she went on before he could answer. "Do you have a plan? A negotiating position? Or are you going to lop off their heads and be done with it?"

Oakheart's eyebrows arrowed together. "Lop their heads off? No! There has been no killing."

Sophy's mouth dropped open. "So you're saying you're at war but no one has been killed?"

"There have been some deaths. Accidents, mostly, and some wounding." Oakheart avoided her gaze. There was more to it. He had mentioned...what were his exact words...molesting of women. *God damn it. Rape?*

"That's because of this binding oath?"

Tilting his head to the side, he added, "Yes. The *given* is less."

Sophy bit her lip. The *given* was less because in her jewel form she had drained much of it from the land. That would affect the oaths, she supposed. No expert, but her oathbond to Oakheart felt the same as it had been, but then again, she never could sense the *given*. Deflated, she sat back on the bed.

Oakheart sat next to her and picked up her hand. "I had been wondering what was bothering me about the situation. If we have chosen not to kill, maybe then the *given* has not left us. You see, it is theorised that the *given* works to tame our more aggressive side. The compulsion either stops us or turns our weapons aside. The *given* is less than it was, but it is not completely gone."

"But the binding oath. Rufus killed," Sophy said.

"He was not bound by the oath."

"So he couldn't break it." Sophy gasped. "I am not bound by the oath either. I could kill."

Oakheart stiffened. "No. You are not bound. Would you kill? Could you?"

Sophy pulled at her bottom lip. "I'm sure I'm capable of it. When threatened." She remembered killing warren beasts and attacking Unesta. "Can I take this oath?"

Oakheart put his arm around her and hugged her to him. "That is a wonderful idea." He frowned and began unpacking.

"What are you doing?"

He sent her a devastating grin. "We will not leave today. I must consult with Lianal about your oath. None have sworn the oath afresh, not since Vorn's time."

Sophy scoffed. "Of course, I just have to be complicated. The *given* doesn't work on me, remember."

Oakheart strode to the door, hesitating before leaving. "Maybe it will not be as complicated as we think. Take the opportunity to rest. I will have more food sent in."

Theatrically, Sophy lay back on the bed. "I intend to rest and eat until my heart's content."

❦

OAKHEART WAS BACK IN TOO SHORT A TIME. SHE WAS DEEPLY ASLEEP and he woke her. "What?" she said when surprised awake.

"Lianal thinks it will be easy for you to take the oath. The First Comers' oathtaking was well documented. You are to kneel by the Crystal Tree and speak the words of Vorn's oath."

Blinking away sleep, she grumbled, "Not the Crystal Tree in the Valley?"

"No, the original tree here."

She closed her eyes and whispered, "Good."

He shook her again. "What?" Her eyes were hard to open. She was so tired.

"All is prepared. You must dress and we will go."

She growled and flung off the covers. "Go? Like now, go?"

Oakheart let out a groan. "Yes. There is no time like the present. You must make your oath. Then there will be a meal to celebrate."

"Do I have to...you know, celebrate? Can't I sleep instead?"

"Truly you do try my patience. If you do not move I will dress you myself and carry you over my shoulder to the Crystal Tree."

"That doesn't sound too bad."

Oakheart dived for her. Sophy squealed as she ducked under his hands and fled to the bathroom. Inside, she found a set of clothes set out for her. Travelling clothes. There was no avoiding this. She washed up and put them on.

❦

ALL TOO SOON THEY WERE STANDING OUT ON THE PROMONTORY, where the Crystal Tree stood. It was weird though, because the tree

333

looked dead and it wasn't adorned with crystal leaves like the one in the Crystal Tree Woods, the one that had so marked her. Oakheart had lectured her on the specialness of the place. Vorn had knelt there, his blood dripping from his wounds as he made his oath to the land. The *given* had answered him by making the tree bear fruit so that he could feed his companions. *Nice story.*

Once kneeling there beneath the tree, she detected a stirring in her. The leaf was no longer a separate thing, she realised. It was now part of her. There hadn't been much time to think about it, but taking the oath would hamstring her. Maybe she could use the sword and kill Hanal and the Puri warriors, but would that achieve anything? She would have to kill them all and that was just unthinkable. She imagined wielding the blade into human flesh and her stomach clenched. It wasn't her at all. No, it was best to take the oath and avoid killing altogether.

Lianal loomed above her. "Are you ready to speak your oath, Sophy, Princess of Silverdale, wife to Oakheart Silverbow?"

"Yes."

"Very well. Speak the words that are in your hands."

Sighing loudly, Sophy looked down at the hand-printed document. Drawing in a breath, she spoke the words: "I give my oath to this land. I will serve it, treasure it, will do no ill to it, its bounty or its people. I forsake hate for this oath and I partake of this place, which I name Argenterra, the land of silver, in its stead. All those who follow after me, who bear my blood, will be bound by my oath."

There was nothing to be felt. She knelt there breathing, hearing the words fall from her mouth. All of a sudden a burning sensation hit her in the breast bone. Her hands flew there. She sought Oakheart's gaze, but the world went white. She fainted.

Next thing, Oakheart was shaking her. "Sophy. Sophy!"

"Damn," she said. "I hate it when that happens."

"Are you well?"

She thought about her answer, squirmed as she checked her arms and legs. "Yes."

"Then it is done."

"Is it? Can you 'see' me? Can you see my oath?"

Oakheart frowned and studied her, his gaze going deep. He shook his head. "No. I cannot 'see' you. But you spoke the oath. You must be bound to the binding oath."

Sophy shrugged and pushed out of his arms. "It figures. I just had to be different. Here I was thinking I could fit in. But no, the *given* doesn't work on me still."

Lianal hovered nearby, overhearing their discussion. "Perhaps the effects take time to appear. We know not if the oath was visible in the First Comers. It was only later it was detected in their offspring, and then only with much study. But speak not of being an outsider. You are the hero of Argenterra, the one who faced the Ancient Evil and won."

Not altogether comfortable being hailed as a hero, Sophy nodded. A pleading look to Oakheart didn't gain her any pity. He was rather fixed on leaving.

"We must go. I cannot delay further, not with my father held as a hostage."

"I thought there was going to be a feast. I'll be tired after that."

He acknowledged her point.

"Tomorrow, Oakheart. Will that do?" She had to face facts. Oakheart wasn't going without her, and if she didn't agree to go he'd carry her off caveman style. His nod was like a salute, and then he drew her close, his arm resting on her shoulder. Sophy went all soft on the inside. Maybe this marriage thing was going to work out .

She turned to Lianal. "Now that we are leaving, can I have my sword back?"

"Your sword?" Lianal squared his shoulders. "I do not know what you mean."

Sophy wasn't going to be put off. "The big guy's sword. The one I brought back with me from Yulandir. I need it."

Lianal recoiled. "But it is a relic of Argenterra." He glared meaningfully at Oakheart then back to her. "You cannot take it."

Sophy pushed out of Oakheart's embrace and stepped into Lianal's personal space. "Actually, it is mine. You can't keep it."

Lianal spluttered.

Sophy put out her hand. "Hand it over, and if you are good I may give it back to you...eventually...one day...maybe..."

"Sophy..." Oakheart's voice held an edge of warning.

"I expect you to back me on this, Oakie. If I have to go to Silverdale so does the sword. I think it might help."

Oakheart grimaced. "She has a point, adept."

Lianal wrinkled his mouth like he was swallowing acid. "I will have it ready in the morning for your departure. It is currently the object of study."

"The morning. Right. Don't forget." She thumped Oakheart on the arm. "You mentioned a feast. Where is it? I'm starving."

They headed back to the retreat and Sophy was quite amenable to food, be it in company or not. She had agreed to go with Oakheart in the morning. Why on earth had she done that? Because she must.

Oakheart carried her to bed once she was too full of food to move. He rolled her gently into the bed, stripping off her clothes and then covering her in a blanket. She sighed. He was so gentle. Then as sleep claimed her, his warm skin touched hers and their legs entangled.

⚜

NEXT MORNING, A GROUP OF ADEPTS WAITED TO SEE THEM OFF. Oakheart cast his gaze over them, wondering if Lianal would comply with his wife's request that he surrender the sword. He could see no sign of it. Sophy was bound to repeat her request and Oakheart was on her side. She was the hero of Argenterra and had brought the sword back with her. If she wanted to keep it, then the retreat had to agree. Maybe later they could negotiate for its return, to study it. Sophy was skin and bone beside him. He wished they could stay longer so she could fatten up and rest. He hated asking it of her, particularly when she was angry with him.

They exchanged greetings. "So Lianal, can I have my sword?"

"I ask a boon of you," the lead adept replied. "Leave the sword with us and we will cherish and care for it."

Sophy shook her head. "No."

Oakheart stood behind her, chin high, eyes on the adepts. At Sophy's words there was a ripple of unease. Lianal dropped his gaze. "Very well."

A younger adept ran from the room. Not long after two adepts came in and approached her, one carrying the sword and the other the scabbard.

Lianal picked up the sword, his gaze travelling over the hilt and then the sleek blade as if in worship. He hesitated. Sophy put out a hand and power crackled from the sword; arcs of power leapt from the sword to her and the blade glowed bluish white. Lianal let out a curse. "Vorn's Blood!"

Oakheart saw that Sophy's skin also glowed from deep within. He wondered at it, until he remembered the leaf embedded within her body. She had Argenterra inside of her. The sword had claimed her. He saw the worried looks the adepts exchanged. Lianal offered up the sword to her and fell to his knees. "It is true. You are the hero of Argenterra. The sword is yours."

Sophy studied the blade, a faint smile on her lips as if it conjured memories.

Lianal stood. "We have brought you the sword's scabbard, the one that Vorn brought with him. May it serve and protect this precious artefact."

Another adept stepped up to her and handed Sophy the scabbard, secured to a newly tooled leather belt. She tied it around her waist and then sheathed the sword. When Lianal's gaze shifted to Oakheart he saw real awe in the adept. It had taken the retreat a while, but they now had respect for Sophy. It was well-deserved as far as Oakheart was concerned.

# 31

## A CONFRONTATION

Aria had accumulated a rather large honour guard as she rode into Silverdale. Thankfully, they had taken another night to camp so that she could appear refreshed and appropriately garbed. With concern she noted the burnt-out farms, the Argenterran people working on the lands and buildings under Puri guard.

In the fields just outside of the main town seemed to be a camp of Puri tents, with the occupants not looking busy at all. Some were just sitting around, idly chatting. In the town proper, although her retinue tended to block her view, she saw enough to give her cause for concern. The streets teemed with Puri men. Whether they came to gawk at her or not, she didn't know. They were taking the shortest route to the palace at the centre of the town. Or was this what the city had "fallen" meant? The Argenterrans were ousted and Puri controlled everything.

Covered in her adept's outer robe, she kept her raiment hidden. She was going to make an entrance, one aimed to impress. As the towers of the palace loomed above her, she had a moment of panic fuelled by doubt. Who did she think she was, taking on the negotiation? She had no skill, no talent and definitely no experience. She punched those negative thoughts down. Now was not the time to be plagued by doubt. That was Dellbright's malice clinging to her. She may not be experienced but she was smart and intuitive. It was her right to help her true father.

Surrounded by her Puri entourage, she was accompanied by Leyla, dressed in her best adept's robes, her long hair plaited down her back. Her honour guards had spent the night polishing their gear so it shined in the light. Their uniforms were travel worn, but being twins and such good specimens of maleness, they were impressive. A bit of dazzle couldn't do any harm and it downplayed her guards' fighting prowess.

In front of the large doors, the last before she would meet Hanal of Puri, she drew off her outer robe. Leyla took it from her and draped it over her arm. The doors swung open and there was a hush around her as she walked slowly, like a bride gliding to the altar. Her hair was clean and lightly oiled as it fell down her back. She had decided against covering her hair in the Puri fashion. Her hair was unusual so she would exploit that, besides, she was not Puri and she needed to make that point. What she wore was decidedly Argenterran, but the addition of the Puri fabric and trousers offered sufficient acknowledgement of Hanal's gift and a placating gesture acknowledging the Puri culture.

In the grand audience hall, Hanal sat on a throne and watched her with his crystal blue eyes. Aria's breath hitched when she caught sight of him. Her gaze travelled down and she had to admit he was a rather impressive specimen of the male variety. Rae had certainly had her head screwed on when she aimed for Hanal of Puri.

Next to him was an amazingly exotic woman. Older than Hanal, Aria guessed, with almond eyes and rich, red lips. The woman's gaze passed over her and Aria shivered: there was something lurking there. From Hanal she could definitely feel some vibration. The woman was more like an itch. The Puri woman nodded to Hanal—a signal—and slipped out of sight.

Drawing nearer, the detail of Hanal's clothing grew more obvious. His robes were impressive, crossing at the front to reveal his smooth-skinned chest. His head was covered in a bright cloth, rich with embroidery. Not unlike the one she wore around her waist. The story of his eyes had been related to her by Rae but even so her own eyes widened when their gazes met. Closer up, Hanal's eyes were startling, such a pale brightness against his swarthy complexion.

Stopping within ten paces of Hanal, she made a bow. Not a curtsey but a graceful bow like a man, toe pointed and arm giving an elaborate flourish with a slight bow of her head. No obeisance for her, just an acknowledgment of equals.

Hanal's expression was closed. His eyes glittered in the light of the firesticks, his mouth held in a neutral expression, although a muscle in his jaw moved almost imperceptibly. Aria had expected more of a reaction to her entrance. She waited. It was proper for him to speak first. Was he trying to psyche her out?

Without warning, he rose from the throne and pushed his outer robes back off his shoulders, leaving them to puddle on the floor. He strode up, his gaze never leaving her. She tried to hold her own, keep her body from reacting to his sudden approach. It wasn't easy for he was formidable. How had Rae softened this man? Thoughts of Sophy intruded. He had hurt Sophy. He could hurt her.

He paused in his approach, quite near, and performed an elaborate gesture, which she took to be a Puri-style bow. "May your waters flow with the *given*," he intoned. "Surely your famed beauty does little credit to the truth. Such hair as you have is most coveted amongst all women, full of gold and sun, a most worthy treasure. Your face so fair puts the dreams men have into the shade. Eyes as green as the finest leaves, rich with bounty. How I wish we had met earlier as we should have done.

"My seer, for all her faults, knew you for an Argenterran without even meeting you."

Aria frowned before she had the wit to control her puzzlement. "I'm sorry." She looked away from him, focussing on the empty throne. "Are you talking about the woman who tortured Sophy?"

Hanal's pleasant expression froze. He swallowed. "That is a delicate matter fit for later discussion."

Keeping her voice as regal as she could, she said, "I have come to negotiate terms for the return of Silverdale." Then, still frowning slightly, she looked his way again. "Although, I thank you for the compliments. They are very poetic." Aria pursed her lips. "Before we start I want your assurance that your seer will be punished for her crimes."

He lifted a dark eyebrow. "Negotiate?" He scoffed and his eyes glittered. "There is nothing to negotiate. I have Argenterra. However, I will be pleased to talk. Although I can say that my seer has already been banished from my side. I hope this is sufficient for you to continue to converse with me."

Aria inclined her head. "It is a start. Let's negotiate."

He shrugged. "What is there to negotiate?"

Aria unclenched her jaw and opened her hands to release the pent-up tension. "I came in good faith to negotiate with you. You could at least hear me out."

"I am listening to every sweet word that drops from your lips. However, you have an army that cannot engage me." He walked around her as if appraising her. He meant to be intimidating, but Aria had suffered worse at Dellbright's hands. She lifted her chin and pretended he wasn't there. "Your forces are caught at the base of the plateau and have no hope of climbing up the By-way to Silverdale, unless they wished to be picked off one by one."

He stood in front of her, his arms crossed at his chest. He lifted an eyebrow. "You seek terms, I suspect."

Aria stood motionless and quiet, her clenched teeth the only sign of her ire.

He studied her overtly, dropping his gaze down her body and up again. "And, as the Argenterrans have sent such a lovely ambassador, it will be a pleasure to listen."

Her gaze flicked to his, a glimmer of hope in her heart.

Acknowledging her with a wave of his hand, he turned away, walking back to the throne. "But do not think for one moment that I have anything to lose. I have already gained what I set out to do."

Fighting her indignation, Aria shivered as she glared at his back. He sounded so confident, so arrogant. He did not have everything. Opening her mouth took effort, but to her ears her voice was controlled. "There may be some room for negotiation," she said, keeping her voice neutral. "There are concessions that can be made on both sides that will benefit all."

Not yet at the dais where the throne sat, he swung around. A faint smile changed the shape of his mouth, altering it from harsh to handsome. "Then come this way," he said, throwing an arm out to her. "Your entourage may await you in your suite."

Recovering from the surprise that her words had some effect, she belatedly understood her position. "My suite?" she said, taking a step. When she reached him, she said in a quiet voice, "You mean my cell?"

His eyebrows rose. "Not at all. I do not think these negotiations," he over-emphasised the word, "will be concluded for many days. I would have you close to me…to discuss the details, of course."

Aria shot her companion a quick look. Leyla's eyes were wide with alarm. Aria nodded at her to let her know she was all right. Leyla had taught her to defend herself. Aria had to trust that Leyla could look after herself.

As she preceded him through the door, she chose to shorten her step so she could draw level with him. She didn't fail to notice the guards following, nor the look on Leyla's face as the door shut behind her. "Please, Hanal of Puri, may I not meet my father?"

A sigh escaped him. "In due course. We shall have our private audience first, if you please."

A chill went through her. Something in the way Hanal studied her made her stomach churn. There was a vee of puzzlement between his brows. Could Hanal see that her oathbond no longer existed? She had been able to fool others, but he was shrewd. He vibrated with energy and something else. The *given*. A sudden fear weakened her legs. "I…er…"

He put out his arm for her to rest her hand. "I give you my word you will come to no harm."

Aria swallowed, looked at his forearm and placed her hand lightly there. She must not betray weakness or fear. "That entirely depends on your definition of harm."

A smile twitched at the side of his mouth and they recommenced walking. "I trust Lady Sophy was well when you saw her last?"

It was difficult to control her emotions. Her eyes widened involuntarily. He knew what she had been thinking. Did he also know that Sophy was taken by the Crystal Gate, or of Oakheart's quest to retrieve her?

"She was recovering very well, when I saw her last. Hanal of Puri…"

"Hanal, will do. I have a feeling we will be friends."

She acknowledged his concession with a slight nod. "I prefer to have my handmaiden with me."

"Your adept?" He shook his head. "That I cannot allow. Not here in this room. You will be reunited with her shortly. First I wish to speak with you…alone."

He wasn't trying to be caressing, but firm. She had to buck up her courage. "Very well, I agree to meet with you privately. For a short time."

Looking earnestly into her face, Hanal smiled. Her stomach lurched. Her heart leapt. This man was dangerous. He had magnetism, but she knew she could not underestimate him. He was ruthless. He had her father captive. He had hurt Sophy. Despite all this, when she looked at him her heart raced as if it had a mind of its own. Fear? Or something else?

Hanal turned to a robed Puri man who followed behind them. "Make sure our Argenterran visitors have everything they need and are treated well." His order was acknowledged with a bow and the man slid away.

The room Hanal led her to turned out to be a small sitting room. It showed signs of hasty redecoration. Most of the furniture had been emptied out of the place and only a few items remained, shoved into corners. Paintings had been taken down and stood with their faces turned to the wall. Large cushions were arranged around a rug, on which also sat a low table. A small brazier smoked under a metal dish. A plate of flat bread stood next it.

Hanal gestured to the rug and cushions. "You will join me in a meal?"

Aria looked around at the room, at the growing dimness outside. "Yes. Thank you."

Hanal indicated with a hand that she should take a spot on the cushions. This she did, as regally as she could manage, moving slowly and gracefully. His gaze burned into her. When she was seated, he positioned himself on a cushion close by her side. His movements were natural and yet elegant. He was used to being watched, she surmised. He knew how to put on a show.

"Will you pour the tea?" he asked, nearly making her jump out of her skin. He had attempted to soften his tone, that much she recognised, but it did not soothe her nerves.

A tea pot sat near her leg with two small cups. It was all uncannily strange: him, the room, being alone. It was definitely intimate. Hanal was even more imposing without an audience.

"Certainly." She bent to the task, handing the small cup to him. "Tell me, is Rae here with you?"

His eyes narrowed and he took the cup, placing it before him. "I forgot she was your maid at Valley Keep."

"My lady in waiting and a good friend. I would love to hear news of her."

"You already glimpsed her and you will see Rae later."

Aria screwed up her face, ready to deny it. Then she knew—the exotic woman in the audience chamber. "So beautiful she is," she said warmly.

Hanal inclined his head, accepting her compliment of Rae. "I am hungry." He picked up a plate. "Would you let me feed you?" he asked lifting a morsel of meat towards her mouth.

She drew back, shocked, and her wariness forgotten. "No! I am quite capable of feeding myself." Her eyes widened. She had blown it. Too late now. She had to continue on this path. "In fact," she added with venom, "I'd rather you just got to the point."

He lifted an eyebrow, his mouth turned up in amusement, his eyes dancing.

She threw a hand out to the room. "I am not comfortable meeting like this, alone. Just tell me what you want and then let me go."

Tilting his head, he lifted the meat and dropped it into his mouth. He chewed and his eyes never left her face. After swallowing, he gestured with his hand. "This is your outlander ways, I suppose. Sophy was more careful how she spoke to me."

Aria drew in a breath. How dare he speak of what he did to Sophy? Before she could open her mouth to answer, he continued. "I heard you were everything that was ladylike and feminine. I admit to being disappointed."

Grinding her teeth, Aria met his gaze. "I am sorry," she ground out. "I am here on business. I have some propositions for you in return for you leaving Silverdale."

His eyebrows mocked her yet again. "Why would I do that? I like it here. Big palace. Lots of room."

"But your people do not. I saw much on my passage through Silverdale and what I observed interested me. No one seems comfortable. The town is in disarray. People mill around in the streets and do nothing, just linger there. Industry is stopped."

He leant back, taking his tea with him, and sipped. "I cannot fault your eyesight. Or your intuition. You have been well primed on what to say, no doubt."

Aria kept her mouth closed. No point in disabusing him. "The high queen offers Fern Ripplebark in marriage to your sister Lyant. He is third in line to the throne of Silverdale, after me." She inclined her head. That was weird, saying it like that.

His face was impassive; her words made no impression on his outer layer. The next bit she did not have authority for. "There will be no reprisals for the Puri invasion."

His mouth turned down.

"Argenterra will cede lands to the Puri. The lands north of the Argent Flow, from the borders of the Valley to outside of Mistletoe."

"How generous to cede land you do not possess."

She wasn't getting anywhere. "You don't possess them! We do."

He sighed and looked to the ceiling as if bored.

Suppressing a growl of frustration, she snapped, "What do you want then? Tell me."

Turning his head in her direction, a big smile adorned his face, before he adopted a serious expression and commented, "An honest request. How lovely."

"Well?"

"I want...you."

Her heart thudded. "Me?" It took a few tries to order her thoughts. "But..."

He sat up straighter, the amused façade dropping away. "You should have been mine if not for all these machinations!"

Genuinely puzzled, she said, "I don't know what you mean. What machinations?"

After studying her for a few moments, his tension fell away and he lazed against his cushion, a hand supporting his head. "Ahh...Tell me this. If you had known you were Veld's daughter would you have stayed at Valley Keep and married Dellbright?"

Her forehead creased and she rubbed at it. "I don't see how this relates to the negotiations."

"Humour me...You are not the true Gift of Crystal Tree Woods. That is known now. You bore the mark of the binding oath. My own seer saw that. I thought I had been deliberately tricked. Now I understand that it was not Veld's design, or Oakheart's. Sophy was the important one. You were just coming home."

She acknowledged his summary. "I didn't know that then."

"Yes, I see that. What I am asking you is for you to imagine what your decisions would have been if you had known. Would that have changed your actions?"

"I hardly see how I could have known. My mother never hinted at it."

"Yes, I understand that. But imagine the what-if."

She stared into the distance, at a small crack in the wall, to order her thoughts. Her response obviously meant a lot to him. "No. I would not have married Dellbright if I had known that I was Oakheart's sister and Veld's daughter. I would have come to Silverdale. I would have come home to see my father." She shook her head. "Sophy would not have married Dellbright either. I am sure of that. We both would have come to Silverdale."

"So, if you had come to Silverdale we would have met. I was here..."

"And..."

"We would have wed. I had been hoping for an alliance through Lyant's marriage to Oakheart, but Veld oiled his way out of it. But if there had been a second choice, you, then I think he might have agreed."

"Sheer conjecture. Many things could have happened. What if I had been born here? What if Prince Daken hadn't left? Dellbright might have been different. I may have married him, after all. Nothing is certain. It's too fluid to predict."

His smile was fleeting. "It certainly is."

"So you want an alliance with Veld's house? But you are already oathbound to Rae."

His mouth lifted in a grin. "The Puri know how to make an oath that allows them more than one wife."

Aria digested this. "Sounds unfair to me. I'd prefer it if a woman could have more than one husband."

Hanal's lips lifted in a smile. "I presume Dellbright is dead. You are no longer bound in an oath."

"Yes." She didn't bother to hide the fact. "You can see?"

He inclined his head and took another morsel of meat.

"I am not part of the bargaining position, but let's leave that issue for the moment. Besides me, what else do you want?"

"I want equality. I tried to get it the Argenterran way through negotiation, through an alliance, through marriage, but the old fool would not listen to me. Do you know what life is like in the wastes?"

Aria was intrigued by Hanal. There was passion in him and intelligence. She didn't understand why there was tension between the Puri and the Argenterrans. "No, not really. I know it is harder to work the *given*, that the land is not abundant with bounty."

"All that is true. It is a hard life. Children die from hunger. People die of illness. These things rarely occur in Argenterra. Do you think that is fair? Our forefathers were amongst the First Comers. I have Vorn's blood in my veins. Why are our people left out in the cold? Why are we so despised?"

His passion washed over her. She had no answer and the one she gave was feeble. "I didn't know. I'm sorry."

"You are sorry. Well, Aria, Princess of Silverdale, it has come to you to fix it." He clapped his hands and she jumped at the sound.

"I think it is time you met your father and thought about your negotiation strategy. What you have offered me so far is not nearly enough."

THE SUITE ARIA HAD BEEN PROVIDED WITH WAS LARGE BUT WAS positioned in the lower levels of the palace. Hence, there was not much sunlight as only small square holes in the top of the wall served as windows. Her eyes had to adjust to the dimness. Was this a prison? A sound at the door startled her. When it swung open, Aria tensed, fearing what? Her hands gripped the back of a chair and then relaxed when her eyes fell on Leyla. She ran to embrace the adept, who squeezed her in strong arms and then held her at arm's length, inspecting her with a critical gaze. "You are unharmed?"

"Why, yes." Her eyes narrowed. "Were you afraid for me? I don't think it is good diplomacy to harm an ambassador."

Leyla's eyelids lowered. "I was...apprehensive." Stepping away, she turned to take in the room. "It is little better than a cell."

"Are there guards at the door?"

Leyla tilted her head. "No, not stationed there. At the base of stairs to the upper floors, yes."

"Then I am free to walk about. I wasn't sure before." Aria walked to the door and turned back. "Coming?"

Leyla was taking in the room, but she quickly met Aria's gaze. "Of course."

It was quiet and gloomy in the corridor. They stepped out and Aria kept her attention keen as she gazed before them. Other doors led off from the hallway. She did not think to explore them. One end of the hallway opened to a room in which stood a round table and a fireplace. Aria walked up to it, Leyla following. The fire was burning. Aria reached out and tested the weight of the kettle. It was full so she placed it over the flames. On the table were tea things and a loaf of bread.

A door hinge squeaked and her head jerked up. An old man stood in the doorway, mouth open. He was largish, had bright blue eyes and lots of white hair. She immediately saw Oakheart's resemblance to him.

She stepped around the table, grasping the back of a chair. "Father?"

"Aria?' he said, and swallowed. "By the *given*! You are so much like your mother I would know you anywhere." He took a step and hesitated. "Would you give your father a hug?"

Aria needed no invitation. She threw herself into his embrace, tears coming along with broken sobs. "Father!"

Veld's large form quivered and she realised he was crying too. She tried to soothe him. "It's all right. I'm here now. We are together now."

He held her tight and she patted his back.

"Why are you here? Now Hanal has you, too."

A bit of squirming and she was free of his embrace. "I came to see you and to negotiate."

"Negotiate? It is too late for that."

"I don't think it is."

Someone else came out of the room. An older woman. Aria blinked in surprise at her colouring, feeling that she must be related to her. Veld shifted aside. "This is my sister. Vola, this is Aria."

"Oh, my child." Vola rushed up and enveloped her in large arms. "Vorn be praised. You are home with us, where you belong." She stepped back and held Aria by the shoulders and gave her a quick inspection. "You have all the arms and legs you need and a pretty face. Your hair," she said taking a hank in her fingers. "What a mass of curls."

Aria nodded. "Yes. Difficult to look after on the road, I assure you."

The kettle boiled. Vola went over to the fire and took it from the flame. "Tea, anyone?" She sniffed and wiped tears from her cheek. "And you, dear, what is your name?"

Leyla gave her name and Aria blushed. She'd forgotten the adept in all her excitement. Leyla sent her a smile and a nod and Aria realised that Leyla understood perfectly; there was no need to apologise.

"Now my child," Vorn said. "Fill me in on what is going on. Where is Oakheart?"

Aria related the position of their gathered forces and the difficulty in freeing Silverdale seeing as they could not get up the By-way to the Upper Plateau. Fighting the Puri raiders was out of the question as the tactical advantage was all on the Puri's side.

"So we have to negotiate," Veld said.

"Yes, but Hanal tells me my negotiating position is weak."

Veld put his hand over hers and squeezed. "It is all my fault, you know. I should have listened to Oakheart but I did not." His eyebrows lowered over his eyes. "Where is he?"

"Rescuing Sophy."

"Yes, but is he done yet? Hanal has summoned him. But if you are here and then he comes, Hanal will have all of my family."

Aria shook her head. "Mother is leading your forces."

"Ahh!" He nodded. "I suppose Hanal must know Maralain has returned. That must be how he knows about you. Did he offer you insult? Did he hurt you?"

Aria sat back in her seat. "No, he offered me no insult. He has taken my guards away, but has allowed Leyla to stay with me."

Veld's eyes shifted to the adept. "And what can your maid do?"

Aria grinned. "Leyla is not a—"

A noise behind them startled Aria. She bit off what she was saying and swung around. "Rae?" Rae had removed the make up and was dressed plainly but she had been in the audience chamber. Aria knew that now. "Oh lordy, it is you! I didn't recognise you before..." She sprung from her seat and launched herself at the young woman. "It is so good to see you."

❧ 32 ❧

## ON THE ROAD, AGAIN

Oakheart stirred the pot, finishing the meal preparation. Dusk surrounded them and a light wind kicked dust over the camp. Sophy was feeding the three horses: two mounts and one pack horse to carry their supplies. So far they had made good time. By his estimate they were half-way there after three days of steady travel. He squeezed dough onto a flat pan and pressed it flat with his fingers. Not as nice as using a rolling pin but he had forgone some luxuries for speed. He had noticed that Sophy did not mind the rough food. She ate heartily.

His gaze focussed on her. She was putting on weight and that was pleasing to the eye. Her thinness, after her ordeal at Hanal's hands and then in the Deadlands, had worried him. While he dished out their food into the metal plates, he watched Sophy currying the horses and grinned. She was so absorbed in the task she did not notice his regard. It meant she had no worries for the moment, lost as she was in her task and relaxed in heart and mind. He turned the flat bread over to cook the other side. He had made extra because Sophy was always so hungry and she liked the flat bread, hot off the griddle particularly.

By the time he was done cooking, Sophy washed up in a bucket and came to sit by the fire. The wastelands were empty of Puri so they could have a fire without fear. It was strange to him to see the land so desolate. Closer to Glass Cutting Canyon, where the Puri had cut a passage through the ranges, he expected they would find more of Hanal's men guarding the way. Once he had identified himself he was sure they would get safe passage into Silverdale and an audience with the Puri leader. Whatever Hanal planned for them, Oakheart was certain he would want to be the one to inflict it. Personally.

Oakheart pushed the worry for his father to the back of his mind. He had to trust that Hanal was taking care of him. Also, he must not worry over his mother and his forces. There was nothing he could do. He had chosen this path to rescue Sophy so there was no point bemoaning it.

Sophy leant over and took some bread, blowing her fingers from the heat of it. "Ow!" She dropped the bread into her plate, and scooped more food out of the pot, a steaming stew made of dried meat and vegetables. Nothing too fancy to be sure, but it was wholesome and filling. "Thanks for this," she said, taking a mouthful and chewing it hungrily. "I'm starving."

"I can see that." As he was the one usually hungry he was enjoying the role reversal. "You are looking good now. Less angles and more curves."

She looked up at him, her dark blue eyes sparkling with yellow light from the fire. "Geometry?"

He tilted his head to look at her. "Not exactly. You are filling out nicely. I am relieved I do not have to worry that you are not eating."

Sophy chewed and swallowed but he saw a change in her countenance, like a shadow.

"What is it? Did I say something wrong?"

"Nothing." She spoke softly, as if gazing inwardly.

With a sigh, he looked down at his plate and played with his food. "Are you sure?"

The Deadlands had changed her, and Oakheart was not sure it was a good change. Her soft edges were rubbed away. The Sophy he knew seemed to be lost in a forest of change. He cringed, still thinking that he was the cause of it.

"Yes." Sophy got onto her knees and scooped more stew into her plate. The food was fair. Nothing to get excited about, yet she ate like it was her last meal. After shovelling several more spoonfuls into her mouth she sat back, nursing a distended stomach. "Oh my," she said. "I think I've overdone it. All that time in the Deadlands I didn't have a hot meal. Not one decent meal. I dreamt of eating food. All I had were those bloody roots."

Oakheart's gaze fixed on her distended abdomen. It was an odd shape. He narrowed his gaze and thought hard. Then his heart rate jumped before settling at a faster rate. He put down his plate. "Sophy, are you expecting a child?"

Her head jerked up and he read the truth in her eyes. She looked down and rubbed her abdomen, let out a sigh. "Yes."

Oakheart stood up, his anger surging. "And when were you going to tell me?" he bellowed.

Sophy flinched, then huffed out a breath and looked away, to the horizon. "I've been meaning to tell you."

"Why? Why did you say nothing of this? I have dragged you away from the retreat, where you should have remained."

Her eyes flashed and her gaze raked him. "I was too angry with you at first and then it was just awkward to own up to it."

"That is not a good reason to keep such news from me." His fists were clenched and his voice held no trace of tenderness. A sense of wounding punched him hard in the gut.

Her head shot up and met his gaze. "It seemed good enough for me. Besides, if I had told you, you would have gone off without me. I couldn't bear that, not after...after..." She lowered her head and played with her fingers.

The tension ran out of him, other more joyous feelings taking its place. "How long have you known?"

"I knew in the Deadlands." She glanced up at him. "I'm sorry."

He stood there rocking on his heels, so many emotions fighting for precedence. Anger because she did not care to tell him something so important. Joy that she was expecting their child. Sadness because she had suffered so much, and still she followed him. If there was any path to re-establish their old relationship, the old honesty between them, he had to tread carefully.

He fell to his knees and lowered his head, finding it hard to keep his breathing slow and his emotions in check. A tear slid down his cheek. "Sophy..." He could not disguise his raw hurt.

Sophy stood up before him. Tension bled off her. "Don't."

Another tear fled down his cheek. Then a gentle touch on his head made him hold his breath. Did he imagine it? The touch grew to a stroke, firm fingers sliding over his head and then gently sliding along the curve of his ears. She let out a long drawn-out breath. "Oh, Oakie. It hurts so much." Her voice was clogged with emotion. His arms flew around her waist and with his face buried against her body, he sobbed. Her repressed emotion, and his own, could not be contained. When she moved to kneel with him he loosened his hold. Together they wept on each other's shoulders. "Forgive me," Sophy said brokenly. "I was wrong at first to be angry with you and then to not to tell you about the baby...."

"Forgive me," he said sniffing and wiping his eyes.

Sophy smiled crookedly. "I know there is nothing to forgive. You have always acted right. Forgive me and let's be done with recriminations."

They clung together, hearts thudding in unison. Oakheart lost all sense of time, then they parted and he looked at her bloodshot eyes, wet cheeks and blotched complexion. He had no idea how he looked to her eyes. He had never wept with such ferocity since he lost his mother to the gate.

Sophy's hand swiped up over her face, pushing back her butchered hair. "I wanted you so much and everything kept getting in the way," she said.

"I know," he replied in a soft voice. "But...now there is nothing to keep us apart except our own stubbornness."

Bloodshot eyes implored him. "Are you sure that is all there is to it?" She thumped her chest. "I fear...oh god...I fear that I will go to sleep and you will be gone when I wake up." He tried to soothe her, but she just grabbed hold of his jerkin and edged closer, face-to-face. "Sometimes, I think I'm back in that place, with Rufus coming for me. It's so hard to conceive of a future for someone as broken as me, let alone us...us and a baby."

He touched her cheek and wiped at a tear. "You are not broken. Hurt, yes. And you will heal."

"Will I? I just don't know."

He held the back of her neck and rubbed her skin with his thumb. "We can be true to one another. Then we can deal with whatever life throws at us."

Sophy returned his gaze and then a smile broke out on her face. "Right," she said, and then let out a laugh. "You're the high king's heir. I didn't know that I'd end up a princess or a queen. I'm never going to be any good at it."

A smile lifted the corner of his mouth. He ran his fingers through her hair and then massaged her tense shoulders. "Oh Sophy, you are already good at it."

She laughed out loud and this time the joy stayed. "Oakheart, be serious."

"I am being serious. I have no experience at being a high king. Maybe I will perform badly."

"Ah come on..."

"We have to tread this day together and the next. Sometimes I will help you and other times you will help me. Mostly, we will help each other. I have always admired your intelligence, your bravery and just who you are. Now I have seen you shine, seen you conquer..."

Her eyes narrowed. "Tell me, Oakheart, can you 'see' me now."

"Yes," he said simply.

Her mouth hungered for his. He tasted it in her kiss. There was no holding back. His mouth devoured hers. Stolen breaths were taken in between or as part of their passion. Tears and cries and fierce holding together. "Oakheart," Sophy said in an emotion-clogged voice.

He nodded and kissed her again, just as ravenously as before. It was as if, should he dare to stop kissing her, the words and the bond between them would dissipate. He did not want to let it slip through his fingers.

They lay together in the night, skin on skin, not wanting to separate. He had been alone so long that each breath was a treasure, each touch a paradise. Now he knew, he thought as sleep tugged away at his consciousness, that he had his Sophy back.

SOPHY WAS AT EASE IN THE SADDLE. SHE SHARED A LOOK WITH Oakheart and sent him a smile. Now that he knew her secret and they'd cleared the air, she was finally at home with him. "Can you tell me a bit more about the situation in Silverdale? What demands has Hanal made?"

"Demands? He has taken Silverdale."

Sophy gaped, shut her mouth. "You mean he just attacked, never asked for anything and just took the whole town? Just like that?"

Oakheart frowned. "Not exactly like that. I could see trouble brewing. He asked for justice and equality and for an alliance."

"Oh, Lyant, I remember. You were sent away."

"I was. My father told Hanal to return to the wasteland and stop bothering him."

Sophy had met Veld. "Ahh...I take it he did not say those things in such polite terms."

Oakheart nodded, bit his lip, his brows full of thunder.

"Look, you're an ambassador, right? It's your job to know what people want. Trade, arms, more land, better land, a marriage, something. Everyone wants something."

Oakheart glanced at her, eyes narrowed. "Sophy, I know my job. My father would not give Hanal what he wanted."

"Okay!" She said it long and slow. "Now that he is a prisoner, would that change his mind?"

Oakheart's hands clenched on the reins. "It must."

"Exactly. How do we get him back if we don't bargain? It doesn't seem right. Hanal doesn't want Silverdale. From what I could see, the issue was more that he thought the way things were divided were unequal. It particularly rankled the Puri that they did not have the *given* in the same amount as Argenterra. That is why he wanted the power inside me and why I agreed to let him try to take it. It seemed to me he had a point. He went on and on about his blood and how he had just as much right to rule as Veld. But he did not say he wanted to rule instead of Veld."

"Rae said that Hanal was honourable. I kept thinking she was demented. When I think about it now, it seems that there is more to it than just revenge or seizing power. What's the history?"

Oakheart furrowed his brow. "My father does not trust the Puri. It is a long story going back to Vorn and Shabra. I think it is silly, but father does not. He would not agree."

"Mmm, things might be different now."

"Perhaps."

"So if you were to talk with Hanal and ask him what he wants, it would be a start."

Oakheart was shaking his head. "I am perfectly willing to. We devised a negotiating strategy but there is so much bad blood now. How can there ever be peace?"

Sophy considered him for a moment. "Oakheart, think about it. As far as I know neither side has done much killing."

Oakheart let out a gasp. "None."

"Thought so. Maiming, hurting, stealing, chasing away?"

Oakheart nodded. "They have taken women who are not bound by an oath."

"Taken them." Her stomach fluttered uncomfortably. "Hanal surely wouldn't allow rape."

One look at Oakheart and she knew it to be true. "But you all have a binding oath. I took it. It said do no ill. Isn't rape doing ill?"

Oakheart's gaze met her. "Yes, I suppose it is. In the past, the term 'ill' was taken to mean killing. The First Comers were fleeing war and such a thought was in their minds and hearts when they swore the oath."

"In my experience...well, not experience...my understanding of war, women are often the victims."

"That is certainly true here."

"Then you need to do something about that."

"What can I do?"

"People need to take a new oath, one that is more specific and includes not harming women. No raping."

His eyebrows drew close together. "Yes, that is possible. The Puri must swear an oath."

"Not just the Puri. Everyone."

His eyes widened. "Yes, I see you are right."

"So no killing. That's something, I suppose."

Oakheart nodded and steered his horse around a ditch. Then he rode up beside her. "The *given* was fading. We thought the binding oath was broken, but we hold true to it. All will lose when the *given* fades. The Puri more so because they will go from little to none at all, as in conquering Argenterra they seek more *given* only to lose it in the end."

Sophy chewed on her lip and slanted a glance his way. "Why do they have little, Oakheart? Why does their life have to be harder than everyone else? I heard them often refer to Argenterrans as fat and lazy. Why do Argenterrans have more of the *given*, the best land?"

"'Tis as it has been. They seemed content with their homeland and their culture. So I thought."

"Not as content as you think, I am guessing. There is much prejudice against them, due to the colour of their skin and their culture. Dellbright was always ranting about them, going off about them as if they were a disease. The people of Gilton Forest do not suffer from the same discrimination. They have the Crystal Tree grafted into their heart tree. The *given* exists there and they live their own lives and have their own culture. Doesn't that seem strange?"

"That is so, the forest folk have ever been friends."

"True, true, and your treatment of the forest folk means that friendship endures. Whatever problem caused the rift with the Puri does not need to continue. You could have a better relationship with them if some effort was made."

Oakheart bristled. "I want that. I have tried for that."

"Try harder. Deal with them, then convince your father. He has not done a good job of it so far."

"You are criticising the high king?"

"I am. And I'll criticise you too, if I want to. There is no going forwards here; it's a stalemate. If you aren't prepared to kill the Puri and suffer the consequences then they have already won. You have lost. You have no home, except what the Puri offer you in the wastes. You could live with the forest folk or ask Dellbright to put you up in the Valley."

"Things are not so black and white, Sophy. There has never been a situation like this before. There have been raids but not an invasion."

"So this is the biggest thing to occur between you? Then think about it. You have it in you to resolve this conflict peaceably. You could give the Puri what they want."

"I do not know what they want. We have only offered what we think they want, what we are prepared to give."

"Exactly. Ask them. Ask Hanal. Ask for their terms."

"My father will see that as capitulating to them."

Sophy let out a pent-up breath. "Maybe that's the only way to resolve this conflict. I don't know. You said Maralain has your negotiating position. What is it?"

"We are offering Fern in marriage to Lyant."

Sophy let out a laugh. "Poor Lyant."

Oakheart growled and nudged his horse ahead. Sophy's horse quickened its step to follow. She'd made him angry. Too bad. Fern was a jerk. But that meant Aria would have to give him up.

"Aria and Fern?" she called out

Oakheart slowed his horse and waited until she caught up. "Over, before it began."

"Because she went back to Dellbright?"

"In part. Mostly because they could not leave Argenterra. Aria wanted to be with her mother, with her family."

"She saw the true Fern then."

Oakheart jerked his chin up, then his shoulders sagged. "I believe so. Fern did not take the situation well. I am afraid it exposed his weakness of character to her sight."

"He's a selfish, nasty—"

"Sophy!"

"Well..."

"Fern will marry Lyant. It will be enough."

"Geez, Oakheart, you don't have to have a wedding to seal the deal. Can't you draw up an agreement and list the things that both parties will do? Why don't you address the source of the issue?"

"Source?"

"Yes, the Puri being outcast. Fix it."

He opened his mouth to speak but she went on. "The *given*, okay?"

Oakheart stared at her and then blinked "Could it be possible?"

Sophy didn't really know, but it was worth a shot. It was why she was willing to help Hanal. "Also, make sure Rae is looked after. Her and her child."

"Rae? You wish me to make Rae's settlement part of the negotiations?"

Sophy grinned. "I didn't think of that. What an excellent idea. You'll make a great ambassador one day."

"Funny," he commented, but by the thoughtful look on his face he was mulling it over carefully. "If I do come up with something, the hardest part will be getting my father to agree."

"You will have to work on your powers of persuasion, then, if the hardest part of the negotiations is getting your father's agreement to his own release."

❧

THEY ENCOUNTERED A GROUP OF PURI WARRIORS GUARDING THE mouth to Glass Cutting Canyon. At first, the warriors were surprised, but then recovered quickly. Battle cries burst out of their throats. Sophy jumped and clenched her jaw, annoyed by their ruckus.

Oakheart hissed at her to take cover. She gave him a fulminating look and dismounted.

"Sophy? What are you doing?"

Sophy unsheathed Vorn's sword, planted her feet in an aggressive stance and waited for them to attack.

Oakheart was too busy preparing his own defence. "We will talk about this, later," he said gratingly.

The first Puri warrior struck. Sophy parried the sword thrust and the force in the sword threw the man up into the air and he landed on his back and was still. While the blow had not been due to her strength, Sophy grinned as she studied the sword. Two other warriors stopped in their track, caught between wanting to attack and fear. "Come on," she said with an evil grin. "I'm ready." She was itching for a fight. "I battled the Ancient Evil and won—want to try me?"

Another warrior engaged with Oakheart but these two warriors just gaped at her. "Come on. It's Vorn's sword and hungry for your blood."

Sophy lifted an eyebrow; so much for her binding oath. She didn't feel any less bloodthirsty than before. The two men were frozen on the spot. "What's the problem?"

Oakheart disarmed his opponent and then noticed the other men just standing there looking at Sophy and the sword. Oakheart narrowed his gaze. "Sophy, that sword is full of power. I can feel it in my teeth from here."

Sophy feinted towards the two warriors. They leapt back and ran off. Sophy blinked. "That's not very sporting of them. I could have done with a workout."

"Put it away, Sophy." The man Oakheart had downed tried to climb to his feet. Oakheart kicked him in the stomach. The Puri warrior fell back and stayed down.

"Yours?" he asked her.

Sophy glanced over at the downed man. He was climbing to his knees. He turned his head, saw Sophy, her sword, and scrambled away. "Cowed, I think."

Oakheart went to fetch their horses, which had been spooked when the swords were drawn. She and Oakheart studied the cutting. A big rent in the mountain range revealed layers of coloured stone. Piles of dirt and smaller rocks were pushed to the side as if a big tractor had been through there recently. Oakheart's frown grew as they walked through.

"What's wrong?" she asked him.

"I have never seen anything like this before. How did the Glasshivermen do this? Why?"

"Because they could I suppose. This sort of thing happens all the time on my world. We reshape the earth, cut into mountains, up the sides of them. We fill in lowlands and make more land. Everything is shaped how we want it. Only volcanoes get left alone."

"Then this is nothing to your eyes?" he asked, gesturing to the high walls of the canyon above them.

"I wouldn't say nothing, but not as shocking as it is to you."

Later, they came across Puri guarding the other end of the cutting as it led to the Forest of Galen. "Wow. Having the Puri come through here must have been scary."

"Yes. More than I can say."

The warriors jostled each other as they neared. Oakheart groaned and they shared a look.

"Perhaps you should call out."

"We come in peace. We seek an audience with Hanal of Puri. I am Oakheart."

The disturbance amongst the warriors continued for a big longer. Then one called out for them to approach slowly.

A lone guard stepped out to inspect them. He eyed Sophy and her sword.

"We are here at Hanal's request," Oakheart explained to the man.

With a nod, he stepped aside. "You will meet other warriors on the way through. Report to the gate."

"Thank you."

They passed along, dark eyes watching them with perhaps a mixture of fear as well as curiosity.

A massive wall of tall trees grew in size at their approach. "Is this where we did our quest?" She was surprised that they were that close.

"No. We are near the outskirts of Silverdale. The woods we used for the quest were on the other side of Silverdale, part of the lands where the keep stands."

Sophy nodded, realising she was directionally challenged. It was so long ago when she had been in Silverdale and it was as if it were another Sophy who had been there. Was there even a part of the original her left? Just the part of her that loved Oakheart. This was where her love for him had cemented. A vision of Rufus's angel came into her mind and she screwed up her mouth in distaste. *Damn Rufus to all the hells that exist.* That bastard had ruined her life. But, she had got it back again. Worse for wear, but did it matter?

Oakheart took her hand and squeezed. She looked up at him, grateful for his support. Thankfully he didn't ask her what she was thinking about.

The path through the forest was well trodden. "Did all of the Puri come through here?"

"It seems so," Oakheart replied. "And where are the Argenterrans? I heard that they had been expelled. We saw none in our travels."

Sophy flashed him a look. "Could they survive in the wastes? I mean, Argenterra is full of food for the picking, and water too. The wastes are not."

Oakheart frowned and looked around him. They could see no one. As they neared the edge of the forest, Oakheart tensed and Sophy put her hand on the hilt of her sword. She may not be able to kill people but she could be very threatening and she understood that lopping off arms and legs was permissible. Her grin was feral.

As they passed through the outskirts of Silverdale, Sophy knew things were different. There were no children running along the road or farmers calling out greetings. The air was tinged with smoke and in the distance she could see homesteads in ruin, or others surrounded by tents. Casting a look at Oakheart, she saw his jaw clench and when their eyes met she sensed the misery in his gaze. He chewed his lip. "Be on your guard."

Sophy nodded and kept her eyes peeled. It wasn't until they reached the town's walls that they were halted and ordered to dismount.

"I am Oakheart, Prince of Silverdale, come to parley with Hanal of Puri, at his request. With me is Sophy, Princess of Silverdale, Gift of Crystal Tree Woods and Hero of Argenterra and Vanquisher of the Ancient Evil. We require safe passage."

The Puri guard's eyes widened and he yelled out an alarm over his shoulder. Sophy stood close to Oakheart as the man looked them up and down insolently. Sophy sniffed and looked down at her clothing. It was hard to see where her clothes ended and her skin began, she was so splattered with mud and grime. Her breeches were stiff with dirt, her shirt torn and the vest she wore was stained. She grinned up at Oakheart. He had been similarly employed in inspecting his clothing.

"Hurry, man," Oakheart barked. "There is no time to waste."

The guard jerked to attention and motioned to four guards dressed in fine robes. "Before you proceed, you must leave your weapons."

Oakheart nodded and undid his sword belt and withdrew his knife. His bow was still tied to his horse. The guard moved closer to Sophy. She smiled at him vacantly.

"You must remove your sword."

Feigning puzzlement, Sophy looked down. "This? This isn't a weapon. It's a holy relic. Hanal will be pleased to see it, I'm sure. He is dead keen about Vorn and related history."

The man's dark eyes narrowed. "Nevertheless, it is a weapon."

Sophy levelled her gaze at him and smiled evilly. "Even if it is, I'm just a girl."

"You will disarm!" The man thrust out his chest and clenched his fists as he bellowed the order.

Sophy stepped back, keeping her hand on the pommel. "It's an artefact of great value. Very old and fragile. I won't take it off."

"Sophy?" Oakheart said.

Turning to Oakheart, she said, "I am not taking it off." She faced the guard and tried for a reasonable tone. "Put on extra guards or tie my hands if you're so scared I'm going to kill someone. If this sword gets lost or goes missing, not only will Adept Lianal kill me so will Hanal of Puri."

The guard growled at her. Next thing, he was tying her hands. Sophy had to hold back a giggle. It was a symbolic gesture. Oakheart could undo it in a jiffy and they dared not tie him up too. Sadly, the guard had the same notion. He undid her bonds and studying the sword, tied the rope around the hilt. Sophy stood calmly while he did this, not bothering to point out that it was totally pointless. They really did need to speak to Hanal and end this whole invasion of his.

"You may proceed."

# 33

# FRIENDS THAT ARE FOES

Aria sat in Rae's small cell, her finger caught in little Lien's grip as the baby slept. A lamp shed light on them. Although the room was small, it seemed cosy. "What are you doing down here with us?" She spoke softly so as to not disturb the sleeping child.

"I am content here," was Rae's reply. She kept her head down, thus Aria could not read her expression. Rae had changed from that young, hopeful girl who had left Valley Keep in what seemed like only yesterday. Aria tried to calculate the time. Two years? Not possible it was that long. But Gilly was walking now, talking.

"I'm surprised you aren't with Hanal. Surely he wants to be with the baby."

"The baby is no concern of his," Rae answered, finally meeting Aria's eye.

Aria blinked a few times as her thoughts rearranged themselves. "Oh, have you separated from him?" That made her sad, because her marriage had ended and she had hoped that Rae had been in a happier place than Aria had been.

Rae's dark eyes glittered in the lamp light. "Separated? I do not know what you mean."

"I mean that your oathbonding hasn't worked out."

Rae's eyebrows shot together and she leant back. "Hanal gave me no oath."

"What?" Aria gazed down at the sleeping baby girl. "But you...you have a baby."

"Yes. He has fathered my child. No oath has he offered me. Now I care not."

Aria removed her finger gently from Lien's grip. "You said Hanal was an honourable man. This makes no sense to me. If he is honourable how could he father a child and not give you an oath?" And he never hinted that he wasn't oathbound to Rae in their meeting. Cunning. Just plain cunning.

Rae's chin lifted. "Makes no sense to you? That is something. He hungers for an Argenterran bride. Not just anyone, either, someone with power. At first, he desired Sophy. Now I expect he desires you. My only hope is that he does not try to break your oath as he did to Sophy."

"Break my oath?" Aria looked into Rae and confirmed that what she said was true. There was no oathbond in the Puri girl that she could detect. "Why would he even try?"

"They say the Puri can make oaths that allow them more than one wife at a time. I never broached the subject with him. I feared he would not ruin his chances for an Argenterran wife by saddling himself with me."

"He mentioned something about making an oath to multiple wives. But he's fathered a child on you and not sworn an oath. That's not nice."

Rae lowered her gaze and picked at the lint on the blanket she was sitting on. "The child was not of his choosing. I used artificial means to conceive."

Aria nearly choked. "Artificial?" Her brows furrowed.

Rae inclined her head. "Umri, his seer. She had ways."

"That's kind of fascinating actually."

Rae sighed. "When we were in the summer tents she was able to take his seed and put it in me. Thus I was able to conceive his child. She told him it was a boy. She was wrong, but her hold on Hanal has not waned."

"Good god. I don't know what to say." Aria tilted her head. "This seer of his was nowhere in sight."

Rae gaped at her, then a pleased smile curved her mouth. "Truly. But she is always there whispering in his ear."

But she wasn't there in the audience hall. "Not this time. He told me she'd been banished."

Rae's expression brightened.

"You still love him?"

The lightness in her eyes faded. Rae shook her head. "No. I do not."

Aria bent her head, while trying to keep eye contact with Rae. "Are you telling me the truth? Is his lovemaking that bad?"

Rae's eyebrows flew up. "Hanal is a wonderful lover."

Aria grinned. "So why don't you love him anymore? Why are you here?"

"I came to Silverdale be with him." Rae turned her head away.

Aria sighed. "He put you in here. Because of Sophy. You helped her."

"Yes, I helped Sophy to escape. He calls me a traitor."

"And now you don't love him anymore?"

Rae faced her, lifting her chin slightly. "In part. At first, he did not acknowledge Lien. I thought his heart would soften when he saw her, but it was hard. I thought he would see Umri's lie, but he did not. He suggested that the child was not his. I nearly died at such a betrayal. But then Lien opened her eyes and anyone could see the child was his. Now, my heart is hard in return."

Aria leant forwards and squeezed Rae's hand. "I am sorry. I can see this situation causes you grief. You have suffered much. I wish there was something I could do."

"There is nothing. We should focus on other things. How is your child?"

Sudden sadness threatened Aria, and tears spilled from her eyes. "I'm sorry." She wiped at the moisture on her cheeks. "I haven't seen my son in quite a while. You probably heard about what happened with Dellbright."

Rae nodded. "Is there nothing cheerful we can discuss?"

Aria put on a smile. "Yes. I am so pleased to see you, to see a friendly face."

Rae embraced her and they hugged each other fiercely. "You will get your son back."

Aria nodded. "I know. One day. Dellbright hid him and although we have sent word, offered rewards, none have come forwards. Gillcress is gone without a trace." She remembered the view she'd seen through Dellbright's death vision. That was her only clue.

"Oh no! My lady, that is more awful than I could ever imagine." Rae stroked her sleeping baby. "I could not part with my child. My greatest fear was that Hanal would cast me out and keep the child. How could you bear it? You, who are now revealed as a princess of Silverdale. Who would have thought tragedy would touch one such as you? I used to envy you and Sophy, and now I find that I do not. While my own life has offered me hardships, they were of my own making. You both have been so caught up in events, it is a wonder you have your sanity."

Aria grinned at her and squeezed her hand. "Life isn't perfect, is it? Now, I hope you don't mind, but I need your help."

"My help?" Rae said carefully, her dark eyes widening.

"Yes. You have lived in the Puri wastelands. I need to come up with some proposals for Hanal so we can negotiate a peace between our peoples. I thought perhaps you might tell me what life is like there. Then maybe I can think of things to offer him."

"But would I then not be disloyal to him?"

Aria's eyes widened. "I can't see how. You are not telling me secrets. Just about the life there and what is hard, and what could be useful to make things better. If anything, you would be contributing to peace. Not defeat."

So Rae detailed the life of the Puri: the harshness of the landscape, the trial to grow food and find water. All the while, the Argenterrans lived with abundance in all things. Rae spoke of how the Puri felt that they were looked down upon and were excluded.

"What are they excluded from, besides Argenterra? They can use the *given*, is that not so?"

"Yes, they can, but none are taught and because the *given* is so hard to use in the wastelands, many never experience the use of it at all.

Although they live close to the retreat, no Puri are taught by the adepts, and the Crystal Tree's influence is cut off by N'Brell's Chasm. It is said the people of the Gilton Forest have their heart tree, a graft of the Crystal Tree, but the Puri have no equivalent. Thus they covet the verdant pastures of Argenterra and consider the Argenterrans as fat lambs grazing with ease upon the land."

"Oh, why is this so? They are marked with the binding oath, so I do not understand." Aria studied Rae, wondering if the girl had some wonderful story from the First Comers to share.

Rae just shook her head. "Something Shabra did, so legend says. Now his descendants suffer for it."

"But...but they are not Shabra. How can they be responsible for something he did? It is so stupid. In my world, in the other world where I was born, there are things like that. Wars fought over historical issues. There are people who have less than others. Wealth and wellbeing are unevenly distributed. I never thought Argenterra was like that. To me, it is a paradise." She frowned. "Now I see that it is not so."

"What can you do?" Rae rested her hand on Aria's forearm.

"I don't know." She lifted her eyes to Rae's. "Something."

Rae smiled, unshed tears glistening in her eyes. "I wish you luck."

Later, Aria spoke with her father. "Tell me," she asked Veld. "Do you have the power to compel the retreat?"

"Why would I want to do that?" Veld poured himself some wine, took a sip and sat back in his chair.

Aria sat on a chair opposite and leant across the table. "I have an idea with regard to the negotiations with Hanal. I need an answer before I propose it."

"Negotiations? You had best wait for Oakheart. He will deal with Hanal." Veld tipped his cup and took another sip.

Aria studied him while biting her lip. Oakheart was more experienced with negotiating, but Aria had ideas. Ideas she was sure would work. "Why? If I can negotiate a peace with Hanal, then we may be free of the Puri before he even arrives."

Veld snorted. "I appreciate your enthusiasm. Oakheart has been my ambassador. He knows how to handle these situations. Hanal is known to him."

Affronted, Aria burst out, "If that is so, why are we in this situation now?"

Veld's cheeks grew a deeper shade of red and he lowered his eyes. "Ah...that will be my fault. I did not listen to him."

"Oakheart's not here. We don't know when he will be. Besides, I have already spoken with Hanal in preliminary discussions, and mother already gave me the negotiating position. She discussed it with Oakheart before he went after Sophy."

"You mean Fern marrying Hanal's sister." Veld pursed his mouth in distaste.

"Yes...and giving them some land."

"Land? What land?"

"Oh, just some land that isn't used much."

"I did not agree to that. What were they thinking of?"

"Your freedom, I expect." Aria didn't tell him that the land was something she'd thrown in.

"Hanal says it isn't enough. So I'm thinking of other things to tempt him."

"Upstart! Tempt him," he growled and took another sip of wine. "He expects too much."

Aria patted his hand. "Father, we have to do something to fix this. Will you listen to me and answer my questions?"

He glanced up at her and narrowed his eyelids. "What do you have in mind?"

Aria squirmed in her seat, aware that her father was regarding her with suspicion. She shouldn't be angry at him for preferring Oakheart. They had a relationship. He hardly knew her at all. "I need to know if I promise on your behalf that the retreat will do something, it will."

Veld stared into space. "The retreat has always cooperated with us, provided advice. We have never tried to force the retreat to do anything." He shrugged. "Everything has been by mutual respect and agreement."

Aria let out a breath and brushed a stray curl out of her face. "That's not entirely helpful. But it will have to do. Oakheart is not happy with the retreat, you know. I think he would be keen to reduce their power."

"What? Why?"

"They did not treat him with the greatest respect. He can fill you in himself, later."

"Why not tell me now?" Veld's voice was quiet, his eyes interested.

Aria sighed. "Because it is Oakheart's story. If only I could confirm with him it is okay to reveal it. Never mind, I will go ahead with my ideas. I will have to place faith in Oakheart's abilities to make the retreat agree."

"That might work. What do you want from me?"

Aria smiled at him. "Trust—and your authority to bind you into an agreement with Hanal."

Veld lifted a hand and brushed hair out of his face. He looked at the table and then looked up at her. "I must confess the thought scares me to my very soul. Very well, you shall have my authority to negotiate. But be careful. Hanal is wily."

Aria hugged him. Veld patted her hand. "One more thing: Oakheart has to agree. He will sign this treaty...agreement on my behalf."

Aria narrowed her eyes. "I will do my best. I'm sure Oakheart will not fault me. I wonder if he is back from looking for Sophy yet."

At Aria's request Rae went up to the guard and requested an audience for the three of them with Hanal. The guard gave a nod, cast them a quick glance and then went away to confer supposedly with someone with more authority. Not long after, he returned and asked them to follow him. Aria linked arms with Rae and nodded for Leyla to follow as they left the lower rooms where they were staying and ascended to the upper levels where Hanal held his audiences. Before they caught sight of the audience room, strange sounds like the clap and clash of wood or cane reached them.

"What is that?" Aria asked the guard.

"Hanal practises with the staves." Rae said this rather flatly and Aria wondered at it.

Aria shared a look with Leyla. Her maid lifted both eyebrows and grinned. Rae's expression lightened. Aria thought they were in for a treat. They were taken to a large room, not the audience chamber they visited on arrival. As the doors were pushed open by two impressive Puri men, dressed in fine robes, Aria determined that this was the ballroom. Its walls and ceiling were painted and finely decorated with murals, and long tall windows let in light. Around the edges of the room stood Puri warriors, stripped down to their trousers, and their elaborate headdresses lay folded on top of their outer robes. Each wore a plain bandana around their head. A clap of wood hitting wood drew Aria's eye. It was Hanal himself brandishing a stave.

Stripped to the waist and wearing only his trousers, Aria got a greater sense of his size and strength. He was impressive. Muscles rippled as he moved with ease across the floor, dodging sideways a thrust of a stave and then ducking under another stroke before he took his opponent under the knees. His hair was free of its cloth and long plaits swung around him as he moved. His opponent got to his feet and bowed, showing a number of bruises across his back and ribs.

Hanal inclined his head and, on turning, saw that they had arrived. He lifted a hand and one of his men ran up to take his stave. Then a servant went and helped the Puri leader into a robe.

Hanal's face betrayed very little of his inner feelings as he walked towards her. Aria stepped further into the room and then re-performed her mash-up of bow and curtsey that she had delivered on presentation to Hanal the day before. Hanal paused before her and greeted her in the Puri way.

"You honour me with your presence, Princess of Silverdale." His eyes ran over Rae and Leyla behind her. There was a mocking texture to the not-quite-smile on his face and the curious way he looked at her made Aria squirm. Her eyes dropped to his torso, visible between the edges of the robe that hung from his shoulders. Red marks and a graze were the only evidence that his opponent had scored a hit. A light sweat settled on his rich brown skin. She realised that all was silent and lifted her head to speak.

"Forgive my intrusion. I seek permission to use the talkstone to confer with the retreat."

Hanal's expression grew thunderous. "I thought you were smarter than that. Is this what you came here for? You are more foolish than I expected." He swivelled away and gestured to a guard by the door, the one who had brought them. "You, take her away."

A hand grabbed for her. "No. Wait. I need to talk to them to negotiate." Whoever held her moved away. Aria sent Leyla a warning glance and shook her head. This was not where she wanted to make her stand.

Hanal moved closer to her, so close she could feel the heat of his body and detect the aroma of spice redolent in his skin. "Tell me then of the innocent reason you wish to confer with my enemies."

Aria screwed up her face. "Enemies? I did not know the retreat were the enemy of anyone." She let out a breath. "Please, you need to trust me."

"No. I have trusted before and was betrayed." His gaze shifted to Rae and then he lifted his hand and Aria was grabbed again. Leyla had already been dragged through the door. Two guards had her and Rae by the arms, but the women were not putting up a fight. They had no choice but to go. Aria was not prepared to fight her way out, even if such a thing was possible. Her father and aunt were downstairs and the people of Argenterra were depending on her to make peace. Struggling against the guard's hold, Aria called back to Hanal: "Don't keep Rae down there, Hanal. She needs the sun and air to keep her love alive."

The door was shut behind them with a resounding boom. Aria shook off her escort's pressing hand. "All right, I am coming."

Back in the room with Veld and Vola, Aria paced the floor. "Where is the talkstone room?"

"You cannot think to use it without—"

"I can so think it. Leyla and I can get ourselves there if you show me where it is in relation to this room."

They had no pens or pencils, but Veld dripped his finger in his cup of wine and used the dark liquid to draw a crude map on the table. "This is the bonding chamber, and this doorway here leads to the talkstone room. There are three attendants: Tru, Basa and Winter. They operate the stone. If they are not there I do not know how you can contrive to operate it."

Aria shared a look with Leyla. "What do you think?"

"If the attendants are not there, then I should be able to use it. I spent time in the talkstone room at the retreat as part of my training."

"When will you try for the talkstone?" Veld asked.

"Soon. The guard is alert right now after Hanal refused my request. I will try tonight if there is no opportunity before then."

"I do not like this. What if you are hurt? Killed?" Veld held out his hand to her. "I could not bear that."

Aria stayed by her father and squeezed his shoulder. "I will be fine. Don't you worry. Hanal won't kill me. I don't think the Puri have killed anyone. Besides, he doesn't want me dead." She hesitated to say that he wanted her in his bed.

⁂

IN THE LATE AFTERNOON, HANAL CAME TO VISIT THEM IN THEIR prison. Aria was with Veld and Vola and Leyla was at the stove boiling water for tea. He did not allude to their earlier exchange but cast his gaze around the room. "Where is Rae?"

"In her cell," Aria answered, noticing that Hanal's mouth tightened.

"Do you exclude her from your company?"

Aria blanched in surprise. "Of course we don't. She is listless and sad. She said she'd rather lie down with the baby than have tea with us. I told you she is finding this confinement difficult."

Hanal drew himself up. "I will speak with her," he said regally and stalked off to Rae's chamber. After some discussion, the gist of which they could not discern from where they were sitting, Rae came out of the room holding the baby. With a quick glance at them, Rae left the room following Hanal.

Aria smiled. Maybe she had achieved something after all. Seeing him with Rae and the baby gave her hope.

As the sun had set below the height of the windows, the light grew dim in their hall. Leyla lit the firesticks, bathing them in warm light. Vola bustled about preparing a meal of roast toffelbread. It was all they had for their captors had not provided any other vegetables or meat that day.

When Leyla touched her arm gently, Aria looked up and saw Leyla's grin. "Time, do you think, my lady?"

With an answering smile, Aria nodded. "I think it is. Rae should keep him occupied for long enough."

Veld spluttered. "What do you mean? Is Rae part of your plan?"

"Not at all," Aria responded. "We haven't even mentioned our plans to her. It doesn't pay to, you know. She's a friend but also a potential foe. She's in love with Hanal, despite his ill treatment of her, and she couldn't help telling him if she knew. Now, we are having a lie down on our beds if anyone asks for us."

Veld got to his feet. "Very well. Vola and I will also lie down on our beds, but will leave our doors open." He turned to his sister and winked. "We will be very difficult to wake, though."

Vola took his arm and they went to their respective chambers. Leyla tossed some leftover toffel into the fire. It smoked horribly and stunk too. She waved the smoke around the room. With a nod, Aria and Leyla went cautiously to the door. It was unlocked but a guard stood on the other side. Two more were down the hall.

"Pray do assist us. We have a problem with the fireplace," Aria said in her best helpless princess voice.

The guard frowned at her. Leyla coughed theatrically and the guard stepped inside to look. The billowing smoke was only slightly impressive. He took another step in and looked back at Aria with a questioning look. Leyla zapped him with the *given* and he fell. Together, they carried him to a nest of cushions and covered him with some of the decorative cloths that were used for dining. Aria wiped her hands after dropping the man's feet.

"How are we going to manage the two guards? Call them in here? Or tackle them in the hallway?"

Leyla nudged the fallen man with her toe. "In here. Can you manage one of them? I can do two, but I do not wish to make too big a display. There is a limit to how much *given* can be expended."

"Then we shall take a detour to the bonding chamber."

Leyla's eyes widened. "I did not know you cared so much for me, my lady."

Aria laughed and covered her mouth to smother the sound. "There is a store of *given* in there. At least, there should be if it is like the one at Valley Keep."

Leyla's eyes rounded. "You astound me. Here we go." She flung open the door. "Scream," she ordered Aria.

Aria did her best girl-in-distress scream, and followed with another.

"Help, please," Leyla shouted. "He is attacking the princess!"

The two guards jerked to attention. "More," Leyla whispered through the door. Then in a louder voice, and waving her arms. "Oh, please do not! Help us! Help!"

The sound of running feet greeted Aria. She took her place behind the door while Leyla, in full actor mode, pointed further in the room and wrung her hands. Both guards ran into the room and pulled up short. With surprised faces they turned around just as they were zapped. Aria assessed the condition of the man she had felled. Leyla was busy checking the corridor.

"Should we bother hiding them?" Aria asked. "Hanal could come back at any time."

Leyla ran into Rae's room and gathered up the blankets. With a toss she covered the two guards and then grabbed some cushions and arranged them around the mound of the unconscious bodies. "That will have to do," she said as she considered her work. "It probably will not fool anyone even for a moment." She shrugged.

Aria ran for the door, poked her head out and pulled back in. "Coast is clear. Come on."

THE SETTING SUN PAINTED THE SKY A MAGNIFICENT BURNISHED orange. The light dazzled Rae as she walked through the quadrangle garden. Lien too, squinted, and then sneezed as the light shafted across her face. A few more minutes and the dark of night would hold them. Even now the dew-laden air kissed her skin. Firesticks flickered along the path, their glow reflected on the surface of the dark ponds that dotted the ground. Rae followed Hanal into the path through tall trees and waving ferns. She stood for a moment, just absorbing the soft afternoon light. It seemed so long since she had been outside. A sigh slid out of her so slowly she barely noticed it.

"I used to walk here when I stayed at the palace awaiting Veld's pleasure. These gardens gave me much pleasure.," Hanal said as they walked.

Rae frowned. For a moment she had forgotten Hanal's presence. On opening her eyes, she found he was regarding her, examining her like she was something new. Her heart thudded because she recalled a moment in his arms, when he had traced the contours of her face. When in his eyes she thought she had seen love—a love as true and as deep as hers had been for him. But that was long ago. A fantasy. A dream from her past. She gazed down at Lien. The child was sleeping, her skin a pale tan warming in the sun.

"May I carry her for you?"

Rae tensed, her mind lost in a barrage of conflicting thoughts. Yes. No. Maybe. Never. Yes. No. Then finally the realisation that, despite the estrangement between them, her daughter had a right to know her father. "Of course," she replied in a shaky voice. She lifted Lien and Hanal took her gently into his arms. He stared at the baby's face for a few moments. Rae thought he had forgotten about her.

"Please, go ahead, take a walk. I will follow with the child."

"You will give her back to me when I am done?"

Hanal's head shot up, confusion marring his features. "Of course. Go, walk. Enjoy what is left of the day."

So Rae gazed around her and breathed deeply. It was a magical place. The gardens at Valley Keep had been fine, but this walled enclosure held so much in a small space, cleverly designed to make it seem larger. She walked over a bridge and looked down at the pond that held so many fat but beautiful fish. She gazed up at the tall trees, fronds leaning down creating curtains where benches hid. Waist-high flowers bowed to her as she passed.

A small cry from Lien made her instantly turn around. Hanal walked behind her and was letting Lien touch his nose. He had a smile on his face, small, sweet and totally unknown to her. "She looks like you," he said when he saw her standing there regarding him.

"No. She looks like you. Besides the eyes, she has your forehead and chin. The nose though..."

"Is yours. Although she may grow into mine. It is so tiny now that it is hard to see."

Hanal did have an impressive nose—regal and proud. Not like Rae's small straight one. Hanal flashed her smile. Her breath caught. She had thought herself immune to him and found herself susceptible. All that time he had kept her confined, her anger had been growing. She must not surrender. Her life was her own. Had she not decided that? Hanal was not here for her, but for their child. He would take Lien from her.

"Rae," he said softly, his gaze returning to Lien. "You shall be permitted to walk here every day."

Rae lifted her chin. "How generous of you." She did not try to hide her sarcasm. She had been around outlanders too long. It was rubbing off on her.

His eyebrows arrowed together. Before he could speak, Lien cried, a loud angry cry. She was hungry. "What is wrong with her?" He hastened over to pass her back.

Rae spied a bench and hurried over to it. "She is hungry. That is all." She undid her robe and allowed the child to suckle.

"Then she has a mighty appetite. I thought perhaps the sky was falling her cry was so loud, so lusty." Hanal sat down beside her and stretched out his legs, giving the impression that he was happy to relax. "It is very lovely here."

Rae blinked. She thought he would absent himself, yet he did not seem so inclined. It was as if he wanted to be there, with her, with Lien. Rae looked around, wondering where Umri was.

"Where is Umri?"

He did not turn to her but lifted his face to the sun. "Why do you ask? Do you want her?"

"No. I do not want her. I was just curious."

"Ah!...Umri is not here."

Rae changed Lien to her other breast. Her suckling was loud.

"The child is noisy as it eats. Is she always like that?"

"Yes, she—"

A shout and running feet interrupted her. "Hanal!"

Rae's head jerked around, her eyes widening. Something was wrong. Hanal was on his feet, the relaxed mood forgotten. "What is it?"

A guard ran up. "There has been a breakout."

"Breakout?" Hanal repeated as if he did not understand the words.

"Men down..."

Hanal grabbed the man by his collar and drew him closer. "Where?"

"The talkstone room."

He shoved the man away. "Get me the palace guards." Hanal spared her an angry glare. "Were you party to this treachery?"

"To what? I do not..."

He studied her face for a few seconds. "Later." He turned to his guard. "Stay here and watch her closely. When she is done feeding the child take her back to her room."

Two other guards stood ready at the doorway. Hanal strode past them, robe flying behind him. The guards turned and followed, trotting slightly to keep up with his long strides.

Rae caressed Lien's head and kept on feeding the child. Firesticks dappled light on them and she stared up at the branches swaying slightly overhead. *Not long before the first moon would rise*, she thought. The guard stood waiting. With a smile, she deliberately ignored him. Hanal had said until she had finished and she was not done. Not yet. Maybe she would never have her fill of this garden.

ONCE FREE OF THEIR ROOMS, ARIA AND LEYLA RACED ALONG THE corridor following the instructions Veld had laid out on the table in wine. It was fairly straightforward. They were on the same floor but in a different wing to the bonding chamber.

A quick peep around the corner and Aria pulled back. She lifted her finger indicating one. With a nod, Leyla stumbled around the corner and threw herself on the floor moaning loudly. Startled, the man came running up only to be zapped by the adept when he bent down to check on her.

Aria and Leyla carried him unceremoniously away and hid him behind some curtains back along the way they had come.

"How long before they wake up?" Aria asked as she dusted off her hands.

Leyla shrugged. "Some take a day, some a few hours. It depends."

They stood outside the door to the bonding chamber. "Do we need more power?" Aria asked.

Leyla studied the door. "I think we have enough to operate the talkstone. More power than time. We must hurry."

They moved to the door of the talkstone room, next door. They had no idea who was inside so they had to go in blind and hope for the best. The element of surprise was on their side at least.

With a nod, Leyla flung open the door. Two Puri guards lounged on seats and an Argenterran man had his head on the table, apparently asleep. He jerked awake at their entry and blinked.

Leyla downed the first man who opened his mouth. She cut off his yell. Aria had the second with a zap to the throat. He fell clutching at his neck.

"Can you use the talkstone?" Aria asked the remaining man. He shook his head and backed away.

She shared a look with Leyla. "Are you the guardian of the stone?" Leyla asked. The man nodded. "Then use it to hail Lianal. Princess Aria needs to confer with him."

He stared at them. Aria shook her head. "We don't have much time."

"But I will be punished."

"So will we. This is for Argenterra. Come on!" Leyla growled at him.

The man, who looked to be about fifty, shuddered and stood up. His thin arms shook within his robes. "Very well."

He went to the stone. Images flared to life and flittered. "We need to speak to Lianal," he said when a face took shape. "I have Princess Aria here." The face in the stone nodded and left.

Leyla leant against the door, not only to hold it shut but she had her ear there listening for footsteps. Aria chewed on her thumbnail. It was taking forever for Lianal to appear. Her gaze went to the inert men. A hand twitched on the one closest to her.

Lianal's face suddenly filled the talkstone. "Princess?"

"Yes. I am here at Silverdale. Father is well. I have to ask you some questions."

"Of course," he replied, eyebrows drawn together over his brown eyes. "What do you wish to know?"

"Is it possible for a graft of the Crystal Tree to be planted in the Puri wastelands?"

The eyebrows shot up. "Planted in the wastelands?"

"Yes. Can it be done?"

Lianal's image wavered in the crystal. "Vorn was the one who planted the Crystal Tree near Valley Keep and the one near Gilton Forrest and also the branches that live in the bonding chambers."

Aria bit her lip. "So are you saying that you can't do it? That only Vorn knew how?"

Lianal's eyes widened. "We have the records. We could study them and then maybe it could be done. Why would we, though?"

It was Aria's turn to frown. "So the Puri can have more of the *given*, and have abundance like in Argenterra. So they will want to go home."

"They have asked for this?" Lianal asked hesitantly.

"Not outright. But what we have offered so far isn't enough. I want to use the Crystal Tree in my negotiations. At the moment Hanal won't budge. He has no reason to, and he's not wrong. We need to come up with a better plan."

"What does High King Veld think of this?"

"I have his permission to negotiate with you. So, can you do it?"

"If we are so ordered by the high king we will do our utmost."

"Right, next thing."

"You have more?" Lianal's mouth hung open.

Aria grinned. "Yes. The next thing I want to know: can Puri study to be adepts?"

"You want the Puri to study at the retreat?"

"Yes, and also I want a school set up in the wastelands so that those who wish to be near their families can do so and still learn."

"No, my lady. The Puri do not have the experience of the *given* as we do in Argenterra. I cannot see why we would trouble them to study at the retreat."

Aria blinked a few times. "I'm sorry, what did you say?"

He repeated his opinion to her.

"Have you met Hanal of Puri?"

Lianal frowned. "No. I have not."

Aria was stunned. "Well, he's the Puri leader—"

"That much I do know—"

"He has very good sight. He can see into people, see their oathbond. I would call that an unusual gift. Also, the Puri can call the waters in the wasteland, where the *given* is weak and the water scarce. I would say that demonstrates a lot of talent, wouldn't you?"

He shrugged. "I suppose so. I never thought about it before."

"Well, is it possible for the Puri to study at the retreat and to set up a school to study the *given* and the history of Argenterra in the wastelands?"

"In theory. The high king would need to make a decree. There are other logistical issues..."

Aria's fists clenched. Lianal was not making this easy. She thought he'd be more forthcoming, willing to do anything to help the Puri and the Argenterrans to come to an agreement.

"Thank you. Oh, one other thing. Is there word from Oakheart?"

A pounding on the door interrupted her. Leyla was shoving hard against a force pushing from the other side.

"Yes, he brought Sophy back and they left for Silverdale, perhaps a week ago. They should arrive soon."

"Thank you."

Aria signalled for the stone operator to end their call. Leyla jumped away from the door and raced to Aria's side. "We will not strike them this time," Aria said. "Best we keep them ignorant of our skill."

Leyla nodded. They held hands and waited. Aria's hands grew moist and her heart rate increased.

The first three guards rushed through the door with their swords drawn. Aria held her breath as the blades drew closer.

Then Hanal stood there, eyes wide, lips grim. "What is the meaning of this?"

He stared at his men, who lowered their swords, and then glared at Leyla and Aria.

"I had to talk to the retreat." Aria squeezed Leyla's hand to calm her own nerves.

"You did this when I expressly forbade you? You expect me to trust you after this?"

"I have new items to negotiate."

"You have attacked my people."

Aria looked at the felled men. "They are not harmed. Except for a headache when they wake up, they should be fine."

Hanal's bright eyes met hers. "You have kept things from me. You have no honour."

Aria gritted her teeth. "I have been working on my negotiation tactics. I had to consult with a higher power before putting my proposition to you. I meant no dishonour...not much dishonour, really. I simply wanted to go forwards in good faith and to be able to deliver what I pledge. Please believe me."

Hanal motioned to more men to come into the room. Aria raised her hands. "Okay. We will go with you peacefully."

Aria and Leyla walked out of the room, curtailing their talent with the *given*.

"We will speak this evening," Hanal said as they passed him by. "I will ensure your good behaviour."

Aria turned to him. "You don't need to do that. You can have my oath. As the *given* is my witness, I will not try to escape. I will not raise a hand to you or your men until we finish negotiating, whether we reach agreement or not. Once we agree we can go no further, then I am free of my oath."

"Your maid?" he asked, as though maid was a dirty word. Leyla repeated the oath. This satisfied him and they were accompanied back to their accommodation.

Rae came running to meet them. "What did you do?"

Aria took her hand. "We need to talk. Can we go to your room?"

Rae bit her lip but nodded. Lien was awake, kicking her legs and waving her arms. "What a dear girl, she is," Aria said, not without a touch of sadness. The thought of Gilly tormented her and filled her with need. But she bit her lip and shook off the feeling.

"Rae...how do you feel about Hanal?"

Rae looked down at her hands and played with her fingers. "That is not easy to answer."

"He took you outside, didn't he? How was that?"

Rae glanced up, her eyes narrowing. "Yes, to the gardens. Did you orchestrate that?"

"Not specifically. I did happen to mention to Hanal that you needed to be outside. I could see that the confinement was wearing on your spirit."

Rae's chin lifted. "So he did not walk with me because he wanted to?"

"He must have. He could have had a guard escort you."

Rae broke eye contact and chewed her bottom lip. "I suppose that is true." She looked hard at Aria. "But you chose that moment to escape. Now he thinks I am complicit."

Aria studied her. "I can't see how. You didn't know what we were going to do. You don't even know why. Please tell me, Rae, how you feel about Hanal? Do you love him still?"

Rae tensed and her eyes flashed. "Why do you ask me? Do you wish to marry him?"

"Wish? No. But I believe that it will have to be part of the negotiation."

"But you are wed to Dellbright."

"Was. Dellbright is dead." There was no need to elaborate that she had severed her oathbond before he died.

Rae gasped and looked away. "Then there is nothing stopping him from having you." Her fists clenched and she looked back at

Aria, face twisted with emotion. "He will have his Argenterran princess."

Aria let out a sigh. "Not necessarily. You know I care for you, Rae. If we negotiate this peace, I believe things will be better for your people. Don't you want that? You helped me come up with these ideas. I haven't spoken to Hanal about them yet, but I am sure they are what he will agree to. I can make an oathbond with you as part of the deal."

"Me?" Rae sat back, chin haughtily raised. "I do not figure into this negotiation."

"But you do; for me you do. I have to know how you feel."

"Why? I am free. Hanal is nothing to me. I will take my child and we will leave this place."

Aria found this conversation difficult. Although Rae denied it, Aria was certain that Rae was just as much in love with Hanal as before. Only her pride and anger were getting in the way. And jealousy, too, if she was honest about it. "Where would you go?"

"Either I will return to my father's house or I will travel to Glasshiver, or perhaps even beyond. You have travelled worlds. There are many places that have yet to be explored in this one."

"Rae," Aria asked softly. "Are you sure? I have seen the way you look at him. I've seen the way he looks at you. There is a tenderness in his expression. Don't throw away this chance out of pride."

"How does he look at me?" Rae's eyes were wide, full of hope.

"Like he loves you."

Her face screwed up and Rae shot to her feet. "No. He does not love me."

"I think he does. He says you betrayed him but he treats you gently. Think about that. You wounded him deeply but he is still considerate."

Rae gazed down at her hands, which worried at her tunic. "Umri will never let me have him."

"Umri. The seer? She's gone."

"He said that to me too, but I cannot believe it." Rae clasped her hands together. "If it is true, then there is hope. She was a bad influence on him. No wonder he was so good to me in the garden."

"Rae, I want to make sure this is a good deal for the Puri and Argenterra. I want there to be a lasting peace."

Rae met her steady gaze. "Truly." A ghost of a smile played around her lips. "Who would have thought that two outlanders would have changed Argenterra so."

Aria leant across and squeezed her hand. "Rae, you have the power to change it too. You can help us forge this peace."

"How so?"

"I can give Hanal the political marriage he wants. You can give him the marriage his heart requires."

Rae snatched back her hand. "I told you I do not want his oath. I will be free. That is my destiny."

"And your daughter's?" Aria let the baby grip her hand. Lien squealed and cooed. "She is Hanal's daughter. Will you deny Lien her destiny?"

Rae shut her mouth tight and turned her head away.

"Think on it, please? It won't work, otherwise. I am not going to be the wife of his heart. It's a political marriage. I don't love him. But I think we could make it work."

Rae lifted her head and stared at Aria as if she had grown two heads. "What are you saying?"

"I'm saying that we both will marry him. He boasts that he can do it so there is no issue."

"Both of us?"

"Yes, I believe it can be done. The way I understand it is that we make the oath together. Then Hanal will have two wives."

Rae shook her head. "You have lost your mind. He will not do this. He would want to have an Argenterran wife, Argenterran ways. It will not be acceptable to him."

"So you won't agree?"

"I will not."

"Are you sure? Would you like some more time to think about it?"

Rae stood up abruptly, edged around Aria and snicked open the door. "I am certain. Please leave me now."

Aria nodded, leant down to kiss Lien on the forehead, and climbed to her feet. "We could make it work, Rae. We were friends once. We could be again."

Rae shut the door in her face.

## 34

# DEALS AND MORE DEALS

A week later after hearing nothing on the progress of the negotiations, a message arrived instructing the royal prisoners that they were to prepare for a bonding ceremony. Fern Ripplebark was to wed Lyant of the Puri. Aria heard this news with mixed feelings. She'd had no idea that Fern had arrived. Hanal must have organised it, even though the negotiations were not complete. Fair enough, she supposed. A down payment on the whole deal. She had the urge to punch someone.

A pile of clothing had been deposited in a heap on the floor just outside Rae's room. Rae had been drawn out by the commotion and stood wringing her hands. Her eyes flashed as Aria came into view. "Hanal cannot mean me to attend this ceremony."

Aria shrugged. "I had hoped he didn't mean me to attend either. How awkward."

Rae's eyes narrowed. "You do not like Lord Fern?"

Aria bit her lip and shrugged. A hint of a smile lit Rae's face. Aria grinned. Rae was thawing out after their discussions about marriage and Hanal of Puri.

Rae ventured closer. "I have not met Lord Fern myself, but I did hear that he was very handsome and well bred."

Aria flushed and put her hands to her cheek, suddenly embarrassed if she had to explain herself and Fern. "Yes, he is handsome. Oh dear, it is not that I do not like him…it is difficult to explain. I once thought myself in love with him."

Rae covered her mouth. "And now?"

"I am not in love with him. But, as you may guess, there will be some embarrassment and anger on meeting him."

"Do you care that he is to marry Lyant?"

Aria searched her feelings. There was some regret there that she had not been able to make the relationship work. Then there was the realisation that she hadn't been in her right mind anyway. Thoroughly battered, she had responded to his kindness, although she did admit he had helped her to find her courage. Did she ever have terrible taste in men. Fern thought about himself first of all. At least now he was putting Argenterra's need before his own. "No. I am over him. It was a mistake. Will she make him happy?"

Rae shrugged. "She is very beautiful and very skilled in the art of loving."

Aria blinked. "What did you say?"

Rae wrinkled her nose. "The Puri consider the making of love an art. They can appear prudish, but the women study the art of making their husbands satisfied and also to…how do I say this…to reach their own fulfilment."

Aria trembled inside. "Did you learn these arts?" That was an education she had missed out on. Her feelings on sex were mixed. Being with Fern had helped a little, but then they hadn't actually had intercourse. The oathbond saw to that. Now she didn't have an oathbond. Hanal knew, but Fern didn't. It was best that he didn't know. It could damage their negotiations.

Rae glanced at her and lifted her chin. "Yes. Umri taught me. It was how I was able to seduce Hanal of Puri."

Aria coughed to cover her gasp. "You seduced Hanal of Puri? Lordy, why did you not say?" Aria was taken aback. Rae was a young, innocent young woman when she left. How had she developed the courage to seduce a man like Hanal? He was so…magnificent. Just thinking about it made Aria quail inside. She was sure she could never be seductive... not after...after Dellbright.

"It did not come up directly in conversation. We were speaking of the conception of Lien."

Aria's face grew hotter and she put her palms to her cheeks. "Right. I see. Well, I suspect you are invited to the wedding." Aria indicated the pile of clothes. "Shall we see what might fit us?"

Veld and his sister emerged from their rooms an hour later, fully resplendent in their royal finery. Aria had to make do with the scrounged items. Leyla assisted her, and with a touch of the *given* to enliven the dye in the gown she chose, she looked respectable in a deep green gown. A golden-edged veil was secured to her hair with a comb.

Leyla wore a white suit made up of trousers and a tunic, not much different to her everyday wear. Her hair was neatly plaited down her back. A gold pin on her breast was the only concession to vanity. They stood waiting for Rae. The guard yelled at them and Veld and Vola stepped forwards to precede them out of the door. Aria's heart leapt. She hoped she would not do anything stupid on seeing Fern again. He'd been so angry at her and she at him. And she and Hanal had yet to negotiate where the married couple would reside.

Rae's door opened and she came out, dressed in a pale lemon dress that floated around her legs and feet. Lien was wrapped in a shawl of the same fabric. Rae's hair was hidden by a Puri head wrap of many colours, which picked up the pale lemon from her dress so that it looked perfectly coordinated. Rae's eyes were darkened and her lips coloured deep red. She looked amazing. No wonder she hadn't recognised Rae in the audience chamber when she first arrived. When she walked Aria could not help but envy her grace. Rae had certainly come into her own after the sojourn into the Puri lands. Lessons in lovemaking, indeed. Aria could do with some of those.

Rae and Aria walked together with Leyla trailing behind. Last time they trod this corridor they had attacked Hanal's men and broken into the talkstone room. Now they were going to the bonding chamber. The room was large with an ornate ceiling painted in blue with various types of harvest depicted on it in white relief. Round the bare stone walls were firesticks in ornate holders, and flowers were decoratively arranged along the skirting. It was simple and beautiful.

Soon after they arrived the room filled up with people, mostly Puri. Fern walked in and passed down a row where the Puri stood aside to let him pass. Aria inhaled at the sight of him. She never seen him so immaculately turned out. He outshone everyone there even as his tanned complexion blended with those around him. He had one Argenterran man to stand with him. Aria did not know the fellow.

Lyant arrived and glided towards the pond. Aria heard gasps from the Puri surrounding her. Lyant was tall and her skin was paler than her brother's, but she shared his proud profile. With dark eyeliner and wine-coloured lip rouge she was beautiful to behold. Her face showed no emotion as she took her place by the bonding pool. Her Puri robes were the finest Aria had seen. Rae whispered to her of her awe. There was not even a sideways glance at Fern. Aria wondered if they had been introduced. Did either of them care?

Hanal told Rae that she was to stand with Lyant in the bonding.

This was news to Rae. She bowed her head and then handed Lien to Aria while she went to stand in her designated place at the rim of the pond. Aria gazed down at the child, thinking she would be asleep, but Lien's eyes were wide open and moving around to stare at the ceiling with a certain wonder.

An adept stood at the head of the pond and the four participants knelt in their respective niches. The adept began the ceremony. Aria looked up and realised it was the cowardly man who gave them such trouble at the talkstone. He called upon the *given* to witness their vows.

As she took in the crowd, her eyes passing over Hanal standing regally amongst his people, she was caught by the sense of him. He was tall, but not the tallest of the Puri she'd seen. He was broad and muscled. Her mind went back to seeing him practising with staves. His was not just a physical force as he had presence and an inner knowing. She was certain he had skill with the *given*, she just didn't know the extent of it. He knew that she was no longer oathbound to Dellbright. He said he wanted her. But was that a wish or a request? She had taken it as part of the negotiation. With a sigh, she decided time would tell.

Fern gazed across the pond at Lyant and Aria fancied she saw desire in his eyes. Hadn't he looked at her like that? Lyant's dark eyes were large and her head, swathed in her headdress, hinted at a dark fall of shiny hair. As Lyant spoke her vows, Aria could discern nothing except intelligence and a touch of excitement in the sparkle in her dark eyes.

Once the vows were done the couple led their wedding party out of the room and up the stairs to the large audience chamber. Aria was stopped by Hanal who stood by the door. "Will you accompany me?"

Aria's gaze shifted to Rae who was walking with Fern's man as was tradition. Aria still carried Lien. "Of course," she inclined her head. "It would be an honour."

"The child looks at home in your arms."

Aria smiled and once more inclined her head, trying to be graceful. "Would you care to carry her?"

"I would, but I have other duties. For now I trust that you will care for her."

Aria nodded and kept her eye out where she was placing her feet as they climbed the stairs.

They entered through the broad doors, she on one side of Hanal. Aria tried to calm her heartbeat. Hanal turned to her as he assisted her to sit in the inner circle. Cushions were arranged in Puri fashion. Aria was seated across from Fern and Lyant and did her best to avoid eye contact. Hanal whispered in her ear, "The first part of the negotiation is complete. I hope you have more to offer for we will conclude our negotiations after this feast."

Rae came over and took Lien in her arms. Aria smiled at her reassuringly. Aria acknowledged her and then her eyes slid to Hanal before she sat back down in her allotted place on the other side of the Puri leader. Rae may say she no longer loved the Puri leader but her body language and her expression of longing told a different story.

Aria leant in closer to Hanal in order to respond to his earlier comment. "I assure you, honourable Hanal, that I have been very busy. The proposals I have for you, I hope, will be entirely acceptable."

He did not smile but his mouth twitched and his eyes brightened. Then he clapped loudly and the food was brought in. Aria ate a small taste of all he offered her. She noticed he was equally solicitous of Rae who sat nearby on his left. For the most part, Rae hid her emotions well during the meal but there had been that look at the start and this gave Aria comfort. When Lien started to fret, Rae rose and excused herself before the meal was over. Hanal watched her go. *He was definitely smitten*, she thought.

Then with a glide of fabric he turned his bright eyes on her. "Shall we retire to the small audience chamber? We are no longer needed here. Lyant and Fern will retire to their suite soon."

Aria put down the cup she was holding. "Yes, by all means." Her heart was really hammering now. She noticed that Veld and Vola were being approached by servants ready to escort them back to their rooms. In deference to their age and station they had been seated at a table with chairs, with servants providing them with all the foods offered to the other guests.

With a nod to his sister, Hanal stood and then drew Aria up with him, holding her gently by the hand. He nodded to the two guards, who opened the doors at their approach. Then he allowed her to precede him from the room. Aria turned but Leyla was not following.

"Your maid is being entertained. Fear not. I will not harm you."

Aria smiled to herself. Hanal did not know it, at least she thought he didn't, but she was well able to protect herself.

They took the stairs to the next level and walked a short way along the corridor where Hanal paused by a door with another set of guards. These Puri men were dressed in fine robes, complete with ornate knives in their belt. Either they were dressed so for the wedding or standards amongst the Puri warriors were improving.

Once open, the door to the small audience chamber revealed a shabby room but in a nice lived-in way. A large chair was pushed back and two large cushions were placed opposite to each other. "Won't we need a scribe?" Aria asked, concerned to be so alone. Her courage fled. Not that she thought he would harm her; she feared he would seduce her. Or, worse still, find out that she didn't know how to seduce him. Then the doubts about her ability flooded in. Who did she think she was, anyway? How could she possibly bring this off? She was a pitiful creature, so useless as to be despised by her husband. A failure as a mother and a friend. A princess? Who was she kidding? The well of self-doubt was overwhelming.

"Do not look so afraid. We will talk, that is all. I do not seek to ravish you."

Startled out of her negative reverie, Aria gasped. "I did not think you would."

"Then what has made you tremble and go so pale?"

Aria kept her gaze averted. "It is nothing, I assure you. I was only hoping I did not forget any details of my proposal. I didn't expect to present it alone."

His eyes dancing, he took her hand and kissed her knuckles, before he led her to sit in the cushion opposite him. Rae's accidental information about love arts made her quail. Despite having been married, and becoming quite close with Fern, she did not feel able to respond appropriately to Hanal's flirting or in any way engage with him on a sexual level. She was too intimidated, not mentally, but physically. She was attracted to him and hadn't been prepared for that. However, she had to put that part of her response to him aside. She was pretty sure Sophy must have felt the same when first confronting Hanal. Had she not said that Hanal was too much for Rae? Yet that little woman had conquered this man's heart. She had no doubt of that.

"You have a question?" he asked, his voice smooth and assured.

"I was wondering where your seer was."

"Umri? She served her purpose and has rejoined her husband. They have left to start their own clan."

"Oh?"

"Oh? What do you mean...Oh?"

Aria scratched her eyebrow, distracted and fighting for calm. "I thought perhaps she would be here."

"Does being alone with me disconcert you that much? If you are really that upset I can send for your maid."

Aria gave a little laugh. "You must think me absurd. I am quite all right. Quite comfortable. Just curious. I thought she was your adviser in all things."

Hanal's smile died at her comment. "You thought wrong."

Then giving himself a perceptible shake, the smile returned and then he lounged on his cushion, propping his head up on his arm, his robe falling open to expose that impressive chest.

Aria rolled her eyes then drew on her anger. He was doing this deliberately. He knew she was distracted by him. Well, it wasn't going to work. While she appreciated his physical attributes she was not in love, or affected by him. Argenterra was at stake and she would do well to remember it. "Very well. You have accepted Fern Ripplebark as the first step in an alliance."

"Yes, and removed a formidable warrior from your ranks."

Aria's head jerked back. "I bargain in good faith."

A smile widened his mouth. "I am sure you do."

"I have the authority to act in these negotiations. When you caught me using the talkstone, it was to confirm that my proposed actions could be achieved and whether the high king has the power to compel them to be done. In coming up with this proposal I have consulted with Rae."

His eyes widened. "Rae? She knows nothing of my desires. She was not born Puri."

"I beg to differ. Rae is observant and has lived amongst your people. She has Puri blood."

Hanal scoffed and waved a hand. "Do get on with it. I have no idea what harebrained scheme you have devised."

"Harebrained? You aren't taking this negotiation seriously. Why am I even here if you aren't listening." Her heart fluttered. She was no good. Useless. Why had she tried?

He studied her face. "Forgive me. I meant no insult. It is just that Rae..." He shrugged a shoulder. "I did not think her politically minded. I am disconcerted, surprised even. Go ahead."

Somewhat mollified, Aria put her thoughts in order. Should she start small and work her way up, or the other way around? She thought a mixture of both would be best.

"Lyant and Fern shall be presented with Valley Keep to live in and to hold for themselves and their offspring."

"What?" Hanal sat up straight. "What of your son?"

"Other arrangements will be made for him. He is Veld's grandson."

"How did Dellbright die?" His eyes rounded. His gaze travelled over her. "Were you there when it happened?"

Aria studied his face. "I was right in my assessment of you. You are very sensitive in the *given*."

"Dellbright?" he prompted.

Aria let out a sigh. "I wasn't there when it happened, but I was connected to him in his last moments. He fell."

Hanal eye lids lowered. "How do you feel about it?"

"Relief." Aria's eyes opened, disturbed that she had been so unguarded. Hanal didn't react to her confession. "Why are we talking about me? We should be negotiating."

Hanal grunted and waved a hand for her to continue. Her doubts fell away. He was listening.

"In her own right, your sister will be awarded the title of Princess of Valley Keep and her children will be part of the royal line."

Hanal's nostrils flared and his eyelids slitted as he studied her. Yet he said not a word. Aria was certain she had his attention.

"The lands traditionally belonging to Valley Keep shall be theirs, except for a small portion of land between the Valley and the plains. This will form part of the lands to be ceded to the Puri for their perpetual use."

He studied her without expression.

"I have a map drawn up but I do not have it with me. However, after you have agreed to return to your lands it will form part of the formal agreement."

"So you think this is sufficient to mollify me?" His voice was smooth and calm. It gave nothing away of his feelings.

Aria lowered her gaze. "I have not finished yet. The retreat will plant a cutting of the Crystal Tree in the Puri wastelands. This will be done at a place of your choosing, thus the *given* will spread across your lands bringing abundance."

His eyebrows rose. "I am told the *given* is lessening."

Aria met his gaze. "I have been told the same and have sensed it to be so. However, it has not waned completely. Perhaps if we can end this altercation without killing then the *given* will remain and perhaps grow once more."

"There has been no killing on our side." Hanal spoke matter-of-factly.

"There has been harm. The Puri will provide compensation for the women who were..." she faltered, "...who were raped. You will also punish these men in your own way and endeavour through your best efforts to ensure that women are respected and not subject to such torture again."

He sat up suddenly. "You are to present terms to me of what you offer. Not demand things from me."

Aria lifted her chin. "Most certainly, but in this circumstance someone has to speak for those injured in this invasion. You may have held true to the binding oath but what of those women? Their terror? The abasement? You cannot know what that is!"

His face softened as he studied her face. "I know what you have suffered," he said softly. He touched her chin gently, just a brush of skin on skin. "It is still written there in your flesh."

His touch sent tingles through her body. At the same time she was horrified by his observation. "No!" Her eyes were hot with unshed tears.

"It fades, but Dellbright's crime is still evident. You have no shame in this, believe me."

Aria was raw, exposed. Looking at Hanal, she experienced a twist in her gut, a feeling of faintness. "I don't want you to pity me." Her voice shook with surprise and anger. "I want you to see me as I am."

Hanal's expression was serious, sincere even. "I do see you as you are. I agree with this condition. Is there more to your proposals?" He sat back and resumed his casual recline on the cushions.

"The retreat will accept Puri as adepts to study at the retreat. In addition, Lianal has agreed to set up a school on Puri lands, if you so wish it, to teach your people about the *given* without leaving their kin."

Hanal chewed the inside of his mouth. "Am I to believe that you have secured these things? Unasked? We do not deal with the retreat. We need nothing from them."

"Then take nothing from them. It is offered. I take it you will accept a branch from the Crystal Tree."

"I would be insane not to. You have provided a vision of the future of my homeland that I have never envisaged. What would my land be with the *given* flowing through it? We have but little that leaks though from the retreat and the Valley."

Aria smiled, because he was enthusiastic. "Is this sufficient for you, Hanal of Puri?"

"Is that all you have to offer me?"

Aria's hand trembled. She knew now he was not speaking of his people, but of himself. "What more do you want?" she asked, meeting his gaze and holding it, even while her heart lurched uncomfortably.

"You."

Her eyes lowered. "You have a wife already."

"I do not." His voice was tense.

She lifted her gaze to his. "You love Rae."

He did not look away or deny it, just held a steady gaze.

"I have negotiated with you in good faith."

He stood up and walked away from her, his robe kicking up against his heels. "You have thought of things I have never considered. For that I honour and thank you." He turned to face her, lifted a hand. "But alas, it is not enough for me."

There was a thump at the door. Aria jumped. A guard rushed through. "Hanal! Oakheart and Sophy, Gift of Crystal Tree Wood, are at the gates. They are being escorted to the palace as we speak."

Hanal frowned. "It took them long enough. I had reports yesterday that they had passed into Silverdale. Bring them here directly."

Aria stood up, all of a sudden agitated. *Sophy! Oakheart!* He had done it. But the timing. She was so close to a deal with Hanal. She was sure of it.

Hanal inclined his head. "The news pleases you, I see."

Aria's eyes lit with happiness. "I don't know if you know the whole story, and now that he is here and safe, I suppose I can tell you. Oakheart used the Crystal Gate to travel to another world to rescue Sophy."

Hanal lifted his chin. "I know part of it. I am also curious to see how they fare. I summoned Oakheart."

Aria frowned. "Was that because you didn't want to negotiate with me?"

Hanal stepped closer, looking down into her face. His eyes were arresting in their brilliance. "Before I heard word of you. You negotiated well, princess."

Then Hanal stepped away and ordered more cushions to be brought in.

Footsteps sounded in the hallway. Aria stood up, clenching her hands. Oakheart stood there with Sophy by his side.

"Sophy!" Aria blurted and ran forwards, leaving her royal negotiator persona in shreds. Sophy eyed Hanal and then shifted her gaze to her. "Aria? Thank god."

Sophy was filthy, her hair was all chopped and askew and, Aria noted, she was pregnant. They hugged each other tightly. Aria blinked away tears, screwing up her nose at Sophy's stench. Then, conscious of their audience, Aria stepped away.

Hanal's expression was full of surprise mixed with anger. "Your timing is out," he said. "You missed the wedding and have come before the negotiations are complete."

Oakheart executed an Argenterran bow. "You summoned me, Hanal. The timing I had no control over. The retreat sent word of my departure, did they not?"

"Well, yes, but you did not come the usual way."

Oakheart's head cocked. "I took you by surprise by using the invasion route?"

The tension between them was palpable.

Sophy looked them both up and down. "Still the same." Oakheart and Hanal started at her comment. Then Sophie gave Aria a long look from head to toe. "You look amazing."

Oakheart put his hand on Sophy's shoulder and addressed Hanal. "I did not intend to sneak up on you and I made sure I advertised our presence as often as I could. Your troops were a trifle...how can I say this...skittish. Is my father well?"

Hanal's expression had turned sour while Oakheart spoke, like he had eaten rotten meat and was required to swallow. At the last he jerked his head back. "As far as I know. Nothing I have done would have harmed him." He turned to Sophy. "I heard that you were taken by the Crystal Gate."

Sophy slitted her eyes at him. "I was. Without much time to recover from the effects of your treatment."

"The power in you is less now." Hanal's eyes slid down her body, assessing. He gasped and fell to his knees. Sophy jumped back, casting him a look that suggested she thought him unhinged. He lifted his hands. "The power is centred here. Your child is ripe with the *given*."

Sophy gaped at him. "What?"

"I can see. It is not all the power that resided in you previously. But a substantial portion grows within."

Sophy looked askance at her swelling mid-section. "You can see that? Funny that Lianal' the head adept' could not. Unesta said a child would prevent her taking all the power."

Aria wasn't quite sure what Sophy was talking about. "Oakheart, I have been negotiating with Hanal for he and his people to leave Silverdale. I thought it was enough, but he says it is not. Father says you must agree to all the conditions."

Oakheart took her hand. "Tell me."

Aria listed all the things she had suggested to Hanal. Oakheart's smile widened. "You have proposed many things that will be of benefit to the Puri. What else does he want?"

Aria bit her lip. "Me."

"You? But you are oathbound."

Aria shook her head. "Dellbright is dead. Hanal can see the bond is gone. I am free."

Hanal looked between them. "It is not for only selfish means that I ask this. It is important for the Puri to be seen as equal."

Aria turned to him. "Lyant is to be a princess. Isn't that enough?"

"Her offspring will be Argenterran. In years to come they will have blended in. What of us Puri who remain in the wastelands? Those of us who wish to keep our identity, our culture?"

Oakheart bit his lip. "What about betrothing our child to one of yours?"

Sophy's head jerked up. "No way."

Oakheart swung around. "Sophy?" he protested.

"No. I'm not promising my unborn child to marry a future someone. You can sack me as a princess, if you like."

Oakheart took Sophy to the side. He argued hotly. "But it is for peace."

"No. I'm not saying that if our child grows up and takes a fancy to one of Hanal's offspring that I'll object. I won't. But I'm not going to tie this baby up in fate."

"I'll do it," Aria said. "I will marry Hanal but I also have a few conditions."

Oakheart's eyes widened. "Aria, are you sure? You have suffered too much. You deserve to be a princess without worry, without care."

"Hanal won't lay a hand on me without my consent."

Hanal's eyebrows winged up. "Of course I would not."

Aria knew she had a means to protect herself, but also suspected that he was honourable. Rae did say she had seduced him and not the other way around.

"Come, take a seat. We shall finish these negotiations," Hanal intoned as he lowered himself to his cushion.

As the guards had placed extra cushions, Oakheart assisted Sophy on to one and himself another. As Sophy sat down she laid a strange sword in a scabbard over her legs. Aria frowned at it, wondering where Sophy had got it from. It practically throbbed with power. Where had Sophy been? Aria was dying to know. But first the future of Argenterra and her own fate had to be decided.

Hanal glanced at the sword in Sophy's lap and blinked. He then squared his shoulders and began. "What do you propose, Aria? You have conditions?"

Aria bit her bottom lip as she considered him. He was an imposing man, but not in the way that Dellbright was. Dellbright was anger and insecurity. Hanal was different. Proud. Sure and very virile. It scared her to the bone. Not that he'd harm her. She didn't think he would, but using the *given* as a weapon as Leyla had taught her would protect her. She had a new confidence now. Nor was she gulled into believing that Hanal cared for her. It was a political marriage. He found her pleasing, but not in a possessive way. His heart was Rae's and that didn't bother Aria in the least. She could do the marriage thing and still be her own person.

"I propose that you take me and Rae of the Valley as your oathbound wives."

Oakheart inhaled loudly. Hanal's nostrils flared and Sophy just gaped.

"It is said that Puri have ways to work their oaths to take more than one wife. You yourself have boasted to me of such. I propose you take us together."

A beat before he replied. "Yes," Hanal said. "I will do this gladly."

"There are a few issues to discuss," Aria added quickly before he could assume that that was all her conditions.

Hanal lifted his eyebrows, his impressive gaze washing over her. "They are?"

"Rae doesn't agree. She does not wish to marry you. Her plans are to leave these lands and take her child out into the wider world, beyond even Glasshiver."

"What?" Hanal exclaimed, his complexion darkening. "That is ridiculous."

"Not to her."

Hanal blanched and after a moment said, "I will talk to Rae. Convince her. Continue."

"We can work out the details in a contract, but basically I stay in Argenterra."

"No, I will not agree to that."

"Hear me, please. I propose that you spend six weeks a year here. I will spend six weeks in your lands...in your tent if you require." She shrugged. "As I said, the details can be ironed out later."

"This is not a marriage you are proposing but a..." he spluttered. "What about children? Do you intend for them to be dragged hither and thither to suit yourself?"

Aria sat back. "Children?"

"Yes, children of the marriage."

"But you will have more children with Rae."

"And with you. Otherwise there is no point to this arrangement. To be equal we need equal representation in the royal house, that means the future royal line."

"Oh," Aria said and chewed her lip more vigorously. While she had thought they might sleep together if they were inclined to, she hadn't put thought into children. Gilly had been taken from her. That was too much to bear. The *given* regulated childbirth. If the Puri lands were under the influence of the *given*, the birth rate should drop there too. She would have to give him at least one child to secure his line with Veld's. She let out a sigh.

"Very well, I will spend six months of the year with you, if I have a child."

Hanal pursed his mouth. "You will spend six months of the year with me before we have a child. After that we will negotiate to increase the time."

"No. That's too long. Three months together."

"That was your first offer. It is completely unacceptable."

Aria clenched her hands. Was she being unreasonable? "All right, a minimum of six months in the year together."

"I will consider this." Hanal sat there, bottom lip in a growing pout, eyelids partly lowered over his simmering eyes.

Oakheart summed up the negotiations. "Are we agreed? Will you take your people out of Argenterra?"

"Yes, this arrangement is acceptable to me," Hanal said curtly.

Aria lifted a hand. "You have to get Rae to agree. And I want that compensation I asked for and the punishment of the men who committed those crimes."

Hanal glared at her. "You dare ask?"

Aria lifted an eyebrow. "I do."

Sophy placed herself between them. "I'm sorry to butt in here, but Oakheart and I have been discussing this same issue."

"What issue?" Hanal asked, expression thoughtful.

"The issue of the binding oath and how it doesn't protect women from being taken against their will. If we truly believe in doing no ill, then the binding oath should cover that."

Hanal blinked. "We cannot change the binding oath. We are born under its rule."

"Yes, I know that," Sophy said and cast a look at Aria. "But we think there should be a new oath, one with more specific wording."

"You cannot make everyone take this oath," Hanal pointed out.

"I know that. But we can. Then our children will be covered by it, and maybe the people will hear about it. Maybe we will tell them and then they will make the oath and perhaps one day in the future we will all truly do no ill to anyone."

Hanal let out a breath. "You two women truly astound me. I can see that your idea has merit. I do not believe that many people will take this oath, Puri or Argenterran. But I will."

"I bet the women will take that oath and bind their future children," Aria added. She was excited by Sophy's idea. It was brilliant.

Oakheart said, "I have already taken this vow, as has Sophy. But if we are mostly done here, I would like to see my father, and Sophy needs food and rest."

Hanal nodded. "I will see to it." He put out a hand to stop them from getting up. "Sophy, please. Before you go. May I offer my sincere apologies for what befell you when you were in my care. I have long since regretted it. I was desperate to avoid this war. You were my last hope. Forgive me." He knelt before her.

Sophy bit her lip, her cheeks turning pink. It was obvious she wasn't expecting this apology. "Umri isn't around here, is she?"

Hanal lifted his face to hers. "No. I have banished her from my household. I am not sure when the mist was lifted from my eyes, from my mind, but I saw her truly when she corrupted my order about the taking of women. It was Rae who made me see."

"Then Hanal of Puri, I accept your apology."

His gaze was drawn to Sophy, to the sword she held. "What is that you have there?"

Sophy's eyes widened. "This? It is Vorn's sword."

Hanal laughed. "I did not know you to be prone to jest."

"I'm not joking. I went to Yulandir through the Crystal Gate and I brought Vorn's sword back with me."

Hanal gaped then covered it quickly. His eyes sparkled as he asked, "May I see it?"

Sophy stared at the sword and gave Oakheart a sideways look as she passed it to Hanal.

When he drew the blade from the scabbard Hanal gasped and

caught his breath. He studied the pommel, brushed a finger across the blade hesitantly and quickly pulled it back. "It is full of power."

"I know," Sophy replied. "I think it took some of the *given* from me. I touched it before Unesta drained me. When I wield it power flies from it. Do you want me to show you?"

Hanal looked aghast at her. "So much power for one such as you. Can you touch the *given* now, Sophy?"

Sophy shook her head. "Actually, I'm not sure. I have taken the binding oath, and the *given* doesn't make me as sick as it once did. The only power I have been able to wield is that sword. The retreat wanted to keep it, but I refused. So they gave me the scabbard that they had in their library as a relic."

"Will you give it to me?" Hanal asked softly, his eyes bright.

Sophy started at him, considering. After a long silent moment she said softly, "Yes. But not now."

Oakheart surged to his feet. "No, Sophy. You cannot."

Sophy whirled around to confront him. "I already did."

"But...it is Vorn's sword." Oakheart's fists were clenched and his gaze shifted from Sophy to the sword now in Hanal's hands.

"Vorn isn't here anymore."

"It is a relic of Vorn. It belongs to Argenterra, either in the retreat or here in Silverdale."

"Who says? If Hanal is to be equal, if his people are to be equal, why can't he safeguard the sword? If he values it and it helps him get his people out of Argenterra then he can have it."

Oakheart breathed out slowly. His gaze flicked to Aria, to Hanal and back to Sophy. "I do not know how to answer you."

"That's a start." Sophy grinned at Aria then turned to Hanal. "The retreat wants this sword. I will make a deal with you. I will bring this," she held up Vorn's Sword, "to you in the wastelands. I think I have an idea that will allow you to keep it forever or until you are offered something better."

Hanal bowed. "Sophy..." He frowned and then sighed. "I have to believe in you."

Oakheart groaned. Sophy swung around to him, fastening the scabbard to her waist. "Stop complaining, will you? I have something the retreat wants." She slapped her chest. "I reckon I can get them to agree to let Hanal keep the sword."

A smile lit Oakheart's face. "And you think you are not fit to be a princess?" He grabbed Sophy to him and hugged her roughly. Then he spoke to Hanal. "You see before you Sophy, Princess of Silverdale, Gift of Crystal Tree Woods, Hero of Argenterra and Vanquisher of the Ancient Evil."

Hanal froze, his eyes flitting from Oakheart to her. Then flinging his robes out behind him, he knelt and lowered his head. "I am honoured to be in your presence."

Sophy's mouth dropped open and she sent a begging glance to Aria.

Aria's heart was light and her eyes sparkled with delight. "This is perfect, Sophy. The adepts will not be able to ignore the Puri now. Your idea with the sword fits in perfectly with the terms of our agreement. You have gained for the Puri a splendid gift."

Hanal stood up gracefully. "Then all that is left is for me to convince Rae and the deal is sealed."

"Yes," Aria said, her heart leaping. "Oakheart?"

"I will discuss everything with my father. It may take some work but I will not relent until he agrees."

Hanal bowed and sent Aria a small smile before addressing Sophy. "I will see that you are escorted to some apartments. You need a bath, clean clothes and food." To Oakheart he said as he inclined his head. "I have kept you long enough from your father, Oakheart. The order in which you do everything is up to you. I must discuss arrangements with Rae." He bowed elegantly and then summoned a guard to escort them.

Aria hurried out with Sophy, hugging her again. "We did it?"

Sophy grinned at her. "How soon before the Puri will withdraw?"

"We are very close. I just hope that Rae agrees. She must know that I could not do anything that would hurt her."

Sophy stopped and grabbed her hand and squeezed. "But marriage with Hanal and also with Rae? Can that work?"

Aria shrugged. "I have no idea. But I think it will work out somehow. If it means peace and harmony between our people then I am willing to try."

Sophy grinned at her and let go of her hand. "I suppose he's rather a lot for one woman."

Aria's face froze. "Oh dear, the things you say. I..." She patted her heated cheeks.

Sophy laughed. The guard led them to some guest quarters, not the cells down below. Oakheart pushed open the door. The room was airy and furnished. Sophy promptly went to the bathroom and water could be heard filling the bath.

Aria pulled back to the door. "My stuff is still downstairs. I will wash and bathe in my own room. I will see you later. The guard is seeing to some clothes for you. From what I can see the palace has been ransacked but I'm sure they will come up with something."

Oakheart came up to her. "I will come with you. I must see my... our father."

"Will you be all right?" Oakheart called to Sophy.

"Yes, I am fine."

Once out in the hall, Oakheart hugged Aria. "You did well. I do not think I could have come up with such a good proposal. Will you come with me to talk to Veld?"

"Brother, since you ask so nicely, I will."

# 35

# THE NITTY GRITTY

Rae had been led to the quadrangle garden. A light rain had fallen, subtly changing the scent of the place. Lien wriggled in her arms so she placed the child over her shoulder so that her young eyes could see the greenery. Pale sunlight gave an interesting hue to the leaves and palms, and darkness lingered in the shade of the trees. She made her way to the bridge. Perhaps seeing the fish would lighten her mood.

It was not long before she heard a step and turned. Hanal stood there, looking regal in his ornate robes, the expression in his eyes soft. "How are you?" he asked in caressing voice, reminiscent of his lovemaking.

Rae looked down at the water, ignoring the shiver of awareness that travelled over her skin. "I am well. Thank you for asking."

"The child? Does she let you sleep?"

Keeping her head averted, Rae replied, "She sleeps a little longer each night."

"May I hold her?"

Rae's heart beat all askew. "Certainly." She drew Lien off her shoulder and into the crook of her arm as she arranged the wrappings. Then she stepped up and passed Lien to Hanal. His fingers brushed the skin of her arm and she blanched, shocked by the touch. She did not need to feel this attraction. Her mind was made up as he had spurned her and his child. "She grows fat," he said as he gazed into Lien's face and touched her chubby cheek with his forefinger. He let her grab his finger and she cooed at him.

"Yes. She is healthy."

"Rae," Hanal said suddenly and so urgently that she instinctively looked up at him. "Marry me."

Rae stepped back. She was not expecting such a declaration without some preamble. "No!"

Hanal's forehead creased. "I have treated you badly. I know this. For that I am sorry. Your betrayal wounded me. Yet, I could not put you from me. You were right about me. Let me prove it to you. Marry me. Take the love I have for you and cherish it."

"No. You only want me to say yes so you can marry Aria. I am not stupid. Aria spoke to me. This is all a political arrangement. Right now, I am free to go where I will."

"Of course, you are free to go where you will. But," he stopped and then knelt in front of her, Lien tucked over his shoulder. "Consider taking me on as a husband. We were good together. When things were simpler we were happy. Aria's negotiations have brought much that will be good for our people. Aria said that you gave her the inspiration for her wonderful proposals. Rae, I did not know such things were possible for the Puri. Consider a future of our lands with the *given*, with abundance. Our people equal with the Argenterrans."

"Aria said I inspired her?"

Hanal nodded and adjusted the baby in his arms. "Please, Rae. Let me be the husband I should have been. Surely you know I have loved you from the first."

"But you never said," she replied, keeping her hands curled tight. "You made me suffer for my love."

"I know. I can claim many things but treating you as I ought was not one of them. My baser desires were encouraged. I acted badly, I see that now. I have weathered my own crisis and I have come out the other side. If not for you, the crisis would not have occurred. And I needed that. I needed to see what the truth was. I sent Umri away once I saw her for what she was and what I saw in me."

"Hanal...I...."

"I was wrong, Rae. Let me make it right. Give me a chance." He reached out a hand to her and she took it, relaxing her fingers. His skin was warm and he emanated strength, something she could not resist. "Aria's proposal includes that you and she are equal. She knows that I love you and that you feel the same way. She suggests that she mostly resides in Argenterra. I have limited it to a minimum of half a year."

Rae sniffed. Tears were burning in the corners of her eyes. "I could be free. I could go away, explore..."

"I know," he said softly, drawing closer. "But stay with me. Marry me. Love me. Please."

The tears escaped and Rae let out a sob. It was some time before she could speak. "If you wrong me, Hanal of Puri, I will leave you. Do you hear me?"

"I hear you." He brushed his hand over her hair, his eyes tracking over her face.

"If I agree to this, will you listen to my counsel?"

"That I will and I will not knowingly wrong you. I swear it by the *given*."

❦

IT TOOK SOME TIME TO SOOTHE VELD. OAKHEART WAS HARD pressed, especially since Veld did not like the marriage proposal. "What was Aria thinking? Here I was convinced she was a smart woman. Surely marrying Fern to Lyant was enough?"

"Aria did what she thought was right for a lasting peace. She attempted to remove the inequalities between our people. To right the wrongs of the past. She surprised even Hanal with her offerings."

"Gone too far, if you ask me."

"No, she went as far as she could. Already the Puri are leaving Silverdale. I saw a number of clans departing from my window."

Veld lifted his gaze to his. "Truly? It is over?"

"Almost. I believe Hanal has convinced Rae to agree to the

marriage. Strange though it seems to us, I think it will work. Aria is just the right Argenterran to pull it off."

Veld picked up his wine and took a long sip. "Ah well, if it is to be that way. How I wished I had listened to you."

"I do not think my marriage to Lyant would have addressed the larger issue. It would have been a bandage on a festering sore. Aria's solution is the one that drains the wound and sets it to mend. Sophy also urged me to address the real problem. To fix it."

"You say Sophy is expecting your child?"

"Yes."

"How is she?"

"She is bearing up. The position of princess is not to her liking. You will find her not very..." Oakheart sought the right word, "...accommodating."

"Spirited thing," Vorn said with a snort. He cast his eye over Oakheart. "The world is topsy-turvy now."

Veld put his signature to the deal, sealed it and took a sip of wine. Oakheart countersigned it.

Oakheart reached out to squeeze his father's shoulder. Joy surged through him. The written agreement lay on the table, signed and sealed. "Aria will be staying in Argenterra for a while. You will have time to get to know her. She intends to look for Gillcress. Then we will travel to the Puri homeland for the wedding, which is to be in the Puri style."

Veld nodded. "I suppose your mother will be here in a few days."

Oakheart grimaced. "Yes. Perhaps you should clean yourself up a bit."

Veld glanced down at his tunic, suddenly noticing that it was stained with food and wine. "Ah well, I have time before I have to been seen to be the high king again. Keep me informed, will you?"

Maralain entered Silverdale with a racing heart. After kicking her heels for so long, readying for a battle that hadn't come, she was overwhelmed. Aria had done it. Negotiated a peace. Pride surged through her. She had to not constrict her daughter so much. She wasn't aware that she had been, but that didn't mean she hadn't.

Her dress was one that was fit for presentation to the high king. Aria had it sent to her in readiness. For that she was grateful. She was not looking forwards to seeing her husband. Fear, embarrassment, shame all warred for the right to be first in her mind.

Oakheart had told her that Veld had forgiven her all, but she found that hard to believe. The corridors were familiar to her, arousing memories from her past. Some were damaged, a testimony of the recent occupation. When they at last turned the corner to meet the doors of Veld's private audience chamber she quailed. It would have been easier to meet in the formal audience chamber with courtiers watching. It was easier to pretend when others were watching.

The doors flung open. She could not run and flee. Would not. Squaring her shoulders, she walked through. The carpet was more threadbare than she remembered. Her gaze fell upon Veld in his chair and he too was more worn that she remembered. He smiled at her and climbed out of his seat. "Welcome home, my dear," he said putting out his hands to clasp hers. He enfolded her fingers in his palms and squeezed them reassuringly. "And thank you. Thank you for all that you have done in my name, rallying the people, leading the troops."

Maralain tried to curtsey but he held her hand firmly. "I... er...I...um."

Then he let her go, to stumble back into his seat. Veld was changed. He was older than her but not by much. What she saw was a man ravaged by time, by wine and by pain. It stabbed through her heart that she was the cause of it. Veld had never been an overly smart man, but he had been kind.

"You are even lovelier than I remembered," he said.

Maralain had a speech prepared but the words dissolved. He cared for her still, just as Oakheart said. How could he forgive all that she had done? Tears welled and her throat grew tight. She had not expected such a welcome. She'd been prepared for recriminations, anger and blame. A sob broke from her and she fell to her knees in front of Veld, leaning her head on his thigh.

As she sobbed, he patted her head. "There, there, none of that. All is forgiven."

Those words only made her sob more. "But...I..." As he patted her hand she could detect he was trembling. It was not easy for him either.

"It was a long time ago, Mara. Let us start afresh...as friends."

She wiped the tears from her face and got her sobs under control. Climbing to her feet, she replied, "I can try."

Veld nodded and led her to a chair placed next to his. "That is all we can do."

❧

ARIA RODE THROUGH THE TOWN, THE FOURTH THEY HAD encountered on this journey to find Gilly. Her entourage spread out; their usual habit was to dismount and ask the locals about Gilly. They had a set of questions and knew when to summon her if the answers indicated a child had been placed there. She looked to the mountains to see if the vista matched the one she'd seen in Dellbright's mind before he died. Nothing quite struck her from her vantage point.

"Anything?" Leyla asked.

"No, not yet," Aria replied.

They had not bothered going to Valley Keep. Not only did she not want to meet Fern again, she wasn't quite ready to face her memories. The keep was beautiful but it would always contain pain for her. Gilly was not there in any case. Fern and Lyant would have sent word if her son had been returned to the Valley.

As she rode down the narrow street, she happened to look to the west, to the mountain range. The sun shone on a particular spot, highlighting the jut of the rock and the sweep of snow. Her heart stopped. This was it. "Stop," she called to her entourage who were already splitting up, and pulled on the reins to slow her mount.

"Aria?" Lyant asked, squinting at the mountains.

"This is the place," she said as she studied the houses.

The call went out and the four palace guards came back to her, led by the handsome twin guards Jael and Kael who had volunteered to accompany her.

414

Leyla dismounted and led her horse down the street and tied it to a post on the other side. Aria moved ahead slightly and then got her horse to back up, seeing the view from either side of the house. This view looked exactly like the last thing Dellbright saw.

Just then, the door to the house opened and a little boy toddled outside, followed by an old woman. Aria's eye was immediately drawn. "Careful, Pert," the old woman said. "There be horses here."

Her *given* sense penetrated the boy and there was the resonance she remembered. "Gilly!"

The boy's head shot up and he squinted at her.

Aria dismounted and Leyla held the horse's head. Before she could do or say anything, the old woman came up and grabbed the boy, holding him tight against her skirts. "His name is Pertwee Rye, son of Dalton Rye. I be called Mistress Dooley."

Aria stared the woman and the wide eyes of the boy. Green, like her own. "Where is this Dalton Rye?"

"Dead. He fell from the balcony and is buried on the common."

While Aria knew it had been Dellbright, she had to do more to convince this woman. "Was he of medium height, curly hair with dark eyes?"

The woman jiggled her shoulders. "Yes. Do you know him?"

"Yes, that man was actually Prince Dellbright of Valley Keep, and this is my son, Gillcress."

The old woman gasped. "The Prince of Valley Keep? Why did he not say?"

"He was not well," Aria said, attempting to be tactful. The old woman continued to stare at her and at the boy. "A great sadness filled him and it changed his heart. He felt compelled to send our son away due to political reasons. Do you understand?"

Mistress Dooley still stared at her, but then Aria saw her compare her face, her hair, her colouring, with that of the boy and, finally, she gave a slight nod. "I don't be understanding why a father would do such a thing, but I can see you be telling me the truth." Her gaze went to her escort of palace guards, dressed in their fine uniforms.

Aria knelt in front of Gilly. "Hello? Do you remember me?"

Gilly shook his head, but reached up and touched one of her curls. "Mama."

Aria tried to control her emotions. "Yes. Gilly. It's mama. I have found you at last." Gilly only squirmed a little when she hugged him.

The old woman had tears pouring down her cheeks. Aria did not want to wrench the child from the woman, who was only doing what she thought was the right thing. Gilly obviously loved her too. "Would you consider coming with us, Mistress Dooley? Gilly would be comforted by your presence. I would treat you well."

The old woman's grey eyes met hers. "I live alone here except for the boy. There is nothing to keep me here. Aye, I would like to come along for a time."

"Very well. I will make the arrangements." She addressed the captain of her guard. "Jael, make arrangements to hire a carriage and consult with Mistress Dooley as to any items of furniture and personal items she wants transported to Silverdale."

Her Guard of the White bowed and then dispatched Kael, his brother, and others to carry out her orders.

Holding Gilly's hand, she smiled at Leyla.

"You did it," the adept said. "He is a bonny child." She bent her knee to greet Gilly and acknowledge Mistress Dooley. To Gilly she said, "We are going on a long ride. Would you like that?"

"Horses!"

Aria relaxed her body, let go the coil of stress that had kept her sleepless for many nights during the search. Now all she had to do was get herself to the Puri summer tents for her wedding. They had to hurry but it wasn't likely that Hanal would start the wedding without her.

## 36

# A WASTE NO MORE

Sophy wobbled on her feet as she walked around Hanal's tent, trying to avoid colliding with wedding guests. To make matters worse, she thought she looked ridiculous, particularly with Vorn's sword strapped around her huge girth. People looked at her strangely, whether Puri or the Argenterrans who had come for the wedding. It had been a long, slow passage across the wastes, but she had been looked after, fed well, and Oakheart had held her in her blankets every night. It was sort of like a honeymoon. They weren't running from anyone. No one was pursuing them and the end goal was a celebration. This was what life in Argenterra was meant to be like.

Aria had joined their entourage midway, bringing Gilly and a nanny to boot. After three months of searching, they had despaired of her ever finding her son or turning up to marry Hanal. Now that her son was found, there was so much happiness in Aria that it communicated itself to Sophy. She didn't have worry about her friend anymore; she only had to worry about herself.

Rae and Lien had travelled with them from the start. They were welcome companions with Sophy edging closer to full term. Rae was full of advice and assurances, which was sufficient to keep Sophy's childbirth anxieties at bay. Hanal had left months before to plan the ceremony, to organise his people, to re-establish them in their homelands. Life in Silverdale was almost back to normal. With improvements that Oakheart had planned, maybe they were better.

"I beg your pardon," an Argenterran wedding guest said as he bumped into her.

"Sorry," Sophy replied and tried to get out of the way.

Rows upon rows of tents surrounded Hanal's large complex of tents. There was no sign of the Crystal Tree that had been part of the peace deal. The retreat was looking into it, they kept saying. Sophy thought they were stalling. She'd told Oakheart what she thought and although he didn't come right out and agree, she could see the subject disturbed him.

Aria came into view, dressed in a dress that was both Argenterran and Puri. *Aria. She is really going to do it*, she thought. *Marry Hanal, and share him with Rae.* Sophy tried not to think about how the logistics would work out. Aria was calm about it and that was all that mattered. The Puri had taken to Aria too, so it looked like things were going to be okay. She treated them with respect and they in turn treated her as one of their own.

A loud guffaw let her locate her husband amongst the throng of wedding guests. Oakheart was babysitting and enjoying the practice. She smiled a secret smile to herself and kept her gaze moving. An adept was there, his white and blue robes making him stand out from the more colourful Puri. He was not there to officiate the ceremony, but to represent the retreat. Lianal had indicated it was a great honour for the adepts to visit the Puri with the reason being Aria getting married. She finally recognised him as Aran, the healer. He caught her gaze, waved and then headed towards her. She remained wary, for the retreat was not happy generally. The new accord with the Puri lessened the retreat's power. Veld had issued a number of decrees. While Lianal hadn't disobeyed them, he'd been slow to deliver. That rankled Sophy. After all that they had been through, the retreat decided to have a low-level tantrum.

Sophy put her hand on the pommel of the sword possessively as the adept approached. By the look of yearning on the adept's face, he'd clearly noticed Vorn's precious relic. The retreat wanted the damn thing but she'd promised it to Hanal. It was leverage. She was going to give it to the Puri leader today. The final item of the peace accord from her perspective. Damn the adepts for jeopardising everything.

It would then be up to the retreat to negotiate for Vorn's sword, if they dared. She grinned, knowing how much they'd hate negotiating with Hanal.

Adept Aran knelt in front of her. "Princess!"

Looking down over his thinning hair, she said, "Just Sophy, if you please."

Adept Aran cocked his head, an amused smile on his face. "If it pleases you, then I will call you by your first name. But it is an insult. You are the bearer of Vorn's sword, Hero of Argenterra, Vanqu—"

She held up her hand. "Stop!"

He inclined his head to acknowledge her request, then he lowered his eyes to stare directly at her belly, eyebrows taking flight on his forehead. What the hell was he doing? Sophy shifted her weight from one foot to another. It was one thing to be near-term pregnant and all that entailed without someone examining her navel.

"Vorn's Blood!" Aran squeaked out, glancing at her face before he returned his gaze to her belly.

"What?" Sophy couldn't see. Was her clothing ripped? Had she spilt wine on herself?

Aran climbed to his feet. "Forgive me, but the child...your baby...it is so imbued with the *given*...it is...it is..."

Hanal walked up, eyes on the adept, and then he flicked his gaze to Sophy, a smile on his face. "I had meant to mention it to you. There is so much *given* centred in your child that he could be Vorn reborn."

"Vorn reborn?"

Adept Aran turned to face the Puri leader, appearing to be lost for words. He pivoted his head between Sophy and Hanal. "Yes, that...that is exactly what I was thinking." He turned back to Hanal, looked him up and down. "How could you know?"

Hanal sighed, his bright eyes assessing the adept. *He did it so well,* Sophy thought, *that he almost hid the condescension in his expression.* "I have talent with the *given*."

Sophy's stomach was queasy. "That's not some sort of prophecy, is it?"

Aran lifted a finger, almost ready to reply, but Hanal waved him down. "I came only to tell you, Sophy, that the ceremony is about to begin. Will you attend?"

"Of course, I'm coming." Sophy looked around for Oakheart and saw him with two elegantly robed women. As she made her way over to him, she realised these were Aria and Rae, resplendent in the richest of Puri robes and the style of Argenterra, embroidered and colourful. Aria's face was made up too, her eyelids darkened with kohl and lips enriched with colour. Rae was radiant, her dark eyes so enhanced that she looked quite different and exotic. Mature. No longer little Rae, but Rae of the Puri. A soft, warm feeling glowed inside. Sophy shifted her feet and belched surreptitiously. It was not heartburn, surely. It was joy and pride.

The tent they entered was as large as a hall. The sides were up so people could gather in at the sides. Red and yellow bunting looped from the corners of the roof of the tent. Firesticks glowed and also torches lit with real flame casting them all into a warm, golden glow. Colourful robes mixed with Argenterran finery.

Vola was there, a handkerchief dabbing at her eyes. Veld did not travel to the wedding and Mara stayed with him so Oakheart's aunt had taken her time, leaving just after Hanal to make her own slow journey to prepare for the wedding and explore the countryside. Turning her head, Sophy spotted Leyla in new adept's robes. Sophy heard that she was to teach the Puri about the *given*. Kushlan stood close to the centre ready to witness his daughter's wedding. His smile so bright, Sophy found him unmistakable. His fine Puri robes of royal blue and violet made him look like a king, rather than a kind of bard, a new position granted by Hanal. Rae confessed that Hanal had developed a liking for the old tales and had commissioned her father to write them down.

To start the ceremony Hanal stood in the centre ringed by people. Sophy was in the first ring, along with Oakheart. The other layers were stacked with Argenterrans and Puri seemingly in equal proportions. Then it just became a crowd that spilled out of the sides of the tent.

Lillia was in the second layer, her smile bright as she represented her queen. They had had a great reunion, catching up on all the news the day before. Sophy grinned at the memory. Lillia had called her new daughter Sophy, in her honour. It was so sweet. Sophy hoped people weren't looking at her grin and thinking she was daft.

Hanal lifted his arms and the crowd grew quiet. "I welcome you here to the Puri heartlands, to our summer tents, to witness this wedding ceremony. I call upon the *given* to witness my oath and those of my brides."

Hanal put out both his hands, offering one to Rae and the other to Aria. "Tu Raenal? Aria?"

Both of the women stepped forwards, a slow walk that showed their clothing to the best advantage, robes draped just so. They each took one of Hanal's hands. Sophy blushed at the look he gave Rae, and then Aria. She couldn't tell that he loved Rae more than Aria. Had Hanal fallen for Aria's charms? Maybe the Puri had the capacity to love more than one person at a time. Maybe he was just an expert in treating people equally.

"As the *given* is my witness, I bind myself in marriage to Tu Raenal of the Puri and to Princess Aria of Silverdale, holding only to them, in body and in spirit, until our essences wane at the end of all things."

Rae and Aria repeated their oath to him. While it was a relief to Sophy not to have so much *given* present in the form of the Crystal Tree in a bonding ceremony, she was sad for Hanal and his people that the retreat had not come through in time with the promised branch. A little bit more *given* would have set them up nicely.

Loud cheers burst from the crowd. That was it. Shouts and cheers continued for some minutes before the feasting began. Some people were already dancing. Aromas of spice and meat teased her nostrils and the sounds of voices raised in song lifted her spirits. Detaching from the crowd of well-wishers, Hanal came up to her with his arm over both Rae and Aria's shoulders. "That is how we make oaths in Puri."

Sophy laughed and then sobered. She had an idea. She also had a back ache and rubbed at her lower back ruefully. "Hanal, could you help me with something?"

Hanal's eyes widened and he turned to his brides. They smiled at him. "Would you permit me?"

Rae and Aria agreed, then went off together arm-in-arm to the feast. Gilly burst out of the crowd, pushing through peoples' legs. "Come back here, little scoundrel," Oakheart bellowed. Yelling at the top of his lungs, Gilly ran rings around Oakheart, who was holding Lien at the same time. The boy was having a fine time. Sophy laughed as Gilly went off to chase a young Puri boy into one of the tents. She had wondered what had happened to her little nephew. Wow. She had family. A real family.

When they had walked a way off and they could hear each other without yelling, Sophy stopped and turned to Hanal.

"What is so urgent that you request my help now, Sophy?" Hanal sounded aggrieved and cast a look back to his tent. "I did just get married to two beautiful women."

Sophy looked around her for an empty space. "I won't keep you long." She pointed to a patch of ground, a bit apart from the tents. "Over here will do, I think." She undid the scabbard from the belt around her waist and then grimaced as another twinge stabbed in her back.

Hanal eyed the scabbard. "What are you doing?"

Sophy sent him a devilish grin. "Providing leverage."

Hanal jerked back. "What are you doing?"

"Just do what I tell you. This is going to work. Has to."

"What is going to work?"

Adept Aran must have been watching them for he came running towards them, waving his arms and calling out. "Sophy? What are you doing?" His voice sounded panicked. She had to move quickly.

Ripping the sword out of the scabbard, she tossed the covering to the ground. Then holding it vertically, she upended the blade and placed the point of Vorn's sword on the ground. "Come on. Put your hands over mind and help me push it in."

Adept Aran was closing in. With a nod to her, Hanal laid his hand over hers and they both shoved. The blade sliced through the earth and sunk two-thirds of the way to the hilt. Sophy gasped at the blue flame that erupted from the sword, which vibrated, sung with the discharge of power. Sophy was lifted up and back by the concussion wave. A loud grumble in the earth continued for some time. One the ground, Sophy rested on her elbow and studied the sword. Hanal had been thrown too and stood shakily as he brushed dirt off his fine robes and stared in wonder.

Oakheart ran over and helped her to her feet. "Sophy? What were you thinking? You could have hurt yourself and the—"

"You should not have done that," Adept Aran growled. His forehead was creased and his mouth tight.

Sophy looked at the adept coolly. "Why not? I figured the sword was full of the *given*. It would provide a stop-gap until the retreat plants a branch of the Crystal Tree. Why should the Puri wait for what is rightfully theirs? I don't think Hanal will let you have the sword back until you deliver your part of the truce negotiations in full. In fact, Hanal, I suggest you don't give the sword to the retreat until they fulfil all their obligations to your complete satisfaction."

"Lianal will not like this." Adept Aran's expression was grim.

"Too bad. It's done." Sophy brushed dirt out of her hair. She gestured to the scabbard. "You can take that back to the retreat to continue to cherish and protect, as before."

Hanal's face was full of wonder. "You...you..." His eyes flicked from her to Oakheart, several times. "We have the *given*," Hanal cried, rapture in his voice. "I can feel it beneath my feet, in the air that I breathe." He fell to his knees in front of Sophy and bowed his nose to the ground. "A miracle!" he said as he raised his head.

Sophy fidgeted, feeling awkward with Hanal's gratitude. "I...er...I'm glad it worked."

Oakheart had a wide grin. "I knew there was a reason you were here in Argenterra." He kissed her lightly on the forehead. Sophy was overwhelmed. She had done something right. Something that others acknowledged as right and good—maybe not the retreat but that did not signify much to her mind.

As Oakheart beamed a smile at her, she knew she was home, really home, where she belonged.

Climbing to his feet, Hanal called out to his tribe leaders and they came at a run. His tribesmen gaped in awe at the *given* flowing beneath them. Hanal took this moment to fall to his knees and speak a new binding oath, one that specifically included women. His tribesmen joined in and repeated the oath.

More voices repeating the oath went out like a wave to the people around them. Sophy smiled so wide she thought her lips would tear, and then grabbed her belly as a sharp pain rocketed through her.

"Sophy?" Oakheart asked, looking from Hanal and the Puri kneeling on the ground to her.

"I must have pulled a muscle."

Oakheart frowned. "You really should take more care." Then he looked around him again and the frown faded and once again his smiled rapturously. "Sophy, you have done a wondrous thing." He wiped at his eye.

Sophy's face screwed up in pain. "Oh!" Her knees buckled and she used her hands so as not to fall face first into the dirt.

Oakheart leant down and helped her to her feet. "You are not—"

"Don't worry, I'm good." She patted his hand and took a step away from him.

Her waters broke. "Ah?"

When she looked at Oakheart, he went pale. Hanal was still lost in wonder, staring at the sword, the finest of tendrils of blue power leaking into the land. His people gathered around him, exclaiming and murmuring.

Sophy couldn't feel the magic, but in looking at Hanal she knew it had worked. She had done right and good. Then a contraction crumpled her midriff, and her mind focussed inwards. Oakheart bellowed for help.

Aria and Rae came running up to her. "You're in labour, now?" Aria was appalled.

Rae laughed. "On our wedding night?"

"Sorry!" Sophy said as she hobbled, then bent over as another labour pain announced itself.

Rae and Aria were to help in the delivery, both having birthed babies previously. An older woman hovered behind them. The Puri midwife, Sophy guessed. She wasn't keen on having a baby with no painkillers. Lillia rocked up, panting a little and dressed in her forest finery. She cast Sophy a lopsided grin. "Don't tell me. The baby is coming now?"

Aria directed them to a tent. "In here. Oakheart, you coming?"

"I don't know. Should he?" Sophy asked as she was bundled into a tent by her female companions.

"It is up to you," Lillia said. "Remember how often he has nursed you in the past." Sophy winced as another wave of pain arrived. "He could be useful."

Sophy grunted and Aria laughed. "He's already done his bit."

Lillia helped Sophy remove her gown and carefully inspected her protruding belly. "'Tis a good-sized child. Sit down here and let's look at you."

During her labour, Sophy was spoiled and rubbed and prodded, and even though she often begged Lillia for Newin's Brew and the oblivion it offered, she didn't get any. The birth happened anyway. It hurt. She screamed a lot. Oakheart was there, holding her hand, cooling her forehead with damp towels and whispering words of encouragement. She would never forget the look on his face when she started screaming. He hated to see her suffer just as much as she hated suffering.

Whispers of "Vorn reborn" could be heard outside the tent. Damn Aran and Hanal for spreading rumours like that. Finally, Oakheart said, sounding stunned, "'Vorn reborn is a girl." He had a stupid grin. Oakheart went outside to spread the news and then came back in, unable to take his gaze off his daughter.

Sophy squinted at the bawling baby as it was placed on her. "Is she really full of the *given*?"

He nodded, his face filled with awe. "She certainly is."

"Speaking of the *given*, Adept Aran has been in touch with the retreat. Lianal is not as upset about the sword as Aran predicted."

"Really? I wonder why."

"Apparently there has been an upsurge in the *given* everywhere."

"Do you mean it is back in the land?"

Oakheart shook his head slightly. "Not back to its prior strength, but more than it was and there is hope that the *given* will grow again in time. Placing the *given* here has connected the retreat and the places in

Argenterra where the Crystal Tree is planted and created a circle of resonance, a kind of loop." He frowned for a moment. "Consider it a healing. Argenterra is now whole, largely because of you."

"I did do something right?"

He nodded. "You certainly did. Again. You have to admit you have acted right on more than one occasion. You were meant to be here with us. You were meant to save us, and you have."

"Oh," Sophy bit her lip, then smiled. "I feel at home now."

Oakheart kissed her full on the mouth, lingering for a moment and disregarding their audience. Then he released her, still grinning. "Adept Aran is very excited. More so than Hanal, I believe, if that is possible." He ruffled her hair. "I believe they are thinking of calling you Saint Sophy now..."

"No way!"

Oakheart laughed at her expression. "I was teasing."

She gave him a playful slap on the shoulder and turned her mind to their child that lay against her breast. She seemed so big. She had a fine, dark down on her head, eyes shut tight in a wrinkled face. "So what do we call her?"

Oakheart frowned as he rubbed his chin. "S'Vorn." He reached over and squeezed her hand. "What do you think?"

"Sounds good to me. Second name?"

Lillia grabbed the baby, wrapped her in a cloth in very quick time with upmost efficiency. Sophy met Oakheart's gaze. "Lillia?" they said in unison.

The forest maiden glanced up from rocking the baby. "What?"

Oakheart took S'Vorn from her. "If you do not object, we have named our child S'Vorn Lillia, Princess of Silverdale."

Lillia glanced at them both and burst into tears. Sophy sat up and put out a hand, beckoning her closer. "Don't you like it?"

Lillia sniffled, wiped her tears, too upset to get any words out although she did sit on the bed. Sophy rubbed the woman's shoulder. "Lillia?"

Then smiling through her tears she said brokenly. "I like...like it very well."

The End
*Please note:*
*British/Australian spelling conventions are used in this book.*
*For example, words like color are spelled colour, recognize are recognise,*
*traveling are traveling and so on.*

DID YOU ENJOY UNGIVEN LAND? CARE TO LEAVE A REVIEW SO others can enjoy it too? Leave a review.

Want to keep up with Donna's publishing adventures then join her newsletter Wing Dust.

# AUTHOR'S NOTE

Finishing this trilogy, a story that spans a good fifteen years of my life, from the very beginning of my writing career (that's called learning to write) until now is an amazing feeling. At first, I set out to write a fantasy with something different in it. I also was interested in types of romantic relationships. If you haven't guessed, there are three types explored in this trilogy: love at first sight, friends to lovers, and hero worship.

I have to admit that I was very in love with the characters and the world. My inspiration comes from a number of places and authors. I really like Stephen Donaldson's work, in particular, the fantasy duology, Mordant's Need. I would totally write fanfiction about that world and the characters. I also have to say that a fair bit of David Eddings's fantasy works would have influenced me because I read all of his work before I wrote this and late Sara Douglass too. Sara Douglass was one of the reasons I started writing. She showed me it could be done by an Australian. Of course, there are many Australian fantasy authors these days and some I count as friends.

I'm really pleased with how the books turned out, and I hope you will be too. I owe a debt of gratitude to my editor, Kaaren Sutcliffe, A.

E., who I've known from my early days of writing. She encouraged me when I was still learning my craft and then later she encouraged me to keep going with this particular series. I don't think I could have completed the trilogy without her. She has offered me praise, told me off for bad habits and even thrown a few tantrums in the margins when I used a word she didn't like. Her expertise with horses also added to the descriptions of horsey things and she is much better at battles than I am, so she doesn't let me get lazy. Most of all her comments made me think about the reader and how to make the story easier to read. Then next up I must praise Jason Nahrung, proofreader extraordinaire. His sharp eye catches the little things Kaaren and I miss and also some biggies.

I need also to thank Nicole Murphy and Aiki Flinthart for their generous reader comments. They helped to shape this last book and took time out from their own writing to help me out. Other beta readers over the many years include Gillian Polack and Helen Brinsmead. Thanks are also required for Louise Cusack and the Envision team. Louise told me not to throw Argenterra in the bin.

The first book in the series, Argenterra, was my second attempt at a novel after my first called Relic, a science fiction novel with romance. I wrote Oathbound in 2003–2004 and part of Ungiven Land in 2010. The stories lay dormant for a while, until 2016, when I attacked Oathbound and Ungiven Land with renewed motivation, and hopefully enhanced skills. And here we are.

Two of the books ended in cliffhangers and try as I might I couldn't get them not to leave things up in the air. Either I had to cut them off before the big moment to avoid a cliffhanger or go on and end up with a novel that was too lengthy. I consider them three parts of one story.

You may be wondering if I meant to discuss feminist issues, like domestic violence, and I can say I did. Did I touch on violence against women deliberately? Yes, I did. I also deliberately touched on racial discrimination and the unequal distribution of wealth and resources. This makes The Silverlands Series a product of the now—2017.

Are there more stories set in Argenterra? There could be...if readers want more then I certainly have the ideas.

I am currently undertaking a PhD exploring the topic Feminism and Romance. If you are interested in following that journey, feel free to visit my blog. http://donnamareehanson.com

Thank you for reading!

Donna Maree Hanson

# ABOUT DONNA MAREE HANSON

Donna Maree Hanson is a Canberra-based writer of fantasy, science fiction, horror and, under the pseudonym of Dani Kristoff, paranormal romance. A traditionally and independently published author, she has been writing creatively since November 2000 and has been a member of the Canberra Speculative Fiction Guild (CSFG) since 2001. She has had about twenty short stories published in various small press and ezines. In January 2013, her first longer work, Rayessa & the Space Pirates, was published with Harlequin's digital imprint, Escape. This was followed by Rae and Essa's Space Adventures in 2015. Opi Battles the Space Pirates was published in 2017. In September 2014, the first book in the dark fantasy Dragon Wine series, Shatterwing, was published by Momentum Books (Pan Macmillan Australia's digital imprint). The second book, Skywatcher, was published in October 2014. Two further instalments in the series will be published in 2017: Deathwings and Bloodstorm, along with the republication of Shatterwing and Skywatcher. In 2015, Donna was awarded the A. Bertram Chandler Award for services to science fiction in Australia.

Donna is currently a PhD candidate researching popular romance fiction.

Argenterra: Book One of the Silverlands, her epic fantasy series, was published in 2016. Oathbound: The Silverlands Book Two was published in early 2017. Ungiven Land is the third book in the trilogy out in May 2017.

You can find out more about Donna on her blog and sign up to her newsletter Wing Dust

http://donnamareehanson.com

Twitter @DonnaMHanson

Facebook https://www.facebook.com/DonnaMareeHanson

# PREVIEW OF SHATTERWING, DRAGON WINE PART ONE

***Deliciously Dark Fantasy!***

The world of Margra is a desolate wasteland after one of its moons shattered. Factions fight over resources as pieces of the broken moon rain down, bringing chaos, destruction and death.

Dragon wine is a life giving drink imbued with the essence of dragons. It is what keeps people alive. But the prison vineyard where Salinda works to grow grapes is in jeopardy. Not only does the Inspector, the sadistic ruler of the prison vineyard, make her life and the life of others a misery, he wants to rule the world by hoarding all the dragon wine. But Salinda has a secret power, an ancient gift called a' cadre', that may one day save the world.

When the Inspector suspects that Salinda has secrets, she may have to die to protect the cadre from falling into his hands...

# THE PRISON VINEYARD

Salinda trod the mud tracks of the vineyard, inhaling air that was fresh and damp from the previous night's rain, dispelling the ever-present smell of sulphur for a time. As the sun notched a little higher over the mountains, the humidity levels rose, making sweat bead on her upper lip and her dress cling uncomfortably to her legs. In the distance, dragons rode the thermals, hunting for prey above the barren plains. A reminder that the Fire Ranges, the geothermal wastes and the dragons served well to imprison them all in the vineyard.

Coming up on the winery building that bordered the staging area, she hid in the shadows and watched as a new prisoner arrived. A gray burden beast whined soulfully as it clawed forward, dragging the wooden cart free of the muddy track. A sudden jerk threw the new prisoner off balance and onto the side railing. Two guards stepped forward, lifted the latch on the cart's rear gate and stepped back as the man tipped himself into the mud.

Ange, the one-eyed guard, stood with hands on hips. "Come on, yer 'ighness. Git up 'n' view yer new princedom."

Salinda clamped down on her revulsion. Next to the Inspector,

Ange was the worst of the vile creatures that passed for guards in this place.

The cut of the prisoner's chamois breeches and embroidered shirt confirmed he was a royal rebel, one from the many dynastic houses overthrown when rebellion erupted, who then in turn became a rebel. On climbing to his feet, the fair-skinned man spat into Ange's weathered brown face. The guard wiped his cheek with a grime-covered hand, looked at his palm in apparent surprise and lashed out with a savage backhander, sending the young man sprawling unconscious into the muck.

Ange's pot belly jostled as he laughed, only pausing when the guard prodded the inert prisoner in the ribs with the toe of his boot. "That'll teach ya, scum."

Curiosity drew Salinda out into the open. Hearing heavy steps behind her, she realized she'd been noticed by the guards and offered little resistance when they dragged her forward. They shoved her down into the pungent mud near the rebel, where she saw the newcomer's bewildered face as he came to. He was young, barely an adult. It had been a while since she'd seen such innocence.

A cloud of smoke hit her in the face and her gaze slid to a smelting fire. Chains lay in a disordered pile, along with some tools propped up against the fence. She shuddered once, remembering her first day when the chains had been fitted. "Stupid whore," Ange growled at her. The rest of the guards laughed and flung curse words at her while she pulled herself up into a squat, indifferent to the mud that clung to her faded and patched pink dress. Tossing her loose braid over her shoulder, she smiled when she caught the young man's eye.

"Welcome, friend," she said huskily, lifting her shoulder invitingly for the benefit of the guards. It served her well that they thought her a whore, and a defective one at that.

At the sound of familiar, rhythmic footsteps, she knelt hastily in the dirt and cast her head and eyes down, surreptitiously keeping the Inspector and the guards in view.

"Inspector," Ange said, dragging his hat off his head to worry it with nervous fingers. The other guards followed suit, grabbing their various dented and rusty helmets from their bowed heads.

The lithe Inspector shot a piercing glance in her direction. "Why is she here?"

Salinda flinched. Ange started. "Her helpmate be dead so we be giv'n Poxy Sal to show the new prisoner the...er...ropes. Tau't it'd please ya, Inspector," Ange said, bobbing his head vigorously. "Ya 'pproved it jus' t'other day."

"Ah, yes. I remember. She was all alone out there on the rim. Good." The Inspector focused his gaze on the new prisoner and slowly and deliberately peeled off his clean, beige gloves. "Prisoner Brill of Duval?"

"Yes," Brill answered as he climbed to his feet and stood unsteadily. His face was swollen around the eyes and jaw. Old bruises lingered, with streaks of purple and yellow staining his pale skin, traces of his interrogation.

"Kin, I think," the Inspector said, slapping a glove against his immaculate breeches before sliding it to join the other at his belt. "But I am not as stupid as you."

Brill blinked and then with slightly hooded eyes examined the Inspector's face, perhaps looking for signs of his noble heritage.

The Inspector smiled thinly. "I am a Karonen of Bristling Flat. My mother was your cousin."

Brill looked ready to smile. But Salinda, still kneeling, warned him with a wide-eyed look of alarm. His gaze shifted toward her, catching her signal, and he kept his mouth shut.

"Good," the Inspector said with a slow nod. "Don't think family connections will help you here. Your father's foolish altruism died with him. Thankfully, all trace of his Highland Confederacy was obliterated."

Salinda saw Brill's fist clench and worried that he might protest. But the young man remained silent, his anger betrayed only by his heightened color.

"I understand you are here because you trusted unwisely." Throwing his head back, the Inspector barked out a laugh. "You've learned too late never to trust another, especially with your life." The Inspector paced by the fire, five steps up and five steps back, his gray eyes intent. All was silent except for his even footfalls. He stopped suddenly and gestured with both arms to the surrounding vineyard, like a shrug. "We make dragon wine here." He turned again and began to walk away, only to return and halt abruptly in front of the rebel, almost nose to nose. Then he rasped out, "You will learn that dragon wine is all there is."

Salinda watched the Inspector, the clenching and unclenching of his hands, the pink flush turning livid on his neck. She had no idea why this particular rebel angered him more than any other, but she sensed trouble and climbed to her feet.

"Yes, Inspector—dragon wine is all there is," Salinda blurted out, bringing the Inspector's attention to her. Breathing hard, she realized she was being reckless, but something about the lad, some gut feeling made her do it, made her draw the Inspector's malice to her and save him from some small part of it.

The Inspector lunged, backhanding her. She fell backward and lay on the ground, dazed. Looming over her, he said hoarsely, "I'm not talking to you, whore!"

Behind her, the guards guffawed and called her a slut and a stupid moll. Brill stood still, dumbfounded, and then when he had collected himself, she saw his gaze shift left and right, measuring up his chances of escape. Salinda worried that he might intervene, making matters worse. Luckily, he didn't.

Blood leaked from her mouth, and she wiped at it as she sat up—a small cut, nothing more. After climbing to her feet, she faced the Inspector, keeping her expression impassive. The mud would dry and brush out of her hair. No harm done. There, she thought as she jutted her chin out slightly, no need to fear him.

Turning to Brill, who stood immobile, the Inspector's face creased with a grin. "Good, good. No heroics from you, as I expected. You're the lazy, self-centered, minuscule prince you always were, living off the suffering of others."

The punch to the gut took Brill by surprise and doubled him up. The kick to the ribs that followed when he was down winded him painfully. He was barely aware when Salinda helped him to his feet. Her hand steadied him as he lurched, keeping his eye on the guards and the Inspector.

"Chain him and set them to work." The Inspector pushed an indolent guard out of his way and marched off.

Ange headed for the fire and grabbed a length of chain. Caressing it, he grunted out a command. "Fust, bring the prisoner. The rest of ya, git."

The remaining guards drifted away sulkily into the vines or wandered off in the direction of the village. Fust shoved Brill toward Ange from behind and then kicked the rebel's leg forward for the ankle manacle. The memory of her chaining returned to Salinda, as acrid as the smoke. The emotion, the utter desolation welled up inside her. She had to breathe through it—push the images, the feelings, away.

Brill screwed up his face as he leaned away from the heat of the soldering iron.

"I'm called Salinda."

Brill nodded and then tensed his face when the hot iron was brought back for his wrist. After tugging on the chains to test them, the two guards stood back. When she saw the metal anklets, the memories surged back. It was long ago and she was free of them now, an earned privilege, but her ankle still bore the mottled, white scars.

"I said git." Ange waved smoke away from his face and the second guard, Fust, heaved a fluid, chesty cough before spitting a glob of green-tinged mucus at her feet.

Ignoring it, she caught the boy's eye again. "Come, I will teach you what you need to know to survive here."

Brill's face was slack with surprise, and it took a moment for him to register what she had said. "What?...I am Prince Brill, late of..."

A thump across his ear sent him reeling. "Save yer 'igh talk 'til later. She's a poxy whore...nuttin' else. Ya know—tavern slut. Don't go puttin' yer rod in there or it'll drop off. She's diseased." Ange spat at her and walked off, rubbing his groin. If any prisoner was still abed, they would suffer Ange's attentions that morning.

Brill moaned slightly, once again claiming her notice. Salinda put her hand under his elbow to support him. He lifted his wrist, testing the heavy weight of chain linking it to his ankle.

"The chains are more for show, you know. Walking is possible once you learn how to manage the weight."

He gaped at her in disbelief while flexing his bicep.

"It's true. There's no point in preventing you from working, is there? They hinder rather than prevent escape. It's all in the mind—don't let it get to you."

Closing his mouth, he nodded and cast a look around him, the dark shadows beneath his eyes a telling sign of his despair. He leaned on her and then gradually worked out a rhythm with the chain, looping the slack over his arm so he could walk. A chained prisoner couldn't run from a dragon on the plains, nor could one climb down the side of Crawlers Gorge, even if they found a way to it through the maze of mud pits, boiling pools of water and hidden steam vents. The road was guarded by more than the Inspector's men. Fear and degradation created worse prisons; they entrapped minds.

As they passed in front of Fust, he glared at them with red-rimmed eyes.

"Move," he yelled after them. "Or I'll chain ya together 'n' make ya dragon fodder."